WARP WORLD

KRISTENE PERRON
JOSHUA SIMPSON

Cover designed by Miguel S. Kilantang Jr.
Email: megryanchapelle@gmail.com

ISBN   978-1-55120-050-7
www.warpworld.ca

JoKri Publishing
PO Box 478
Gardendale, Texas 79758

Kristene

For my father

Joshua

For the kiddo.
Writing was your idea.

ACKNOWLEDGEMENT

Kristene

To thank every person who played even the smallest role in seeing this novel come into existence would require several pages and a list that stretches back to my kindergarten teacher, (thanks, Mrs. Townsend!). Instead, I'll offer a general but heartfelt *thank you* to all those in my life who have ever inspired, encouraged, or kicked my butt onto the writing path, and move right along to more specific notes of appreciation.

I might as well give up all hopes of winning the lottery since I used up all my luck with the various editors and readers I found for this novel. Deborah O'Keeffe, Mickey Novak, and Sharmaine Grey all took a turn at shaping and polishing the story and our writing. Thanks for your editorial prowess and your patience.

Anne DeGrace, Rita Moir, Jennifer Craig, Vangie Bergum, Sarah Butler, and Verna Relkoff constitute the writing group I was fortunate enough to be invited into (twice), and I love them all for much more than just their Brilliant and Insightful critiques and delicious soup.

When literary agent Morty Mint took Josh and I on as his clients, I didn't realize I was meeting the man who would become one of my closest, and most entertaining, friends. Thanks for always being in our corner, Mr. Mint.

It's handy to have a paramedic as a good friend when you are constantly wounding your characters. Thanks to Darcey Lutz for his medical input. And while I've spent a lot of years in, on, and around water, I am not a sailor. Thankfully, Michael Skog is and he was kind enough to point out my gaffes and offer clever suggestions for Ama's boat.

To my dad, Bob, and my sister, Kelly, there aren't enough words in any language to tell you how thankful I am to have been raised by people who loved me so unconditionally, encouraged my crazy imagination, and made me feel as if being adopted was not just normal but wonderful. I regret that my mom, Lorraine, did not live to see this novel published but thanks Mom, I miss you.

My writing partner and friend, Josh, in a short time, has become one of the most important people in my life. Without his persistent suggestion that we write a "short story" together, *Warpworld* would not exist. He is a brand of crazy that fits perfectly with my own, he tolerates my bad jokes, makes me laugh when I most need to, and puts up with my obssesive workaholic tendencies. For the latter, he deserves a medal. For the rest, he has my gratitude and love for all time.

I saved the best for last. My husband, Fred, swept me off my feet fourteen years ago. Literally. Through our unconventional and adventurous life, he has been my biggest fan and best friend. The sacrifices he made to ensure I had time to let this story use me to write itself went above and beyond supportive. No critic's praise, five star review, or bestseller status will ever mean as much as the smile on Fred's face as he turned the last page of this manuscript. To the love of my life, thanks for sharing this journey with me.

Josh

Two and a half years ago, in another job and another life we started a series of books. At long last, the first one goes out to the world.

I'd like to thank my English teachers for their infinite patience. I'd like to thank the army of assistants that Kris noted, though I mostly only directly interacted with Mickey and Morty. This book definitely had a village behind it, a village of helpers and well-wishers that helped us get through the ups and downs of production.

I'd like to thank my parents Kenneth and Linda for all their encouragement, not to mention the land to park on while I went back to college. Yes Mom, we corrected the 'site/sight' error.

Likewise my aunt and uncle have been extraordinarily helpful and supportive in my life. Barbara and Don, you're wonderful people.

Friends. I don't count many people in that category, but the ones I have are priceless. James, Tom, Billy, Chelsea, Josie, Garvin, life is better having known you.

I'd also like to thank my friend the Norseman for helping me make sense of the HTML.

Kris. Where to start? She's crazy. Seriously folks, she's the crazy one. But this wouldn't have happened without her. I had an idea, together we made a story. (And several more to come.)

CHAPTER 1

The sky was blue, he should have been prepared for that. All those years of preparation— simulation, training, reading, lectures, images—fell away as Seg lay on the moss at the transit point. The cool morning ground soothed his body while the roar of the nearby ocean quieted his thoughts.

Rolling onto his back, he blinked once more against the clear, unshielded sky. Unusual. For the first time in his life, Segkel Eraranat of the Cultural Theorist's Guild felt at peace with the world, even though this world was not his.

Squad Leader Kerbin squatted down next to him, facing the opposite direction. "Snap out of it, Bliss kid!" she hissed, and jabbed his shoulder with the butt of her rifle, "locals might have seen us come through." She stood upright and glared at the large trooper hovering over Seg. "Manatu, you were ordered to make sure he took his stim pack! Damn it, if we lose the Theorist we might as well set up camp here permanently. The Guild will sell our organs to the highest bidder."

Kid? Yes, Seg supposed that, to Kerbin, he was a kid. At twenty-one, he was just beginning. His first mission as a graduated Theorist, the final test. Succeed and fulfill his life's ambition to work in the field, succeed far beyond expectations and he could elbow out the rearward thinking fossils and take the seat of Selectee for Field Research. Fail and—no, that was not an option.

The beginning. Of his career, certainly. And, judging from the wonders that now surrounded him, perhaps even his life. He looked up and over at the squad leader. How old was Kerbin? Thirty? Thirty-five? Memory eluded him. Old enough to be angered by inexperience or whatever else had dug those lines over her brow and on either side of her mouth.

He closed his eyes and took a deep breath of this new air, so clear and fresh. He thought he had trained for the Bliss—the euphoria, the debilitating euphoria his People experienced when they traveled through the warps—but no drug could replicate this feeling.

"Vita." He inhaled again, and swore he could taste the substance in the air. Vita, undetectable to the human eye, was the energy imbued on anything of cultural or spiritual importance, and necessary fuel for the continued existence of his People. This was what they had come for. And though he had studied vita, even visited the Central Well where it was fed to the ever-hungry Storm, at this moment he could actually *feel* it.

Seg lifted himself from the ground, sat upright, and watched as Kerbin gestured orders to the recon troops, fanning them out around her position. Had he really thought of her, during their prep sessions, as colorless and bland when he could now see her crisp efficiency and competence?

Her uniform, set to woodland camouflage, hid any evidence of gender but her almond eyes and high, sharp cheekbones betrayed Kerbin as distinctly female. Seg was at least a head taller than the troops, with the exception of Manatu, that were assigned to his mission, though not nearly as filled out. Despite the difference in size, Kerbin was formidable. She knew well what she was doing.

An avian flew across the sky in the distance; Seg stood as if to follow its direction. Manatu grabbed him by the collar and pulled him behind cover while, next to Seg, the signals operator began a broad-based passive sweep, his equipment sucking down any emissions the locals might be making.

Pre-transit, Manatu's only redeeming quality had been his imposing size but now Seg watched, with admiration, as his assigned bodyguard swept his weapon across the treeline. A stalwart and steadfast protector – who could not respect that?

"What society awaits us?" Seg wondered aloud, then moved his tongue around his mouth and lips to taste the salt-tinged air. Manatu gestured with a hand sliced across his throat to indicate an immediate need for silence. Seg realized his mistake and pressed his lips closed. But the Bliss overwhelmed him again, spinning his thoughts off into happy contemplation.

There were thousands of worlds out there, from high-tech wonders that dwarfed his people handily, to aboriginal primitives who had barely progressed past the use of flint. The basic human phenotype had, surprisingly, remained consistent from world to world, with only a handful of cases of extreme adaptation. Fortunate, as successful infiltration would be impossible otherwise.

Outers, that was the People's name for any humanoid species from other worlds, and Seg looked forward to seeing his first one. He wanted to see them in their environment, a race as yet untouched, naïve and pure. These were not processed caj, the slaves of his World. These were raw Outers in their natural state.

He pressed his hand to the tree Manatu had placed him behind, marveled at the ridges and knobs of the bark, and put his nose up to the surface for a long sniff. The scent was rich and earthy. His world had nothing like this.

If only his People could simply pick up and move, reestablish their society in a place such as this. An impossible but tantalizing dream, the fancy of first year cadets before their instructors slapped them with the unforgiving hand of simple math. All other sound reasons aside, to extrans ninety million People through the warp? Never mind equipment, supplies or caj. The amount of vita required to fuel that journey was laughably unattainable.

"Signals, what've you got for me?" Kerbin asked, her voice low but urgent as she crouched near the operator, occasionally casting angry glances in Seg's direction.

The troops had formed a perimeter in the forest, covering their sectors with the professionalism and wariness of veteran raiders. *Anything* could happen on a new world; Seg remembered that now.

"Getting high band traffic over here," the signals operator replied. "VHF/UHF. Got some shortwave too. Nonrepeater, definitely comm signals. No signs of satellite comm."

"You with us yet Theorist?" Kerbin snapped.

Seg bristled, the effects of traveling through the warp quickly draining from his body. He ignored the squad leader, adjusted his gear, and wiped away bits of moss and dirt. As he tugged at the edges of his coat to straighten it, he willed his head to clear.

How long had he laid there, Blissed out, endangering himself and the squad while Manatu had watched over him? Mistakes irritated him and his mistakes, however rare, most of all. Now that he was free of the fog, he re-evaluated the circumstances.

He recalled Kerbin's earlier snide remark, and frowned. Who was this insolent bitch who dared address a Guild Theorist as if he were a common raider? To say nothing of the clumsy idiot they had assigned to guard him. *Manatu*, the name of an extinct, lumbering, land mammal from the World's ancient past. Fitting name for one so dim.

His decision to forgo the pills designed to counteract the Bliss had been an error. Nevertheless, he shot the Squad Leader a withering stare. First or fifty-first, this was *his* mission, every responsibility and outcome—from collection of vita-related data to the selection of strike points—rested firmly upon his shoulders. Kerbin should know her place.

He screened the scenery with new eyes. It was lush here, vibrant and alive. Was this some residual Bliss informing his opinion or merely the strong contrast to home? Either way, it was that vibrancy they were here for.

As he slid his visor down, Seg was already contemplating what the standard cultural practices of residents of such environments would be. Systems of trade and transportation, myths and religion, mating rituals, all aspects of a society hinged on its surroundings.

"Any visual signals?" he asked the comm operator.

"Negative."

According to the drone signal captures, the locals obviously had problems with the regulation of their signal traffic, with a messy clutter of bands often clashing into each other. "Sloppy organization," Seg remarked to Kerbin. "Promising. Between the signal capture from the drone and this, we've got a start on language capture."

She nodded. "We'll review the plan, then make the initial move-and-acquire."

The troops clustered around Kerbin as she went over the first stage of the mission with them. Seg listened but his eyes were fixed on something he could barely see through the thick foliage.

Water.

Initial drone penetration and its environmental readings of this world had shown a high ratio of water to land. An estimated seventy-two percent of the surface was covered by salt water, with countless island chains and six major land masses, the largest of which had been chosen for the transit site. Seg had known the geography going in— the drone was programmed to determine if a world were a viable vita source and to assist the recon squad with preparations—but now that he was here, the word had taken on a threatening tone.

Water.

Endless quantities of it rushed by, roiling uncontrolled and undirected. It lay within an easy walk of their location, a loud, flowing menace. The rational, educated part of his mind knew full well that it wasn't likely to come flooding their way and wash them out of their hiding spot but the animal part felt both challenged and daunted by its presence.

There were worlds where Outers worked on water, even lived on it in various temporary and permanent structures. It was strange, reckless behavior, even for primitives.

"Okay, we're thirty out from the nearest piece of settled ground," Kerbin said to the gathered squad. "Eyes and ears open. There are Outers on this world just waiting to kill every kargin' one of us. Don't give them a shot. We're the hunters; they're the meat. Keep watch for dangerous bioforms. Plants, bugs, water, even the Storm-cursed dirt. We've lost troopers to every damn thing there is on a planet and there's always a new way to die out here. Don't be the idiot who finds it!"

Unlike the rest of the squad, Seg sat a slight distance away from the squad leader, watching the perimeter with his bodyguard. The danger curve for a fresh extrans through the warp spiked in the first hour, declined as the Bliss faded, then spiked again within the next eight hours as attention drifted and the first glimmers of familiarity led to the early dangers of relaxation. Kerbin knew those statistics as well as he did, and she worked to keep her veteran troopers sharp and alert. Her cadence and emphasis were born of training, practice, and experience, and served to command the attention of her people.

Well, at the very least, she had his attention. He had come to this place to facilitate conquest and capture, not to die in any of a million different barbaric ways such as pleased the local primitives.

"We stick to plan. What's the first objective after successful extrans?" Kerbin asked.

"We make a grab on an Outer and pull the language out of 'em," a small, wiry trooper replied. He was the squad's long-range weapon specialist. On the other side, he had a relaxed demeanor. Here, however, he was all business, head moving in a slow, continuous motion as he swept the area with his electronically enhanced senses.

"Okay," Kerbin said, pulling her visor back down, "let's go collect the Theorist a specimen."

Ama walked the fifty-foot length of the *Naida*, satisfied that the latest 'temporary' repair job to the skins was holding. There was a good wind blowing from the southwest; she gathered her loose, light blonde hair in her hand and twisted it back into a knot. It was the perfect day for a devotional cruise; her Damiar customers would get their money's worth. As she reached the set of stairs leading from the dock to the upper deck of the boat, one of the passengers called out to her.

"You there, girl. Help Lady Uval with her bags," the long-faced Lord ordered, waving his hand as if shooing away an insect.

"Captain," Ama answered, forcing a smile. "You may call me *Captain*...Your Lordship."

She grit her teeth, slung the heavy piece of luggage over her shoulder and made her way up the steps to the *Naida*. Why did these fat-assed Dammies think they needed so much fluffery for a flat-water day cruise?

"Captain Kalder!"

Constable Provert's voice, just what she didn't need to hear. Tossing Lady Uval's bag to the deck, she hopped back down to the dock, out of hearing range of her much needed, paying customers.

"Constable," she said as she shifted her bandaged right hand behind her back and raised her left palm skyward, "blessings of the Shasir upon you and—"

"You are on notice." He dropped a folded piece of paper into her hand. "Again."

"Is that all?" she asked, passing the paper back.

"No," the Constable replied, his pleasure obvious even beneath his flat expression as he thrust the paper back into Ama's hand, "Judicia Corrus has reduced the term of your license. You have thirty days to be off the water, permanently."

"What?" she stared down at the paper, mouth agape.

"Girl!" one of the Damiar passengers called from the deck of the boat, "How much longer?"

Ignoring the question, Ama unfurled the notice and read. Eyes skimming over the list of her current offenses, she stopped at the last two lines.

In light of these and past violations, we hereby give notice that Captain Amadahy Kalder, of the vessel Naida, is to cease commercial operations on the first day of the following month. Failure to adhere to this notice will result in seizure of property and a term of Correction.

"He can't do this; I was promised three months!" she protested, but Constable Provert was already halfway down the dock, weaving through the crowd. As she crushed the paper in her grip, Ama took off after him.

"Girl!" the Damiar called again.

"Provert!" Ama yelled, shoving bodies out of her way, "Get back here and explain this, you coward!" She was almost on him when she felt a set of hands grab her around the waist.

She whipped around, fists raised.

"Ama, what are you doing? Calm down."

"Fa, I..."

Focused on the cause of her anger, she hadn't noticed her own father, Odrell, on the dock. She turned her head to see Constable Provert climb into a cartul and drive away, then lowered her raised hands and let out a cry of frustration.

"He shortened the term of my license. Bloody Corrus thinks he can—"

"Hush!" Her father stepped closer and lowered his voice, "You know better than to curse the Judicia in public."

His eyes directed hers far down the length of the dock, to the very end, where the black and charred remains of a cargo boat jutted from the river like the ribcage of a skeleton. Ama's mouth closed and she felt the usual swell of fear and anger that accompanied the sight of any of the Judicia's warnings.

At least they had taken down the body of the vessel's captain, who had been hung from the bow. Not before all the other captains and crew had gotten a good eyeful, though.

"Besides, you should know by now that getting angry isn't going to help your case." As he spoke, he lifted her right hand, his mouth slipping into a smile at the site of the blood-speckled bandage wrapped around her knuckles.

She shrugged, "Some Westie called my *Naida* a floating scrap pile."

"Tadpole," he sighed, "your brother is one moon away from ascension and you have offers of marriage, good offers. Why can't you put this aside?" He gestured to the non-stop bustle of the Banks: boats docking, casting off, loading, unloading or being repaired.

Ama tugged her hand away, "You don't understand."

"No, I understand too well," her father said, placing his large hand on Ama's shoulder and brushing the leather nove she wore around her neck with his thumb.

All the Kenda wore some form of the traditional collar but only Odrell understood the significance of his daughter's decoration. The nove, well worn with use, had once graced the throat of Colwyn Kalder, his wife, Ama's mother, who had taken her own life when Ama was just a child.

"I have a cruise," Ama said, looking away, swallowing the lump in her throat.

"Go on then. I only came to make sure you're still coming for family meeting tonight."

"Gods beneath the waves," Ama cursed, "I forgot." Her mood sank even further. Thanks to the meeting, she would have to give up her planned paddle down the east fork of the Brahm.

"Language, Ama, language," he said, and tugged sharply on her ear.

"Ow! Sorry Fa."

"You'll be there?"

"Yes," she said, drawing out the word to two syllables.

"Blessings of our beloved Shasir'kia, for safe journey," he said, turned his palm upward, then pulled her into a hug and whispered in her ear, "Nen guide you, my daughter," in the secret language of the Kenda.

Her smile was bittersweet as she pulled away from her father and strode back to her anxious passengers. *Put this aside.* Yes, that is exactly what she had planned to do once she had made enough coin to refit the *Naida* and leave the Banks for good. How could she tell her family that, especially her father? The news would break his heart, which is why she had found too many excuses to postpone the telling of it. Not that it mattered now; Judicia Corrus would make sure she was trapped on shore forever.

"Girl! This is unacc—"

"My sincere apologies your Lordship. We'll be off in a drop," she called up to the Damiar pacing impatiently on deck, his many layers of robes flapping in the wind, like the plumage of an exotic bird.

Ama motioned to the dock runners to help her cast off the ropes, offering a quick whistle to the Captain of the neighboring cargo boat, by way of greeting.

"Another devotional cruise, sure you can handle that all by yourself, Kalder? I could send a man to help you." Captain Brant Tather took a moment from directing his crew, as they hoisted a load aboard the *Greehm*, to take a jab at the *Naida's* captain.

Ama smirked, "If you can find a real man on these docks, please, send him on over. I'm dying to meet one."

"Another love letter from the authorities?" Captain Tather pointed toward the piece of paper in Ama's hands.

"Yeah," she said, crumpling the notice into a ball and tossing it in the river, "they just can't stay away from me."

"Hmph," Tather snorted and moved closer, kicking aside a broken shell, the remnants of some gull's breakfast, "you and the rest of us." He looked left and right, then spoke just loud enough for Ama to hear, "Cargo levies were raised again and the fleet limit is now four boats. The Shasir won't be happy until every last Kenda is crawling on their hands and knees like a Welf." At the last word, he spit on the wood plank near his feet. "No disrespect to your brother," he added, then returned to his work.

Ama nodded. No one could disrespect her brother Stevan's esteemed place among the ranks of the Shasir holy men more than she already did but she was at least wise enough to keep her tongue stilled on that matter.

"Lords and Ladies," she called, rousing herself to act the part of cheerful guide, as she climbed aboard the *Naida*, "the Halif River awaits!"

Leaping to cast off the lines to the dock runners below, she paused briefly at the stern, made sure none of her passengers were watching, then leaned over, and knocked twice on the hull for safe journey. It was a silly old superstition but these days she could use all the help the ancient Kenda gods could offer.

Ama pointed to the treetops, "There's a blue hweztel, they come to the Halif this time of year to feed on the spring fry." Above, a pair of sapphire blue wings circled over the water.

"How marvelous," one of the Damiar Ladies replied, allowing her eyes to flick upward for a second before turning back to her companion. She fanned herself briskly, "I'm sure I'll faint if we don't find some shade soon."

"Mm, I warned Flavert about these kinds of devotional tours," the Lady next to her commiserated. "We pay our dues at the Sky Ceremony and that is more than sufficient devotion if you ask me."

Not fifteen minutes earlier, Ama had listened to the same two women complain of the cold. Before that, it had been the seats (too hard), the drink (too bitter), the wind (too windy) and so on.

Only the stop at the Ymira Pavillion excited them as, swarmed by Welf servants, they were ushered off to be fed and waited upon under the shelter of canopies, overlooking the river.

Once they had gorged and drank themselves to their satisfaction, and had paused to leave a token offering at the temple, the passengers shuffled back aboard. Ama tossed a small bag of coin to the Pavilion's caretaker and pushed off for the return trip downriver.

Beneath the weight of their petticoats and dresses, their bellies full of roast game meat and benga bread, the Damiar Ladies and some of the older Lords drifted off to sleep, in the way of the privileged classes.

Boring. Stupefyingly boring these devotional cruises were, and yet the Shasir would take even this away from her. As she rested her hand on the wheel, Ama let her gaze roam, watching the familiar trees scroll by and the hunting hwetzels circle overhead.

Even with the time she had originally been allotted, she would barely have been able to make enough coin to refit and stock the *Naida* for the voyage she had planned. And now? In thirty days?

Closing her eyes for a moment, she imagined—as she always did on the long, silent stretches of the river—extending the skins and pointing the *Naida's* bow west. One day she would leave the docks of the Banks for good.

"Any more grint, *Captain*?" a man's voice asked, too close to her ear.

Ama jumped out of her daydream. "Forgive me, Lord Uval…er, hold on, I'll fill your cup."

When she held out her hand for the Damiar's cup, he grabbed her by the wrist and licked his lips. "Such fine bones you have. However do you manage this beastly craft all by your lonesome?"

Ama yanked her hand away. "I grew up with five older brothers. I know how to handle myself, your Lordship."

The man's long, sallow face, split into a wet grin. "I bet you do."

She snatched his cup away, held it under the wooden cask on the transom and opened the nozzle. A moment later, she smelled the sour stench of old wine as Lord Uval pressed his face against hers and whispered, "Interested in side coin, after the voyage?"

There was always one. Always. Why were men so rutting predictable?

With a practiced movement, Ama's hand flew to her waist, unsheathed the blade secreted on her back, and brought it around until the point rested against Uval's crotch.

"I am *interested*," she said, quietly, between gritted teeth, "in getting you to shore in one piece, without any unnecessary displays that might attract the attention of your wife."

Uval scowled and retreated a few steps. Ama passed him his cup of grint and tucked the blade back in its hiding spot. She watched him fumble his way back to his snoring wife, with a lack of grace typical of those who lived off the water.

No doubt he would be filing a complaint with the local authorities before departing the Banks, but what was that to her? They were already taking away her living and her freedom, how else could one lecherous Damiar possibly hurt her?

"Watch your step now. Hope you enjoyed the tour – tell your friends to ask for the *Naida*, everyone on the Banks knows me." Ama might as well have been talking to herself.

On the dock, she watched an elderly Welf struggle to pick up a large bag. His legs shook beneath the weight and he teetered momentarily before dropping to one knee. Somehow, he managed to hold onto the load, but his leg was gashed open from the rough wood.

"Lazy klutz," one of the Damiar Lords spat out, poking at the servant's midsection with his walking stick, "get up or you'll be swimming to Alisir." The Damiar turned on his heels and strode away, pushing through the cluster of servants who were following their masters and mistresses.

Ama offered the old man her hand but he refused, righting himself with a series of low grunts before rejoining his fellow Welf.

Slaves. Ama shook her head, as she watched the servants trudging up the ramp.

She was ready to finish folding the skins before hurrying to her father's house but then she saw Lord Uval turn from his wife and walk purposefully toward her. What now?

He held out his gloved hand, "Lady Uval insists we tip you for the lovely journey and charming banter."

Coin was coin and now, with the term of her boat license reduced, she couldn't afford to be fussy about its source. Ama held out her hand, ready to deliver the most sincere thanks she could muster but Uval flipped the coin into the air and it landed in the water, sinking into the dark green.

"And *I* insist you remember your place, Kenda whore."

Fists clenched, she forced herself to turn away. By morning, he and the rest of his party would be sailing for Alisir, on to one of their many seasonal homes. It was best to let him go. Besides, it was one thing to brawl with her fellow mariners in the Port House, quite another to attack a Damiar Lord. The former earned her a set of scraped knuckles and a warning from the authorities – the latter could see her swinging from a rope.

From outside her father's cottage, Ama heard her brother's voices competing for attention. These family meetings, supposedly to decide important personal and business matters concerning the various members of the Kalder clan, more often than not ended as an excuse to drink too much praffa wine and boast of some recent misadventure.

She used to look forward to them.

Now she paused, her hand on the door, hearing Geras's voice above the rest, speaking her name. Nen's death, not another lecture from the oldest of her five brothers, not tonight. A too-familiar feeling gripped her insides.

"Cruise went late," she announced, as she pushed open the door. The room fell silent.

"We thought you might be hiding from us," Geras chided.

"Tadpole never hides. She's a fighter!" Thuy said, leapt out of his chair and ran across the room to tackle his younger, smaller sister.

The two tumbled to the floor, knocking aside the low table where their father's pipe and tins of leaf rested.

"You see, this is what I'm talking about, Fa," Geras said, his voice sharp. "We treat her as a man and wonder why she's turned out as she has, why she's always in trouble."

"Now, now," the elder Kalder said, both hands in the air in a placating gesture, "your sister may not behave like other women but she knows her duty to her family."

"Does she really?" Geras continued, his voice reaching the far side of the room, as Ama pulled herself away from Thuy. "Does she care how people talk about the wild Kalder girl, drinking and fighting and charging money for tours on that sad excuse for a lumber pile she calls a boat?"

"Does her gresher-brained brother know that the last person who insulted the *Naida* lost two of his teeth for it?" Ama asked, elbowed Thuy in the stomach and ran to the table to steal his seat.

"My apologies, sister. Are you quite finished your wrestling match?"

"Yes I am." Ama sat and poured herself a cup of wine, as she kicked Geras under the table. "Apology accepted. Aren't you supposed to be on your way to the land of cloud sniffers to hawk your wine?"

"I leave for T'ueve tomorrow."

"Give my regards to Stevan," Ama said, her face a parody of good cheer.

Geras gave her one of his trademark nods that meant he wouldn't expect any less from someone as uncultured as his sister. Visits to the domain of the gods were only considered for few very circumstances – blessings for births and marriage, prayers for the newly dead. It had been almost a year since anyone at the table had even set eyes on Stevan, and that had been at a Sky Ceremony, from a distance.

"And tell Brin he still owes me four coin for that game of Yoth he lost," Ama added.

"Your wagers with our cousin are your business." Geras turned to Odrell, "Gambling, another of her many virtues."

A weighty and uncomfortable silence stretched across the table.

Mirit, the smallest of the mighty Kalder brothers, looked at Ama with his eyebrows drawn closely together, "I'm sorry the Judicia reduced the term of your license."

Ama looked to her father but he shook his head, "I didn't tell them, Tadpole. You know how news spreads on the docks."

"Son of a whore!" She banged her cup on the table. "It's hard enough to attract passengers without this news to scare them off."

"Language, Ama!"

"It's not fair!" How could they all sit there so calmly? How many times had she heard Fa or one of her siblings complain about the authorities poking their nose into Kenda business? Some change had taken place over the last five months; their family meetings had grown progressively more conservative and, for the first time in her life, Ama felt as if she were standing outside her family.

"Stevan is very nearly a Shasir'threa; no Kenda has ever reached that level of ascension," her father cautioned.

"Hey, maybe there's some way we could change Geras into a Damiar," Ama said. "He has the right attitude."

"This is serious, Ama. It's very important how people see Stevan's family and that includes how we earn our living."

"So? Geras gets to sell his wine, Afon and Mirit can crew the cargo ships, and Thuy still works the charting runs. All of you can make your living how you want but I can't. Why is that?" Ama asked, looking each of her brothers in the eye, daring them to challenge her.

Geras was the first to answer, pointing an accusing finger at her, "Because, like it or not, you are a woman and an unmarried one at that. Kenda women do not earn their living as boat captains, especially not alone, out on the river with strange men."

"Oh please, you make it sound as if I'm doing something dirty."

"You might as well be from what they say about you," Geras snapped back.

She opened her mouth and stopped. From the way her brothers and her father lowered their eyes, she could tell Geras spoke the truth. She nodded, slowly, imagining the wagging tongues around the Banks. "I see."

"It's all dung, Tadpole. Don't let stupid rumors bother you," Thuy said, looking at Geras.

"No, it *should* bother her," Geras countered, his voice escalating in volume as he spoke. "It should bother you," he said, leaning across the table toward his sister, "that I have to listen to people talk about my sister as if she were a Welf whore."

"Geras, enough!" Odrell bellowed at his son. "Enough, all of you." He paused as his offspring settled – all but Ama and his eldest, who glared at each other. "Ama," he placed his hand on his daughter's shoulder, "we have always looked after each other, looked out for each other. If you are...wild, the fault is mine, I know it."

"Fa, that's not—"

"Let me finish, daughter. Your brother Stevan has spent his life studying the ways of the Shasir; his ascension will be an important moment for our family, for our people and an important step toward equality. Some things are bigger than you, bigger than all of us here. You must understand that. I know it won't be easy but you must behave as a respectable Kenda woman."

Odrell rose. The same shoulders that had carried his daughter easily as a child now sagged slightly with the weight of mere words. "I am telling you, as your father, that you must abide by the decision of Judicia Corrus. Furthermore, when your license expires, if you do not choose to accept any of the offers of marriage put before you, then you will sell the *Naida*, return to this house and live under my roof as an obedient daughter. No more running to the rivers to paddle and swim, no more nights at the Port House, no more fighting, no more cursing. You will dress properly, you will attend the sky services, you will cook and associate with the other women, as you are meant to." When he sat, the air of the room swarmed with unspoken thoughts.

"And if I don't?" she asked, staring at her hands, both gripping the cup of wine.

Thuy cleared his throat and shifted uneasily in his chair.

"Then," her father said, with a sigh, "you will be cast out. You will be dead to your brothers and me."

At this, she raised her head, eyes wide in disbelief. Looking from one face to the other, she knew they had decided this long before her arrival. No threat but this could have persuaded her to obey her family's wishes, and they knew it.

"Well, I see you've all figured out my future for me. How convenient."

"You know it's for the best," Geras said, leaning back in his chair.

Ama looked to Thuy, who was busy examining the grain of the wooden table. "Even you, Thuy? Would you shun me?"

"The choice is not mine," he grumbled.

"Don't be angry, Ama. Fa's right; this is bigger than us. Stevan has been chosen by the gods," Afon finally spoke up, his lips struggling to smile.

"Angry? Why should I be angry? I should thank you all for helping a stupid, wild girl learn her place."

"When you stop acting like a child, we'll stop treating you as one!" Geras said, jabbing his finger in Ama's direction once more.

She kicked out her chair and stood, face burning, "What do you know of it, Geras? What do any of you know of it? No one threatens to take away *your* freedom!"

"Gods beneath the waves! Your brother would offer a bridge between our people and the Shasir and all you can think of is your own petty desires," Geras said, standing as well.

"Why must our people bow to those spooks?" she asked, pointing her finger toward the sky.

"Ama! Watch your tongue. That's blasphemy," Odrell said, his voice sharp.

She lowered her voice but it lost none of its fire. Ama leaned in and looked at each of the men before her as she spoke, "Blasphemy? We still pray to Nen, we still speak our own language in whispers, we keep our ways in secret and teach our children the war songs. Fa taught every one of us here to use the seft – a forbidden weapon. We are all blasphemers and may we always be. Our family has a proud history of opposing the Shasir and their Damiar puppets but now we throw that away because having Stevan among their numbers makes us respectable? If this is what the Kalders are to become then you may as well shun me. I want no part of it."

"If I didn't know you were speaking from anger, I would order you out of this house," Odrell said.

"Fa, we should listen to Ama's words," Thuy said.

"Words spoken by the girl who earns her coin from Damiar. High talk of rebellion but only when it suits her. Selfish. Just like mother," Geras said, shaking his head.

Ama swept her cup of wine off the table and hurled it at the wall behind Geras's head. "Take that back!"

"Stop this!" Odrell yelled.

The room fell silent. Ama's chest heaved as she fought to contain her emotions. For a long moment, everyone just stared. "It isn't true," Ama muttered, then turned and ran.

"Ama!" Thuy cried after her but she was already to the door.

Half blind, she ran—her heart and chest tight and painful—back to the only friend she still had.

Below deck, by the light of a lantern, Ama tore off her clothes, hurling them in a pile on the bed in her sleeping berth, while she muttered curses. When she was down to her waterwear, she reached her hands behind her neck and tugged impatiently at the laces holding her nove in place. They were tight – how long had it been since she had last taken it off?

The wide piece of leather fell away and her dathe, the thin slits of skin halfway down her neck tingled as air tickled them.

Her dathe, a remnant from the ancient, water dwelling Kenda, allowed her to breathe underwater. Their tiny vibrations created pictures for her, outlined shapes of a world she could not see otherwise.

They were also one more mark of difference between her and the rest of her people – no one had dathe anymore, not for centuries. Since she could remember, her mother and father had warned her to keep them hidden, from everyone. No chances could be taken, not even her own kind could know. Were the Shasir to learn of her 'abomination', they would claim she was a demon, one of the O'scuri that dwelt below ground and feasted on souls. She would be sacrificed to the gods, along with the rest of her family. All of the Kenda would be suspect, all would suffer because of her.

She was careful to hang the concealing nove on the hook next to the likeness of her mother. Her fingers drifted over the age-stained paper that prevented her mother from leaving her completely.

Tall and slender, with eyes that changed colour with her surroundings, Colwyn Kalder stared down at her daughter. She had golden hair tied in a knot because, like Ama, she could never be bothered to fuss with it. She wore a smile that hid her dissatisfaction with the life she had been herded into. Here, aboard the *Naida*, Colwyn Kalder was alive and well in her daughter.

"I won't let them," Ama whispered, her fingers moving from the paper to the worn wood of the *Naida*'s hull. "I won't let them separate us."

There was only a sliver of a moon, the docks were empty, nothing could be heard but creaking wood and lapping water. As she hurried above deck, Ama kept a watchful eye. It was dangerous, exposing herself as she was. One never knew where Shasir spies might be hiding, but tonight she needed release. More than that, she needed to forget.

In a motion as familiar as breathing, she sprung up onto the bow and dove into the black water with barely a splash. Her second eyelids—the thin, filmy layer that protected Kenda eyes from salt and cold—were up before she hit. On her neck, the freshly exposed dathe went to work pulling oxygen from the water and sounding the area so that Ama could 'see' the world below the surface.

She dove deep, letting the current sweep her toward the Big Water. She would not go that far, though she could, and without raising her head above water once.

Praise you, Nen, Water Father, she thought, shocked at the depth of the gratitude she felt.

But why shouldn't she be grateful for her gift? An onom turtle swam by, she could tell from the shape of its shell and flippers. A lucky sign. Onoms were rare, hunted nearly to extinction by the Damiar. In the water, they were almost impossible to catch but on land, where they nested, they were slow and awkward. An entire colony could be taken in a single day and so they had been. For all she knew, this one could be the last of its kind. Just like her.

She pumped her legs harder and caught up with a spinner; the two of them rolled and twisted around each other. Eternally playful, spinners frequented the rivers, though they preferred white water and waves, anything to surf or leap out of.

If she were to encounter a person down here—one of the Nen-tribu, *tribes of Nen*, that lived beyond the Rift, the long ago home of the Kenda—what would she do? She knew the history, knew about the civil war between the Kenda-tribu and the Vakua-tribu that had driven her people across the Rift and onto the land; her kind had good reason to be wary. Even though the nove—the collars they had worn to hide their dathe after their exodus from the deep, countless generations past—

was now merely decoration, the old fear persisted. The Kenda's ancient rivals no longer hunted them. Good for her people. Only, on nights like these, she wished she didn't have to be like the onom turtle. Alone.

According to Kenda prophesy, their exile from the water would not be permanent. One day their savior, the Kiera-Nen, *Nen's chosen one*, would appear and lead an army against their enemies. Would lead them home. That story had been enough for her to cling to as a child, but now that promise was beginning to sound as empty as any of the Shasir's.

As it slowed, the spinner dipped beneath Ama and let her wrap her arms around its neck. With long, languorous pumps of its tail, the animal turned and carried his passenger back in the direction of the *Naida*.

Praise you my brother, Ama thought, stroking the slick fur of the spinner's belly, a long-absent sense of calm returning. She would swim for hours tonight, to wash away the day.

"I have the target," the lead trooper called. Moonlight washed over the valley, the water gurgling as if issuing threats, or so Seg imagined, though the others were more used to it and did not seem perturbed. "Do I acquire?"

"Hold," Kerbin ordered, her voice terse. "Flankers, clear?"

The flankers chorused that their areas were clear, there were no witnesses lurking around to reveal the existence of the recon squad once they made their move. Seg glanced at Manatu, who sat immobile, eyes flickering constantly in a state of ready vigilance. He glanced at Kerbin; her stillness mirrored Manatu's.

First acquisition was rife with peril. Aside from the potential for their presence being revealed early and compromising the mission, there was the tremendous uncertainty as to what they were really facing. All the troopers sat as still as stone pillars. Vigilant.

Kerbin's head jerked in a slight nod. "Acquire."

"Moving."

CHAPTER 2

S eg stared at the film overlay in his palm, cupped toward his chest so the faint light didn't give away his position. The thermal readout indicated the relative positions of the trooper and his prey. The stunner the trooper carried required him to move within an arm's reach of the target; a heavy dose of voltage would handle the rest. Through the audio pickup, Seg could hear the trooper's regulated breathing, the water, and a faint splashing as the trooper's target moved through it. He sucked in a breath, wondering if the trooper would have to enter the water and risk exposure to whatever hostile fauna lurked within.

His stomach clenched, muscles locking in a small spasm that made him shudder. Time was crawling. Couldn't the trooper move any faster?

On screen, the trooper's icon moved in on the target. The audio pickup caught the sound of the stunner discharging. There was a loud splash, a muttered curse, then the sound of sloshing water.

The trooper had entered the water; Seg's stomach tightened further at the thought.

"Acquisition made," the trooper reported. A long pause followed and then, "Going to need some help hauling him back. He's a heavy bastard."

Ama paused only to squeeze the water from her hair before she finished climbing the rope ladder dangling from the stern of the *Naida*.

"Enjoy your swim?"

She gasped; the disembodied voice came from somewhere midship. She shook her hair forward and smoothed it to cover her dathe as she squinted into the dark.

The outline of a man stepped to the portside, his walk casual, his posture relaxed.

"Whoever you are, get off my boat before I throw you off!" Ama's voice faltered slightly. In her anger and hurry, she had left her knife, over-clothes, and nove below deck, in her quarters. The forbidden seft, hidden in the transom, could have her sent to Correction and therefore was for only the direst of emergencies.

"I think you are mistaking me for a threat, Captain Kalder. This is a friendly visit."

Now she recognized the voice. She took a step back as the man stepped forward, hands raised to show his innocent intentions.

"Judicia Corrus," she said, her voice higher than normal. Had Uval complained to the local Damiar enforcement after all? "Blessings of the Shasir upon you." She looked over each shoulder. If Corrus were here then his Head Constable, Dagga, would be too. "Your notice said I had thirty days, I—"

"You have your thirty days, Amadahy. Have no fears there."

His tone was obviously meant to be reassuring but Ama felt no such thing, as Dagga finally appeared from out of the hatch that led below deck. Moonlight reflected off his bald head, which sat on his neck like a block of stone and was thatched with thin scars. He didn't speak, didn't even acknowledge Ama's presence as he clomped his way to her side, where his body eclipsed hers.

"Should I have fears somewhere else?" Ama's eyes flicked down to the large blade sheathed on Dagga's hip.

"Witty, I like that," Corrus said, and stepped forward again. Now the moonlight caught his face, casting his soft features in harsh shadow. To Ama, Judicia Corrus had always seemed like a shard of glass – smooth and clean, but so sharp it could cut you almost by looking at it. Even now, the shine of his black and silver hair threatened to draw blood. Most on the docks feared Dagga, but it was Corrus who had always sent ice through Ama's veins.

"I came to talk to you about the notice, actually. As a friend," he continued.

"A friend?" Ama ducked her chin to keep her hair forward, over her dathe, and inched sideways, away from Dagga.

"Is that so strange?" Corrus raised his palms; his eyebrows also rose. "Ama, I have no grudge against you, I don't draw up notices and fines because I enjoy making your life unpleasant. As a representative of the Shasir, among the people, I have a duty to enforce the laws and ensure order. I am the hand of the gods, a responsibility I take seriously. And you have to admit," he smiled, his white teeth gleamed, "you can be boisterous, disruptive, even a little wild, from time to time."

He waited for her reply.

"I guess so," Ama said after a pause. Her bare thigh was pressed against the transom. If Corrus or his pet monster made a move, she could always dive overboard.

Corrus tossed his head back and laughed, "Look at you! So nervous. Come now, I've heard tales of your Port House antics. Timidity doesn't suit you."

"What do you want?"

The laugh stopped. "The better question is: what do *you* want?"

"To keep my license. To keep sailing and earning coin, as I was promised I could."

"And I want that for you as well." Corrus smiled at her tilted head. "I want everyone to do their jobs, make an honest living, stay in line with the laws. I want peace, Ama. But," he sighed dramatically, "there are those who want to keep all of us from getting what we want. Traitors in our midst. Kenda who defy the will of the gods and jeopardize the well being of their own kind. Remnants from a less civilized past who would undo the unity our beloved Shasir'kia brought to the land. And I would search them out, expose them and see that they were properly corrected, if I could. But, as you know, your kind can be…secretive."

"I don't know what you're talking about."

"Oh, I think you do. Don't you, Constable Dagga?" Corrus asked.

"Buncha filthy, sneaky water rats," Dagga said.

"I'm not a traitor or a heretic; my brother is a Shasir'dua. I attend the—"

"I know all about your brother. He's a fine example for all of us. No," Corrus placed his hand on the wheel, "I'm not accusing you, I'm asking for your help. You're a devout believer, obviously, but among those you associate with, well, I'm sure you hear things, see things. All I'm asking is for you to keep listening, keep watching, and then come to me, as a friend, and share what you know."

He tightened his grip on the wheel and inhaled deeply.

"Gods above it must be invigorating, being out on the water all day. The freedom," he sighed again, a lock of hair slipped out of place, "how I envy you! But, I'm getting carried away. You watch and listen, tell me what you see and hear, and I," he knocked on the wheel, "will make sure that you stay free and sailing."

"You want me to spy for you?" Ama's eyes were dark, she fought to keep her fists unclenched. "You want me to spy on my own people?"

"I want you to help your people. I want you to protect them from those who would force me to use less civilized measures to keep order."

"Like burning boats?" She regretted the words the moment they slipped out.

"Yes. Like that," he replied, the friendly tone seeping out of his voice.

"No."

"Think about this Amadahy."

"I have." She kept one eye on Dagga, "I said no. You're not my friend and I'm not yours. I'll follow your rules but that's all you can make me do."

"Sure about that?" Dagga muttered.

Judicia Corrus tipped his head to one side then the other, "Well, I had to try, but I can't say I'm surprised. Stubborn." He lunged forward without warning, until his nose was almost touching hers. "Just like your mother."

Ama gasped, which elicited another gleaming smile, this one predatory.

"You…" Ama's heartbeat sped up. She tried to move but Dagga's hand clamped on her elbow and held her in place.

"Stubborn, proud, secretive, yes, you're just like her." Corrus said, then smoothed the undisciplined lock of hair back into place. "But perhaps you have slightly more concern for your family than she did, hm? Why don't you take some time to think about my offer?"

"Get off my boat," Ama said, her voice barely restrained.

"Your boat, yes, she's a beauty," Corrus said, then turned to Dagga. "Let's leave our friend to consider her future. Oh, and Amadahy, if news of this friendly chat should reach any other ears, then those ears would find themselves at the mercy of my Head Constable. Understood?"

Ama's heart felt as if it had stopped beating. She nodded, unable to speak.

"Good!" Corrus strolled away as casually as if he were in his own home.

Dagga released Ama's elbow with a shove, pulled a match from his shirt pocket and struck it on the cask of grint. He held the flame in front of Ama's face, she leaned away from the light to keep her dathe hidden. Dagga let the match burn right down to the end, to the tips of his finger and thumb, without flinching. When the flame died, he placed the blackened stick on the helm, worked up a mouthful of spit and hacked it on the deck.

"Thirty days, Amadahy," Corrus called out from the stairs, without looking back. "Thirty days."

She watched the men leave until the night swallowed them. Then she hurried below deck, to her quarters, where she re-fastened her nove with trembling fingers.

"Rutting Judicia," she cursed.

She thought of Dagga, pawing through the insides of her beloved *Naida*, and was filled with an urge to dive overboard again and scrub herself clean.

Had they been watching her? What if Dagga had shown up while she was still onboard? She grabbed her knife off the small table in the corner and clutched the hilt.

Thirty days.

She couldn't tell Fa or her brothers about Corrus's threat, or she would put them all in danger.

Overhead, the lantern painted the small berth a dismal orange. Ama sighed, as she looked around at her home. What were her choices? Whether she married or not, it would mean giving up the *Naida* and everything she lived for, with no way to ensure Corrus would leave her alone. If she could make enough coin, if she could only do that, then she could run, take herself and the *Naida* out of Corrus's reach. Beyond the Rift Tribu, if it came to that.

Thirty days.

Or she could betray her own people.

She stared at her mother's likeness; Corrus's words filled her head. No one in the family talked much about the suicide but Ama remembered, vividly, the last day she had seen her mother. She was five; it was her first day at the Lesson House. It would also be her last. She was folding her lesson sheet into a paper boat and gazing out the window, dreaming of distant lands, when her mother appeared, the seed winds whipping her hair in a frenzy. Her mother's smile was sad. She touched her hand to her heart, then her forehead, the Kenda gesture for love that transcends words, then knelt down next to a large stone, removed her nove, and left it there.

"Amadahy!" The Lesson Master's sharp voice called her to attention, and she looked away from the window.

When she looked back, her mother was gone. Ama never saw her again.

Jumped, off the bluffs, downriver from the docks, witnesses said. Swept away forever by the river below. People said it was no surprise, Colwyn Kalder had never been happy.

Was it true? Or was there more to the story, as Corrus had intimated.

"I won't let him," Ama whispered, determination edging back into her voice. She closed off the lantern and lay down on her bed. She didn't know how, yet, but this was her home and no one would take that away from her.

Lugging the Outer to shore had been a chore for the troopers. Once he had regained consciousness, the real work had begun, and that was proving even more difficult.

"Talk, damn you!" a trooper growled, prodding at the native.

Their first acquisition was a short, stubby man of indeterminate age, who murmured fearfully but who spoke only in unintelligible bursts, no matter how roughly he was handled.

Samples of live conversation were necessary to help tune the implanted translators, known informally as *chatterers*, which they all wore. No matter how fitfully the native gasped and rasped, though, it was obvious he had no language and the best he could manage was disconnected sounds. One of the troopers raised a rifle butt and Seg, finally deciphering the clues, raised his hands to stop him.

He motioned for the man to open his mouth wide and when the prisoner complied he looked inside with a knowing nod. "He can't speak properly, you halfwits." He gestured to the Outer's mangled tongue. Whether it was a birth defect or the result of some form of primitive punishment was impossible to say. "You've abducted a partial mute." This was not the most promising omen for his first venture across the warps. So far the operation had been short and simple. They had gathered a great deal of radio chatter, almost entirely communications based. The inhabitants of this world obviously didn't go in for transmission entertainment – a notable point, which Seg had filed away. The gathered data revealed that the technology level on this world was generally low, speaking to either a technocratic upper class, or a pattern of cultural divisions between nation states, some possessing more modern accouterments than their primitive neighbors. However, it was still too early to say.

Accurate tuning of the chatterers was impossible from broadcast communications alone. Or perhaps it was possible but his people would never know how to achieve it – such were the failings of stolen technology. Nevertheless, the data from the chatterer had suggested a complex, nuanced language that seemed adjective-heavy, indicating an artistic or religious bent.

Perfect. Seg felt there was a rich mine to be plumbed here, and he was as eager as the recon squad to start digging into it.

"So what do we do, boss?" a trooper asked Kerbin.

"De-pop," she answered, tapping the butt of her rifle against the sheathed knife on her hip. "Wait," Seg said, holding up a hand. He looked at the native cowering on the ground, making noises that were obviously pleas for mercy. It wasn't pity that drove him to stop the execution, he assured himself, merely calculation of the odds. Each abduction of a native involved the risk of exposure, and if the squad had a resource at hand they needed to make full use of it. "Even with the defect, I can work with this. Get your cretins away from him, Kerbin. Signalman, I'll need your assistance." Seg crouched down in front of the native and switched the chatterer on. He could tweak it based on the responses he was getting, he was sure. It would take a while longer to extract language this way, but he was nothing if not patient, especially in the face of potential wealth. "I need you to work the modulation," he explained to the comm operator. "We'll be using verbal and non-verbal, and I will provide missing elements of sound where possible. It will give us a rough working approximation of his language." "Whatever," the comm operator said, grabbing up his equipment while casting a sideways glance to his fellow troopers. Seg didn't miss the look that broadcasted the comm operator's feelings about Theorists and their penchant for what so many of his ilk considered esoteric nonsense.

After three hours of patient exchanges between himself and the Outer, Seg managed to establish a rapport.

Welf, that's what they called themselves. Surreptitious observation combined with the modulated chatterer allowed the troops to pick up a rudimentary understanding of the local language. He wasn't sure if Welf was a species term, tribal/national term, or a caste term, but it was a start.

Seg conceded that he had gained as much information from the native as was possible under the circumstances. A trooper motioned for him to stand back, raised a combat blade and dispatched the Outer with a flick of steel. With his boot, he pushed the body aside, then buried it in the shallow grave that had been prepared, covered the grave with greenery, and rejoined the rest of the squad. By the time the body might be discovered, the squad would be a safe distance away.

The Outer was of no further use to the mission and was too feeble and simple to make any sort of useful caj on their World – but the death bothered Seg in a way that he couldn't quite define. The universe was harsh and unforgiving, and his World, the apex world across all dimensions, survived on the basis of capture and sacrifice. It was the nature of things, though wasteful. He had seen death before, in the arenas, from a distance, but he had never seen a man bleed out right in front of him, with all the associated sights, sounds and smells. The body had still been twitching as he had walked away from it. Such was the nature of this work, though, and Seg reminded himself that the ensuing raid, once he gathered the necessary information, would be far from bloodless. "We have to make track," Kerbin said, interrupting Seg's thoughts. "If the local primitives haven't noticed your pet mute went missing yet, they will soon enough." She tapped a button on her wrist; a holographic display sprung up and floated between them. "It's your show, but I recommend we cut north and track along this river." "Why?" Seg asked, studying the map. "Because," she said, in a voice that reminded Seg of someone trying to explain why the shielded sky was copper to a small child, "Outers like this run to the rivers. We can move down, acquire one that actually talks, and then get on with our business." "No." Seg's eyes remained on the map. "No?" she asked, shaking her head. He had no time for interdepartmental prejudices. "No, not north, scroll northeast," he said, pointing to the display. "How far did your survey drone go?" "It dropped at seventy kilometers to recharge. Give it twelve minutes and it'll be back up again." "We have a developing mountain range here." "So? Mountains mean a tough trail." Kerbin wiped her forehead; they were all sporting glistening skin, unused to air so moist. Seg watched as the display scrolled. "Primitive Outers tend to place value on mountains and caves. Our radio frequency signals are coming from northeast, twenty kilometers out and increasing. We move this way, examine the base of the range for artifact sites, then cut back to follow the river track. It's not just the Outers we're here for." He slipped into a lecturing tone, "We're here to scout out their vita sources, and following the primitives along the river won't take us there." He could feel her glare on his back as he turned away and reviewed the feeds from the visual monitoring.

Another self-referential was emerging from the collected comm data: *Shasir*. Fascinating.

The squad was only an hour into the hike up the mountain when a trooper's scream violated the air.

"Damp that!" Kerbin ordered.

Manatu rushed forward and clamped a hand over the man's mouth. The trooper flailed wildly as the rest of the squad moved up and grabbed his arms to help restrain him. Even Manatu's bulk could not contain the trooper's frenzy.

Herma, his name is Herma, Seg thought as he pulled his pack down and reached in for his auto-med. On Kerbin's nod, he wrapped the sleeve around Herma's forearm. Herma struggled to pull his arm loose but the other troopers held him firm as Seg initiated the auto-med by pressing a large green button. It was a simple machine, designed for ease of use under trying circumstances — a design Seg could now appreciate in more than theory. The cuff clamped down as the machine gathered vital information.

Kerbin snatched the control box from Seg's hand to study the readings. Her grim expression betrayed the trooper's prognosis as she jabbed the touch-sensitive screen and chose the option the machine gave her.

"Poison," she said. "Likely vector was at the calf. Possibly insect-based. Clear back and let him go."

Herma was already going slack, the drugs pumping into his system relaxing him. That or the poison was finishing him off, only Kerbin knew at this point. She stepped back, eyes flickering between the victim and the auto-med. Herma shuddered, all color drained from his face.

"Get out there and set the perimeter," she ordered the troopers. "And don't let any kargin' bugs get on you."

The troopers dispersed, moving into position. It would be a perimeter smaller by one man now, Seg noted silently. He gestured at Herma. "Is he…?"

Kerbin nodded, her face harder than he had seen it before. "Yeah, he's done for. The machine's already got antivenom formulated, but the venom got into his heart tissue. Too late for him," she said, as she jabbed another button, "but we'll be protected."

He couldn't help noticing she didn't seem comforted by that fact. Seg crouched down next to Herma, stared at him a moment, then grasped his shoulder. "Sleep," he said quietly, as Herma's eyes fluttered.

Kerbin swore softly behind him. Seg glanced back and addressed her in a low tone, "Anything can kill when you're extrans."

"I know that damn well better than you do," she said. "I'm not the first-timer."

"We need to keep moving. Let's get him cleared and buried." He reached for Herma's pack and began pulling it off.

"You could wait until he's dead!"

Seg looked back at her, briefly, then resumed his work. "He can't feel it now anyway."

The sunlight filtering in through the trees was coming in at an angle now, but even after four hours it had lost none of its intensity.

"We need a Shasir," Seg said to Kerbin, as they waited for two of the squad to cut a path through a wall of fallen trees and thick brush. "That seems to be a position of some importance to the Welf primitives. We must acquire a Shasir or someone closely connected to them."

"Better to grab assistants," she said. "When the big figures go missing, there's usually a stir." She swatted a flying insect away from her face.

"We don't know how big a figure the Shasir represents just yet. If they're a broad-spectrum religious caste, then losing a minor functionary is less likely to draw attention."

Kerbin cleared her throat, "That sounds dangerously close to an assumption, Theorist."

"Missions turn on inference," he answered. Leaning closer, he looked her in the eye, "Risk is factored into the mission."

"You don't have to remind me about that," she said, pointing to the men clearing a section of woodland debris from their path. "We're already off the safest path. Listen, this is your first extrans. It's my thirteenth, for recon alone."

"But only your second as squad leader," he pointed out. "You've lost one of your troopers. You're showing signs of shying."

Kerbin's dark eyes narrowed but she didn't reply.

"This is my mission," he said. "The choice of path was mine and the responsibility mine."

"You're going to push for catching one of these Shasir regardless of protocol. Unortho."

He leaned back, wiping the sweat from his face with the sleeve of his uniform. The same word always came up for him. *Unortho.* The label had pursued him throughout his training, and of course it would arise on his mission. "Protocol is a guideline, not a control graft. We will continue to assess the situation, and if taking a Shasir, which appears to constitute the best information source, presents itself as an opportunity, we'll move on it. It will entail risk. We accepted risk when we walked through the warp gate."

Kerbin was irking him more and more with every exchange. He didn't need to put up with balking now that they were out in the field.

"Perimiter clear, lead," a trooper reported, his chest heaving from the strain of the work.

"Let's move," Kerbin answered, swatting the air around her face again. "At this pace, all we'll have to send back through the next warp is bugs anyway."

Challenging had turned out to be a gross understatement to describe the terrain. Once again, years of training proved to be a pale imitation of the real thing. Layers of decomposing vegetation made the ground wet and soft. Walking on it was like walking through a field of wet sponge. It also hid possible hazards, a fact that made all the troopers skittish, especially on the heels of Herma's death.

Seg knew of trees from his studies but he had never conceived they could function so perfectly as obstacles. The thick, green canopy overhead let in only the thinnest beams of natural light, the trunks and branches limited the field of vision, roots hid beneath foliage to trip unwary feet and the trees size and spacing often dictated sweeping detours. Formidable, these structures.

Between the constant buzz of insects, the slow travel and the humidity, Seg was beginning to question his decision to move inland until a voice in his ear announced that the lead trooper had spotted a target.

"There's a lot of 'em," the lead trooper called out, as the rest of the squad halted. "Visual and scan puts it at over five hundred."

Everyone waited while the information came through. Kerbin glanced back at Seg, who nodded. She cued her transmitter.

"Observation positions and coverage everyone. The Theorist and I will go into primary observation position."

At the words, the troopers fanned out, and Kerbin led Seg up to a small outcropping on the side of the mountain. In the distance, in a wide valley, hundreds of dots moved like a slow whirlpool. When Seg lowered his visor, and tapped his wrist controls to zoom in, the dots became flesh. Another few taps and he could make out individual features – leather and rough fiber clothing, dark hair and eyes, the lean, protruding muscles of a working class, females wide at the hips with generous breasts, indicating healthy breeding stock.

"Trooper," Seg said to the man hovering behind him, "bring me a recharge cell."

The man nodded once and hurried away.

"We have names, you know," Kerbin said to him.

"I'm well aware. I know them all. I know your service histories, familial affiliations, service sectors, and full backgrounds. Probably better than you do," Seg said, observing the unfolding scene.

"Really," she said. Seg couldn't see her face, but her tone was one of disbelief and, if he was not mistaken, tinged with fear.

"Really," he answered, not moving his gaze from the spectacle below. "Tell me, what do you know of me?"

"You're a Theorist and an obnoxious, self-congratulatory prick, and you'll be even worse now that you've actually gone and found something. But we need you on this, and hey, you know what? You need us too."

He considered that as he watched the solemn procession chanting and droning. It wasn't a particularly colorful display, given the nature of the environment. He would have expected more primary colors, more body paint. The Welf were entreating the Shasir, from what he could gather of the rough translations.

"You're correct, Kerbin, I do need you and your troops," he said, focusing on the primitive gathering. "Somebody has to carry the equipment."

She snorted at that and he felt her face move closer to his. "Y'know, Theorists aren't soft—the Guild trains you hard—but most of 'em I've had to shepherd on jobs like this, they wouldn't have looked to march straight into the weeds like you did. They're usually fine with taking the easier path. You didn't cry about it, just grabbed your gear and moved. Much as I hate to admit it, I'm impressed." She stared into his eyes, her own dilating as she waited for his response.

Kerbin's proximity and tone of voice were unwelcome. He had been prepared for this eventuality; extrans missions often inspired sentimental notions of bonding, which escalated with stress and danger. "I'm not interested in you," he said.

He watched the features of her face widen in disbelief, then narrow in anger. A predictable reaction.

"Go play with yourself, you self-absorbed little shit," she said, pulling away.

Seg resumed his observation, satisfied that the relationship was back in proper working order.

"I think things are about to get interesting," he said, pointing. Kerbin's eyes followed his finger to the airship in the distance. Now that, *that* had some color going. It was a crude thing, by the standards of his World, but functional. The ship drifted along sedately as the chanting picked up.

As the airship neared the gathering, a burst of brilliant light exploded from the bottom, showering down in streams. The mass of Outers leapt into a frenzy, raising their hands skyward and cheering.

"Loud noises and bright lights are primal human triggers," Seg said. "The more advanced the society, the more ostentatious the displays tend to be. And we can assume, from the pyrotechnics display, these Shasir have familiarity with black powder and weapons of that nature."

Kerbin rocked onto one elbow, "Primitive weapons."

"As Squad Leader, you should know better than to underestimate the damage such weapons are capable of," Seg said. Kerbin was silent but he could feel her resentment. "How long until warp window?" he asked, after a moment. Once they had acquired a prisoner for proper interrogation, they would have to hold the Outer until such time as they could send it back to the World. All the while evading contact and pursuit.

"Seventeen hours," Kerbin answered.

"If I'm correct, one or more of the Shasir will be aboard that airship."

"You're still set on getting one?" she shook her head.

"At least one." He tapped a button on his wrist to switch his visor to photo-capture mode. A few more taps and he could make out a young Outer woman, swaying to the chanting, winding her way up a set of stairs toward a large tent erected beside what was obviously the landing pad for the airship. Tapping another button, he captured the image and transmitted it over to Kerbin.

"There, that structure. That's where your troops will find a Shasir."

"You want the girl too? Ever had one? This could be your first?" Kerbin asked, one corner of her mouth tugging upward.

The insult was an obvious attempt to gain ground over him. "I've had partners." He looked Kerbin up and down, "Though I prefer girls that aren't built like boys."

She bared her teeth at him, then pulled her visor down with a snap.

"Just the Shasir," Seg said.

Kerbin turned and issued orders to the squad without another word to him.

Ama lifted the empty cask off the transom, dropped it to the deck and rolled it toward the bow. More grint. More expense. She was barely scraping any profit from these tours but they were all she had. Without a crew, she couldn't run cargo and the *Naida* was too small and unappealing to the Damiar for Big Water transport. And she was sure Judicia Corrus was well aware of these facts.

"Miss Kalder?" a man's voice called out from the dock below.

"*Captain* Kalder," she raised her head and stopped the cask mid-roll, "are you looking for a tour?"

A face came into view. Ama frowned as Wirch Jorret—the least palatable of the men who had burdened her with an offer of marriage—stepped aboard, carrying a handful of cut flowers. She resumed her chore.

"You're looking…healthy, Miss Kalder."

"It's bad manners to come aboard without asking the captain's permission, you know," she said, without looking at him. She had had enough of uninvited visitors.

"This is an urgent matter," Wirch said, following her at a trot. "Your brother Geras informed me of the latest change in your circumstances."

Ama rolled her eyes. Leave it to Geras to make a bad situation worse. He had to be blind not to see that Wirch's only interest in her was her family name.

"My circumstances are none of your business. I told you last time I wasn't interested in your offer Mr. Jorret." Tipping the cask on end, she stood and faced him, hands on her hips. Over Wirch's shoulder, she could see Captain Tather on the bow of the *Greehm*, watching her. Having a good laugh too, she was sure. "I think I was even polite about it. Now if you'll excuse me," she strode past Wirch, "I have another cruise tomorrow and I have to—"

"I have an addition to my offer, something that will make us both happy," Wirch called, jogging after Ama again. "I understand the Judicia is taking away your license?"

Ama spun around, "And?"

"And I have a solution!" Wirch's smile was practically swallowed by his cheeks. "If you agree to my offer of marriage—an offer, I should add, that most women of your age would be pleased to receive—you can sign this vessel over to me. With my position, I'll have no trouble securing a commercial license in my name. You can keep this as a side business, for pocket coin. You see how perfect my plan is?"

Ama crossed her arms in front of her chest and leaned back, taking in Wirch's self-satisfied expression with no small measure of skepticism. "You won't have a problem with your wife working as a boat captain?"

"Work? On this boat?" Wirch let out a high-pitched laugh, "Oh goodness, no, no, whatever gave you that idea? I think you mean to tease me, Miss Kalder, but I'm not so easily fooled. Of course you couldn't remain doing…this," he swept his hand to indicate the whole of the *Naida*, his mouth puckering as if he had bitten into the bitter sac of a jinje fruit. "It wouldn't be proper. No, we'll hire a captain to run these quaint little tours, someone qualified. But I assure you," he reached out with his free hand and touched Ama's elbow, "all of the profits would be yours to spend as you wish."

Ama looked down at the hand on her elbow, not as large or forceful as Dagga's but every bit as unwelcome. "So, if I marry you, give you my boat and quit my work, you'll let me keep a few coins?"

"For whatever you fancy," Wirch said, nodding his head eagerly. "Geras mentioned that you are strong willed but you can see I am no tyrant."

Geras was going to get an earful, or worse, when he returned from T'ueve. "Thank you," Ama said, pulling the flowers from Wirch's hand, "for your *generous* proposal."

"Is that a yes?" he asked, following behind her as she walked to the port gunwale.

"What do you think?" she asked, dropped the flowers overboard and brushed the debris from her hands. When she looked back at Wirch, his mouth hung open, making his loose flesh droop even more. "Now," her face hot, she stepped forward, forcing Wirch to step back, "get off my boat. This is still *my* boat, Mr. Jorret. Mine. Remember that."

"Well, this is...I never...you..." Wirch blathered as he retreated, nearly falling as he reached the steps to disembark. "You'll receive no further offers from me, no matter how high your brother may ascend, I can tell you that!"

If only that were true.

Wirch half marched, half wobbled off the dock, accompanied by the sound of Captain Tather's laughter.

"Always happy to amuse you, Tather," Ama said, flipping an unmistakable hand gesture toward the bow of the *Greehm* before turning away and walking to the bow of her own boat.

"Don't ever marry, Kalder. I'd hate to lose my entertainment!" he called back.

Hands gripped on the rail, Ama stared off to the horizon. A Shasir skyship was floating inland, probably to the Ymira valley and the Welf village there. Soon, Stevan might be up there among the robed spooks, bringing the blessings of the gods, the Shasir'kia, to the poor and downtrodden. For a price, of course. Always for a price.

Wasn't that the way? The less you had, the more you were expected to give up.

Wirch's flowers drifted by below. Ama shivered. There would be more offers, from him and others. As distasteful as her occupation was, she would soon be the sister of a Shasir'threa, and at the 'old' age of twenty, men would assume she was anxious to be wed.

Everyone wanted something from her and they didn't care what they took from her to get it.

Well, there was always one option, something no one could take away from her. Her eyes moved past the flowers and stared into the dark water as her thumbs rubbed the leather of her nove. Disappearing was as easy as removing her collar, diving into that other world, and leaving everything behind. The question was, how far was she prepared to go?

The troopers, still riding the adrenalin leftover from their infiltration of the Welf gathering, busied themselves setting up the field warpgen, which converted stored vita to power the warp gate, as Seg examined their primary acquisition.

There was a loud *ahhh-kreee* from some nocturnal animal above them, probably avian, which made the anxious troopers even jumpier.

The Shasir Outer was unconscious. He was a scrawny thing, withered and aged. Seg wondered how he managed to carry all his ceremonial bric-a-brac, but lifting the robe he realized it was fairly lightweight. Most of the shiny parts were hollow and light, designed to awe and impress and not function for anything. He shook his head at the artifice and at the gullibility of the Outers who fell for it. Worshiping these people as conduits to a higher power? The natives were idiots. "This is the control unit," he said, pulled off a star-shaped box, the one functional device in the collection of shiny junk, and passed it to Kerbin, who was holding a hand over her earpiece.

"We've got maybe thirty-five minutes until they sweep our way," she said. "When that happens, we'd best be gone, unless you want a hundred dead Outers and a lot of trouble down the road."

"Warp window in four and a half minutes," Seg said, feeling much calmer now that the objective had been achieved.

From the observation point, he had watched the raid. The troopers had moved with honed precision, waiting until the right moment to isolate the target. That part had gone smoothly. On the other hand...

He looked at the whimpering girl, bound hand and foot and gagged.

"I didn't request that one," he said.

Kerbin smirked, the troopers tried to mute their snickers but it was clear they found the scene amusing. "She was in with the ugly Outer. Finding the holy or something like."

"Yeah, found it on her knees, under his robes," a trooper added, sparking another round of quiet laughter.

"Troops figured they'd get you your first caj," Kerbin said.

"What?" Seg raised his hands in frustration.

"First mission. Your trophy."

Seg looked from Kerbin to the girl. The first mission trophy was a Theorist tradition that went back centuries. And while it was true every Theorist still took a trophy caj on their first field mission, there were few that bothered 'hunting' their own anymore. Generally, the Theorist was given first pick of any caj brought back after the raid, keeping their trophy long enough to parade around at the Victory Commemoration. This had been Seg's plan; he had no intention of taking caj for himself.

"This is not the time to be marking and collecting yet. We have work to do," he said.

"Oh Storm, if you don't want her, we'll just keep her then. Have some fun after recon's done," Kerbin said. Her words were met with enthusiastic murmurs from the troopers. She pushed the Outer over with her boot, exposing her heaving bosom to the sky. "They're all just the same anyway."

"No," Seg said. He looked down at the fear-stricken face and imagined a heavy metallic graft being implanted on the back of the Outer's skull and neck. "No. That is sloppy thinking, squad leader. She moves as mine, but the transit comes out of your portion."

"You can't do that!" Kerbin pulled her helmet off to get close, stared up at him and impaled his eyes with hers.

"I most certainly can. You disobeyed my orders," he said, his tone icy, maintaining his calm demeanor even as he fought down the impulse to reach for his sidearm. "It's in your contract. Read carefully next time." They glared at each other for a long moment. "But I will give you and your lot a chance to make it up to me."

"Two minutes, boss!" one of the troopers called out.

They stared at each other a moment longer, before Kerbin broke away. She grabbed the Outer by the hair, hoisted her to her feet and shoved her toward the warp gate. The girl squealed through the gag and tumbled forward, landing on her face, then tried to squirm away. Kerbin planted a boot in the middle of her back, pinning her in place.

"Oh and mark her: *Do not process*," Seg added.

"Would you like to hold its hand as it goes through, as well?" Kerbin asked as she pulled a band from her pack, scribbled Seg's instructions on it and clipped it around the girl's neck.

Behind her, Seg didn't bother with a reply but he relaxed his shoulders a fraction.

He watched as the warp gate opened and the Outers were thrust through. The priest was due for a bad end. He would be processed. The Guild would empty his brain for a quick culture dump, then shoot the information back to Seg so he could begin the next step in the process. The husk that was left would be shipped off to the huchack ponds, the mines or the recyclers to haul metal and toil until the body followed the dead spirit.

Such was life.

As for the Outer female, he would deal with her when he got back. There had to be a better fate for her than being used and discarded by raiders.

Kerbin tugged her helmet back on. "Pack the warp gate, we move. NOW!" she ordered her troops. She didn't speak to Seg at all, obviously willing to leave him to the mercy of the local search parties if he didn't follow.

The squad had backtracked down the mountainside. The natural contours of the mountain offered them a strategic camp site for the night, though no one was letting down their guard just yet.

Morning passed slowly as they waited for the next warp window and the interrogation data that would determine the course of their mission. When it came through, Seg spent the better part of the afternoon speed-reading, as he had been trained to do for work in the field, with Manatu parked annoyingly close by his side.

The reading wasn't a full digestion, not at this rate, but it was a hearty skim that would give him a wealth of details. The Shasir was a perfect snatch, full of information. There was a good deal of caste bias to weed out but it was enough to put them onto the major vita sources of this world.

He split the display, again, opening the global map with the suggested hotspots the analysts back at the World had put together for him. Grudgingly, he could admit that they had done a good job. But then, this was about as easy an analysis as one could do. This world was rich, rich, rich. Loaded. Perhaps the best strike in over a hundred years or more. Almost enough to justify return visits, but that policy was sacrosanct. One in, one out.

However, he had an idea he had nourished since their arrival and now he was confident that the risk was worthy. He stood and headed straight for where Kerbin sat, back resting against her pack. Manatu followed in his wake.

"We're going to split up," he told her.

"What?" she asked, nearly choking on the ration bar she was chewing.

"You know, where you and your team go one way, and I and…he," he pointed at his bodyguard, "go another."

"Out of the question. Completely unortho," she said, standing. "Don't you people have rules about that kind of thing?"

Exactly the response he had anticipated.

"Rules that can be modified in-field if necessity arises." Among other things, the necessity to get this exceedingly dangerous woman away from his back before she could follow through on her strong impulse to shoot him.

His mind raced, sequences and prospects competing for his attention. What he was contemplating was not done anymore, as it resulted in disaster more often than reward. The last few attempts had been confined to the work of veteran Theorists, and a string of failures had resulted in the deaths of dozens, and on one occasion—the infamous Lannit raid—several hundred had died. People, that was, not Outers. However, the successes had been the greatest bounties of any raids. It was the ultimate in risk/reward, and his best chance to impress the Guild.

"We're going for a multi-strike," he told Kerbin. "For that, we need to each scout a half dozen sites over the course of the next twenty-one days. We need to set up a remote comm—"

"You're kargin' joking with me!" Kerbin hurled the ration bar at Seg's feet.

"Do I make many jokes, squad leader?" Seg asked, his tone even. "Remember when I said you'd get the opportunity to make up for that trophy caj fiasco? Here it is. In any event, I trust your operator to set us up with a long-range signal system that will evade local detection. You'll guide to the targets I vector you on, make the local sampling required, then we'll meet and intrans back to the world."

"No, we will not," Kerbin said, jabbing her finger into Seg's chest.

The troopers, who had grown used to their squad leader's spats with him, were perking up and taking notice. For their benefit, he kept his temper. When it came time for the Question, the formal Guild inquiry at the end of the mission, he would not have witnesses accusing him of emotional outbursts. Unortho but logical, that is what they must say.

"This is what we're doing. I have operational control here. Every order you give," he stepped closer to her and lowered his voice, "is an order I allow you to give. But consider this: if it works, all of you will make enough to retire on. Off one mission."

Behind her dark eyes, Seg could see the wheels turning. Nothing motivated troopers like money. Nevertheless, Kerbin was career military; it would take more than greed to win her.

"Consider this, as well," he pulled up the holographic map overlaid with the Guild's suggested vita hot spots, "on foot, as we are now, we are limited to the following sites." He pointed to six, glowing red dots. "But by water we could feasibly survey at least twice that, maybe more, including the biggest two, here and here."

"By water? How in the name of the Storm are we going to arrange that miracle?" Kerbin dug out a piece of ration bar that was stuck between her teeth, then sucked it off her finger.

"Not *we*, squad leader…me. You and your troops possess no cultural training beyond minimal survival skills. I will take only my bodyguard and charter a vessel—"

"You'll what?" Kerbin let out two loud barks that were her equivalent of laughter. "Cultural penetration without us to cover you? You're insane, Theorist. First mission and already cracked."

Seg continued, unfazed by her disrespect. "When we are finished here, I will send a comm to the world with a list of the necessary cover elements. We'll travel over land together, as far as here," he pointed to the map again, "where we'll wait for the next warp window. Once I have the necessary equipment, we'll part ways – you and the squad will head to this inland site first," he indicated a red dot, "and Manatu and I will take appropriate cover roles and travel to this river port settlement to secure transport."

"Too dangerous," she said, shaking her head, all traces of merriment gone. "I don't care if you *are* the Guild's wonder boy; our job is to stick close to you when you infiltrate and be ready to pull you out if things get ugly. What you're proposing—transit with Outers on a waterborne vessel, with a single trooper—is beyond unortho. Without a full squad to cover you, you could blow this mission for all of us and get yourself killed in the process. Not to mention, if anything happens to you, it'll be my guts on the table."

"Regardless, this *is* what we're going to do." He gave her a long, thoughtful appraisal. Her apprehension was small-minded but not unreasonable. Theorists were trained to blend with Outers of all descriptions but even the best sometimes found themselves compromised. "I will make sure to note your concerns and your formal *disapproval* of my decision, Squad Leader."

That seemed to appease her but her jaw remained set. "I want a worst-case scenario back up plan," she said, after a moment's contemplation. "If we lose comm, I am not risking my squad by traipsing all over this insect-infested water hole looking for you."

A reasonable precaution, and one he had not considered. Seg performed a quick calculation of distance and time, then zoomed in the holographic map to an area on the other side of the mountain range they were camped against. "We'll set up a rendezvous point. In the unlikely event that something should run afoul, we'll meet here," he pressed a button to mark a spot on the map, the coordinates jumping to the foreground as he did so, "in twenty-one days—the mission deadline."

"I won't wait a minute longer. You don't show before sundown, we leave your tender ass behind. And I want all this on record."

"I assure you, I've made note of *everything* we've discussed."

Kerbin's face twitched slightly at that. She sized him up for a moment – Seg knew she was assessing the threat implied in his statement.

"Fair enough," she said, after chewing on the offer. "It's still insane. Totally unortho. But I'm sure you've already thought of that." She stepped closer, her voice low and prodding, "I don't have to tell you that if you karg this up, changing the rules as you go, making things up as it suits you, you'll be the joke of the Guild, the laughing stock of the World. Lannit made a mess but he was an experienced field Theorist, his risk was based on a career's worth of successful missions. The People still speak his name with a grain of respect. You? First time extrans?" A low, menacing chuckle. "They'll invent a new word for *disgrace* to describe the depth of that kind of failure. You make it back alive after that and you'll wish you didn't. They won't just strip you of your title and hold you up for the World to see just what happens when People turn their back on orthodoxy, they'll also make sure you live a long, long time in the worst misery possible and that every day will be a humiliation, that every day you will be reminded of your mistake." She broke away, her tone shifting back to a more casual air, "But, like I said, you already know that, don't you?"

Seg stared through Kerbin before speaking.

"My last teacher said I'd either make a large impact or be the victim of one." His face was immovable but he wondered if Kerbin could see through the facade.

Her words were true, entirely true. His plan was insanely ambitious. Injury or death, those possibilities were vastly preferable to the fate that awaited him should he fail and live to tell of it.

There was also the terrifying prospect of traveling on water. Something he refused to dwell on.

But it was all right in front of him, and he couldn't let a world and an opportunity this rich go to waste. Maybe he was overstepping his bounds here, and maybe he was getting too ambitious for a barely-released Theorist.

Segkel Eraranat, Selectee for Field Research, youngest Theorist to ever hold the position, he imagined the newsfeed would say one day. Youngest and boldest. Fear and thrill wrestled in his stomach. Thrill won easily.

"Get to work on the communications," he ordered.

With the squad settled in for the evening, except for two troopers standing watch, Seg finally had the opportunity to review the data from the Shasir priest without being disturbed. Always the same stories, world after world – the conquerors and the conquered. Though the story of this world was no different from a hundred others he had studied during his time training at the Guild, this time the details mattered, not simply for good grades but for survival.

Coming from the brain of the Shasir, the facts would be slanted in the direction of his kind but that's where training came in.

A hagiocracy, a society governed by holy men, with three races and four classes. From top to bottom: Shasir, Damiar, Kenda and Welf. Easy enough, though there were a legion of sub-classes within each, to be sure.

The Shasir's home territory was on the opposite side of the planet; they were old hands at the game of world conquest. In areas such as this, inhabited by primitives, they simply announced themselves as gods upon arrival, then smothered any resistance with their vastly superior weapons and technology, which they passed off as 'magic'. Food, labor, natural resources, all were easily extracted and exploited once the population was suitably awed.

The Damiar were a sub-set of the Shasir, a class of nobles set up to act as liaisons to the holy men and gods. Bestowed with power and privilege, they looked after the practical, hands-on business of running an empire.

According to the data from the priest's brain, this technique had worked well elsewhere but when they had arrived here they ran into an obstacle: the Kenda.

The Welf were largely peaceful, uneducated and agrarian. They were naturally inclined toward belief and superstition, and had been subdued and seduced easily by these new gods and their magic. But even with a Welf army, the Shasir made little or no progress against the independent and seafaring Kenda, who had the clear advantage of geography and experience. Shasir boats, designed for ocean crossings, were large and slow, unsuited for the many inlets, rivers and tight channels their foes had spent generations navigating, and the Welf, who had their own unpleasant history with the Kenda, maintained an unshakable fear of the open water. The conquest was a near disaster.

Until the airships had been constructed and launched.

Shasir technology, from everything Seg had read and observed, was rudimentary compared to that of the People, but on this world, against enemies who were unprepared to defend against even a simple air assault, it was more than sufficient. The Kenda fell and the gods reigned.

"Clever," Seg muttered, as he read on about the Shasir's unification process.

Kenda who accepted the Shasir'kia as their gods and agreed to live under Shasir rule, were allowed to keep their boats and engage in trade and commerce on the water, according to Shasir law, which was enforced by the Damiar Judiciary. A ploy to make the high-spirited rebels believe they maintained their freedom, which, for the most part, was successful. Those who refused the Shasir's offer, or broke their laws, were executed publicly, as their boats burned before their eyes.

Unification included everything from religion, to language, to currency, and law. *S'orasa* was the Shasir name for this planet and *S'ora* the official language, to be spoken by all. Another piece of good fortune, as no further language sampling would be required. (Though, should he encounter other languages, Seg would be sure to collect samples for study.)

Likewise, all four classes were humanoid with no extreme genetic mutations. The Guild had spent decades perfecting cultural infiltration. On worlds where they could not physically blend with any Outer groups, Theorists would return home for a session of surgical body modification, then return to the recon. An extra expense, but direct contact with Outers was invaluable. Only rarely were all Outers so physically different that infiltration was unfeasible, in which case recon was conducted from a distance.

On this world, he could easily pass for one of the Shasir or Damiar, who were of the same race, (or mix of races, more accurately), and those castes had access to any of the prime vita hotspots.

As rigorous as the Shasir had been about cultural unification, they protected the secrets of their technology through even more extreme means. Lengthy torture, death and a promised eternity of suffering in the afterlife, had served well to keep their magic out of the hands of those they ruled. A necessary precaution, since even primitives could eventually figure out the mechanics of things such as steam engines, lift gas (such as hydrogen) or advanced metallurgical methods, given enough time and exposure.

A reasonably formidable band of Outers, these Shasir, Seg had to concede. Though, in their position, they would have been better served doing away with the Kenda completely. Once a rebel, always a rebel – history taught that lesson well.

He rubbed his eyes from the strain of reading the small screen. He knew he should take a som tab to help him sleep but what he was attempting was beyond unortho, it was dangerous; he needed to be prepared. His mind drifted back to training, as he considered the history of these Outers.

"Despite typically professing a desire for peace, every culture thus discovered has maintained some capacity for violence. Given our notions of evolutionary adaptation, it follows that the pressures of competition, internal and external, ensure that no humanoid population of sufficient size will ever achieve any modicum of perpetual peace."

Jarin. His mentor was brilliant, unquestionably so, but Seg did not expect he would approve of his plan any more than the thickheaded Kerbin. House Haffset, the raid's sponsor, would offer resistance, as well, at least until Seg could show Haffset how much wealth was to be gained. He suspected he would have only detractors until that time. Prodigy or not, no one on the World would count on a Theorist to bring in much above quota—if that—on his first mission. He would simply have to prove them wrong.

In order to do that, though, he would have to lay the groundwork on this world. Tapping a button on the screen, he reviewed the list of items he had requested from home. Clothing to disguise Manatu and himself—the Damiar were the class most suitable to imitate for this venture—local currency and an assortment of the nonsensical items these self-imagined nobility were so fond of. Large quantities of everything, in keeping with the Damiar custom of excess for the sake of excess. All could be manufactured, (ironically, by the caj of other worlds the People had conquered), well enough to fool the Outers.

Thanks to wide geographical and cultural differences, he could use his own name and Manatu's as part of their cover, which gave him one less detail to remember.

The list of weapons was restricted to those that could be easily hidden. Two micro-chacks, two pistols - the former were more powerful and the best choice for a primary weapon, latter were smaller and could fit inside a pocket or boot, a perfect back-up defense. However, both weapons were reliable and near silent, firing toxic huchack spines that easily sliced through flesh and poisoned the blood. There were also a selection of micro grenades on the list, (smoke, concussive and fragment); eight chack cartridges and two forearm straps to conceal the weapons; six blades; another pair of stunners; a chack for Manatu and some remote micro-dets. They weren't going to war, and if they had to use any of their arsenal then things would have gone drastically wrong by that point and the weapons would most likely be useless anyway.

The Signals Operator had incorporated a means of text-based communication, via Seg's digipad, to keep him in covert contact with the squad, and he had also put together a larger audio/visual comm unit, which in an emergency would allow him to communicate with the World. As per protocol, he kept a set of digifilms to record the details of the mission – information that was the property of the sponsor House. He had also requested another warpgen and warp gate. That would raise some questions and it would be bulky, but if he needed to get back home in a hurry he couldn't depend on rendezvousing with the rest of the troops.

He had already stashed an auto-med in his kit as well as the standard selection of medication; field rations; map disc; and VIU - Vita Indicator Unit, for scanning vita sources.

He was ready for any eventuality. One more day of travel, one more night of study and he and Manatu would be on their own. Tapping his digipad, the new world returned to darkness.

Seg laid his head on his pack and looked up at the night sky. Stars were visible to the naked eye. Strange. Could a Person get used to such a thing? Closing his eyes, he reviewed the list in his head. Yes, it was complete; there was nothing to add.

He was ready for anything.

CHAPTER 3

The Central Well dominated the landscape more than any other structure on the World. Towering over seventy stories high, it transmitted a continuous, translucent stream of vita into a shimmering aperture projected over its height.

Efectuary Jul Akbas always found the sight a testament to the will of the People and their superiority over the greatest force of nature in existence. The Well was power, a flag of defiance against the Storm – the force that had threatened to consume their World for over a millennium.

No one knew when the Storm had first appeared, those records— as was the case with so much of the People's history—had been lost. What they did know was that the black, howling monstrosity had once ravaged the land, destroying cities with its insatiable hunger for vita, and the People had fled, hidden or been consumed in its path. Billions of People had perished, entire continents had been rendered uninhabitable. Then the Well had been constructed; at last the Storm could be fed, directed, controlled.

Of course, as a natural phenomenon, the Storm could not be completely contained, but shield technology had eventually been developed to cover all the inhabited areas of the World. The people had triumphed.

And who had led this triumph? Who processed, disbursed and controlled the collected vita of the World? The Central Well Authority, of which Jul Akbas had been a member since her graduation from Orhalze Scholastic Academy, sixteen years ago.

The CWA administrative facility included an observation deck, where high-level management could take in a meal and look out upon the main instrument of their power and position in the World. As of today, that senior administration included Jul Akbas.

She shifted her focus and examined her reflection in the thick wall of glass, to ensure everything was in its place, organized. Like the Well, she stood tall, polished, productive. She looked back out at the Well and felt the pride of her personal achievement mirrored in that iconic edifice.

The observation deck was sparsely populated at the off-hour. Light, repetitive tones of music droned in the background, while well-trained serving caj padded silently on bare feet to refill drinks or deliver meals.

She held the rail with one hand as she looked back toward the entrance. The man who entered was lanky, taller than most, with neatly-trimmed grey hair and a sculpted beard. Supervisory Gran Fi Restis smiled as he approached.

Until thirty minutes ago, Gran Fi Restis had been her superior.

"Efectuary Akbas," Gran said, stressing the title. "Congratulations. Taking in the view for the last time?"

She nodded and slipped away from the rail toward one of the secluded booths. As with so many products on the World, the booth and cushions were blended from extruded huchack fibers, and bleached free of the toxins the creatures left on everything they touched. However, for the upper echelons of the CWA, the material had also been laboriously softened – an expensive process few could afford. Draped over the plain seats were shimmering fabrics, the spoils of some raid.

Jul sat first, according to protocol, a reflection of her new rank and superiority to the man who slid in across from her.

"Supervisory Fi Restis, thank you for coming. We will be able to do great things in Orhalze," Jul said.

The center of the table lit up as they sat, revealing a selection of glowing icons. Gran waited while Jul pressed an icon for her drink order before he made his own choice.

"Well, the visit isn't all pleasure," he said, then passed his digipad across the table to her. "One last impression, then your duties here are complete. Standard forms, code transfer approval and the like."

Jul knew he expected her to press her thumb to the document without so much as a cursory glance. That was why Gran Fi Restis, ten years her senior, would forever remain a Supervisory. She read through the entire document, gave her impression, and slid the digipad back without a word.

"When do you meet Director Fi Costk?" Gran asked.

"In twenty minutes," Jul answered, the mixture of pride, excitement and fear barely detectable in her tone.

Adirante Fi Costk, Director of External Affairs, was perhaps the most powerful of the five CWA Directors, power accrued over the course of decades. A hard and challenging man who did not tolerate failure – admirable qualities.

The drinks arrived and Gran lifted his glass to Jul.

"We will be discussing the latest acquisition cycle," she said, after a small sip.

"Have you made your assessments of current raids?" Gran asked.

"There are four recon missions in progress. Two are led by veteran Theorists known for making safe, conservative assessments that lead to minimal expenditure and minimal gains. Both noted for breaking even." As she spoke, her hand flexed around her glass. "The third is a corporate-sponsored raid. A possible option, but we are prioritizing the Houses."

There were two entities on the World who sponsored raids: Corporations and Houses. In the actual process, there was no difference between the two. They both bid for the right to sponsor a raid; both hired Theorists and recon squads to survey the targeted world and determine the best sources of vita; both designed their raids according to information provided by the Theorist; both sold the recovered vita to the CWA, technology to the Guild or the CWA, and auctioned caj and materials on the open market.

The difference lay in the structure. Corporations had multiple owners, strict contracts and complex ties that made them resistant to takeovers. Houses were familial, hereditary units, with a hierarchical system that left even the strongest vulnerable. Both entities would take all measures to avoid a takeover but, under the right circumstances, Houses were the easier prey.

"And the fourth recon is House sponsored?" Gran asked.

"Yes, and led by a young Theorist on his first mission – one of several promising factors. First, this Theorist, Segkel Eraranat, is a former student of Senior Theorist Svestil, known radical and risk-taker. Second, the sponsoring House, Haffset, hopes to leverage a successful raid for elevation to Major House status. Finally, junior Theorists will take more chances, to prove themselves."

"And if they fail…" Gran led.

"We move in," she said, with a sharp smile. "However, we are also prepared to disrupt a raid at the planning cycle, before forces are committed. Properly handled, we will demonstrate that the Guild is less functional in vita assessments than we are, and that our own services can be more profitably substituted for theirs."

Gran chuckled. "Theorist Jarin Svestil. I met him once. Radical, yes, but hard. There was some scandal that the Guild concealed, I understand." His smile faded. "You know, if we dislodge the Guild from their position, the financial fallout of that failure would likely leave many of their senior members exposed to reclamation. I would actually visit the huchack ponds, just to see those 'intellectual elites' mucking around, collecting the fibers."

"Visit the ponds?" Jul's nose wrinkled. "We are above that. Certainly the ponds have vid feeds, to monitor the caj? If not, we would insist on their installation."

Fi Restis laughed quietly, then sobered. "I have every confidence in your success, Efectuary, but bear this in mind when you deliver your briefing to Director Fi Costk today: he knows the cycles well. He will want you to show sufficient mastery of detail to demonstrate that you understand the finer points of this operation, down to all the names of the Theorists involved, House Masters, and so forth. However, he will also correct you for being over-explanatory at some point, to demonstrate the value of his time. Fi Costk operates on the principle of keeping everyone in his sphere off-balance and uncertain."

Jul nodded as she finished her drink, then dabbed the corners of her mouth with a cloth napkin. "Thank you for your concern, Supervisory Fi Restis"

They rose together. His smile was warm, genuine and too familiar.

"It has been a pleasure working with you, Jul. You should be proud. You're climbing the final layer, and the position you're in gives you a clear path to the Directorate."

Jul's smile tightened as her eyes narrowed. "Certainly closer than you ever reached, Gran." She soaked in the wounded confusion in his eyes before she added, "A productive day to you, Supervisory Fi Restis."

Jul felt his eyes on her back until she boarded the lift to take her to the topmost level of the administration facility.

Whisked silently upward, Jul contemplated that the majority of People on the World would never stand at this height in their entire lives, and now she would be working here. The air felt different somehow, cleaner and more sterile.

She exited the lift and stepped into the security cordon. Sharply-dressed security staff scanned her and checked her credentials, then a caj stepped away from the wall to guide her to the scheduled meeting. She stared at the golden metal graft implanted in the back of the creature's head. Such fine quality!

After passing through a series of doors, she arrived at Director Fi Costk's temporary office. He sat at his desk, a bulky man with a shaven head, who radiated authority. He glanced up as she entered and gestured absently toward a chair.

The office was a study in simplicity, dominated by a single large window that encompassed the entire rear wall. She had heard that his regular office, in Orhalze, had a special projector system built into it that made the floor appear invisible, as if the office hovered over the city, so that all who entered walked on air. Adirante Fi Costk liked to loom over those he ruled.

As she thought that, he rose to his feet and looked down at her. "Efectuary Jul Akbas," he said gruffly, "impress me."

As they neared the bustling center of the river city, Manatu slowed and Seg ordered his bodyguard forward. Unlike Kerbin, Manatu was unimaginative and simply responded to authority. He was brainless enough to be caj, but that made him useful for such things as carrying bags full of gear and absorbing rocks and arrows and whatever else the natives might decide to hurl Seg's way.

Seg understood Manatu's discomfort, though. Dressed in their impractical Outer attire, they stood at the threshold of a dock that sprawled for at least two kilometers along the bank of a wide river. Attached to sturdy, wood pilings, the structure was stable—as evidenced by the number of Outers traversing it with carts full of goods—but that didn't make its location, over the water, any less intimidating.

There was also the crush of Outers. Observing the group of Welf Outers from a distance had felt not much different than classroom study but being here, among the throng, it was immediate and real. Although the port city was primarily populated by the Kenda—tall, robust stock, golden haired and skinned, faces weathered early by ocean travel—there were a good share of Welf in the mix. By contrast, the Welf looked as if they sprang from the very soil they farmed, with dusky skin, dark brown hair and eyes. They attended their Damiar masters as porters or guards, or saw to the menial tasks of the docks, tasks traditionally reserved for the lowest classes.

Damiar were scattered throughout the crowd, as well, Seg was relieved to see, since his goal was to blend in as fully as possible. From passing observation, he could tell that the Damiar here were either travelers passing through on one of the many vessels, merchants, or what constituted the upper ranks of the local legal authority. Welf, being expendable, were used for general enforcement – Seg couldn't help a slight smirk as he passed a uniformed constable, the dim expression and hulking frame were so similar to Manatu's.

Seg's senses had never been so engaged. Savory wafts of frying breakfast meat intermingled with the musky smell of the animals pulling carts and the tang of the salty air. Bells rang, sails snapped, boots clomped, hammers pounded, birds cried, mariners shouted and whistled to each other from vessel to vessel. The sky was a painful shade of blue and the sun—the sun, what a novelty—brought all the colors of the river city flashing garishly to life.

How does any culture evolve amid such confusion? The thought skipped over Seg's consciousness as he continued his walk, thankful the social status his wardrobe signified forced the lower orders to move aside as he passed.

Soon they arrived at one of the walkways leading down to the dock.

Just as Manatu was about to step forward, as ordered, Seg stopped him by placing a hand in front of his chest. "Remember, you're mute. You don't talk. *At all*. Understand? Nod if you understand." Manatu nodded, frowning. "Good man," Seg said, in what passed for an encouraging tone for him, and raised his hand to let Manatu pass.

Taking his first steps onto the gently sloping ramp that led to the dock below, Seg kept his focus on the vessels. He had vague familiarity with waterborne craft, having studied them in training. Of course, studying images and reading about watercraft was entirely different than actually approaching one. Bobbing in the water, they were at once cryptic and confusing. How to assess the quality of each craft?

Seg pondered the question as he ignored the creak of his footsteps on the wooden planks and the spaces between the planks that showed the water, clearly, beneath him. It occurred to him that the best means of judging a vessel was to judge the commander of the vessel. What was true when navigating the skies had to be true here as well.

Water. It was daunting. Worse, by far, than trees. The World's seas were now no more than large lakes, their rivers reduced to trickles, dead things, used only for shipping by the lower classes until even that had no longer been feasible. He had never known them as alive and rich, such as what he saw before him.

From the top of the mast, Ama hooked her leg over one of the thin-but-durable lengths of bonewood that made up the 'bones' of her sail, then lowered her upper body until she was hanging upside down. With one hand, she maneuvered a wide patch, slathered in epoxy, into place on the thin membrane, made from garzine skin. The tear had re-opened, yet again, on the return trip the previous evening. More trouble and expense she didn't need. It was bad enough that today's tour consisted of only three passengers and she had nothing else booked for nearly a week but now, with a gaping hole in the main skin, there was no way she could make it upriver if the wind died off.

"Told you it was time to replace that skin," Captain Tather called up to her, from the bow of the *Greehm*.

"Skin's fine," Ama lied, wiping her brow with the back of her hand. "Just routine maintenance."

"Routine maintenance my hairy hindquarters!" Tather laughed. "That crate's more patch than boat. You should start taking those marriage offers more seriously."

"I'll do that," Ama called back, "when you start bathing."

She righted herself, then scurried to the top of the mast, pushed off and dove head first into the water. Underneath, she examined the hull of the *Naida* as she swam. Satisfied, she kicked to the surface, sucked in a lungful of air and climbed the ladder to the dock, where Tather's men were hooting at her jibe. She raised her arms over her head in victory, "Captain Kalder wins again!"

She soon realized she now had a slightly bigger audience. Two foreign looking men were staring at her.

"Can I help you, good sirs?" she asked, wringing the water from her hair.

The men, two Damiar, one young, one somewhat older, possibly from the South judging by the style of their dress, said nothing.

The tall, thin man, his limbs slightly overlong, stood closest to her. His hair was a light brown and silver color that reminded her of the winter coat of a volp; hair that was thinning already to leave a distinct widow's peak. He had an angular face with strong, pronounced cheekbones and his eyes, which were much the same colour as his hair, remained fixed on Ama as if she were an apparition and he was waiting to see if she would suddenly vanish.

His companion, a monolith of a man, was older and more wary. His eyes shifted from Ama to the surrounding boats and back.

She found the thin man's gaze unsettling – he lacked the social consciousness of most normal people who would maintain a mutual gaze for a few moments before a subconscious mental impulse would direct their eyes elsewhere. For a Damiar, especially, to pay so much attention to a Kenda woman in public, even one so underdressed and sopping wet, was unusual. His mouth hung slightly agape. Ama could sense that in some fundamental way, she had shocked him.

"I, ah, that is—" he said, before shaking his head and composing himself visibly. "Yes, we require a private charter of your vessel."

"When, where and for how many hours?" she asked, sizing up the amount of luggage the larger man was toting. Excessive for a day trip, even for Damiars.

"We would depart immediately," the thin man began.

Ama cursed silently. "Ah, that's too bad, I already have—"

"I want to travel for about twenty days in total," he continued.

Twenty days? A twenty-day charter? Ama's heart leapt inside her chest.

"Why don't you gentlemen go aboard and I'll consult my itinerary to see if I can fit you in," Ama said, offering the two men a warm smile as she ushered them toward the stairs to the *Naida*. "I'll return in a drop," she called, then jogged to Captain Tather's boat.

"Finally come to ask for help?" Captain Tather teased as Ama climbed aboard the *Greehm*, still dripping from her swim. "Wouldn't blame you, that big cloud sniffer looks like he could tip your floating crate to one side – make sure he stays midship in rough water." He gestured toward the men who were waiting for Ama aboard her boat.

"Look Tather, I'd rather spend a month on shore polishing the Judicia's boots than ask you this but…" she looked down to her feet, then back up at him, crossed her arms in front of her chest and squinted with one eye.

"Don't worry, I'll tell your scheduled passengers you had an emergency and point them down the dock to one of the other, more reputable, charters." Before she could ask how he had known what she wanted, he continued, "Whatever those Dammies are looking for, you'd better haul back on that enthusiasm before you wrestle them for a price. Too obvious."

"Twenty days, private charter," Ama said, as she toned down her visible excitement.

Tather let out a long, low whistle, "Not bad, especially considering what you have to work with." He tilted his head in the *Naida's* direction.

"You're lucky you're doing me a favour," Ama said as she put her hands on her hips, the scrapes on her knuckles still visible.

"Hmpf," Tather snorted, then crossed his arms and stared once more at the men on the *Naida's* deck. "Strange looking pair. I'd say they're Southies, if I had to guess. Don't get many of them up our way. And that one," he indicated the taller man with his chin, "I didn't realize they grew Dammies that tall. Awfully young for a cloud sniffer to be on his own so far from home. Half coin says the big one is a guard Mommy and Daddy sent with him. Not a terrible looking fellow, the thin one, kind of regal. You be careful not to be dazzled by his good looks when you negotiate."

Ama rolled her eyes, "The day I fall for a cloud sniffer is the day you can burn my boat." She turned to leave, then called over her shoulder. "Thanks Tather, as much as it kills me, I owe you."

"Just fall madly in love, that's all I ask, and I'll keep some fosfol and matches handy."

As she climbed back aboard her own boat, Ama gestured to the seats, "Make yourselves comfortable, please." She hurried to the stern, toweled off and slipped into a dry shirt and trousers.

Neither sat. The older man was silent and sour looking. Unlike his partner, his eyes roamed everywhere, taking in everything. His companion, the tall one with the hard face, was watching his feet and holding one of the side rails.

Tather was correct, they were dressed like Southies, and the accent fit, but something was off about them.

"You, sirs, are very lucky," Ama said, as she returned to finish the deal, "I did have a devotional cruise booked for today but the clients are regulars of mine and entirely forgiving of schedule changes." It was a blatant lie but hopefully Tather would keep his word. In any case, she would deal with the consequences later. "And it looks like the Shasir have blessed us with a perfect day for travel," she touched her forehead and looked upward, in a display of respect for the lords of the sky.

"Indeed they have," the thin man returned the gesture.

"So, where are we going on this finest of days?"

"I am a negotiator," he said, after a lengthy pause, "representing the financial concerns among the Damiar of my home. We have an interest in some mercantile arrangements along the northern seaboard, as far as Malvid, and up certain rivers. Our itinerary will require a large degree of discretion on your part, Captain, as well as a tight schedule to make all our pre-arranged meetings. The payoff will be quite handsome, and, as I mentioned, the retainer will extend to twenty days of travel. Can you take us where we need to go?"

Ama heard one word: discretion.

When customers wanted discretion, they usually didn't goff about paying for it. This could be good. Better than good. If she played this right, she might make enough to pay for the refit of the *Naida* – to the depths with Judicia Corrus and his threats. She could set sail in time for the seed winds and get herself beyond the reach of the authorities.

Of course, discretion often meant trouble, as well. Trouble she could ill afford. It was a matter, she decided, of setting the price high enough to justify the risk.

Don't murk this one, Ama, she thought, as she pretended to contemplate the offer.

"Well…it would mean canceling future bookings with some of my regular clients. And I'd have to miss the Shasir Sky Ceremony, which I look forward to every year." That she attended the annual Sky Ceremony against her will, only for the sake of Stevan and family peace, was a detail Ama chose to leave out. "But I'd hate to leave you sirs at the mercy of some of these shady types on the Banks," she jerked her thumb in Captain Tather's direction. "Speed and discretion *are* my specialty. This girl may not look like much," she patted the *Naida's* handrail, "but she's got triple-cured skins and a shallow draft; she nearly outruns the luxe cruisers on a good day." Sucking on her lips for a moment, she pretended to calculate figures in her head. "A thousand coin and the *Naida* and I are all yours."

The thin man opened his mouth to speak but she cut in, "Oh, and of course I would need half of that up front. Just in the most freak happenstance that you and your friend decide to make wake at some port down the way and leave me out of pocket."

"Actually," he said, with a trace of cheerfulness, "one of our planned meetings just so happens to be set for the Sky Ceremony. So you won't be missing that. And I'm thinking that being able to tend to our devotions would make six hundred coin a reasonable offer, with a one-third advance. Given that you're charging near to double rate for this special charter, it wouldn't exactly hurt your finances to lose us at the first stop, now would it?"

Ama looked to the horizon, pursing her lips. Not bad. Could be he didn't know much about boats but he did know negotiating. Six hundred was good coin but she could do better.

"I do tend to charge a bit more for *discretion*. You sirs spin a fine tale but for all I know there could be some shadier business on your schedule – not likely you'd tell me about it ahead of time, now is it? If I'm to risk my boat, I want a fair shake."

The men grimaced. And Ama caught something else. At the mention of 'shadier business', a twitch of the mouth—not from the thin man, he was blank slate—from the big man.

This was no merchant run, she would bet her life on it.

"But since you're not depriving me of the Sky Service…" damn her ancestors, now she would have to sit through three hours of chanting and gesticulating, "I guess I can come down to eight hundred. Do we have a deal?"

"I think seven-thirty and bump the advance to forty percent, and we'll both feel somewhat taken advantage of, yes?" he countered.

He raised his hand in front of his stomach, back of his hand facing her, pinky curled in, other fingers splayed out. Ama's breath stopped for a moment. The hand gesture was one of mutual assent…and pure Shasir. Though not technically incorrect, certainly not a gesture that was used on the docks or for negotiations as casual as these. Her instincts hadn't failed her; there *was* something more sinister going on here. Even as she smiled and returned the gesture, her brain was churning. Who, exactly, was he and why was he here, on her boat?

He was too young to be put in charge of complicated trade negotiations. Could he be a Shasir spy? Fa had warned her to be cautious and certainly she and the rest of the Kalders would be monitored for the slightest hint of dissention now that Stevan was preparing for ascension.

Perhaps he was in league with Judicia Corrus?

Her free hand drifted to the small of her back and rested on the blade hiding there. She would watch these men closely and watch her step.

"Soon as I have my coin, we can push off. Just tell me which way to point the bow. The head's below deck and there's some sleeping quarters in the bow and the stern, nothing fancy but warm and dry. Oh, and there's grint in that cask at the stern and another cask below deck. I won't always be free to serve it up, so help yourselves. I've got a few supplies but depending where we're headed I can always load up on foodstuffs at the next port. Anything valuable you want to store, let me know and I'll lock it up for you. Doubtful that pirates will bother with a vessel as small as this but I've got a few hiding spots for special trinkets, just in case. There's no crew so you might have to pitch in now and then. That's about it."

As she waited for the man to offer up the promised deposit, Ama noted every move and stored it in her memory. She glanced at the bigger man and deadpanned, "And I'm sorry but you are just going to have to keep him quiet."

It took a few beats. The thin man with the hard face gave her a twitchy smile that was as false as his cover story.

"Anyway, I'm Captain Ama Kalder. And you sirs would be...?"

"I am Lord Segkel Eraranat," he answered, bowing graciously.

"That's a mouthful."

"You may call me Seg, for the sake of expediency on this voyage," he said, with an attempt at a smile. "This is my companion and bodyguard Manatu Dibeld. And you may call him very, very quiet because he's mute. Right Manatu?"

Manatu nodded and pointed to his mouth, opening it and making no sound.

He produced a cash-purse, counted out the agreed-upon deposit and displayed plenty more available. "And now," the purse closed with a *snap* and he fixed his stare on her again, "you and your ship belong to me."

Ama's jaw muscles tensed briefly but the moment passed like a thunderclap and Seg the Damiar resumed his previous attempt at cheer.

"Manatu will see to our luggage."

Ama bowed slightly. "And I'll see to extending the sk—"

"Water rat!"

Ama's head whipped around, at the sound of Dagga's voice. As he climbed the stairs to the *Naida*, Dagga cleaned the dirt from under his nails with his knife. She turned her right palm skyward. "Constable Dagga, blessings of the Sh—"

"Pushing off?" Dagga pointed his knife toward the large bags on the dock below.

"I have a charter, yes," she replied, her tone respectful.

"Where? How long?"

"Twenty days," Ama answered, "I don't know every stop yet, since you interrupted my dealings, but as far as Malvid. Anything else I can help you with before you leave, Head Constable?"

"Got business in Malvid?" Dagga asked, pointing the knife toward Seg, an eye on Manatu.

Seg's hand slid back and touched Manatu's arm, as if to stop him. "You may point that elsewhere before I officially notice it," he said, indicating the knife with his chin. With that, he looked back out at the water, the constable once more in his peripheral.

"May I?" Dagga grinned, then flipped the knife, until it was pointing away from Seg. "Now, as I was asking…"

Seg looked back, as if seeing Dagga for the first time. "Oh, yes. Who are you and why are you holding up my charter?"

Ama turned away to hide the smile that rose to her lips.

"Manatu, go collect our things," Seg continued.

Manatu stepped forward but Dagga blocked the stairs. A miniature war waged in the eyes of the two men and Ama held her breath.

Dagga finally stepped aside with a false display of courtesy and turned his eyes to Seg. "I'm Head Constable Dagga," he offered, "here on orders of Judicia Corrus."

"Ah," Seg said. "If the woman is a problem, I can have my man restrain her for you. Is she in trouble?"

Dagga's smile looked as if it had been wrung out of him. "This one?" he pointed the knife at Ama now. "She's always in trouble."

Ama straightened and shifted her weight to one side. "Constable," she said, her tone placating but with an edge beneath it, "let me consult with my passenger and then I'll give you our full itinerary."

Manatu pushed past Dagga with four bags. At the same moment, Ama crossed toward the stern and beckoned Seg to follow.

She transcribed the list of destinations as Seg recited them to her. When he finished, he pulled a watch from his coat pocket and frowned. "Should we anticipate issues of law at each stop?"

"No," she flashed a glare at Dagga, her animosity unveiled. "And my apologies about the delay."

She strode quickly back to the constable and passed him the folded piece of paper, which he took his time reading. "Is that satisfactory? I'd like to push off before dark."

Dagga tucked the paper inside his shirt pocket, and offered Seg a conspiratorial look, "Can't be too careful with the water rats." He rubbed a hand over his head, then redirected his attention to Ama, "I better see this hunk of sticks tied here before your time's up. You got any notions of running, I'll be having a chat with your father. Savvy?"

Ama's reply was a forced smile.

"'Course, that's assuming this junk heap doesn't come apart the minute it hits the Big Water." His laugh was half growl. "Pleasant voyage your Lordship."

"And a pleasant…whatever it is you do," Seg said, turning his back on Dagga. "When do we leave?" he asked Ama.

"Now," she said, her voice and face hard, her eyes monitoring Dagga's departure. "If Manatu is finished with your bags, I'll cast off the ropes."

"He's finished. Carry on, Captain Kalder," Seg said, then looked downriver, to the horizon.

Ama moved swiftly to extend the skins and summon the dock runners to help her cast off the ropes. That monster, Dagga, had nearly ruined her opportunity; the sooner she got out of port the better.

As she winched the wide, wing-shaped skin fully open, she caught a glimpse of the Damiar, Seg, watching her, his mute companion hovering nearby. No, not just his companion, his bodyguard. Tather's guess had been correct.

At the thought of Tather, she locked off the winch, ran to the stern, whistled and called out his name. His head appeared at the bow of his boat and Ama took a deep breath. She was already one favor in debt with him but this was different, this was far more important. "Tell my family to keep their eyes on the horizon for my return," she shouted.

There was a significant pause, then Tather nodded.

"You'll have their eyes, Kalder," he answered. She waved her thanks, then knocked twice on the outside of the hull. Sometimes you can't have too much protection.

Out on the open sea, the *Naida* rode effortlessly on a warm, west wind that blew steadily at about ten knots. Nen was feeling generous today. Ama worked hard to repress a smile as she watched Seg standing at midship, fingers clutched to the back of a wooden seat. Since leaving port in the morning, he had made a valiant effort to appear at ease, though she wondered why he bothered – Damiar didn't care what people like her thought of them.

There were a great many things she wondered about this Damiar, not the least of which was that he had given her leave to address him so informally. *You may call me Seg.* Not Lord or even Segkel, but 'Seg', as if he were a crew member or family. Well, that could be his age speaking, or perhaps manners in the south were different.

That he was traveling without servants and that his lone companion was mute could be due to the secretive nature of his supposed business, though her suspicions about that remained in place. If his business was so important, why wouldn't he have scheduled a proper charter, on a proper cruiser? The *Naida* was seaworthy, for short passages, but hardly the type of vessel any self-respecting Damiar would lower himself to travel on for more than a few hours.

He hadn't balked about the cramped berth, (her berth), in the bow, though he had cleared his throat, several times, as she had gathered her scattered belongings and attempted to give the space some sort of order. When she had shown him the small bunk in the stern, (which she had been using to store tools and charts), for Manatu, he had been equally unperturbed and even his guard had seemed untroubled by the rustic conditions.

Of course, they would likely find their own lodgings whenever they were in port, she didn't expect a Damiar to sleep on a boat like the *Naida* by choice.

He had even inquired as to where she would sleep. His reaction, when she explained she had a hammock she would string up above deck, was a long, silent stare – a response she was growing accustomed to.

Above all, what bothered her most about Seg, the so-called Damiar, was the way he looked at her. Ama was used to men staring at her, as the only female captain around it was to be expected, but this man was different. There was no lust, no malice, no disgust, not even plain, old curiosity in his gaze. His eyes didn't look *at* her, they penetrated her. For any Damiar that would be unusual, for one who couldn't be much older than her it was both unusual and vaguely threatening.

His age was also a question. Physically, he was in the prime of youth, beardless, lean and strong. And, as Tather had said, he wasn't terrible looking. He lacked the ruggedness and brawn of a Kenda man but there was indeed a regal quality to his features. However, his mannerisms, tone, carriage and attitude belonged to someone much older and wiser, someone who was comfortable with great power and responsibility. The contrast was mysterious.

He had insisted on following on her heels as she made preparations to push off. It was as if he was studying her, and each time she felt those eyes on her she grew more unnerved by them.

And each time she thought of speaking up about it, she remembered that purse full of coin. He was her ticket to freedom; he could stare if he wanted to.

"How is Manatu?" she called out against the wind.

Seg looked back at her and shook his head. He took a long stride toward the helm, tugging down at the edges of his coat, but he was far from acquiring his sea legs and stumbled sideways. On his next attempt, he grasped any available handhold and after a slow progression he stood next to Ama. "Not well," he said, nodding in the direction of his guard's body, which was slumped into one of the seats.

"If I'd known he got wave sick, I would have given him some dried genga root before leaving port. Unfortunately, it's too late now. Just keep him above deck, unless you want to clean up his mess," she said.

"Is it usually so...chaotic out here?" he asked.

"This?" Ama looked out to the seas around them. "This is calm. We couldn't ask for better conditions." Seg's brow furrowed slightly. "You've never sailed before, have you?" she dared to ask.

Again, the silent stare.

"I've been on the water since, well, since I was born. My father was a chartsman, he taught my brothers and me how to sail when we were small. You see how the skins are billowed out full like that? That's perfect, it means we're getting just enough wind and it's a westerly, which means it's coming at us like this," she lifted one hand from the wheel and placed it at a ninety-degree angle to the boat. "Garzine skin is tough but flexible; this sail," she pointed forward and above them, "is kind of like a giant binta wing. I can extend it if the wind is light or retract it if the wind is strong, just as the binta's do. Think of it as flying on water. Here, why don't you take the wheel for a moment while I trim the skins?"

For a moment it seemed as if Seg would refuse but then his features brightened faintly, as if someone had lit tiny fires behind his eyes, and he let Ama guide his hands into position.

"Just hold her steady, like that. Perfect." She offered him an encouraging smile to counteract the stony look of determination etched on his face. "Since I have no crew, I had to set the *Naida* up to be sailed solo." She reached for the winch on the port side and told Seg to keep his eyes on the main sail. "I've got two skins, but I only use the secondary for traveling upriver, and they're both set up on a winch system, so I can extend or retract them right from the helm." She gave the winch a quarter turn and the far ends of the skin lowered, "See that? The way the folds at the tips are flapping? That's too much; we've lost surface area and power, which means we lose speed." She flicked a lever and winched in the opposite direction until the skin tips stretched back into place.

He was watching her, as his hands held the wheel, and though he didn't speak Ama could tell Seg was beginning to relax. Helming the boat returned to him the element of control she guessed he was accustomed to.

Seg was surprised at the sensation of steering the vessel. It was almost as if he were directing and controlling a living creature. There was more to this sailing business than simply raising the sails and steering the craft. It was science – primitive science but science nonetheless.

She was talkative, this Outer, though he had to admit that learning about the operation of the boat was vastly preferable to the choice of either staring out at the churning water or watching Manatu turn a deeper shade of green. The simpleton had forgotten to take his anti-nausea meds or they had failed him. In either case, there was nothing to be done now.

It would be appropriate for him to now offer something in the way of conversation. She had spoken of her family more than once, had even made a point of calling to one of her cohorts to pass on a message to her kin before they had left the port, so obviously that was a desirable topic.

Family. He barely knew his. After qualifying for the Guild basic at the age of ten, he had moved into the dorms with the other students. As to his siblings, he had no idea what became of them. His parents, he had barely known. His father had been an overseer at a recycling facility his entire life, driving caj on endless shifts to keep their output of material flowing in usable form. His mother had died when he was very young, lost in an autotrans accident.

He didn't really understand the concept of family unity. The competition between all of his siblings had been ferocious and he had learned to play them off against each other. Even as the middle brother, he competed with his older sister for dominance of the clan, and got his way more often than not.

The brutal inter-family wars had sharpened him and prepared him well for his eventual immersion with the other brilliant students of the Guild. He had learned early on that even those who seemed most intelligent, most promising, were all still creatures of human desire. Jealousy, pettiness, lust, anger and greed could drive them to stupidity.

He liked to think he had transcended that. His goals were clear and any emotions that did not serve them were ignored or discarded. A philosophy that had served him well enough to bring him here.

He watched the girl as she fiddled with the winch again. The data from the Shasir, he was discovering, lacked much detail about the Kenda. For example, she had very deliberately and discreetly knocked twice on the outside of the craft before they had departed. There was no reference to the knocking in the data from the Shasir they had captured and drained. Local superstition? Personal belief? He resolved to study it further. If she had a favorite spot to knock, it would leave a small, faint but discernible vita trace. If it was something more widespread among the mariners, it could well represent a seagoer tradition. Probably nothing that would amount to anything worth harvesting but he liked having all the data he could lay his hands on. He was notorious for chasing every lead, back in training, to the point of exhaustion. He had been called over-thorough.

Well, he had graduated. Now it was time to see if there was such a thing as over-thorough. He didn't believe it.

"Your father taught you to sail?" he asked, after some time had passed.

"He taught me everything," Ama answered.

"You are close to your family, then?"

She looked off to the undulating horizon. Her *yes* came out only after a significant pause and her seemingly perpetual smile wavered. The subject, one he assumed she would be happy to discuss, had driven her to silence. His impulse was to push the matter, but he refrained.

"We're making excellent time; you'll be in Alisir by tomorrow, right on schedule," she said, changing the topic as she took the wheel again.

Alisir, his first target.

CHAPTER 4

Inside the shelter of a cove along the coast, Ama dropped anchor. They were ahead of schedule and could enjoy some rest, particularly Manatu who was too sick to move from the upper deck. She had left him up there, with Seg, while she ducked down to the galley.

The stove had ample fuel. Good. It would be a simple supper— smoked fish, fried vegetables and some leftover bread—all she could do with so little warning. Not that she could have prepared a feast even if she had had the warning.

Grabbing a knife, she peeled and chopped potato and blemflower into large, uneven chunks.

What was it about the Damiar, Seg, that suggested a sense of superiority beyond title or physicality? He had driven away Dagga, but he had also started asking questions about her family, which no Damiar ever did. Unless they had plans for such information.

She brought the knife down on the block with a heavy thud, sending the two halves of the potato tumbling to the deck. *Damn!* Ama gathered them up and wiped them off on her trousers.

It's like swimming with a drexla. At the thought, the scar on her calf throbbed and her mind drifted to a summer day off the island of Lind.

She and her brothers had gone for a long swim, riding the waves to shore with their bodies. As usual, she had needed to outdo them all, kicking her way out further and further until she was past the break. And alone. That's when she spotted the drexla.

With her dathe covered by her nove, there was no way to sound the surrounding water, she could only keep swimming and keep her eyes open. Every now and then she would catch a glimpse of a dark shape—a long, thick body ending in a winding tail with spines running the length of it—but then it would disappear. Shore was far in the distance, as were her brothers. Showing off had left her at the mercy of a predator. At least she had been wise enough to strap her blade to her calf but, as she clutched it in her hand, she realized how useless her tiny weapon was going to be against all those teeth and the poisonous spines. No matter how vigilant, how prepared or brave she might be it was only a matter of time until the drexla attacked.

More frightening, though, was how her heart raced, how a dormant part of her came burning to life in the moments before she felt those teeth, and how much she enjoyed the thrill, the danger.

The drexla had taken her blade in its eye and Ama had escaped with only a gouge on her calf, from its teeth, and a good scare. She had been lucky, the teeth had caught her but she had avoided the poisonous spines along the tail. Even a scratch from those meant death.

Now, that same sensation was rising in her again, that feeling of being circled, hunted.

A gull cried as it flew by the open porthole to the galley, startling Ama back to her chore. The knife, she noticed, was clutched so tightly in her hand that her knuckles were white.

Closing her eyes, she whispered, "You don't scare me, drexla."

Seg descended the stairs to the lower deck. He could see the girl was hard at work butchering some sort of vegetable and hadn't heard him approach. He paused to watch her. This was a new and pleasant situation for him, observing an Outer in its natural environment.

The only Outers he had dealt with were caj that had already been captured, processed and fitted with control grafts. Caj that functioned as servants and pleasure-caj for the Guild were trained at the finest academy, at Hebreck.

They were also broken. Boring, vacant and beyond shame because they knew that in their station literally nothing was beneath them. They were simply soulless husks who obeyed because they knew their owners could end their existence at the touch of a button.

He continued watching the girl in silence as she chopped the vegetables.

From the moment he had seen her dive into the water, he had been seized with some undefinable emotion. She swam. Swam. Not under threats or orders, not out of necessity, but for pleasure. Even now, watching her, he could scarcely believe he had witnessed such a thing. He couldn't remember the last time anyone had left him speechless, as this Outer had.

She was different. A challenge.

And, with every exchange, he was gathering clues about her. Her spirit was sumptuous.

The food, on the other hand, smelled abysmal.

He saw her start at a bird's passage, and heard her whisper. Something about a *drexel?* He couldn't think of any food rituals or deity invocations involving that name, and wondered what it meant.

"That smells adequate," he announced. She jumped, startled once more.

"I'd be more careful sneaking up on someone when they have a knife," she said, with a slight laugh he was learning to read as discomfort.

His cue to move closer. But not too close. She chopped faster and with less accuracy. A piece of vegetable dropped to the deck and this time, knowing he was watching, she didn't just wipe it off, she tossed it aside.

"I heard you talking to someone," he said.

The knife slipped, slicing open a small cut on her finger. She stuck the finger in her mouth and fumbled around for a cloth.

"No," she said, holding a rag to her wound to stop the bleeding, "just talking to myself. I'm used to being alone."

The kitchen was small, the ceiling low; he was not ignorant of how his tall frame loomed over her, how she might perceive herself as penned or cornered. A theory confirmed by the subtle shifts she made to distance herself from him.

"Can I assist you with anything?" he asked, keeping his tone deliberately light, non-threatening, as he inched forward another step.

"Uh…no, thank you." She wiped the knife clean, then made a show of lighting the stove and moving some pots and pans around on the stovetop.

He waited another few beats before speaking again, "Well then, I shall retire to my quarters and let you finish."

It had been a pleasing bit of indulgence, studying the girl, but there was work to consider. He wasn't here to sightsee or frolic with the locals; Kerbin's warning echoed in the corners of his mind. He could not fail.

The Outer had provided him with detailed maps of Alisir and there was time, before the wretched looking meal was served, to study them.

After a night of tossing and turning, Ama had woken before the sun. The winds were perfect and she pulled anchor.

You didn't battle the Big Water, Fa had taught her that. People tire, water never does. If you want to ride Nen's back, you learn to read his moods. When he is sweet, you can relax, catch your rest. When he is ornery, you stay vigilant and respectful, you let him direct you. He was being sweet now but Ama knew she would have a hard time convincing poor Manatu of that.

The wind had picked up slightly since the previous day, blowing at about fifteen knots and gusting higher. They would make good time to Alisir. Unfortunately for the sick flatlander, bigger wind also brought bigger waves and since the rollers were running north-south and the waves were hitting them from the west, the *Naida* was dipping and rolling as she cut through the blue water. Manatu's stomach was obviously doing much the same, as he clung to the rails, heaving up nothing but air and foam until exhaustion claimed victory and he sunk down into a giant heap of flesh.

Seg, to Ama's surprise, was making a decent showing of himself, even taking on some of the minor tasks she had demonstrated for him. Not bad for a flatlander. Nevertheless, water legs took more than a day to develop and his discomfort appeared in brief flashes that were quickly and consciously subdued. He was at the mercy of her world now and that obviously didn't suit him.

Her world. Ama licked the salt spray from her lips as she gripped the wheel and concentrated on keeping them on course.

Seg stared down at Manatu, who was sprawled out on the deck, half dead and useless. Some bodyguard.

The menial work the Outer had shown him was far more suited for Manatu's ideal combination of strong back, weak mind, and agreeable servility. For that matter, Manatu might as well be caj himself.

The notion actually surprised Seg, who had been raised on the sharp class distinction. There were People and there were caj. To believe otherwise was to betray the People; to speak such a belief aloud would be treason.

Admittedly, some of the work Ama had asked him to do was not unpleasant. He especially enjoyed manning the wheel, and learning the basics of the geometries of the skins gave him a whole new respect for her learning capacity.

In truth, he was finding it difficult *not* to think about her and this new world she was showing him. The only daydreams he had ever allowed himself revolved around his career and tangible, achievable objectives. And yet he had caught himself, the previous evening, wondering how far this vessel could travel and then entertained visions of directing Ama and her boat on a course of exploration beyond the boundaries of the mission.

These imaginings had offered a pleasant two-minute contemplation before he had finally gained hold of his senses again and resumed calculating potential vita loads from the preliminary data Kerbin had transmitted through the digipad. Using the comm, in such tight quarters, was too risky but from the text of her dispatches he could tell she was flogging the squad hard, covering tremendous amounts of ground on foot. Lacking his direct supervision, they avoided making any public appearances; they had made their first read at a distance. This was not as reliable as the sort of close-in readings he would be taking, but it would give him a rough picture.

House Haffset had a limited resource base but excellent credit accounts. His plan would take some convincing but, if they were willing to gamble boldly, they could strike at least a half-dozen choice targets in a single go. It was up to him to winnow out the richest sources.

He grasped the handrail and left Manatu to his misery as he returned to the rear of the boat – the *stern*, as it was referred to.

"Getting close," Ama said, as Seg arrived at her side, then pointed to a large, rocky outcropping in the distance. "There's the Killing Cliff."

A small wave blew sideways across the stern, soaking them both. Ama's second eyelids were up before it hit. Seg ducked away from the spray.

"Sorry about the ride," she said, glad for her Kenda eyes, so well adapted to water, "Price you pay for speed."

"Never mind the ride. Comfort is secondary to getting business done. Tell me more about this Killing Cliff."

The Killing Cliff, Ama knew two versions of that story – the accepted one everyone spoke out loud and the darker one, whispered among her people.

"Before the Unification, before the Shasir brought us together in peace, some of the Welf tribes around Alisir used to practice human sacrifice. Usually it was a single infant and no one really knows why, since the Welf have no written history. The story says that the Welf believed their gods required servants, so they would 'send' one of their children to live with the gods and serve them. That cliff was a holy place to the Welf, a meeting of mountain, water and sky; that was where they would…"

She stopped, assuming Seg could fill in the missing detail.

"In their legends, in return for the sacrifice of a child, the Welf would have a season of healthy crops and protection from plagues and storms. When the Shasir came to our land, they put an end to that kind of barbarism." Ama lifted her palm skyward, hating the gesture but determined to put on a good show, "Praise to the Shasir'kia."

After the previous evening, she was even more convinced that her passenger, if not a spy for Corrus, had some equally threatening Shasir alliance.

"Your first stop, the Temple of Shasir'Pei, in Alisir, was constructed shortly after the arrival of the Shasir. So now, instead of murdering babies, the Welf sacrifice food, gifts and whatever pitiful amount of coin they manage to put away during the year." Damn it, why couldn't she ever keep her tongue under control? That last part was unnecessary. No wonder her family worried about her. That kind of blasphemy could get her sent to Correction.

But she couldn't pretend she didn't know the other half of the legend. Yes, the Welf, brutes that they were in the black times, had sacrificed an infant every year and the Shasir had stopped that practice but that had not put an end to the murder at the Killing Cliff. The Shasir used Welf labor to construct their temples, their skyships and devices for their magic, but they forbid anyone outside of the Shasir to know their secrets. Any workers privy to Shasir magic, when they were no longer useful, were herded off the Killing Cliff, their disappearances explained as magical ascensions to the Cloud Temple in the realm of the Above — one of the reasons many Welf made the yearly pilgrimage to Alisir, in hopes of their own magical ascension.

Ama had no proof of this, no one did, but the Kenda had strong memories and their own secret history.

"Good fishing in front of that cliff, too," she added, to lighten the mood. "Maybe there's some magic there, after all. Alisir has a large Welf village, so I'll be able to get some decent food for us. There should be lots of kembleberries still on the vine. I'll make sure to get more genga root for Manatu, though I don't think it's helping him much."

And maybe I'll have some free time to paddle the Gwai tributaries, she thought with no small degree of anticipation. Her paddleboat was strapped to the stern. The water level wouldn't be as high as she would like but tackling some whitewater would be just the diversion she needed to shake the tension her latest passenger stirred within her, and the Gwai's secondary rivers had more than enough monster waves to do the job.

"You study history, do you?" she asked, now curious, against her better judgment, to decipher Seg's intentions.

"I enjoy local lore," he said noncommittally. "Folk tales, legends and myths. A hobby of mine." He waved a dismissive hand, but there had been a gap, a hiccup in his response, large enough to suggest his interest was more than a hobby. "So, you feel that perhaps the Welf would be better-served by being allowed to keep more of the coin they earn?"

Now she was having a hiccup of her own. Her honest answer to his question was one she would never share with a stranger, especially a non-Kenda stranger.

"I feel…" she considered her words carefully, if this man was a Shasir spy the wrong words could mean Correction, "I feel that all people would do well to improve themselves and sometimes that takes coin." Treading dangerous water. "However, spirituality *is* the core of life, the Shasir'kia are powerful gods, and the Welf seem happy with their lives, so perhaps it's best they place more value on worship than on material goods. And they'll be well rewarded in the Cloud Temple, when their days are over."

What a pile of dung.

The invasive stare; he was making her twitchy again. That and the wind was picking up even more. They were coming down some of the rollers too fast for her liking. If the *Naida's* nose dipped under she could drive them underwater and that would put an abrupt end to this cultural tour of Seg's.

Damn, maybe she should have given up some of the coin and taken on a deckhand for this charter. At the thought, a sudden push of wind prompted her to turn her head to the stern. A wall of black was bearing down on them, one of the late spring squalls that drop out of the sky with no warning.

"We've got weather coming in," she told Seg, her tone firm but not panicked. "Take the wheel for a drop," she ordered, dashing to the stern locker as soon as his hands were in place. She pulled out three oilskin coats and pressed two into Seg's hands as she repositioned herself at the wheel.

"We need to lock down the secondary skin and close the hatches. Do you think you can do that on your own? I need to keep us pointed into it." Manatu was still crumpled in a heap at the rail. "Move Manatu back to midship, put the extra oilskin over him, and lash him to something solid so he doesn't get washed overboard."

Seg nodded but paused. He laid his hand on her arm, opened his mouth as if to speak, then just as suddenly he closed it again. His body stiffened and he hurried away.

Ama stared at the spot where Seg had grasped her arm, as if there might be a mark there, an imprint of his hand. Where had that come from? Like a jealous lover, the Big Water demanded her attention, though, and she slipped into her oilskin and pulled her eyes to the horizon once more.

She shivered, but not from the wind.

As he slid into one of the coats, Seg berated himself for the impulsive act. He had stopped himself just before speaking, thankfully, but had he not, he would have offered her some kind of reassurance. When he had asked her about the Welf, she had quite obviously censored herself for his benefit, believing him—well, not *him* but his current incarnation—some kind of threat and he had been moved to assuage her fear.

A ridiculous impulse; in reality he comprised a much worse threat than any she might imagine him to impose. The timing couldn't have been less appropriate.

The pitch of the boat was frightening and yet exhilarating in a way he had never felt before, and he was torn between a self-interrogation over his impulsive move and the realization that they were perhaps getting into something dangerous and therefore exciting.

He secured the open hatches and turned to make his still-clumsy way back to Manatu. It would serve the parentless wretch to let him drown, but in addition to their gear, there was a load of superfluous junk tacked on for their cover that Seg had no intention of lugging around himself.

"Hold still, you lackwit," he muttered as Manatu twitched and expelled more bile onto the deck. Hands hooked under the large man's armpits, he dragged him toward the center of the boat. At least he had managed to maintain his cover of being mute thus far. Be thankful for the small favors.

Ama gripped the wheel; the squall was almost on them and things were about to get tricky. Likely it wouldn't last more than an hour but it would be a fitful hour. The secondary skin was locked off and the main was almost fully retracted – it wasn't about speed anymore, it was about control.

Seg was sealing the last hatch. He was no mariner but he was a quick learner, and a willing one – an anomaly among the privileged classes. His hard face fired up with the storm, as if he were a man meant for challenge. Ama knew how that felt, to only come alive when life was at risk. She bit her lip and again felt his absent hand on her arm.

The rollers grew steeper and tighter as if the Big Water was folding in on them. The *Naida* fought her way up each face, then slid off the back side and plunged toward the dark grey of the next wave, as if she would punch through it. Wind blew the tops off the waves and soaked the upper deck. Ama's second eyelids flicked up and she gripped the wheel even tighter.

"Seg!" she yelled, her voice all but swallowed by the squall. He looked her way, one hand clinging to the mast and one hand covering his eyes to shield them from the stinging salt water. She waved him over to her, urgently, and he stumbled his way back, grasping onto whatever his hands could find.

Even side-by-side, she had to shout. "Stay back here now, the stern's the safest place. Hang on!" The *Naida* shot over a wave, screaming her way through the water, which was almost black now in the shadow of the clouds. "Yeee-aaa!" Ama yelled, as if she were at a raucous party and not in the middle of a tempest. "We're ripping now!"

Her smile was savage; she was riding the beast. She whipped her head around to face Seg, her wet hair plastered to the side, eyes wide and bright silver, "Isn't this great?"

He was grinning from ear to ear. The smile didn't look in any way appropriate on his face, as if he had never done it before. His hair was plastered to his head also, water dripped down from his forehead to his chin, and as he looked at her one corner of his mouth quirked up even further.

For a moment, his face frozen in an expression of feral rapture, he held her gaze, real desire and passion rolling off him, uncontrolled, before he turned away to stare into the belly of the beast, and another wave broke over the bow.

For over an hour, Ama guessed, (though time stretches inside a squall), she and Seg had held on at the stern, while, at midship, wave after wave washed over Manatu. Then, in the way of spring storms, the clouds broke, the wind died and the *Naida* was gliding peacefully over long sets of low rollers. Ama, her two passengers and every inch of the upper deck were drenched but the sun, burning against a pure blue canvas, would sort things out soon enough.

Some unspoken connection had evolved between Ama and Seg during the squall, and now, in the calm, she felt awkward and self-conscious. And exhausted. Prying her fingers from the wooden wheel, she asked Seg if he could take over the helm for a moment. Thankfully he obliged, though he was obviously spent.

"I'll just check to make sure everything's in one piece," she said, flexing her cramped arms and fingers, making her way, first, to Manatu.

What a mess. He was still breathing, thankfully, but he was waterlogged, white as the clouds and shaking with cold. "I'm going to get some blankets to warm him up," she called to Seg, as she made her way to the hatch and ducked below deck.

Quick as her aching joints would allow, she grabbed two thick, praffa-cloth blankets from storage and scurried back up to the ailing man. She sat Manatu upright, untied the rope from around his waist, wiped his face dry, removed the oilskin coat Seg had covered him with and wrung as much water as she could from his clothing. He weighed a solid ton and maneuvering him around was like moving a dead whale, but she was used to doing things alone and so she managed. Once she had a blanket beneath him, she laid Manatu back down, then covered him with the second blanket, tucking in the edges to keep it secured. Smoothing the wet hair from his face, she rubbed his cheeks with her hands to warm them up.

His eyes blinked slowly open. "Hey big fellow," Ama said, "almost there. You'll be on dry, flat land soon, sure as I can whistle." She pursed her lips and blew, making a wet, *whooshing* noise. "Maybe that was a bad example."

A weak smile came to his lips.

Wrapping part of the blanket around his head, she rubbed his shoulder, stood up, and prepared to leave. Then he spoke.

"Hhhnk oouugh."

"Manatu?" she asked, but his eyes had closed and he was asleep. Had he spoken or was she hearing things? There had definitely been a noise. She was sure of it.

Puzzled, Ama set about putting back in place anything the squall had knocked loose. *I'm just tired. I'm imagining things*, she thought. But she had doubts. Now that the skies were clear and the sea was calm, she extended both the skins. Finally, she coiled up the last bit of loose rope and returned to the helm, where she took Seg's place.

"We'll be at the mouth of the Gwai River in less than an hour, and in Alisir shortly after that, I expect. You might as well get some rest. Your friend is asleep and…" *I heard him speak*, "…he's fine, just fine. Thanks for your help."

She was tired and confused and babbling. This had been a strange crossing.

Having surreptitiously popped a stim tab, for energy, while Ama was busy, Seg felt lively. He would pay for the chemical assistance later, with a period of sleepless shakes, but for now he was bright and alert.

He wondered how she would react to the Storm of home. The Storm was the only remaining item of deification left to his people, and it was a monster, flesh-stripping howling madness that plunged the World into darkness. None ventured into the Storm and survived, at least not without protective Storm-cells, but he had always had that urge. He wanted to face the darkness, to challenge and master it.

Much as he had mastered this. He was feeling ten feet tall and invincible, and for that matter powerfully aroused. He turned to stare at her, casually stepping back from the wheel, sensing her weariness. Her scent was that of strong exertion, overlaid with a rinse of salt tang, her hair tousled and crusting with brine. She was a mess, but that was exactly what appealed to him. He sensed a need from her, too; there was something lurking underneath the strength and determination.

Enough idle fantasy. He shook his head. There was work to be done, and no room for distractions. And yet he brought his hands together and forward, in a low clap, then nodded at her and sauntered away.

For such an old soul, in that moment, he felt so very young.

Ama had not visited the Alisir docks this season and had forgotten how busy and animated they were. As they approached port, she ran up the yellow flag with the red stripe, to alert the Port Captain of her need for a slip, as well as to indicate the size of her vessel. When they had finally gotten close enough to make out individuals, it took her a good five minutes to spot the runner on shore, as he was lost in a sea of bodies, cargo, livestock and vendors. At last she picked out the small, stringy Welf, who waved an identical flag to hers, frantically attempting to get her attention. He ran down the crowded dock and guided the *Naida* to an empty slip, where a crowd of dockhands waited.

Manatu had perked up noticeably once their journey had made the transition from the Big Water to the flat calm of the wide river, though he was seriously dehydrated and physically wrung out. From her position at the helm, she had watched Seg talking to him and wondered what he was saying. From the way the big man sluffed off the blankets she had given him, and struggled to sit upright, she imagined it was some kind of hard-assed pep talk.

Right at this moment, she sympathized with Manatu. The squall had drained her and she had taken no more than one brief break since it had passed. She still had to collect some supplies before sunset, make sure they were properly registered with the Port Captain, pay the heaps of fees charged by the local governing bodies, and prepare dinner for her passengers before she could pour herself a mug of praffa wine and collapse into her hammock.

Safely secured in the slip, Ama hopped down to the dock, double-checked the lines the dockhands had tied, (which were never done as well as she liked), and helped position a moveable set of stairs for her passengers.

Every now and then she glanced up at Seg, who was drinking in the scene at the docks as if he had just been freed from a life in prison.

"Can I trouble you to run my creds to the Port Captain and sign on my behalf?" she asked the runner, an aimable old Welf who went by the name of Jibri. "Quarter coin," she added, though she guessed Jibri might do it for free. "Half coin if you can send someone to help me with provisions."

Jibri fell into paroxysms of delight as she handed him the leather folder with the *Naida*'s legal documents in it. "Fast as I can run, yup!" he answered, showering her with a series of symbolic hand gestures before tearing off down the docks. *Maybe I'll toss him another half coin if he can find someone to cook for me as well.*

"Soon as the runner returns, I'll fetch us fresh provisions for dinner," she told Seg, as she dashed up the stairs and back on deck. "In the meantime, you and your friend are free to do as you like."

He seemed anxious to get on shore; Ama couldn't wait to see it.

"And please let me know if you require anything else of me," she added, sincerely hoping, through the fog of her exhaustion, that he did not.

"Finish taking care of the boat," he said, "and then get rested. Manatu and I will take our refreshment in town." He turned to Manatu, "Come on you, we've got work to do."

Manatu, pale and visibly miserable, followed along.

When he stepped onto the solid pier, Seg staggered sideways and nearly wiped out in spectacular fashion before he grasped a post and hung on the brink of going over into the water. Manatu, already weakened and disoriented, staggered forward a few steps and fell to his knees, shaking his head.

From the deck of the *Naida*, Ama watched Seg and Manatu making their way on land like a couple of drunks and ducked her head so they wouldn't notice her spying and smirking. Flatlanders don't realize how their bodies adapt to the constant movement on water, and how that affects their transition back to land. She could have warned them, she guessed, but then she wouldn't have had the satisfaction of watching the man who had made her so uneasy in her own galley, with his innate sense of power and entitlement, experience a bit of unsteadiness himself.

Between the comic display and his assistance during the squall, perhaps Ama could consider the score settled. The rest of the journey could proceed in peace.

Perhaps.

If only the nagging voice in her head would be quiet. She set about her chores as the voice continued to harass her.

Why are they so unused to water travel? If they really were from the south, they would have made at least one or two passages to get to the Banks.

As she locked off the skins, she caught herself gritting her teeth. And what of this odd itinerary? The Shasir'Pei Temple? A Shasir temple, yes, but one that was almost exclusively the domain of the Welf. What trade would they find there? Few of the stops on their route were of any great importance for trade. She tugged hard on the tie for the skin, knotting it more tightly than usual. Also, there was the matter of Manatu's muteness, though she now had her doubts about that. Was she making too much of this? Pulling her hammock from the stern locker, she thought of Seg. An odd man. Difficult. And yet...

Her fingers drifted over the mesh of her 'bed'. *He notices me.* That was what she couldn't understand. The agenda of men was never difficult to fathom. They wanted her body, her boat or her family name and those were the only attributes they paid attention to. But Seg, with that penetrating stare, he seemed to be only interested in the workings of her innermost self.

On first meeting Seg, she had seen an old man in a boy's body. But during the squall the mask of restraint and studious contemplation had fallen away, revealing a spirit as wild and youthful as her own. Wherever he came from, she guessed this part of Seg was not allowed to show itself, at all. She understood how that felt, too well.

Worst of all, he made her want to know more about him. In fact, he made her want things she had never considered before.

"Captain Kalder!" Jibri called her thoughts back to the business at hand. "Papers, I have them! Assistant, too, yup." The runner waved her leather folder and pointed to a tall boy, who pushed an empty, wooden cart.

Ama dropped the hammock and made her way to the dock. Both men lowered their eyes when she stepped in front of them. "You can look me in the eyes. I rarely bite." The Welf did so, smiling nervously.

"This be Tev," Jibri said, patting a hand on the boy's shoulder. "He'll take care of all you need, well and true."

She paid out the promised coin, plus a bit extra – an act of kindness to exorcise her bad thoughts and suspicions. To the boy, she gave a rough list of required provisions, as well as license to pick out a few extra treats if he thought them worth the coin.

Lord Flavert Uval pressed his lips together in a smile only his wife would fail to recognize as disingenuous, as she held up yet another bracelet for his approval. Was there no end to his wife's hunger for trinkets?

"I simply cannot decide. Let's see them all again," he heard her say, as he turned from the merchant booth and pushed his way through the crowd of walking human refuse, two of his guards and a servant on his heels.

How he hated this stinking Welf port. If Hertia's father had not graced them with the use of the summer estate at Alisir, he would be content to never set foot among this rabble again. When the old tyrant died, he had every intention of selling it off and relocating to T'ueve or Malvid.

To one side of him, he could hear a couple of Welf jabbering away at each other excitedly. Was there anything that didn't excite them? One of the dirt lickers had been given a tip from some boat captain and you would think from his retelling of the event that he had been named Judicia instead of being tossed a meager half coin.

"Put it right in my hand, even asked my name, she did, yup!" the Welf repeated for the third time – enough to ignite the headache that had threatened Uval all afternoon.

Pinching the bridge of his nose, he turned to leave. Unfortunately, the obnoxious Welf had decided to sprint off at the same moment and crashed into him, knocking Uval sideways. He turned to glare at the man who had been so negligent. The Welf bowed repeatedly and apologized, raising a palm skyward as he begged forgiveness. "So sorry, my Lord. My fault, all my fault. Wasn't watching my step. So sorry."

Uval scowled. Greedy, nattering vermin. "Clear my sight," he ordered, waving his hand impatiently.

The Welf nodded two or three times then backed away.

"Wait!" Uval said, stopping the man in his tracks. Could it be? In his annoyance, he had almost missed an important detail of the dirt licker's otherwise inane story. The *she.*

"My Lord?" the Welf cowered, obviously expecting a thrashing.

"I couldn't help but overhear your good news. Which Captain gave you the extra coin?"

"Captain Kalder," he answered, tightening the hand that held his payment.

Uval smothered a grin. "Really? My dear acquaintance, Captain Ama Kalder, here in Alisir? And where would she be, pray tell?"

Relieved to escape a beating, the Welf pointed, "Down there, next to the scrap hauler. Just got into port."

Next to the scrap hauler. *How appropriate.*

"And does Captain Kalder have passengers?" Uval asked, feigning a benign interest he most certainly did not feel.

"Two," the Welf, answered. Uval couldn't help a slight frown. Passengers would complicate matters. "Fine Damiar gentlemen, such as yourself. But they both got off, gone now, yup. She's all alone if you wants to visit her."

Of course they had left, probably at a run. The men had obviously been in some desperate straights to travel so far on that wreck of a boat to begin with, but no Damiar would lower himself to actually sleep on the thing while in port. Even a dirt pile such as Alisir had lodgings vastly more suitable for men of his class. Which meant they would be gone at least until sunrise. Good.

"Oh, I do want to visit her, and thank you so much for your kind assistance..." Uval gestured for the Welf to supply a name.

"Jibri, I be, my Lord. Jibri Bel."

"My thanks to you, Jibri." Uval reached a gloved hand into his breast pocket, pulled out a half coin and held it out toward the Welf. "But don't tell anyone, if you please. I would prefer to surprise her."

"Swear to the Sky Fathers, not a word to no one, no, no!"

Uval grinned as he dropped the coin into the man's outstretched palm. Parting with the coin didn't bother him; he would send one of his men behind the Welf, to slit his throat at the first opportunity. Silence is priceless.

The Welf bowed and thanked and blessed his way away from Uval, who was already whispering instructions in the ear of his guard.

He wound his way through the bodies, to the railing overlooking the pier. There it was, that claptrap of a boat, on which the water rat had threatened him. Him. A Damiar Lord. And with a weapon no less.

What good fortune. What lovely happenstance. He still couldn't believe his luck, to have the Kenda whore right here in Alisir.

Uval stood next to a piling, licking his lips. He would have to keep Hertia from spotting the slut she had found so 'charming'. He couldn't very well slit *her* throat, now could he?

Ama. *Captain* Ama...lest he forget. All alone. Yes, the self-righteous bitch was alone, but not for long.

CHAPTER 5

For the trip to the temple, Seg hired a cartul and driver, as Ama had suggested. On this world, a 'cartul' was slang for any type of mammal-drawn transport and he had discovered that there were endless variations on the theme. The bulk of the cartuls for hire were simple, open-air affairs, drawn either by scruffy yet durable equine hybrids or the fat, plodding greshers that were also used for meat and heavy labor. Though the common cartuls were adequate for two travelers with no baggage, Seg also needed to consider his cover. From what he knew, both from his quick study and from observing the local Damiars, he decided on something much larger and more elaborate than was required. The benefit of this choice, he discovered, as they rumbled up the winding, mountain path in the relative comfort of their covered carriage, was that he and Manatu could sit out of listening range of the driver.

"You'd best have taken an anti-bio med," Seg muttered quietly to Manatu. "Your death would be most inconvenient at this juncture. If you'd doubled your anti-nausea meds before we left port, as I'd told you, you might not have been stuck out there." Idiot. At least, for the moment, a silent idiot.

As they drew closer, Seg could see the temple grounds. A large complex surrounded by rolling hills, his first target, the temple of Shasir'Pei, was situated in the heart of Welf territory. Its geography, combined with its historical significance, meant that the vast majority of the temple's worshippers belonged to the lowest class. Many referred to it simply as 'the Welf temple'. Since the uneducated Welf were the class most susceptible to Shasir trickery and propaganda, the temple promised to hold significant amounts of vita within.

The open design of the structure was ideal for the Shasir to pack in tens of thousands of soft-brained Welf Outers for indoctrination, mass religious ecstasy and hysteria. However, prime season for ceremonial gatherings was not for another week, and therefore the grounds were occupied only by a small number of Welf pilgrims and the occasional Damiar sightseer paying token devotions. Although the timing suited Seg's schedule, the lack of bodies made it difficult for he and Manatu to hide in the crowds. He was very careful when taking his readings. The probe was concealed in his voluminous sleeve, and the VIU was giving him high readings of vita, to the top scale.

This strike alone would justify the mission, and he was only at the perimeter. He would have to move in closer to identify the tangible items the troops could carry away. Undoubtedly large parts of the very architecture would be moved out, which would require a major force package and at least a day's occupation. But it could be done. Nothing was more frustrating to a Theorist than to find a vita-rich location that could not feasibly be moved through the warp. The Killing Cliff Ama had told him of would be such a structure, too big to extrans but rich in what he sought; human sacrifice unfailingly produced dense vita crops.

Seg moved closer to the fearsome looking statue standing guard at the gates to the temple's interior. Arms spread, palms skyward, the stone likeness was that of a man, likely one of the Shasir leaders of old, judging by the attire. At the base of the statue, devotees had left offerings of food and drink, flowers, baskets, even articles of clothing. Seg looked down at the VIU, then up at the chiseled face, with a smirk. The statue was saturated with vita; its devoted worshippers had unwittingly marked it as a prime target.

As usual, such choice targets also bore the risk of fanatical defense, in this case the descent of thousands of maddened Welf upon the strike force. The devoted believers would not stand by and let their holy grounds be desecrated, that was a certainty.

A properly equipped expeditionary force could handle a rushing mob. It was the potential Shasir response that would be the concern for such a lengthy raid. In response to a full day's occupation, the Shasir would have time to mobilize whatever toys they possessed capable of causing havoc.

As he contemplated the options, Seg proceeded further into the temple grounds.

Tev returned to the *Naida* with surprising speed. He helped Ama unload the supplies out of the cart into the galley and cargo hold, singing merrily the entire time. She thanked the boy and offered yet another half coin. Not in her right mind today. The sun had set; she would gather her soap and fresh clothes and dive in the river for a quick swim and bathe. Then wine and sleep. Lovely, lovely sleep.

As she reached for her clothes, from the cubby next to the head, she glanced over at the locker where Seg and Manatu's larger luggage was stowed. Were the answers to her questions in there?

She could be quick. Just a peek to unravel the mystery of her odd passengers. Put her mind at ease. Yes, that was what she needed. She padded over to the cargo locker and traced her fingers over the latch.

This is crazy. Don't do it. You're already in enough trouble at home, she thought, as she worked the latch open and lifted the door.

Inside, there were four large bags, all made of sturdy leather decorated with fine gold stitching, long tassles dangled from each end. She opened the first and examined the contents, which were stacked and stuffed in such a way it was a wonder the bag could stay closed.

"Damiar junk," Ama muttered, plucking at a swathe of gold fabric she assumed was a sash of some sort and moving aside bottles of scented oil. Just the usual heaps of fluffery so esteemed by the upper classes.

As she dug through the unremarkable contents, her guilt gained the upper hand on her suspicions. After all, she shouldn't be poking through the private belongings of her paying customers. She had resigned to pack up and attend to her much-needed bathing, when something caught her eye. A glint of metal.

Ama pushed aside the fluff and finery, reached down and felt something hard. With a quick glance over her shoulder—that Seg had a way of sneaking up on her—she made sure she was alone. No one. The men hadn't taken any of their belongings to shore with them, which could only mean they planned to return sometime this evening. Nevertheless, above deck, she had hooked up the boarding bell on a thin, trip wire. An old Kenda trick for solo sailors; anyone who stepped aboard would knock the line, ring the bell and alert her to their presence.

The box she pulled out was about the length of her forearm and constructed of some kind of Shasir metal, such as the wealthier Damiar sometimes used. There seemed to be no way to open it, which was unusual. She turned it over slowly in her hands but all she could detect was a small pad that had no lock or latch. Shasir trickery? It had to be.

There was another identical box beside the first and she examined it thoroughly with the same results. Stymied, she nestled both back inside the bag, taking care to place everything back as it had been.

Well, they're merchants, so of course they might have artifacts I've never seen, Ama scolded herself but that answer felt too easy. She moved to the next bag. This one must be Manatu's, she guessed, by the size of the garments within.

She didn't waste time looking through the trinkets but pulled aside everything to get to the bottom layers. Peeling back a heavy coat revealed a row of knives of various sizes. "Son of a whore," she whispered.

Around the knives, there were other objects she assumed must be weapons, though most she had never cast eyes on nor even imagined. Even among the elite Damiar guards, the most advanced weapons were bangers. She picked up a small, round object and cradled it in her palm. It was heavy for something so tiny and made of metal just like the mysterious boxes. What was all this?

A loud laugh peeled from somewhere outside the galley porthole. Nen's death, what was she thinking? Seg and Manatu could return at any minute. Private belongings or not, if she was caught touching Shasir magic without permission, the penalty would be death. Her heart pummeled the inside of her chest. Instead of easing her worries or answering her questions, the contents of the bags had only heightened her suspicion. Hurriedly but with care to put everything back exactly as it had been, she packed up the contents, closed Manatu's bag and sealed up the cargo locker.

Calm down! There's probably a reasonable explanation.

Ama grabbed her clothes and towel. She hurried back to the galley, fished a bottle of praffa wine from the cupboard, popped the cork and took several long swigs.

I'll swim and bathe and sleep, and in the morning I'll probably realize I was worrying about nothing.

Assuming, of course, she could sleep.

Seg was coming down hard from the stim dose he had taken after the storm. It was all he could do to lift one foot in front of the other as he walked the final stretch of dock on the way to the boat. A major effort of will was required to control the shivers, and he couldn't stop his hands from shaking. Manatu looked abysmal as well.

The find at the temple was rich. There were statues, devotional tables, an offering tray and the main lectern from which the Outer high priest undoubtedly babbled about the magic of the Above and thrilled the fools with opulent fakery. There was much more, all of it drenched in vita. All of it would have to be taken.

His sluggish mind attacked the problems, working through the manpower ratios that would be required. At least a hundred and forty troops on the passage. A hundred just to hold off the teeming hordes of Welf who would throw themselves at the perimeter, plus whatever tricks the Shasir came up with. Ideally the Shasir would be distracted by the nature of the raid. That was for the military men to figure out but Seg would demand some control.

He kept shifting between watching his path and working the problem, which led to several restarts on the thought process. After too many attempts, he abandoned thoughts of the raid altogether as they tromped up the stairs to the boat.

He had figured out the physics behind their disorientation upon reaching land, and hadn't missed Ama watching and snickering. Well, there would be no more mercy or consideration for her.

A bell jangled and he stopped, stared at it, blinked a few times, wondered what in the name of the Storm it was about, then turned to Manatu. His guard waved his hands, trying to sign something, and Seg stared at him vacantly until the trooper gave up and threw his hands up in frustration.

"Is it safe?" Seg asked, his voice thick and weary. Manatu looked at him for a long, hard

moment, then nodded reluctantly. Seg knew well the axiom of all training excursions: 'It is never safe when extrans' but for now he only needed to know if the bell was connected to some immediate threat. Assured that it was not, he proceeded onward toward his bunk below.

This was going to be a long, twitchy night. He smoothed his hair with a shaky hand and wished the damn bed wasn't so far away.

The bell. Ama choked on her mouthful of wine, coughed and spat. She cast a quick glance over her shoulder to make sure she had indeed re-locked the cargo locker. She had, but that didn't stop her heart from crawling up into her mouth.

With a residue of guilt lingering in the lower deck, she rushed up the stairs to escape it, and ran into a wall of Seg when she finished her ascent.

"Oh! You scared me," she exclaimed, realizing a moment too late how stupid that must have sounded, since Seg had obviously tripped the bell.

He looked like twelve shades of death. For a second she panicked and wondered if he had somehow been spying on her through the porthole before she remembered he couldn't have seen her from that vantage.

"I…" she held out the bundle of clothes and her towel as an explanation while her mouth and brain scrambled for words, "I'm going to swim. You know…uh, just going to bathe and then sleep." Ama was not only tired and nervous, she was now, thanks to the bottle of wine still clutched in the hand holding her clothes, more than a bit tipsy.

Seg glared and shook. Ama thought Manatu now looked positively radiant compared to his companion.

"So, um…"Ama's mouth formed a crooked smile, "goodnight, then."

Seg pushed her aside. "Get some sleep," he ordered. "We leave tomorrow. Early."

Feet dragging, he climbed down the stairs and didn't look back. Manatu, on the other hand, lingered, eyeing her suspiciously.

It was the shock of Seg's shove, not the shove itself, which Ama recoiled from. As she headed for the stern, she glanced back and saw Manatu, still watching her. Once again her heart headed into her throat and her pulse sped up as she remembered the rows of knives in his trunk. She took another long pull off the wine.

Her swim and bath was not the languorous affair it usually was. She finished her scrubbing, climbed back aboard, dried quickly, dressed and fell into her hammock. Shouts, laughter, music, the sounds of brawls and celebrations from the street and the nearby Port House filled the night air – Alisir was never quiet. Nevertheless, sleep took her, despite the noise and her fears, and she slipped into dark dreams.

Lord Uval arrived at the pier, with three of his guards, in time to see Ama climb up and over the stern of her vessel. He waited, hidden, while she dressed and flopped into a hammock strung near the helm. His men practically pawed the ground like rutting beasts and though Uval was also ready to pounce, his motivation was something more sophisticated than primitive lust.

Let one Kenda scum run over you and you might as well let them all move into your home and eat at your table. Welf were vermin but they were useful and obedient vermin, such as the three men with him this night. These Kenda, always aiming above their station.

He had heard news of the Kalder family's good fortune, their rise into the upper echelons of scum. A Kenda Shasir'threa? The thought made him ill. It was one matter to let the water rats into the ranks of the Shasir'dua, to keep their ever-hungry egos pacified. But allowing them into the upper and esteemed ranks of the Threa, riders of the skyships, one step removed from the gods, was treasonous. This night was about more than petty revenge, (though he was owed a good portion of that), it was a lesson and a warning.

Uval waved his men forward. His belly was hot with disgust as he rolled the hastily put together plan through his mind, yet again. She would be laughably overwhelmed. *Let's see her try her knife stunt this time.* They would drag her below deck, far from prying eyes, and spend the night using her body as a receptacle for their savagery. She was not to die, he insisted on that, but she wouldn't walk away whole either. Perhaps he would slice that cocky smile off her face or maybe an eye would make a nice souvenir? Before sunrise, they would string her body from her own mast for all the lower classes to witness. How proud would she be after that?

A hard message to miss.

The men, stealthy for their size, made their way aboard the boat— avoiding the ridiculous trip wire boat captains so haplessly relied on— as Uval strolled down the dock, scanning for unwanted onlookers.

Not that it would matter, if he were seen. He was a Lord; who would dare confront or accuse him? But the authorities, should they get wind of this, would have to make a show of disciplining him, attention he would rather avoid.

He licked his lips again. *Oh my pretty Kenda whore, I'm going to rip you to pieces.*

Someone was holding her head underwater; drowning her. Ama scratched to pull off her nove, to free her dathe, as she felt the current drag her down.

No! Not drowning.

She awoke to the smell of human flesh pressed to her nose – a large hand clamped over her mouth. Her hands flew to where she knew her blade was hidden. What was happening? A set of hands grabbed her wrists before she could reach her weapon and another meaty set fastened onto her ankles as she tried to kick.

Even restrained as she was, she screamed against the hand and thrashed with all the strength she possessed to free herself. It was dark, but she could make out men's faces, at least three, illuminated by the moonlight. She couldn't pick out their features but she could smell them: rancid, unwashed.

Then, a familiar face appeared. The narrow jaw and wet smile were unmistakable. Lord Uval pressed in close, until his nose was inches away from hers.

"Time to learn your place," he hissed, as he shoved his hand between her legs and tightened his grip.

Ama thrashed again, managed to get one leg free and dealt one of the attackers a solid kick. The blow was next to useless and her leg was soon imprisoned, but the momentary distraction allowed her to work her head free enough to sink her teeth into the hand over her mouth.

"Gaaah!" her attacker howled, as he yanked his hand away from her gnashing teeth.

"SEG!" Ama screamed, shocked that his name was the first word that came to her mind. But as soon as the name was out, Uval's hand clamped on her throat. She opened her mouth to gasp for air but he had grabbed a rag from atop the cask of grint and shoved it in her mouth, almost down her throat.

"None of the other water rats can hear you," he told her, and nodded in the direction of the other boats around them, all dark and quiet. "They're all off whoring and drinking, as your kind likes to do. No one is coming to help you." He turned his face to the man with the bleeding hand, "Keep her quiet and hold her still!"

This time the man grabbed a fistful of her hair before slapping his good hand over her mouth. Ama was stretched taut, immobile. Uval reached down and undid the belt from her waist. Her eyes widened. *No, this isn't going to happen.*

Uval slid his hand around her waist, producing her hidden blade with a *tsk, tsk, tsk.* He unsheathed it and pressed the tip between her legs, as she had once done to him.

His wild eyes reflected the moonlight. "My turn."

Miserable, fatigued and twitchy, Seg stared at the ceiling and wished he could sleep. Or think straight. Or do anything. He rolled over to one side, pressed the pillow around his ears and groaned.

Manatu had passed out almost as soon as he had hit his bunk, arms and legs dangling over the edge, obviously the aftereffect of all the exertion and exposure. Seg couldn't focus on much, but knowing the stupid oaf was deep into sleep stirred pleasing notions of drowning him.

"SEG!" he heard Ama shout, the sound muffled.

"What?" he muttered into the pillow, as if she were in the room. It took him a moment to realize she wasn't. Was she having some feverish dream about him?

He shook his head. Manatu, with the preternatural awareness of a veteran, was already awake, and at the hatchway to his quarters. "Trouble," Manatu mouthed and Seg suddenly realized that, yes, a screaming woman in the middle of the night often did herald some sort of disturbance, and pulled himself upright. Since he hadn't bothered undressing, the stunner was still strapped into his sleeve. He lurched up, adrenaline coursing through his system, and staggered out of his quarters. Manatu followed in his wake and put a hand on his shoulder.

"I should go," he whispered, the first words Seg had heard him speak in two days.

"Shut up, idiot," Seg whispered back and shook him off. When he had climbed high enough, he could see figures silhouetted by moonlight where Ama slept. He signaled behind him to Manatu, in the field code in which he had been trained. *Four. Armed. Kill when I signal.*

Before going further, he took a moment to force the shakes down, then climbed above deck. The adrenalin had cleared his head but he still couldn't steady his hands, so he clasped them behind his back.

"EXCUSE ME," he bellowed, in his most imperious voice. The men froze, looking back at him in surprise and, in at least one case, fear.

"I am Lord Eraranat, Kinston of the South Duchy and Inheritor of the Clay Mount, and that is my vassal you are disturbing without making proper recompense."

"What?" asked the man who had a knife pressed against a most vulnerable spot on Ama's body. The man was obviously a Damiar and, by their dress and size, Seg guessed the other three were his Welf thugs.

"That Kenda," Seg said, pointing helpfully in case Uval did not grasp to whom he was referring, "is contracted to me. Where I come from, that means she belongs to me. And if you wish to use her, you need to make arrangements beforehand. Thirty coin a night, *per person*. I would charge more but she's rather unenthusiastic, has two strange birthmarks and, despite repeated washings, she bears a peculiar odor in the nether region. In any event, if you wish to mark her, the price rises to seventy per person, and I must insist that you leave her in a functional state as I will need her navigational skills in the morning."

"This is none of your business, Lord Eraranat."

"I'm sorry, Lord…?" Seg began, "I didn't catch your name. Did you wish to negotiate a lower price on by-the-hour usage?"

"This is ridiculous," Uval said. "Kill him."

One of the thugs lunged toward Seg, who lurched toward him at the same time, stunner ready beneath his sleeve. Behind him, Manatu groaned.

The two men met, there was a crackling sound and both went down in a tangle of arms and legs. Seg was still moving with control, his opponent was not.

Pinned beneath his unconscious attacker, he saw Manatu toss a stun grenade to a point just ahead of where the other thugs stood, timing his move so that the loud flashbang effect preceded him by a second. The other two released Ama, drew their knives, and turned directly into the face of the grenade.

Manatu moved more swiftly and efficiently than seemed possible for a man of his size, his knife glinting in the moonlight as he charged toward his blinded and deafened foes. The blade was barely out of one man, leaving him to fall to the deck, gushing blood and steaming entrails, as Manatu slashed it across the throat of the other.

Arterial blood sprayed across Ama as the body dropped onto her legs.

Uval had gathered his wits enough to try to escape, but as he moved to step across Seg, a shaky hand grasped his ankle and the stunner discharged once more, dropping his ungainly bulk right across Seg's upper body.

Manatu grabbed the limp Outer, lifted him away from the precious Theorist, slammed him against the hatch and prepared to thoroughly eviscerate him.

"Wait," Seg said, "let me get up." His voice was thick and slow, but the rush of excitement had cleared any remaining fog from his mind. Killing some thugs was one matter, he wasn't so sure killing local nobility wouldn't cause them some serious problems. As he struggled to his feet, he noticed Ama pushing the Welf body off her.

Seg hadn't escaped the skirmish unscathed. A long line of crimson was etched across his forearm; the blade of the first attacker had neatly sliced through his sleeve and into the flesh below. The stunner harness and assembly was exposed. Flat black, with a pair of metal prongs connected to a slim battery pack, attached by three retaining straps to the forearm, the harness and assembly were made of stouter material than mere flesh. He slumped against the gunwale as he considered what to do with this Outer who had attempted to damage his captain.

Ama was at the opposite gunwale, throwing up. She wasn't there long. She turned suddenly, wiping her mouth with the back of her hand as she did, crouched down, scooped a stray knife off the deck and charged at Uval's slack body. Her body shook. She was soaked in blood that looked black in the moonlight, as if rage had painted itself across her.

Manatu held her back, grasped her by the scruff of the neck and lifted her clear while he held Uval against the hatch with his other hand. Seg pushed himself off the starboard gunwale and staggered toward them.

"Go ahead," he slurred. "Let her do it. She has my permission."

Manatu looked dubious, but dropped Ama back to the ground and released his grip on the unconscious Damiar a moment later.

Seg shook his head. Storm take it, they were blown one way or another. Silencing the Damiar was a reasonable precaution. Worse come to worse, they could pin the murder on the girl and escape.

"Deaaahd." The Damiar wheezed out the word as he came back to consciousness. "Kenda...whore," he rasped, obviously not yet awake enough to comprehend his position. "I'll see you sent to As'Cata for this. You'll be hung and torn and—"

"My turn," Ama said, then thrust the knife into the man's stomach.

Seg glanced to the bow as Ama finished off her attacker; there were men gathering at the pier, carrying various heavy and edged objects from their boats. Kenda, he assumed, drawn by the noise and lights of Manatu's micro-grenade.

Things were about to get even uglier. "Manatu," he said quietly, "be ready."

"I'm bleeding, Theorist."

Seg's head whipped around. When he spoke next, it was in his own language. "You idiot! How bad is it?"

Manatu's hand came back from his side, covered in blood. He answered in the same language. "Bad." With that, he slumped to the deck.

Seg eyed the crowd again. The situation had just gotten extremely untenable. The first Kenda hopped up to the deck and stalked forward warily with a boathook in hand. Seg checked the charge – one shot left on the stunner. It was an emergency weapon, small, not designed for prolonged conflict.

At least he had transmitted enough data to Kerbin for a good raid, if not as good a raid as he would have conducted.

Like gutting a fish, that's how Ama processed the moment she drove the blade into Uval's stomach. No longer unconscious, he had let out a strangled cry the moment the blade pierced him. How many times she plunged the blade in, she would never remember, only that he had gurgled like a rukefish.

Eventually her arm dropped and she stared at the dead flesh on the deck.

Her mind drifted too slowly back to anchor. There was too much noise. Turning as if she were turning in water, she saw Manatu collapse. Seg's back was to her. Was he bleeding or was that someone else's blood? Someone else was on the deck, too. An armed figure, heading toward them, brandishing a weapon.

Calm washed over her. Knife in hand, dripping with Uval's blood, she stepped around Manatu, past Seg, and walked out to meet the attacker. She was ready to kill again; her heart had slowed to a crawl. This man would not harm her or her passengers.

"Get off my boat."

The man froze in place. "Captain Kalder?" Silence. "Ama, are you alright? It's me Captain Jefir, of the *Lasathe*."

"Jefir," she said, numbly.

"You gave the signal and when…"

Jefir carried on but she had stopped listening. Signal? What signal had she given?

Connections began to snap into place. Back on the Banks, before pushing off, she had called out to Captain Tather, *Tell my family to keep their eyes on the horizon for my return.* A piece of code, one of many the mariners used to pass secret messages. Her 'family' was the Kenda, and her request was a signal that she had passengers she did not fully trust and wanted eyes to watch over her. *You will have their eyes*, he had replied, another piece of the code. As was tradition, Tather would have spread the word to every Kenda on the docks, including all outbound vessels, and word had made it to Alisir. "Jefir. Yes, I know now." Her voice came to her from somewhere deep under water.

Seg was injured. Manatu was…was he dead? She had killed a Damiar Lord. A crowd of Kenda were gathered around the *Naida*, her maritime brothers she had unwittingly summoned.

"You're covered in blood, are you inj—"

"No," she cut him off. Seg and Manatu were her first priority. "Jefir, I need you and the others to keep the authorities busy. I'm going to push off; I'll need help with that, as well. If anyone asks, tell them my passengers had a family emergency to attend to." She glanced back at Seg, and was immediately struck by the situation she had put them in.

"What's happened?" Jefir asked.

"Bad trouble."

Jefir nodded, understanding perfectly well what 'bad trouble' meant to the Kenda. "Go. I'll have my crew help with the ropes and I think we can work up a brawl big enough to draw the attention of the constables away from you. Be careful out there in the black."

She didn't linger to thank him. That could be done at another time, in another port. She heard the Kenda men disperse.

The blade dropped from her hand, she hurried to Seg, tearing the blood soaked shirt off her body. "Give me your arm. We have to go. Now." She gripped his wrist and pulled his arm toward her. "Is Mana—"

Her voice dropped away. She felt his arm, flesh and blood, but there was something else there too, something metallic. Her eyes found his and she opened her mouth to speak. Manatu emitted a low moan.

There would be time for questions later. "Whatever that is, take it off so I can bandage your wound," she ordered.

He was strangely tranquil and stared at the deep slice with an air of detached curiosity. "In my luggage, there are two metal boxes," he told her, then went on to describe the featureless boxes she had puzzled over. "Bring those to me. Then get us out of here. I'll take care of things from here."

As he detached the mysterious object from his injured arm, Seg groaned. Ama watched as it fell and clattered to the deck. "Go," he ordered. "We still have a schedule to meet."

On his command, she sprinted below deck to the cargo locker. She was thankful now for her snooping, as she knew exactly where to look. When she reached to unlatch the locker, she was surprised to see her hand shaking violently. Odd, she felt so calm.

It took both hands to open the latch. Images flickered across her eyelids – noise and a bright light, Manatu sweeping through her attackers as if they were insects, like a trained soldier but beyond any soldier or guard she had ever seen, Manatu speaking, both he and Seg talking in gibberish, some kind of language she had never heard.

Never mind. Do your job.

She fished the boxes from the trunk and hurried them up to Seg, without speaking and barely looking at him. They would speak later; right now they had to get out of port.

The blood was sticky on her body. As she cast off the lines, she thought of the water below and how much she would love to clean herself. No time. This would be tricky, navigating the river by moonlight. Even more dangerous would be their passage out into the Big Water. She didn't relish the thought of tackling any standing waves, formed when the incoming tide met the outgoing river, in the dark.

Uval wouldn't have been foolish enough to tell anyone where he was going, she was positive of that, but evidence of his visit was splattered all over the *Naida*. As soon as she could find a safe hole to hide in, she would drop anchor – she was in no shape to be at the helm but they needed to get off the river and away from Alisir and the authorities.

Ama extended the main skin and guided the *Naida* back onto the river, praying that there were no deadheads in their path.

Bad trouble. Yes.

She had three dead Welf and a dead Damiar on her boat. Dead by her hand. She also had two passengers who were, she was beginning to understand, infinitely more dangerous than any Lord.

As she strained to see downriver, Ama wondered what Seg was doing and if he could save his friend. She wondered if he knew how grateful she was to him and why he had let her kill Uval, one of his kind.

She turned the wheel and focused on the job at hand. After all, that is what she was being been paid for.

Seg pressed his thumb to the smooth pad of the auto-med case and it opened silently. All extrans units were fitted with print scanners to prevent Outers from accessing them, should they fall into the wrong hands. As he fitted the auto-med sleeve on Manatu, he took stock of the situation. Manatu was alive, for the moment. Ama was in shock but unwounded. The Kenda were, if not allies of his, allies of hers. They could make their escape.

From the nature of the attack, it seemed Ama had some secrets of her own.

With Ama busy at the wheel, he spoke to Manatu in the tongue of the People and not the local language.

"Your liver is punctured," Seg said.

"I don't want to die here," Manatu said. "Not here."

"You won't." He snapped the medical system shut. "The auto-med has you stabilized. You'll live long enough to make the next warp window." It wasn't a complete lie; he might make it.

"But," Manatu said, "who will protect you? I have bond-mission."

"You can't protect me if you die, can you?" Seg said curtly. "Don't think. Obey. You'll go back. Your portion comes from the derived intel of the mission. If I die tomorrow, this raid will still pay out enough to let you live comfortably for a good while, even taking out the cost of a new liver."

"This is unortho," Manatu protested.

"If you haven't noticed," Seg said, with a trace of mirth, "that seems to have become my signature style."

The auto-med readout of his own wound matched his initial assessment – unpleasant, but nothing serious or life threatening. He debated whether to retain the scar, but decided his stupidly impulsive act of charging into the fray first didn't merit such a keepsake. The sealer tacked the skin together with a faint hiss as he clenched his teeth against the burning sensation, ignoring the thin stream of wafting smoke and the smell of burnt flesh.

Why hadn't he let Manatu precede him? Simple mathematics dictated that the life of a trooper was infinitely less valuable than that of a Theorist. There were plenty of Manatus in the World, and only one Segkel of the Guild.

Ama had called his name.

He had, somehow, come to see her as his responsibility. A person under his charge had been at risk, and he had acted rashly. It wasn't emotional; Seg refused to allow such petty things to override his judgment. A man protected those under his charge or else he had no claim to manhood. Much the same, he would see to it that the simpleton trooper was provided for.

He looked at the bodies on the deck, his lips and nose crinkling as he did. The dead men were already reeking of offal and gore, and it was only going to get worse. He opened his mouth to order Manatu to dispose of them, then remembered that the trooper should be laid up.

"Get back to your bunk," he ordered Manatu. "I'll handle this."

Seg cut a portion of his sleeve free and tied it around his face to protect his nose, then dragged the first body to the rail to toss it over the side. Let the local carrion-eaters handle this lot.

After four splashes, he had a new appreciation for the term 'dead weight' and just how difficult it was to handle lifeless bodies. Even though he had been the smallest of the bunch, the Damiar that he had let Ama kill was annoyingly limp and heavy. With a grunt of exertion, he heaved the last carcass over the side. He considered cleaning up, but it was her boat; she could clean the damn thing. Besides, she had made the biggest mess of her kill.

Belatedly, he realized that the one he had stunned hadn't even been dead when he tossed him over the side but dismissed that with a shrug. The water would finish his work.

Ama was at the wheel; he stepped up beside her and she turned her face to his. Both of them were coated with the gore of the evening, her eyes were wide with—he didn't know what. He realized he still had the piece of sleeve he had used as an improvised mask tied on his face and reached back with trembling fingers to undo it. Balling up the rag, he threw it over the side.

Her eyes returned to the river, as did his. This was no time for words.

CHAPTER 6

J arin Svestil sat back, monitoring the reactions of his fellow Theorists as they discussed the news of his student's plan for a multi-target strike. In the confines of his office, where he diligently performed regular security sweeps, they were safe to speak of such matters openly.

"He's overreaching," Ansin said, unsurprisingly.

Jarin shook his head, "I beg to differ, honored peers."

On the other side of his desk, the three others, Ansin Sael, Maryel Aimaz and Shyl Vana, waited for him to finish his thought. The Theorist's Guild had a loose management structure, given that it was organized around independent action by its individualistic and brilliant members, but he and these other three constituted a powerful bloc on the Advisory Council that ran the day-to-day affairs of the Guild. "Segkel Eraranat is ambitious, but he has always been completely aware of the limitations of extrans operations. If he is planning a multi-strike—"

"With six targets, at least," Maryel, pointed out. She ran a hand through her iron-grey hair. "Six. Nothing like that's been attempted in fifty years."

"And we know well how that came out," Ansin added dryly. Slight of build, he was the conservative member of the group, the risk-assessor, which, to Jarin's way of thinking, was why Ansin sat here instead of seeking plunder in the field.

"Lannit's strike was too ambitious," Jarin said, weighing his words carefully. Whenever talk turned to multi-strikes, Theorist Lannit's monumental mission failure was always the first to be discussed. "The Storvids were a class eight developed society. To try to infiltrate the strike forces prior to the raid was an unconscionable risk." Lannit claimed that his plan would have worked brilliantly, but for one stroke of bad luck, overlooking all the other potential strokes of bad luck that could have derailed the mission. Lannit did overreach. Jarin was confident that Segkel, for all his inexperience, would not.

He hoped.

"I'll remind you that much of the same was said about Lannit, once upon a time," Ansin said. "A brilliant assessor. A brilliant Theorist. In the same way, much has been said about Eraranat, that he is a prodigy—"

"He is," Jarin confirmed.

"He is," Shyl chimed in, surprising Jarin. Her soft features were a contrast to her sharp mind and keen understanding of the politics of the Guild and the World. He never quite knew which way she would jump. She was enigmatic and played her games far below a measurable level. "I've observed his results. Inexperienced, brash, arrogant but a prodigy. He and that other young one, Mastel, they were the only ones in the past five years to correctly answer the current permutation of the Enginal Test."

Jarin couldn't repress a grin at that. Mastel had intuited the answer, and Segkel, in his own meticulous way, had laboriously sifted the data until it came to him. That was the difference. Mastel would not be going for the multi-strike. If that hothead had this assignment, he would have already called down a raid on the 'Welf' gathering place. Those readings alone would have guaranteed a tidy and certain return for a successful strike. It was the sort of assignment a Theorist loved, one in which the vita simply overflowed and could be easily pruned.

Segkel being Segkel, he was going for all of it. He wouldn't succeed, but the harvest he was planning to reap from a single raid would exceed an entire decade's income from most Major Houses. The House he had contracted to was understandably nervous, but these were the sorts of gambles that separated the lessers from the greaters. House Haffset was determined to fall into the latter category and, based on the limited information that had already been sent through, they were busy borrowing and outfitting troops, awaiting the go from their Theorist.

"Perhaps we could send Eraranat an advisor," Maryel said, leaning back in her chair. "If the fields are so rich, and according to the preliminary data they are *very* rich, a reinforcing presence, a senior presence, would be best for the situation. I know we don't work that way—"

"Because the Theorist is the senior authority in the field," Ansin pointed out. Regardless of his misgivings about Segkel, he could be counted on to uphold the sacred tradition of field control. Ansin seldom let the unortho actions of another taint or influence his own decision-making.

"Therefore, we have two options," Jarin said, "we let him continue, or we call the abort and make the raid on the data we have now."

The others looked among themselves.

"Let him go," Shyl said. "He will either succeed or die trying."

"Agreed," Jarin said.

"We have no overriding cause to pull him out," Ansin said. "Though he will have to answer to critique when he returns, regardless of the outcome. We should not wait for the Question. His actions have been highly unortho."

Jarin muted his surprise.

Maryel took a deep breath through her nose. "The defender of orthodoxy would dispense with orthodoxy here? No, his critique will come as it always has for us, with the Question. As Lead Questioner, however, I can ensure that his breaks with protocol are scrutinized rigorously. He may be a brilliant young man, but we have orthodoxy for a reason. It has allowed us to survive and thrive for centuries."

What they had done, Jarin mused, was slowly slide downward for centuries. A stagnant culture, living on the backs of unsuspecting neighbors, and succumbing inevitably to the forces of entropy. Segkel had not quite articulated that for himself, but at a fundamental level he knew it. Jarin had never told him as much, but he had planted the seeds in the young hellion. For the world to survive, 'good enough' would no longer suffice. They had to excel.

And they had to start looking at other ways to do so.

"I believe we are agreed, then. And as we go on this, so will the Council," Jarin said.

"The Council…" Maryel said, tapping a finger on the table. "You realize, of course," she spoke to the group but Jarin knew her words were directed to him, "that once news of a multi-strike is shared with the Advisory Council, we will attract the attention of the CWA?"

"You may rest assured their attention has already been attracted," Jarin answered.

"And you are confident this will present no complications?" Maryel's eyes moved left to right, only once but rapidly, betraying to Jarin a significant degree of concern.

"Confidence is the province of fools and politicians. The CWA has recently engaged in a new acquisition cycle, where they will look to move on a failing House or raider unit for absorption. During these cycles, they tend to move quietly and avoid provocation, which could create extra complication and cost. At this point in time, I believe the CWA will take care in acting in ways that would upset the delicate balance between our organizations."

"On the contrary, I would argue the CWA would seize on any chance to upset the 'delicate balance between our organizations' in their favor. Prior to Lannit, we were in charge of revenue distribution from raids, and the loss of that function cost us fifteen percent of our revenue stream. The Guild has never fully recovered from that loss but, far worse, Lannit's raid provided the CWA with the necessary grounds for equal authority over raid planning and execution. And they wasted no time seizing the opportunity to undermine the Guild's one remaining political advantage," Maryel countered.

"*Quick to seize opportunity*…the Eleventh Virtue of a Citizen," Shyl added wryly.

Jarin did not leap to defend his position. Maryel had not been appointed Head Questioner by accident. "Lannit…" he sighed. "We have allowed one man, one mistake, to cripple us through fear and superstition. Theorists should study myth, not propagate it." He placed his palms flat on the table, "I cannot speak for the rest of you, but I believe it is time for the Guild to look forward, not back. The CWA will do what the CWA will do. As House liaison, I can keep a close eye on the mission and be in a position to counter them."

The bloc murmured, then nodded their agreement.

"Let us carry on to the next matter of business." Jarin said, glad to be done with this latest topic. The carefully maintained veneer of caution and orthodoxy slid back into place.

Who are you?

The question swirled around and around, as Ama dumped another bucket of water on the blood-soaked deck, then scrubbed the hard bristles of the brush against the wood.

They had made it to the mouth of the Gwai River at the top of the flood tide. Not ideal conditions but passable, and the timing worked in their favour. The Sokolo Islands were close by and on the slack tide she was able to sneak through Ripple Narrows and anchor just off a sheltered beach, in the lee of the wind. On the slim chance they were being followed, no one would be able to pass though the channel once the tide turned, and that would happen shortly.

Seg had stood by her side for the entire journey, assisting her when she asked for help. They spoke only in moments of necessity. After anchoring, she had immediately begun hauling water.

"In a few hours, we'll have enough light to travel safely," Ama had said, as she splashed the first bucket of water across the deck. "Uval didn't tell anyone what he was up to, I'm sure of that. As long as this is gone," she gestured to the mess at the stern, "and we keep Manatu hidden, there will be no ties to us. Alisir's a busy port; boats come and go all the time, and the other Kenda will cover for me. But we'll pull anchor as soon as the tide lets us, and get cruising to T'ueve. The more distance we put between us and Alisir the better."

Seg nodded, "I'll see to Manatu."

Neither moved nor spoke. Seg opened his mouth but a long, low groan from below deck halted his words, and Ama returned to her scrubbing.

Now, as the last bits of blood disappeared beneath her brush, Ama's thoughts returned to questions of Seg.

He was a dangerous man. He and Manatu both, whoever they were, and who knew what kind of business they were up to; she would be smart to flee. But these men had also saved her life.

She rested against the handle of the brush, lifted her head and stared up at the sky, the moon long gone, the dark black fading to grey.

Who are you?

Seg found Manatu awake and aware. He was sweating profusely, a product of the medication as much as the injury. A neuroblock was taking care of the pain, but it couldn't eliminate all the discomforts associated with a severe internal wound. He needed cleaning, a task that Ama was far more suited for, by Seg's estimation. On the edge of the bunk, he sat next to Manatu, and shifted the man's sleeve to access the hidden auto-med readout.

"Blood pressure elevated," he read out, "blood toxin level climbing, early indications of infection."

Manatu moaned.

"According to the machine, without prompt care you have approximately thirty-six

hours to live," Seg lied. "We should have you back before then, though."

Back on the World, they would replace Manatu's liver with a cloned organ, created before the man had extrans'd and stored along with other vital replacement organs.

Everyone on the mission, Seg included, had a bank of spare organs waiting for them, all the vital organs except the brain. In theory, brains could not be replaced but, looking into Manatu's dull eyes, Seg pondered the prospect that it might be possible under certain circumstances.

"You keep looking at me, Theorist," Manatu wheezed, a note of question in his voice.

"Simply assessing your condition," Seg answered. "Do you need anything? The auto-med indicates against eating, but you are permitted water."

"I have water," Manatu answered, with some effort. "How much longer?"

"Six hours until warp window. I'm going to initiate comm soon and inform the House that you're returning."

And probably be requested, forcefully, to either abort or reconnect with Kerbin. He could tell from the last comm with Jarin, before he and Manatu had ventured off on their own, that House Haffset were extremely wary of the unortho path he was taking on this mission. It was only the promise of the data he was feeding to them that had kept them from pulling the plug and calling for intrans for the entire squad.

Just a little longer.

Without another word to Manatu, he stood, walked to the locker that held their baggage and extracted the large unit that could be configured to function as comm or warp gate. From the extent of the mess above deck, he estimated there would be ample time to send a comm before Ama returned below deck. Not that Ama's eyes were a concern any longer, more so the concern was that those back on the World would see he had exposed their technology to an Outer, prior to the raid, and let her live.

In reality, Manatu had perhaps ten hours or less to live, and Seg would have to move up the transit window in order to save him. This was going to complicate everything, bring more questions and more potential disruption.

Storm take the idiot. Better if he had died. Better to just let him die. But he had not died, and now Seg would not permit him to do so. Once he was no longer Seg's problem, he could go and get himself punctured and killed as he pleased, but until then he must live.

Assembly of the large, rugged framework was tricky without help. A set of skinned knuckles later, he had managed to put it together. He sat down and waited for the comm, wishing he could just pass this up and let the Guild Council stew while he carried on with his business.

Once he had established himself as a field Theorist, it was his plan to keep comms to a minimum, outside of emergencies such as this one. He glanced over at Manatu, who was babbling softly about his mother or some such nonsense. The sooner he got the feverish trooper off the boat, the better for his state of mind.

Time. He pressed the glyph sequence in the prescribed order, as the carrier signal punched through the warp from the other side, creating a pinhole connection between this planet and the World, allowing crude but functional visual communication.

Of course it was Jarin, who was handling customer liaison for this contract, who answered.

"Segkel," Jarin said.

"Jarin."

"You are creating quite the stir."

"I'm not aborting." Jarin made him feel as though he were still a pupil, still a step behind. By his mere presence, Jarin overshadowed him. "The mission planning is sound, the targets are viable, and the payoff will be incredible."

"I hope so, for your sake. What is your status?"

"There was a local conflict. Trooper Dibeld was critically wounded. I need to move up the warp window." *Leave it at that, Jarin.*

"That will be costly," Jarin said, "but it can be done. Obviously the situation on the ground has shifted and become more problematic. Will you be linking up with Lieutenant Kerbin?"

"No." Seg watched carefully, but Jarin showed no reaction.

"Unortho. Your post-mission critique is going to be heavy with that term."

"Along with words such as 'unprecedented success', I'll wager," Seg said, defensiveness creeping into his voice. "I've got it under control, Jarin."

"You are on your first mission extrans, you are deep in Outer territory and your bodyguard is wounded badly enough that you must ship him back. You have sent your escort squad off haring about, taking vita readings, while you propose to solo the rest of your self-assigned portion. You are not in control; you are riding the Storm-crest right now. I know you, Segkel."

It was undeniably true. It was also irrelevant. Manatu's injury aside, he was under control, and so long as he was under control, he could bend the mission to his will. "I'm not aborting and I'm not reconfiguring, Jarin."

"Were you wounded as well?" Jarin asked.

"No!" Seg said, fingers curling into a fist out of Jarin's view.

Jarin sighed. "Then we will proceed as per the directions of the Field Theorist. I told my associates as much before the Council ratified your continued mission support an hour ago. It is for the best that they were unaware you were about to send this fellow back with holes in him."

"One hole," Seg corrected.

"Critically wounded," Jarin continued, "and unable to continue the mission. I have faith in you, Segkel. If you fail, though, this will end your career in an inglorious and ugly manner."

"If I fail, I'll die," Seg said, with the confidence of a young man who did not accept the prospect of death.

Now Jarin reacted, a touch of some more personal emotion crossing his eyes. "Be careful, pupil." He paused before adding, "There's one last thing."

Seg repressed a sigh.

"Yes?"

"This woman you sent back."

Woman. While Seg did not embrace the practice of keeping caj for himself, he accepted it as a societal norm. Jarin, on the other hand, was more radical in his beliefs. He had issues about Outers and caj. He didn't use the term 'caj'; he preferred to refer to them as though they were People. It was his own quirk of unortho. He also didn't own any, and generally avoided partaking of caj labor when he could. He didn't advocate for their release or anything that insanely outlandish, so his eccentricity in this area was tolerated, though it was the source of quiet and covert comment. Nothing too loud – Jarin had eyes and ears everywhere, and was noted for his ruthless retribution in the political arena.

"What about the Outer?"

"You didn't send her for processing. I was wondering if you had considered some of the ramifications."

Seg opened his mouth, then closed it. What was the old man referring to? "What sort of ramifications?"

"She was violently abducted, physically abused, her first introduction to our world was a humiliating and impersonal decontamination process, and then she was essentially sent to holding quarters and left alone."

"And?"

"Segkel," Jarin said, with another sigh, "you fail to consider human factors at times. If you leave a person in that state for a month, what you are going to end up with is an insane, gibbering wreck when you return. There is a reason the typical method is to send your captives in for processing. At the very least they receive human contact."

Storm take me. Jarin had caught something he hadn't considered – again.

He hadn't even wanted to abduct the Outer to begin with, but that was not information he would share over an open comm. At this stage in his career, he could risk no questions or speculations about his loyalty to the People's doctrine. Damn Kerbin and damn him.

"What do you propose?"

"I will take care of her until you return, and see to it that she is in some sort of workable condition for your *amusement* when you get back."

Of course Jarin would assume the worst of the situation, the worst of him.

"Thank you," Seg said, the words ashes in his mouth.

"If you need to clean up I've brou—" Ama's voice halted. Seg turned to see her standing on the bottom stair, bucket in hand, eyes fixed on the gate he was assembling. "What are you doing? What is that?" she asked, when she found her voice again.

He nodded toward the crossbar he was struggling with. "Come here, pull that out of the socket for me."

Ama lowered the bucket of water slowly and stepped forward, then paused before her hand contacted the metal. "If this is Shasir magic..."

"The Shasir have no magic. What they have, among other things, is simply complicated metal, metal alloys, as this is." He jerked his head toward the tube again. "We have to hurry. Manatu is dying."

Ama looked over her shoulder at Manatu, then grasped the metal rod and tugged until it was free from the socket. "You're not Damiar," she stated, as he motioned to her to hold another piece of the odd mechanism.

He stared intently at the disjointed pieces of metal before him as he reconfigured the system from comm to warp gate and considered his reply. This was the most dangerous moment yet, the moment that could damn the entire venture and lead to hundreds of deaths, including his own.

He checked the alignment of the accumulator arms, then nodded and wiped his hands on his trousers. "No," he said finally, "I'm not Damiar. Or Shasir. Or Welf. Or Kenda. Or anything else you've ever met."

"Very well, you come from...from a far part of the world that is unknown to me, but how is this...thing..." she gestured to the machine as he passed her a handful of small parts to hold, "going to save Mana—"

The metal bits clattered to the deck as she grabbed his forearm and stared.

"Where is your wound? Who are you?" Ama demanded, her hand clamped down on his white skin.

"Segkel Erarant, Guild Theorist," he said, pulled his arm away and held it up for her to examine. "And yes, I am not from anything you're familiar with. Help me finish this, and you'll learn."

Ama didn't move. "Where did you get this magic? Where are you from? Why are you here? On my boat? What—"

"AMA!" Seg grabbed her wrist, squeezed hard and shook her. He lowered his voice but fired out every word, "Save your questions. Manatu is dying. Now help me!"

She blinked as if she had just awoken, looked at the machine then back to Seg, then helped him collect the rest of the dropped parts. "Can this magic heal him?"

"This will take him where he can be saved. And stop calling it magic. You know your world, S'orasa, is round, correct?" he asked, as he clipped the power pack into place.

"Of course."

"Do you know that there are other worlds in the sky?" he continued, facing away from her as he checked the control screen and ran diagnostics.

"Just the Cloud Temple."

He rolled his eyes, "Yes, the cloud temple." The last two words rang with contempt. "Turn that piece there." He pointed to a dark grey circle, the size of a saucer. Ama rotated it but Seg stopped her. "No, you slide the cover plate eyeward," he said, referring to Coriolis rotation back on the World. He sighed and, realizing that she had no clue what that meant, reached over, his hands over hers, to demonstrate the proper direction. His hands lingered on hers for a moment.

A sheen of sweat covered her face and bare arms, mixed with flecks of blood she had not yet washed away. Manatu's groans and the slap of water against the hall muted; the only audible sound was that of breathing, hers and his. Her eyes were a dark blue, he watched her pupils dilate; she made no attempt to pull away her gaze or her hands. The primal need for her he had experienced after the Storm returned, more intensely now that he had killed to protect her.

A warning chirp from Manatu's auto-med dispelled the momentary attention lapse; he looked away from her and busied himself with the remainder of the assembly.

"Help me get Manatu," he said when he was done. "We're going to place him before this opening."

Assembly complete, the warp gate resembled a small, semi-circle resting on projecting conduit feet, designed to keep the unit stable even in muck and mud. This was the transmission matrix. Attached to that was the box-shaped generator unit, the warpgen, which held the power pack and vita cell. The metal framework could be raised high enough for even the tallest trooper to walk through or lowered right to ground level for delivering wounded back to the World. Such as now.

Manatu was muttering to himself and a dark stain of sweat spread out from where he lay. Ama placed her hand on his wide forehead, "Shhh, be still."

Seg stepped over the profusion of gear on the floor and grunted as he strained to lift Manatu from the bed. The trooper was even heavier than he looked, his bulk comprised mostly of solid muscle. "Come... on," he grunted, as they dragged Manatu toward the portal. "Smaller... bodyguard...next time," he muttered.

They reached the edge of the machine and Seg stopped. Ama's eyes moved between Seg and the warp gate. "I don't understand," she panted, "where can he go?"

"Home," Seg said. He turned the control panel over and tapped the keys in a memorized sequence, which unlocked the warp gate for this usage. "Now."

The air began to shimmer in the middle of the circle, shimmer and distort. As it shimmered, it began to opaque and prism, with colors that vibrated between the rings. The generator unit hummed and vibrated as the accumulator fed and converted the stored vita in the battery pack into the ghost of a warp gate connecting with the World.

As soon as the view behind the warp gate disappeared, Seg lifted Manatu's arms and stuffed them through, then tugged at his torso.

"Help me move him!"

Ama was transfixed by the swirling colors, but the moans of the dying man refocused her attention.

On one side of Manatu, she grunted as she lifted him. Together, inch by leaden inch, they fed him into the center of the ring, the heat from the warpgen drawing even more sweat to the surface of their skin.

As they fed him through, Seg felt the handlers take the weight on the other side. Medical technicians would be on standby to assess and begin treatment even as the decontamination cycle was carried out. As soon as Manatu's boots disappeared, Seg settled back on his rear and tapped the sequence to close the gate. The warp faded in the same way it came in, slowly shimmering away. He let out a long breath. One less concern.

"I come from another place," he said. "Another world, like this one."

Ama continued to stand. She moved to the other side of the warp gate and stared, then reached out a tentative hand and touched the metal frame.

"Did you come here through this?" Her voice was hushed, awed.

"Of course not, I came through a much larger one on the other side," he said, his tongue running before his mind worked the question through. He was too tired; he needed another stim dose to stay functional. "But something like it, yes."

He stared at the warp gate for a moment longer before shifting onto his knees to begin the process of disassembly.

Ama moved to assist him. "But…that doesn't make any sense. If you can travel through this, why do you need my boat?"

"Because it costs too much. The Warp gate uses fuel like a fire uses wood, and burns it quickly. The fuel is expensive and difficult to obtain. It's also the entire reason I'm here."

"Fuel? That's why you're visiting the temples? Is it the Shasir? Are they keeping some kind of magic fuel there?"

He slid the pieces back into the kit, puzzling over the arrangement, as he considered an answer she might comprehend. "Let me start at the beginning. My People travel across the dimensions. There are worlds, next to each other, worlds beyond counting, and the barrier between them is like—like the separation between water and air. It is a different world below the waves, no? And these worlds, they have a fuel on them, we call it vita."

"Vita," Ama repeated. "And there's vita at the temples?"

"Yes, at most places of religious observance. Places where people gather and believe and worship." He stood, stumbled to his quarters and returned with his map disc, which he set on the deck. He pressed his finger to a button and smiled slightly at her gasp as a holographic map of S'orasa appeared, with the selected reconnaissance targets highlighted. "My people," he explained, "are as far beyond the Shasir in development as the Shasir are beyond you and the Welf. And very soon, we will come to take the vita from them. When my People come, nothing will be able to stop them."

"You'll come and take this vita from the Shasir and then leave?" Ama asked, as she stared intently at the globe.

"More than that. They, we, will also take people, thousands of people, and any useful technology we can lay our hands on. I doubt there will be much technology to be found here, though samples will be taken of course. And the process will not be easy or peaceful. My People will come with fire and they will destroy anything that opposes them."

Ama's mouth came unhinged. Her head turned slowly and she stared at the spot where Manatu had disappeared. "I see," she said, her voice hollow. "And you're the leader of this...exploration?"

"Not precisely. More like the scout. I'm a Cultural Theorist; I'm here to find the vita, as part of a team. Manatu was my bodyguard, and now he is gone. That's why I'm telling you about all this, because I need your help."

"What about your team?" Ama asked, her tone guarded. "They can't help you?"

"They have their own assignment." He deactivated the map. "I want you to understand, the target assignment process has begun, the forces are being assembled, and the planning is going on right now. When my People come, it will be with skyships of metal far beyond anything the Shasir can field. Unstoppable, they will go where they please and take what they want. Even I can't stop the process at this point, only guide it to the proper targets."

"And you expect me to help you? To help you conquer my world?" Ama didn't wait for a reply; she snapped around and thundered up the stairs.

"If you'll calm down and listen, I'll explain." Seg jogged up behind her.

"Don't bother," Ama said, the morning wind lifting her hair. When she turned to Seg, her usually animated face was sober. "You're going to tell me how helping you is for the good of my people."

"It can be," Seg said.

"I've heard that before. I believe it now as much as I did then." The strain of the past twenty-four hours showed plainly in her eyes. She looked past Seg, to the horizon. "But I understand. Your magic is greater than ours, as your gods must also be. I would offer some resistance but..."

"You can't."

Ama's expression was tired, defeated. The first beams of sunlight washed across the deck, shabby in comparison to the light of the warp. "The sun's already up, we need to pull anchor and get moving if we're going to make T'ueve before dark." Her eyes moved from the bow to the stern, then back to Seg. "If I do as you ask, you have to promise you'll protect my people, the Kenda.'

"You have my word, the Kenda will be spared."

"Good," she said, swallowed and nodded. "We've wasted too much daylight. We can talk more once we're moving. I'll extend the skins, you winch the anchor."

At the bow, Seg cranked the handle of the winch to raise the anchor. All things considered, she had taken the revelation better than he had anticipated.

"In any event," he said, after a pause, "the Shasir are much better targets, in general, than the Kenda; the Shasir and the Welf specifically—"

Something sharp, pressed into his lower back, stopped his words. Seg froze, his hands still on the crank.

"Get. Off. My. Boat." The defeat and acquiescence were gone from Ama's voice. She jabbed at him with the weapon. "OFF!"

The imminence of death gave him a strange clarity. He could see the individual ripples as the water waited to enclose him, suffocate him. "I saved your life."

"That's the only reason you're still breathing."

"I can't swim."

"You should have thought of that before you came to pirate my world." She pressed the blade harder against him.

"Wait!" Seg shouted, as his upper body was forced further against the rail. "Kill me and the raid still happens. But let me live and I can direct the strikes away from your people." He turned around slowly, hands held high.

"Just like the Shasir. Lots of promises. All lies."

With a quick movement, she flicked the weapon, a gracefully curved blade at the end of a long staff, and slashed across Seg's shoulder, then repositioned the tip of the blade under his chin. "You've already lied to me once. I may not be able to stop your people but I can warn mine. Now jump, or I'll send you over in pieces."

He winced at the cut and fought down the impulse to raise his hand to it. "Your warning won't change anything. When the raid ends, your people will still be under the boots of the Shasir. I'm offering you a chance to topple their order, an opportunity for real freedom."

Ama kept the pressure on the seft but at the last word she flinched noticeably.

"Freedom," Seg repeated, seizing the word that had stalled her anger, "for all of the Kenda."

"If I help you," Ama said, her voice wary, "what do you want from me?"

"I need someone to assist me. Be my extra eyes. Help me transport my equipment while I pursue my targets. Once the information is collected," he shrugged without thinking; the cut's sting, heightened by the briny air, brought on a wince, "we won't need you for the raid. Couldn't use you anyway. Get low, stay away from the target areas, and then whatever comes after is the business of your people."

"And if you change your mind? If you decide the Kenda would make good slaves after all?"

"I understand my word means nothing to you, but it's all I have. You've spoken of your family, I know you care about them. Refuse my offer and you put them all in danger," Seg said.

Ama's eyes darkened. "Enough!" She spun the weapon and cracked him in the ribs with the handle.

The blow knocked the wind out him, he ducked forward to catch his breath. "Wait…" he wheezed, and raised a hand.

She dropped the weapon, lunged forward and shoved. He was a tall man with a high center of gravity; he went over the rail with barely an effort.

The world slowed for Seg as he dropped over the side. Over his head, he saw the water rush toward him, a giant, gaping mouth ready to swallow him whole. The water parted around him and shocked his entire body with cold. Wrapped in the cold water, he lost orientation. Up? Down? He had no way of knowing. He thrashed his arms and legs as he tried vainly to remember the basic elements of swim training he had received as a cadet – they hadn't even actually gotten into water.

He had not caught a breath before he went in and inhaled his first burning gulp of seawater. Panicked, he increased the thrashing and somehow managed to surface. Water spewed from his mouth and he coughed uncontrollably as he struggled to stay aloft.

One sip of air was all he took in before he sunk under again.

From the rail above, Ama watched the water churn around Seg. She had seen men go overboard before, but not like this. He hadn't lied about his inability to swim, at least. His arms flailed, wild and helpless – a cloud of blood spread from the cut on his shoulder.

She stepped away, as if to pull the anchor, then stopped.
You can't trust him.

She turned back to the water and couldn't see his head. He had gone under. She waited a second. Nothing.

You killed Uval; you can do the same again.

"Nen's death," she cursed, climbed up on the rail and dove overboard.

Her second eyelids flipped up as she went under and she spotted Seg, still thrashing beneath the water, hands clawing desperately for something to grasp. Careful to avoid a stray, panicked fist to the face, she hooked herself under him and lifted him to the surface.

"I'm going to regret this," she said, as she swam them both toward the ladder – a difficult task given Seg's size. As she made slow progress, Seg coughed and hacked.

Then, in the distance, she spotted a ripple in the water. A thin line of flesh broke surface, a tail. Along the tail, a row of spines glinted in the morning sunlight.

Drexla.

She kicked hard, aware that the vibration would only excite the predator. There was no way they could both make it out of the water in time. She reached for her knife realizing, too late, that it was still on the *Naida*. If she let go of Seg, left him to die, she could escape.

The ladder was a few strokes away but the beast was closing the distance fast. It would circle once or twice before striking, if only...

Ama's free hand moved to Seg's waist and groped for his blade. "When I get you to the ladder, get out of the water! Fast!" she yelled as they approached the bottom rung.

Though he couldn't speak through his coughing, Seg nodded his agreement. He let himself be pulled by her, then lunged forward when the ladder came within reach.

Ama dove down, Seg's knife clutched in her hand, as the long body of the drexla, carved through the water next to the ladder, it's razor teeth clamping down just as Seg's foot lifted out and away from of its grasp.

She was pinned under the boat now, the beast somewhere circling. If only she could sound it. As she kicked in the direction of the ladder, the drexla swerved by, blocking her escape.

She reached back to untie her nove but the laces wouldn't let go. Air, she needed air, and she needed to know where the beast was lurking.

Eyes darting in every direction, she kicked her legs and reached up with the knife to cut the leather free. Her nove fell away with surprising ease; Seg's knife was exceptionally sharp. At last the collar was off and she could breathe. Severed nove clutched in one hand, knife in the other, she sounded the water for her foe.

Ama saw the outline of the serpentine body, coiled and ready to attack. After the lunge, she would have time to get to her destination, while the drexla turned and composed itself for the next strike. If she survived.

Every instinct told her to flee but she held steady, sculling the water to hold her position, her dathe emitting the low vibration that came whenever she felt threatened. Then the drexla struck, uncoiling and jetting right at her.

Ama ducked, kicked her legs, and slashed with the knife. A glancing blow that left not even a scratch on the drexla. But now she had an opportunity and kicked hard to the ladder.

She tucked the knife in her waistband, clamped the nove between her teeth, leapt up, grabbed a rung and climbed frantically as the drexla swooped by again, lashing out with its spine-covered tail.

Alive, she was alive. She climbed over the stern and collapsed onto the deck. Her body shook, her exposed dathe flared. She was only vaguely aware of Seg staring down at her.

Seg slumped down to the deck and curled around his stomach, which had decided to empty itself moments earlier. He felt sick, wrung out, and pained, but Storm only knew what mischief she would get up to next. Throwing him over was an act he could respect – in fact, it would have been exactly his response to that sort of ultimatum. But saving him? That was a mystery.

He lay there, shivering, and stared at her gills. Across the dimensions, the basic human genotype occasionally exhibited strange alterations. He had seen many but this was his first exposure in the wild. The neckbands seemed common among the Kenda, though many were no more than fancy pieces of string – decorative, not functional. He wondered how many Kenda might have the adaptation.

He scuttled sideways and wrapped his hand around the weapon she had used against him. Holding it, he stared directly in her eyes a long moment before he reversed it, handle held out toward her. "I'd sooner have my weapon. More familiar."

Ama looked up, now gasping for air, and waved off the weapon. She rolled to the side; three long tears in her trousers showed red scratches where the beast had opened her skin.

"Poison," she gurgled, her mouth filling with foamy saliva.

"Karg," Seg muttered. He lifted himself up by the rail and scrambled to the hatch. "Stay there!" he called over his shoulder.

Was anything on this world *not* poisonous? He remembered trooper Herma's sudden and violent end, and sped his weary legs.

Below, he tore through his kit and extracted the auto-med, powering it up as he climbed back up and ran to her side. She was convulsing and it was an effort to hold her arm steady. After a few failed attempts, he wrapped the sleeve around and cinched it down. As soon as the sleeve was in place, he hit the button. Hopefully her anatomy was not too far from baseline human stock, (as defined by the People, of course), to operate.

A filmy second set of eyelids, were half way up. A reaction to injury? He watched as her body jerked and she clawed at her neck, struggling to breathe. There was nothing else he could do; her salvation rested in the hands of technology now.

A moment later, she sucked in a deep breath and her eyes closed. Strangely, he felt himself inhale with her, unaware that he had been holding his breath.

For several minutes, she laid there, face pressed to the deck.

"Okay," she gasped, after her strength returned.

Seg stared, speechless, for a moment, then laughed and coughed as he fell back against the rail. "That was a great deal of drama for an agreement. Is there some token 'imperil the life of your business partner' tradition among your people?"

He watched the readouts from the auto-med scroll by. She would live, though she was fortunate that a more complex antivenom was not called for. The machine was not magic, no matter what her primitive mind might think.

He coughed, his throat still burned and his voice was rough and gravelly. "Don't make threats you're not willing to follow through on." He pointed to the seft, "You're no cold killer."

She raised herself into a sitting position, studied the cuff on her arm, then looked at Seg. "I know," she said, wiping her mouth, "but my family…" her voice trailed off. "Don't hurt them, that's all I ask."

"Between us, we can make sure they're in a safe place. A safe place that I do not have to know about."

He checked the auto-med once more to make sure she was out of danger, then removed the sleeve from her arm and wrapped it on his own.

First order of business was a fresh stim dose. He still had the manual stims in his kit, but the auto-med was just that much closer and more convenient at this exhausted moment. As the cold drugs washed into his system, he shook his head to clear it. Next, the machine delivered antiseptic agents, anesthetic and antibiotics for the cut on his shoulder – he would seal the skin later.

Medical needs seen to, and refreshed by the stim dose, he pulled himself up. "Now, let's get back to work."

Ama nodded, and rose on wobbly legs. The sun was high, a steady wind was blowing. "We should make good time to T'ueve, if I can stay awake," she said, then tucked the weapon into a hiding spot at the stern. "Kenda weapons, like this seft, are forbidden," she explained. Then she pulled the knife from her waistband and held it out to him, hilt first. "This is yours."

"In the future, use caution around this," he said, holding the knife up for her inspection. "The blade contains huchack toxin, the slightest cut will kill the surrounding flesh and, without treatment, lead to blood poisoning."

"Full of surprises, aren't you?"

Seg slid the blade back into its sheathe, without response, then unwrapped the auto-med as he looked out at the water. Something lurked beneath the surface, something that desperately hungered to consume him.

Judicia Serval pressed his index fingers to his temples; the morning had been a long one. Being stationed in Alisir was bad enough without being dragged from his bed before sunrise to deal with a brawl on the docks. Bloody Kenda, always causing problems. He had a good mind to keep all of the troublemakers locked up but after sorting through the many conflicting stories from the suspects and the constables he came to the conclusion that the skirmish on the docks the previous evening was simply another case of excess of alcohol and lack of sound judgment. Some water rat likely insulted another water rat and it had escalated from there.

He would have to give all of the parties a fine and put them on notice but he had no intention of clogging his jail with a dozen loud-mouthed mariners, whose various employers would shortly be petitioning for their release.

"Issue fines and notices," he said to the constable standing in front of his desk, waiting for his orders, "then release them. Be quick about it."

"Yes Judicia," the man bowed and exited.

"Now, Constable Dagga," he turned his well weathered face to the large man in front of him, "what brings you to Alisir?"

Dagga passed over a folded piece of paper, "This."

More paperwork, this day got more annoying by the moment. Judicia Serval pushed his glasses back up on the bridge of his nose and read. His brow furrowed into deep rows with each line of text. "A Shasir'threa? Kidnapped?"

"Or worse. In the Ymira Valley. Got word yesterday. None of the dirt lickers saw nothin', or so they say. Found his guards dead, not a mark on 'em."

"And Judicia Corrus thinks the culprits might be in Alisir?" Judicia Serval read the missive again, his headache pounding even more ferociously.

"Got someone we been watching for awhile. Water rat captain, name of Kalder. Brother's a Dua, supposed to ascend next moon; but the family has a bad history. Whole thing smells foul. She was on her way here. Judicia Corrus sent me to…keep an eye on her."

"Well," Judicia Serval refolded the paper and passed it back to Dagga, "I'll send a runner to the Port Captain and—"

"Judicia!" A constable burst through the door, shouldering a man of considerable size.

"What is this?" Judicia Serval asked, waving his arm, palm upward, at the man being supported. The unknown man was wet and tracking a good deal of mud in with him.

"Sir," the constable began, huffing from the strain of helping the man leaning on him to walk, "a Damiar Lord's been murdered. This man was among his guards, he was found washed up on the river bank."

Judicia Serval straightened up, cast a glance to Dagga, then focused his attention on the muddy Welf, "You were a witness?"

The man nodded, though the motion elicited a wince of pain, "I saw everything."

CHAPTER 7

J arin watched the young woman, on the monitor. He masked his displeasure at the sight of the prostrate primitive, who begged the forgiveness of her deity and prayed for deliverance from this terrifying afterlife her imagined transgressions had doomed her to. As usual, the wheels of bureaucracy turned slowly, as he waited for his former pupil's caj to be delivered into his care.

His first caj; Segkel had wasted no time. Jarin shook his head and turned his eyes away from the pathos he had witnessed too often for his liking.

Had he gone too far with the boy?

Segkel's comm haunted him; that fiery intensity in his eyes. *An intensity you encouraged*, he chided himself silently, as he wandered to the other side of the small office of the Caj Processing Officer and pulled up a screen displaying the list of caj currently awaiting claim. All of the others had been grafted and processed, he noted, as was to be expected. Only Segkel had specified to keep his property untouched.

Well, perhaps the boy was not beyond all hope.

How clearly he remembered the first day he had taught Segkel – transferred to his student unit because of his ratings of 'sufficient' in courses such as Fundamentals of World Affairs and others that held no interest for his sharp mind. Jarin's willingness to take on the more troublesome Guild students was one more quirk of character he knew his peers joked about behind his back.

His first thought, at the sight of young Eraranat, was that he needed several good meals to fill him out. The boy was quiet, almost sullen, as he surveyed the room, finally choosing a seat away from the other students. As with all student uniforms, Segkel's was recycled, but the frayed cuffs and sagging collar marked it as sixth or seventh generation – those worn only by the few students from the lowest ranks of the social strata. The other students also noticed these details; after all, class and caste recognition was an important aspect of their studies.

It would have been easy to feel sorry for him—a skinny loner from a poor family—but what happened in that first class quickly changed Jarin's mind on the matter.

For the last half of his lesson, Jarin presented a question to the class, to be answered in essay format. The assignment concerned the nature of vita assessment without the use of equipment, using their own World as a model. It was also a ruse. A test beneath a test.

As always, the students were nose-to-digipad for the remaining time allotted for the class, many frantically typing as the chime sounded, indicating that they must now send their feed to their instructor. Except for Segkel. He had sat back in his chair in contemplation, typed for a few moments, then spent the rest of the time staring down his new instructor.

After the cadets filed out, Jarin scrolled through the answers, rolling his eyes at the calculations and hypotheses. Then he arrived at Segkel's answer.

The World is a barren wasteland with little to no natural vita worth harvesting.

A smile creased Jarin's face as he read the sentence over and over again. Truth, such a rare commodity on the World. Traitorous, most would call the young man's answer, a fact Eraranat had to be aware of, which made the act that much more impressive. At last, his search was done; he had found the student he was looking for.

Turning back to the monitor in the Processor's office, he watched the young woman try to flee from the guards sent to collect her. She ran to the corner, lashed out and screamed until they were forced to stun her. Then, without production, they lifted her limp body from the floor.

Segkel; unortho and brilliant, rebellious, a gambler, competitive, and with a chip on his shoulder big enough to ensure that he would forever push to prove his worth, that he was better than the House brats and fifth generation Theorist offspring whose crisp uniforms would always remind him that he was the son of a recycler overseer, who could barely afford his tuition. He could have been softer on the boy. He could have revealed to him the truths he himself had learned the hardest way possible, could have guided him down a more empathetic path, been more of a companion and less of an antagonist, perhaps even offered him that ingredient most absent from his life: love. But love and empathy were not what would drive Segkel to the ambitious extremes he would need to enact change on this World.

And so he had, according to the plan formed years before Segkel's arrival in his class, exploited the boy's nature and shaped him into the kind of Theorist who would plan a multi-strike raid on his very first extrans and venture off solo among primitive Outers. Primitives who were dangerous enough to severely wound a veteran recon bodyguard.

Naturally enough, Segkel did not share all of Jarin's unortho views on caj, though his choice to refuse the ownership of caj was one area in which he had always believed he and his pupil found common ground. Admittedly, such a choice bordered on radical unorthodoxy, and only Jarin's prestige and notoriety allowed him to carry on in a manner that would be considered scandalous in a newly graduated Theorist.

Regardless, he would have to keep his tongue on the matter. Were it to be known that he was corrupting his students with his viewpoints, even his esteemed seniority would not be enough to protect his position within the Guild.

Rebelling against the caj system was tantamount to rebelling against the entire underpinnings of their society. The People justified their every action on the basis that they were superior to all other inhabitants of the universe. Therefore, making prey of those other inhabitants was likewise justified. Breaking out of that nigh-religious conviction took more than rhetoric, it took personal experience with the process.

And as well as he had succeeded in the direction of his student's other traits, Segkel's anger and arrogance still required a degree of control that he had not yet achieved. In truth he had not yet even recognized the need for control. For the boy's sake and safety, Jarin hoped Segkel would keep these more volatile aspects of his personality in check at least until his first mission was behind him. But, once again, these were traits Jarin had encouraged when they served his purpose.

He had made Segkel logical, hard and cold. For the good of the People, for the good of the World.

"Your caj will be awake in about twenty minutes, Theorist Svestil. Can we load it into the trans for you?" The Processor jarred him out of his thoughts.

"Yes, thank you," Jarin answered, and pressed his thumb to the digipad held out to authorize the girl's release.

"Are you certain it's not to be processed or grafted? If you were watching the monitor—" the Processor gestured to the screen that had shown the girl's hysterical state.

"Quite certain. If that is all…"

"We'll forward the registration documentation to you and a copy to Theorist Eraranat."

"Good," Jarin said, then offered a curt nod and passed through the open door.

For the good of the People, he thought, his mouth turned down in a frown as he climbed into the private trans and stared at the unconscious body of Segkel's first slave.

Fees paid and registration complete, Ama tucked the leather folder containing the *Naida*'s documentation under her arm and ran down the steps of the Port Captain's office to the line of cartuls waiting for passengers. Back on the boat, Seg lay unconscious in his quarters; she felt a slight pang of guilt about that.

From the selection, she chose a small, open-air cartul hitched to a lean and sturdy looking half-horse. Speed was paramount and her cousin, Brin, lived well outside of the sprawling city. The ride would cost her twice as much as it would have in Alisir, one of many reasons she hated this place.

T'ueve, beacon of civilization. Gleaming white, it rose like a drexla's tooth from the water. High above the city, the Sky Temple loomed – the sharpest point of the tooth, silhouetted against the setting sun. As the cartul rumbled over the cobblestone streets, Ama raised her gaze to the distant temple. Somewhere behind its walls, Stevan Kalder was busy with his daily rituals, believing himself chosen, protected, unique. For his sake, she hoped her brother was enjoying his remaining moments among the elite.

Guilt tickled her once more, as the driver slowed for a procession of luxe, Damiar cartuls that clogged up most of the other side of the street. Stevan would miss his ascension, he would never be a Shasir'threa, something he had studied, trained for and dreamed of most of his young life. But his temple and his fellow priests were a target for Seg's invasion; regardless of their differences, Stevan was family, and Ama couldn't risk losing him.

Which is why she had concocted her plan.

As they had approached T'ueve, she and Seg had talked in more detail about his mission, specifically his plans for his next destination, the T'ueve Sky Temple. According to him, he possessed some piece of equipment—not magic, there was no such thing as magic, he constantly reminded her—that could detect the vita he sought. The closer he could get to the sources of the vita, the better.

"T'ueve isn't like Alisir," she had informed him. "The Sky Temple is the training ground for the Dua, the repository of their knowledge, and a port for the skyships. You can't just walk in uninvited. Even disguised as a Damiar Lord, you won't be allowed in."

And then, before he could reply, she blurted out, "Unless you want to marry me."

Seg's eyebrows rose as he pondered the suggestion, then his face fell back into its usual state of composure. "You have a plan?"

"I do." She didn't, but one was forming. "Take the wheel. I'll go fetch us some grint then I'll give you the details."

When Ama returned from the galley, she pressed a hot mug into his hands and hooked the wheel on course.

"My brother is a Shasir'dua on the verge of ascension, he's lived at the T'ueve Sky Temple for two years. It's rare for a Kenda to be accepted into Shasir schooling at all, and rarer still for our kind to ascend into the ranks of the holy men, let alone to make it as far as the Dua."

Seg raised the cup to his lips then paused, his eyebrows rising a few degrees.

"Believe me, my family was ecstatic when Stevan was chosen to be sent there. They practically interrogated him for details. I know more about the T'ueve Sky Temple than I ever wanted to. Of course, I, being a lowly Kenda woman, can't just go strolling onto sacred grounds for a friendly visit with him. There are only three ways I can ask for an audience with my brother. I can come to notify him of a death in his family but chances are they wouldn't allow me to see him for that; they'd simply pass along the sad news." As if the Shasir would mourn the death of a Kenda.

"I can bring a new child of mine for his blessing." Seg nodded, understanding this was an impossibility. "Exactly. Which leaves us with option three. I can ask him to bless my marriage. The best part of this is I'm expected to bring my future mate with me for the blessing." She paused a beat, "That would be you...sweetheart."

Momentum was on her side.

"Once we're inside the inner gates, we'll be alone with Stevan, in his sanctuary, for the blessing. As with all Shasir nonsense, these blessings take an eternity, which will work in our favour. All we need is a way to knock him out for a short time. I have some furien—that's a drug—if we're able to slip it into his ceremonial tea, that would do the trick."

Ama was surprised at how quickly the wheels of her mind were spinning, as if she were born to this.

"From Stevan's chambers, you can access any of the inner rooms of the temple, to do…whatever it is you do. So, what do you think?"

"I think," Seg said, as he considered her idea, "that you'll also want to extract your brother from the danger zone as well. If your brother is among the Shasir, his life will be at risk." He took a long drink. "We can drug your brother, or I can immobilize him with the stunner if I can get to within arm's reach. If there is a way to get him out of the temple, you can deposit him where you will, and he won't be taken for caj if he's among your people."

"Yes, that's…" the words stopped in Ama's mouth. The entire reason for her plan was to alert Stevan to the danger, which she would have done using Kenda code. But Seg didn't know that. "That's a good idea. I'll find a way to get him out."

Seg swallowed the rest of the grint in a fast gulp. His throat was still raw from his near drowning and the heat of the liquid drew a grimace. "You'll teach me the protocols expected in such a situation. I can't risk discovery; our cover must be flawless." He blinked and wobbled slightly.

"Are you alright?" Ama asked. "You look tired, maybe you should lie down."

"I'm fine. Now, I'll need you to go through the wardrobe I've…" he teetered again, the empty cup fell from his hand, and Ama caught him just before he dropped to the deck. His weight pulled her downward until she was on her knees.

"Sorry," she said, as Seg hung limp and unconscious in her arms. "Maybe I can trust you, maybe you will spare my people, but I can't take that chance."

As soon as she was docked, she dragged him below deck and dropped him on the bed. In truth, she envied him, she couldn't remember feeling more fatigued in her entire life, especially after the tedious process of hauling him down the stairs. But rest was not an option. With the amount of furien she had slipped into his drink, he would be out for four or five hours; perhaps the only time she would have alone before his people attacked her world.

Light from the windows of Brin and Perla's cottage was the most welcome sight Ama had ever seen, she swore she could smell Perla's famous cooking long before the cartul rolled to a stop. She hopped to the ground, legs nearly buckling beneath her, and tossed the driver his coin. Her stomach growled as she approached the front door. Laughter echoed from inside.

There wouldn't be much laughter after her visit, she imagined.

She leaned forward, head against the wood door, one hand smoothing over her nove, which she had repaired before arriving in port. Maybe she should have just taken her chances with Seg? Did she really have to involve her cousin and spoil the circle of bliss that was his family?

Before she could answer, the door opened.

"Ama?"

Brin filled the doorway, his thick mane of hair glowed gold in the lantern light of the cottage.

"I need your help," she said, took one step forward, and collapsed into his arms.

Lady Uval blew her nose, yet again, into Judicia Serval's hankie. "I can't believe it. No, I won't, I won't!"

A Welf servant fluttered nervously behind her, waiting for the hysterics to subside in order to hand her mistress the cup of tea she had demanded. The hysterics, however, showed no discernable sign of abating.

"Dead? My Flavert?" she launched into a fresh round of sobs, as Judicia Serval and his two constables shifted uncomfortably in their chairs.

"I'm afraid that's not the worst of it," the Judicia said, leaping on a quiet moment.

Lady Uval sniffed, and raised her face. "What...?"

"Your husband was murdered." He paused as she gasped. "One of his guards escaped the attack and swam to shore. He told us everything."

The tears stopped, Lady Uval's eyes widened, her lips formed the beginning of a word, several times, before she finally spoke. "Murdered?" she whispered.

"You and Lord Uval recently used the services of a female Kenda for a devotional tour on the Halif River, is that true?"

She nodded. "Captain Ama. She was charming, for a Kenda."

At the last word, the Judicia frowned. "Well, she was docked here, at Alisir, and your husband, according to his guard, went to meet her to arrange a private charter for the two of you."

"He never mentioned..."

"It was to be a surprise, a gift, I'm told." He glanced at his constables, certain they could guess the dead Lord's real intention for keeping his visit with the female captain secret. "When he and the other guards boarded the boat, they were attacked by a pair of thieves. It seems this Captain Ama lured your husband onboard for this purpose. He was robbed of the coin he was carrying, murdered and tossed overboard. I'm sorry, I know this is horrible news I bring you."

"I gave her a tip," Lady Uval said.

"Your husband's men did their best; they managed to kill one of the brigands but the thieves had Shasir weapons, stolen weapons. His men were outmatched." The Judicia tugged down on the lapels of his robe, with both hands. "These outlaws will be dealt with, severely. You have our assurance of that."

"I should expect so," Lady Uval said, sitting upright, all traces of her weeping vanished. Her mouth puckered. "You show a little kindness to these..." she turned and glared at the Welf girl, "...these mud kissers and water rats and they walk all over you. Ungrateful filth." She whipped her head around to stare at the Judicia. "You have them then? The murdering witch and her partner?"

"No, but there is a man on the way to T'ueve at this very moment to track them down and apprehend them. He is a specialist at this sort of thing."

The Lady stood and the three men hurried to follow her lead. "Judicia Serval, I am a woman of influence. You bring me that piece of Kenda filth and I will be calling you Commissioner Serval very soon. I want to see that woman torn and hung."

Judicia Serval raised his palms and bowed respectfully. "Captain Kalder and her partner are as good as dead, my dear Lady."

"Eat!" Perla ordered and dropped a large slice of meat onto Ama's plate. "Gah, so thin! I should keep you here for a month to fill you out properly." She ladled thick gravy over top of the meat.

Ama's instinct was to protest, she had news, important news, and not much time to share it, but Perla's round face shone down on her like a miniature sun, softening all urgency with its warmth. Next to her, Brin leaned back in his chair, while his two young children, Dalit and Nixie, vied for the coveted seat on their aunt's lap.

"Rough crossing?" Brin asked.

Ama, her mouth full, nodded. They exchanged a look between them – hers filled with the significance of her unexpected visit, his assuring. They would speak alone soon enough.

"You didn't come from the Banks by yourself, did you? During squall season? In that…boat?" Perla asked, ready to chasten once more, as she filled Ama's cup with wine.

"No." Ama swallowed and passed another silent message to Brin.

"Did you fight pirates, Aunty Tadpole?" Nixie asked, eyes wide as she squirmed on Ama's leg.

"Only one," Ama answered, with a smile that wavered, then raised her fork like a sword and poked the girl in the ribs.

Not to be left out, Dalit, who hovered at Ama's side, piped up, "Uncle Geras says you gonna get married and not be a captain no more."

Ama stabbed her fork into the meat, "Uncle Geras is a —"

"I think it's time for chores and then bed," Brin said, over Ama, to Nixie and Dalit. "Go on, say goodnight, then off to the kitchen to help your mother."

Perla shepherded the children away after an extended farewell. When the room was clear, Brin leaned forward. "Geras doesn't know you're in T'ueve, does he?"

"Damn it," Ama muttered, "I forgot he was here. Is he staying with you?"

"Yes, but don't worry, you're safe. He's busy at the Terithe estate this evening; we don't expect him back for hours. And I won't tell him you were here but…" he rubbed his beard, in thought, "there's nothing I can do to help you, Tadpole. You know that, don't you? I would much prefer my favorite cousin remain a wild, vagabond captain, roaming the seas, but this business is between you and Uncle Odrell."

Ama looked past Brin, her eyes moving over the details of his home, so much like the one she had known as a child. As she spied what must be his evening chair, and the table beside it stacked with documents, it was hard to believe that she and Brin had once planned to sail the world together, battling pirates and exploring undiscovered lands. She had ended up a glorified babysitter, herding Damiars up and down the river, scratching for coin to keep the *Naida* afloat; he had taken over his father's boat building business, the welfare of a wife, children and a roster of workers all upon his broad shoulders. The dreams of children were so fragile.

"I'm not here to ask you to help me with family matters, cousin" she said and pushed away her plate, with a longing look at the savory meal.

"Oh?" Brin's always-merry eyes, sharpened.

Ama took a deep breath, "We're in danger. All of us. I…"

Now that she had arrived at the crucial moment, words evaded her. Every possible explanation seemed beyond belief and her mind was muddied with exhaustion.

"Ama," Brin's voice was soothing, he rested his hand on hers, engulfing it, "you've had a tiring journey. Why don't you stay the ni—"

"Look," she yanked her hand from beneath her cousin's, leaned down, tugged off her boot and lifted the bottom of her trouser leg. Three long, red scratches were etched across her calf. "Drexla spines," she said simply.

Brin bent forward and studied the marks. "Impossible, you'd be dead. There's no cure for drexla venom."

"I would be dead," she agreed, "if it weren't for the passenger I'm carrying, and his magic."

"Shasir?" Brin jolted up in his seat.

"No. Seg's people have magic far beyond anything the Shasir know, beyond anything you or I could dream of. They're coming here, to invade our home." Ama lowered her voice, "And I'm the only one who knows about it."

Brin looked over his shoulder, to the kitchen, then back at Ama. "Is he still on the *Naida*, this Seg?"

"I slipped some furien into his drink; he'll be asleep for a few more hours at least."

"Good thinking. I won't ask where you got the furien, probably best I don't know." He stood, fingertips on the table, "I'll round up some men, we'll get him while it's still dark and he's out. You should—"

"No," Ama stood and gripped Brin's wrist. She looked up into his pale eyes, "You can't tell anyone about him. Not a word. And any man who tries to harm him will have to go through me first."

Brin dragged his hand through his hair. "Damn my ancestors, I'm beginning to understand Geras's frustration with you." His eyes rested on hers, the unspoken connection they had always shared did the talking. He raised his eyebrows, "Is it a long story?"

"Very."

"Come on then," he crossed to the door, pulled a lantern off a hook, lit it and gestured for Ama to follow him outside. "Going for a walk to the river," he called to Perla.

"Don't you let her leave without a basket of food! I know how she eats!" she called back.

Brin shut the door and wrapped his arm around Ama's shoulder. "What she means is she knows how you cook."

Ama allowed herself a smile, both at her cousin's joke and the welcome break in the tension. Something Brin had always excelled at.

"Now, about that very long story…" he said, as he led her along the path to the river.

Seg's head felt as though large Outers had stomped on it for the better part of a day. He opened his eyes but couldn't see. Where was he? A shiver of unease told him to sit up but his body failed to respond to the cue. He concentrated on one arm and eventually felt it inch toward his face, though there was a disconnection to the movement, as if he were manipulating someone else's limb. His eyes began to pick out shapes in the darkness; he wasn't blind, at least.

His nose was against something soft. A mattress? He inhaled. What was the scent? Musty and old but layered over with something sweet, something vaguely familiar. *Ama.* He forced his thoughts into order. The boat? Yes, he was still aboard. Aboard and, by the lack of movement, somewhere sheltered. A dock?

"Manatu?" he croaked, then reproached himself. Manatu was gone, sent back.

The throb in his head refused to subside. He curled up on the bunk, hands clasped around his skull, fingers probing at the back of his neck to try to relieve some of the tension.

"Ama?" he murmured.

A voice buried deep in his mind ordered him to get up, get his auto-med, get moving. He was vulnerable like this. But the relentless throb held him in place.

She's done something to you, you fool. Get up!

Summoning all his strength, Seg bolted upright. His head screamed and a wave of dizziness washed over him. Then, as if a giant hand had swatted him, he fell back to the mattress. Out cold.

Eyes open again, Seg was aware of some passage of time but had no way to know how long he had slept. The pain had faded, but in its wake came a dull confusion, as if his thoughts and memories were wrapped in a thick layer of gauze. He groped around in the darkness, his hands found the edge of the bunk, his feet swung over and located the floor. There was an amp-light in his pack; he focused on that fact, as he used the contours of the bunk to guide him. One hand on the bunk, he reached out with the other until he felt the edge of the small table. He let go of the bunk, crouched down and groped blindly under the table for his pack. His fingers fumbled through the contents until they located the small cylinder. A press of a button lit up his surroundings.

Better. Now what?

Auto-med.

Another round of fumbling, this time aided by the amp-light, produced the auto-med. Once the sleeve was in place, Seg watched the readout and waited for relief. Then he frowned. *Insufficient data.* He stared at the screen with his mouth hanging open, blinked a few times, then pressed the button again. The readout flickered then came up the same.

Insufficient data. He groaned as the pieces fell into place. Whatever that treacherous woman had used to knock him out, it was too complex for the auto-med to counteract.

"Karging, untrustworthy..." Seg muttered, and punched up the sequence to deliver a stim dose.

There was the usual cold rush and a less than usual sharpening of his senses, but along with that another wave of dizziness, and now nausea, smacked him hard. He groaned and dropped to his knees.

Maybe she hadn't drugged him? Maybe he had succumbed to some local ailment. Where was she? Was he in danger or not? Maybe...he shook his head and immediately regretted it. He couldn't order his thoughts.

I have to find her.

He clung to that one clear idea as he staggered out of his quarters and up the stairs. Hand on the hatch, he stopped before he opened it. He was forgetting something. The light shone on the metal handle. The light. He doused the amp-light, then lifted the door and climbed out. According to protocols, he shouldn't have unpacked even that small piece of the People's technology in the first place, but at least he had remembered to shut it off before he wandered out into the night.

So hard to focus. He rubbed his hand across his forehead.

There was light out on the dock, on other boats and from a small city.

A search, end to end, of the upper deck produced nothing and he returned below. He called her name, shone the amp-light in all corners, but found nothing. She wouldn't abandon her boat. He must have been out for hours; if she had gone to summon her fellow mariners, they would have already taken him by now. *Is she in some kind of trouble? Again?* He let out a long breath and sat down at the galley table.

For the first time he could remember, he had no answers to any of his questions. He rubbed his face, which was still slightly numb, then took a long slow look around the interior of the boat.

"She's gone," he said, the tone of his voice as empty as the galley.

With an effort uncommon for him, he considered the possibilities. She had betrayed him, or she was in some kind of trouble. Either way, he couldn't stay here. He had his stunner and his Damiar persona as protection; he had to leave immediately, had to try to find his missing assistant.

A moment later he found himself staring at his fingers, tracing the grain of the wood table, and slapped his face to sharpen his focus.

The safe parameters of a recon are more intuition than logic. Nevertheless, when extrans, should any of you feel that I would be peering disapprovingly at your actions, then you have most likely exceeded those parameters.

Jarin's voice. He felt his mentor peering disapprovingly.

"Get moving, you fool," he ordered himself, and staggered back to his quarters.

CHAPTER 8

The grass was cool, Ama's legs dangled over the edge of the bank as the low rush of the river filled the silence between her and Brin. She had always loved this spot, an oasis in the middle of the stark coldness of T'ueve, though she wondered that Brin, with his thriving business and wealthy clients had chosen such a meager house, away from the city.

She had given him the story as quickly as she could, leaving out certain details, such as her plan for the Sky Temple, and fending off the inevitable questions in order to reach the end. Now that it was done, Brin simply stared out into the dark.

"He said he would direct these attacks toward the Shasir and spare the Kenda if you help him?" he asked, without looking at her.

"That's what he promised," Ama answered.

"Do you trust him?"

She paused, "I don't know. He could be the opportunity our people have waited for. A chance for the Kenda to know real freedom."

"Or he could enslave us all." Brin faced Ama, the lantern on the ground sent dancing shadows between them. "With the magic you've described, we would be helpless against his kind."

"Seg says it's not magic. He says it's science and…" she dropped into a whisper, "that the Shasir'kia aren't gods, they've just used their science to trick us."

"I believe that much from him." Brin shook his head, "A strange story you've brought me, Tadpole. Now I wish you'd just come looking for a way to get out of marrying one of those poor fools who dote on you." The two shared a smile at that.

"I wouldn't have brought this to you, but you're the only person here I trust."

"And I won't betray your confidence," he said, placing his hand on her head. "So, if I'm not to harm this man, how am I to help you?"

Ama picked up a stone and turned it over in her hand. "I'm honor bound to Seg but not to his team. I don't know who they are, or how many, but I think I know where they are and where they're headed next. The map he showed me had two sets of lines on it – one matched Seg's path, the other diverged and turned inland, toward the Galich settlement and temple. If we could send a group of Kenda to find and capture them, maybe we could learn more about this invasion, about these people. At the very least, if Seg is lying and reneges on our agreement, we would have some of theirs as prisoners."

Brin scratched his chin through his beard. "Possible. Difficult but possible. I have some men I trust."

"Warn them to be cautious. These people…their weapons are nothing we're used to. They have some as small as this," she opened her hand, to display the smooth stone, "that make sound and light as loud and bright as the Shasir's shimmer-fire. Others can knock a man down with only a touch."

Brin's eyebrows drew together sharply, "You're in dangerous waters, Ama. I don't like this."

Ama tossed the stone into the river, "I have to get back before he comes to."

"I'll hitch up my cartul, you can tell me more about this team as we travel." Brin stood, brushed the grass and dirt from his clothes then offered his hand to Ama. "And you'd better go collect your basket of food before Perla locks you away in the pantry to force feed you."

Viren Hult chewed on the end of a benga stick, the bitter pulp mixed with his saliva. The stick, harvested from the dried, inner core of benga tree branches, was a mild stimulant and perfect for times when wits needed to be sharp. He let the juice sit on his tongue and enjoyed the slight tingle as he listened to the muffled shouts and laughter from the nearby Port House.

Night always smothered T'ueve like a heavy blanket. Along the main streets and avenues, constables patrolled; their footfalls and the distant surf break the only sounds. What life remained awake and energetic after the eleventh hour, naturally gravitated to the Wharfinger Block. Centered around the Port House, the Block was a stain on the otherwise pearly city. The stain was tolerated because, though auspiciously a Kenda haven, those Damiar who sought the ills of drink, opiates, gambling, fighting or flesh for hire, would often find themselves 'lost' in the dirty corner of the city.

Among other titles, Viren considered himself a shepherd for these lost souls.

A lean man with a shaven head swaggered around the corner; Viren spat out the benga juice.

"Prow, you've come armed I hope?"

His companion tilted his formidable chin downward, and smiled as he patted the breast pocket of his shirt. "My lucky deck."

"By design, I'll wager," Viren said, his eyes roaming the narrow, dimly lit streets. "Gods beneath the waves, it's been ghostly around here lately. How's a man supposed to make a dishonest living?"

"Sky Ceremony's comin' up," Prow offered. "Lots of bored cloud sniffers'll be looking for amusement."

"I like your optimism. We should…" Viren paused and cocked his head, "I spoke too soon. What do you see there?" He pointed down the street with his benga stick. A lone figure staggered a few paces, stopped, looked left, then right, then left again.

"I see a friend we need to make," Prow answered, interlocked his long fingers and cracked all his knuckles at once.

The men exchanged a smile then strolled down the street.

Viren held his delight in check as he approached the newcomer. Perfect. Young and, judging from the colors and design of his coat, foreign to these parts. Probably some wealthy Dammie visiting members of his Line for the upcoming ceremony and festivities.

Viren smiled broadly as he neared. "Evening, fine Sir. Pardon my bluntness, but you seem lost. I know these parts well, is there something, someone or somewhere you're looking for?"

The Damiar opened his mouth, his eyes shifted from Viren to Prow, drifted away from both, then returned and narrowed. "I am armed," the Damiar answered, his voice thick.

"A wise precaution in this part of the city," Viren said.

The Damiar sized them up for another moment then seemed to come to some important decision. "I'm looking for my boat captain."

"Well," Viren's elbow nudged Prow's, "if it's a captain you seek, I know just the place for it. My companion and I were just on our way home—morning worship comes early, praise to the Shasir—but we'd be happy to escort you there."

The Damiar swayed slightly but his eyes narrowed. "You're scoundrels," he said, straightened up and stepped back.

"Scoundrels? Scoundrels!" Viren raised his hand to his heart in distress, then burst out into a round of deep belly laughs. "We are at that." He slapped a large hand on the young man's shoulder, "But we're friendly scoundrels and you are in a most unfriendly part of this good city. My name is Viren Hult, my friend here is Renten Jask but we call him 'Prow', on account of the…" He stroked his chin and nodded to his companion's most noticeable feature.

The Damiar stared uncomprehending, then blinked and lost focus once more.

"And whose acquaintance do we have the pleasure of making this fine evening?"

"I am Seg…" there was a pause, as the Damiar collected himself, "Segkel Eraranat. Lord Segkel Eraranat."

Prow let out a low whistle, which Viren didn't react to though he understood the code. The Dammie was already under the influence of something.

Or pretending to it.

"Always an honor to welcome a Lord to our corner of T'ueve. Come, we'll take you as far as the Port House. If the captain you're looking for isn't there, I'm sure we can find someone who knows where he is."

"*She*," Seg corrected. Viren and Prow exchanged glances. "I will be watching you," Seg informed them, "but I appreciate your assistance. You are Ken...kindly. Kindlier, than I would expect."

"I was new here myself once," Viren said, as he led Seg up the street, toward the Port House. "T'ueve's a safe city, not like some of those northern ports, but every city has its dark corners. Isn't that right Prow?"

"Dark and dangerous," Prow said, with a nod.

"Do you hail from the south?" Viren continued. "I spent some time down south, lovely countryside, beautiful women."

"Yes," Seg agreed, "there are many beautiful women at home. And yourself? Where are you from?"

"Originally from Malvid," Viren lied. "Have you been? Now, if you want to talk about beautiful women..." he made cupping motions over his chest that indicated the particular type of beauty he referred to, elbowed Seg in the ribs and let loose another booming laugh.

He pattered on with the friendly banter until they reached a large set of wooden doors. Viren stepped forward just as the doors flew open; two men tumbled out in a heap onto the road. Neither man made an attempt to stand but instead, the moment they untangled from one another, both launched into a flurry of punches. A small crowd had followed them out and were cheering, though it was impossible to tell if anyone had a favorite competitor or if it was merely the brawl itself that excited them.

"Here we are!" Viren said, with a flourish, and ushered Seg inside.

The Damiar hesitated, swept his eyes across the scene, then stepped through the door. With a practiced hand, Viren guided his charge through the mob of revelers. The fight had cleared a few tables and he set a course for one in a quieter corner. A cackling laugh caused him to glance over his shoulder in time to see one of the older whores tousle Seg's hair, eliciting a frown. He chuckled at the young man's attempt to pull away, as he steered him into an empty chair.

Prow righted an overturned chair for himself and Viren pulled his own close to Seg's, the scrape of the wood legs against the floor drowned by music and voices.

No sooner had they sat than Viren felt a familiar set of fingernails crawling over his shoulder and down his chest. He grabbed the hands before they could venture further south.

"Mira, come say hello to my friend," he said to the woman behind him, swinging her to one side. "Lord Eraranat is a visitor to our fair city."

"Your Lordship," the woman cooed, and swayed herself beside Seg. She bent forward, her breasts spilling from the dress she barely wore. "Looking for a friend?"

"Yes," Seg said, staring at the abundance of cleavage. "I mean, no. Not you. Her. Ama."

"You can call me Ama," the woman purred.

"Mira, my lovely water nymph, be a dear and send us over some refreshments would you? Lord Eraranat's been walking a fair distance, he could use a drink." Viren said, gently redirecting the woman away from Seg. She could have the Dammie later, once he and Prow were done with him.

He kicked Prow under the table, and his friend reached for the deck of cards in his pocket.

"Ama you say? That's your friend's name? Can you remember which establishment she worked at?"

"Not an establishment," Seg sighed. "She's no whore. As I explained, she's a captain."

"My deepest apologies. I am, as you mentioned, a scoundrel."

A tray of drinks arrived at that moment, convenient timing. Viren knew who the female captain was, though he had never met her. And he wasn't about to share this knowledge with the Dammie. As he recalled, she docked in the Banks, solely a river rat. The poor fool had probably bedded her and now, a few drinks in, was pining for her company.

Viren raised his glass and nodded to Seg to do likewise, "To friends old and new."

Seg lifted his glass high and drank, mimicking Viren. His host, however, noticed that the drink was only a token sip, a ploy to avoid the spikers sometimes used to knock a man out and rob him. Clever boy.

"Nevertheless," Seg said, "she shouldn't be hard to locate. Not many women captaining ships, no?"

Beneath the haze of the intoxicant, Viren recognized the calculation in Seg's eyes.

"No. None that I know of. Thank the Sky Lords for that! The Big Water's no place for such delicate creatures." Viren took a long drink, then wiped his beard with the sleeve of his shirt. "Besides, if they knew how easy it was, our stories wouldn't be as impressive, would they?" He slipped a sideways glance to Prow, then took another drink and scanned the room. "Tell you what, I'll go make some enquiries." He stood and placed a hand on Seg's shoulder, "You stay here, this isn't the kind of crowd you want to get lost in."

Prow split the deck and banged the cards against the table loud enough to draw Seg's attention.

"You play?" he asked.

Seg shook his head. "Not these games, no. But thank you."

"Easy as falling down," Prow said, dealing cards as he spoke. "We'll play a round for fun, while you wait."

Viren took his cue to leave. Prow was a miser with words until the cards were on the table. He was that rare con who could spin a web with such grace the victims wouldn't even struggle once they had been snared.

He found Mira lingering on the wooden staircase that led to the rooms above. She dropped her butt down onto the step, pulled her dress up to her thighs to reveal her bare legs, and peered out at him through the wooden spindles.

"What have we here? A wild animal in a cage?" Viren pulled the benga stick from his pocket and pointed it at her.

She snatched the stick from him, clamped her teeth down on it and growled.

"I need a favor or four from you, my saucy beast," he said, drawing close.

"And I need something from you." Mira opened her mouth and rolled the stick across her tongue.

"Business first, you know the rules," he reached through the spindles for the stick but she held it away from his grasp.

"You gonna give me the Southie?" she nodded to where Seg sat.

"Of course," he smiled and she passed the stick back into his hands. "Once Prow and I get our share out of him. Don't pout, I'll make sure there's plenty of coin left for you." He slid his hand between the spindles. His index and middle finger pressed against the underside of her chin and coaxed her head forward, his lips aimed for hers, which parted in anticipation, but detoured at the last moment to whisper in her ear, "I've got something special for you in my trousers."

"Oh yeah?"

"Go on." He angled sideways, displaying his pocket.

Mira licked her lips, pushed her upper body against the spindles and slipped her hand inside the pocket.

"Got it?"

"Yes," she said. Her smile fell away.

"You know what to do with it."

She withdrew the folded piece of paper, carefully palmed so none of the other patrons could see, and tucked it up under her skirt.

"Nen curse you, Viren Hult."

He reached both hands through the spindles, pulled her head close before she could leave and kissed her deeply. Nose to nose, he held her there, "I am a shameless scoundrel, or so I've been told."

"What else do you need?" She bit down on his upper lip.

"The Southie needs a kiss."

"Not drinking up like a good boy?"

"Pretending to drink, and doing an admirable job of the charade."

Mira pulled away slightly, "Suspicious."

"Yes. When you get him upstairs—"

"Be extra friendly, get him talking, find out who he really is," Mira rattled off.

"That's why I adore you."

She ran her finger over his nose, as prominent as Prow's chin, "Me and half the doxies in the Block. Go on then," she pushed him off, "I'll be 'round shortly."

Viren returned to find Prow sulking as the Damiar spread out cards before him in complicated patterns.

"It's about knowing the combinations better than your opponent," Seg said, as he gestured toward trios of cards. "For example, if you play the vestk, you turn your assembly into Black House, which is a very potent presentation. However," he tapped the cards he had lain in front of Prow "from here, you have three possible counters to Black House, though the odds of drawing to a Seizure are," he paused, "seven thousand to one on a fresh draw. However, the Seizure is virtually the ultimate hand and is only trumped by Refusal."

Prow scratched the stubble on his head, "Yeah…"

"No luck finding your friend yet," Viren said, and flopped down into his seat. "There was one promising lead but the captain apparently just 'looked' like a woman. Not to worry, word is out and she will be found." He glanced down at the mess of cards on the table, "A new game?"

"His Lordship is teaching me one of his games from home," Prow said, his tone dismal.

"Ah yes. Where exactly did you say 'home' was again?" Viren asked Seg.

Seg waved his hand without looking up from the cards, "Down south. Now, this is the most important combination to remember…"

Viren raised one eyebrow just enough for Prow to read. *Bad trouble.*

"I found a friend for you!" Mira's voice arrived ahead of her. Her arm was around the waist of a young, dark haired woman who was all curves. The new woman was sucking on a plump kembleberry, the juice trickled down her chin. Without waiting for an invitation, she plunked herself onto Seg's lap, pulled the berry from her mouth and pressed her equally juicy lips to his.

He struggled to lean away from the girl. "This is not what I came for," he told Viren. Blinking, he raised a hand to his lips, as if to stroke sensation back into them, and wavered in his seat. "You idiots," he slurred, "I don't have any coin."

"Mira!" Viren stood, towering over the woman. "Did you try to take advantage of our new friend?"

"I…" she looked to the woman with the berry, who was running her hands over Seg's body in an approximation of seduction. The berry girl pulled her hand from the inside of Seg's pants, turned and scowled – the Dammie was coinless. "I'm so sorry! She's new, half Welf, shouldn't have trusted her!"

Mira grabbed the berry girl by the arm and yanked her off Seg, "Get upstairs and wait in your room. Dirty mud kisser." She shoved the girl away. "So sorry, your Lordship, so sorry."

"How do you feel?" Viren waved a hand in front of Seg's face, then turned to Prow. "We should leave him, poor fellow. I think he's had enough of us for one evening. Mira, please look after Lord Eraranat." He pulled out a coin and dropped it in her hand, "Whatever he needs. My treat." Both men stood, as Prow collected the cards.

Seg slumped back in his chair and cackled incoherently. "Very, very bad scoundrels." He lolled his head forward and directed his eyes, as best he could, at Prow. "Remember the game. Very few can master it, and those who do can make quite the comfortable living."

"He's cracked," Prow whispered to Viren.

"Good luck with your search, your Lordship, we'll just be—"

"You'll just be staying right where you are, Viren Hult, until we're square, please and thank you." Five men had formed a semi-circle around Viren and Prow, inadvertently trapping Seg with them. All five were Kenda, and all looked ready to remove limbs with their bare hands.

As she had often done, Mira made herself inconspicuous, slipped between the men and back into the crowd.

"Hudish," Viren addressed the obvious leader of the group, a man absent his left hand. "I think there's been a misunderstanding."

"I understand," Hudish growled, and raised the wooden stump, jabbing it at Viren then Prow, "that you and your worthless partner cheated my nephew out of a month's wages. And who's this?" he asked, peering over at Seg. "Dressing your crew up like Dammies now, Hult?"

"They were just leaving," Seg slurred. "Do you know Ama?" He rose to his feet, tipped to one side, and grabbed the table just in time to keep from toppling over.

"He's not with us," Viren said, stepping in front of Seg. "Damiar Lord, visiting the city. Had a bit too much to drink, few holes in the hull too," he tapped his forefinger to his temple, "if you know what I—"

"Shut up!" Hudish yelled. "All three of you, outside, now!"

"Now wait, we can…" Viren stopped and raised his hands as the men facing him drew blades. "Outside, outside it is."

From the entrance to the dock, Ama could see the *Naida* was dark, and allowed her heartbeat to settle. Seg was still asleep. She shouldn't have been surprised, the amount of furien she had used, combined with his own exhaustion, would likely keep him snoring until dawn. She had an alibi cooked up for her absence but preferred not to use it if possible.

Brin passed Perla's basket of food down from the cartul. "You're sure I can't carry this? I think it weighs as much as you do."

Ama took the basket and once again her knees almost buckled; he wasn't joking.

"I know you won't listen to me but be careful, Tadpole. This is no notice from the authorities you're dealing with now." He nodded to the darkened boat.

"Don't worry, I promise I'll—"Ama dropped the basket at her feet. The authorities. She had been so wrapped up in these new events that she had forgotten about Corrus's threat. "There's one last thing," she climbed back up onto the seat. "The *Naida* has to be tied up back at the Banks in twenty-five days. If something happens, if I don't make it…"

"Judicia Corrus?" Brin kept his voice low but it had a hard edge.

Ama nodded, "Make sure you warn Fa and my brothers."

"Of course I will, but you get yourself back there, even if you have to leave this Seg behind. His invasion may or may not be real but Corrus's threats are always genuine."

"I know." She embraced her cousin, then hopped down again. "Nen protect you," she said, in the Kenda tongue.

He opened his mouth, then closed it, and smiled, "And you cousin."

Ama lugged the basket up the stairs to the Naida, not as grateful for Perla's gift in that moment as she knew she would be later. The food was divine but what she craved more than anything right now was sleep.

She rubbed her hand on the *Naida*'s rail, an act that always calmed her. Home, she was home.

Then she saw the open hatch.

She lowered the basket to the deck, padded to the helm, retrieved the lantern she kept there and lit it. A quick survey of the upper deck revealed nothing unusual.

"Seg?" she called as she climbed down into the belly of her boat. Nothing was out of place. She tiptoed to his quarters and poked her head inside. The bed was empty. Holding the lantern aloft, she stared at the jumble of the blanket, the contents of his pack half spilled on the deck. If it had been a robbery, there would be more missing, which could only mean…

"Son of a whore!" She sprinted above deck but by the dim lights of the city she could see Brin's cartul was long gone.

As was Seg.

Just as they had with the previous skirmish, a small crowd followed Viren and the others outside, into the street. The unconscious body of one of the last combatants was still sprawled on the ground; Viren stepped around it.

"If this is a matter of coin—and I assure you Prow played fair against your nephew—in this instance, I would be glad to compensate for his losses," Viren assured his assailant, eyes darting over the spectators to locate possible allies.

"That's a start," Hudish said.

"Well," Viren said, palms up, "I'll have to run and fetch that for you. Don't carry that much on me, not in the Block. But, here," he grasped Seg's shoulders and pushed him forward, "you can hang onto him as collateral."

"He tried to drug me for my coin," Seg informed Hudish, as he made elaborate and nonsensical gestures with his hands. "I have the most sincere doubts about his concerns for my well-being once he's out of your sight."

Hudish looked Seg up and down, then delivered a swift, hard punch to his stomach with the wooden stump. "I have sincere doubts about you opening your yap anymore. I saw you all chummy with this one," he jerked his thumb in Prow's direction. "Teaching him new tricks and whatnot."

Viren winced as Seg doubled over and stumbled backwards. "We don't have your coin on us, Hudish. And your nephew should know better than to be gambling his wages, especially around here. But if you want a piece of flesh," he pushed up his sleeves and stood up to his full height, which was impressive even among the Kenda, "you can try to take it out of me."

The men, all but Hudish, shifted their feet and tightened their grip on their knives, one man took a few small steps back.

"Your ego is almost as big as your mouth, Viren." Hudish let out a loud growl and charged forward.

Viren easily sidestepped the blade and drove his fist into the man's solar plexus, knocking all the wind from him in one blow. The other men moved in but now Viren and Prow had their own blades drawn.

"Two to one, better odds than usual," Viren called to Prow, who sidestepped to avoid a lunge and took a knife in the chest. He and his attacker both looked at the spot where blood should be pooling, the tip of the blade firmly wedged in the deck of cards.

Viren wasn't so lucky, a wild slash opened up a cut on his shoulder and, as he backpedaled to avoid another attack, he tripped over Seg and crashed to the ground. "Be useful or get out of the way!" he barked at Seg's hunched form.

As he righted himself, Seg grabbed one of the attacker's ankles. There was a faint crackle. A moment later the man's arms flew out, his head snapped back, and he tumbled sideways to the ground. Seg scuttled backwards, propelling himself to his feet in time to back into another of Hudish's men, who raised a bottle and brought it down, grazing the side of Seg's head. The hit sent the Damiar back to the ground.

The man with the broken bottle lunged forward to finish Seg off but Viren caught him by the back of the collar and swung him into the stone wall of the Port House. His head connected with the wall with a solid THUNK and the man fell sideways like a sack of laundry.

Viren spun around, stepped onto Hudish's back, as he tried to raise himself off the ground, and ducked beneath the blade of another attacker as it arced toward him.

The tide was definitely turning in his favor, then someone in the crowd let out three shrill whistles.

"Constables!" Viren called out to Prow. Everyone stopped in place.

All except for Seg, who was on all fours, vomiting and coughing.

The crowd at the door shoved at one another to get back inside, Viren's attackers fled down the darkened street, dragging their wounded with them.

Prow jogged away, then looked back and saw Viren wasn't following him. "Viren, make wake!"

Viren looked down at Seg and shook his head. He was sure he had seen the man take down an attacker with no more than a touch. A trick of light most likely.

"Viren!" Prow called, more urgently.

If Lord Eraranat was what he claimed to be, he would be fine. The most the authorities would give a Dammie was a good *Tsk, tsk, tsk*. If he were lying, Correction for posing as one of his betters would be long and painful.

Out of my hands. Trouble with the local Judiciary was a risk he couldn't take.

"Cloud sniffers," he muttered, then ran.

Ama considered running back to Brin's but knew she would drop long before she reached him. And to wander around the streets of T'ueve was only to invite questions and problems with the patrolling constables.

But she had to find Seg. If he had woken early from the dose of furien, he wouldn't be thinking clearly. He would be a target both for the authorities and for the criminals and petty thieves of Wharfinger Block.

But at least there, in the Block, among the lowlife of T'ueve, she might find help locating him.

She took off down the dock at a trot, knife secured in its usual hiding spot. Hopefully, even under the fog of the drug, he would have the good sense to stay low and out of trouble.

Seg flopped onto his back as the Outers made their escape. He groaned, the starless sky spun, his stomach ached, his throat burned. The stim dose he had taken before leaving the *Naida* had probably been enough to prevent him from succumbing completely to whatever narcotic the whore had used to try and knock him out, but his thoughts remained blurry. He wished that scoundrel Viren had taken a knife for the trouble he had caused him.

A group of six constables came around the corner, stopped and surveyed the scene. Seg made no effort to move.

"Go on," one of the men gestured to the Port House doors with his weapon, some kind of black powder gun, "round up a few dock rats. Make a show of it." Three of the men entered the Port House, two stayed close by their leader, who kicked the bottom of Seg's boot. "They rob you?"

Seg laughed, which made him cough. "Those idiots couldn't rob a blind man. Now, help me up." He extended a shaking hand and marshaled what authoritative dignity he could in his condition.

The constable helped Seg to his feet. "You'll have to come back with us, even so. We'll need your signature and statement, the usual procedure."

"It was dark and I couldn't make out the faces," Seg said. He parted his hair to show the bloody welt the bottle had left on his head. "And they got to me quite early in their melee, which was with each other and not myself. I was simply caught in the press of the brawl. I'd be much happier returning to my charter, if we could come to some understanding on this."

The constable stared at Seg as if he was speaking another language. "I want faces, any faces. I want you to point out those faces and sign a declaration. Then I will let you clean up and go. Unless you have something to hide. Forgive me, I didn't get your name…" he looked upon Seg with new interest.

"Lord. Segkel. Eraranat." Seg said, biting off each word with emphasis. "I did not get yours, either." He was tiring of bullies of all flavors tonight, but bureaucratic bullies with whom he had some false rank? Those he could push back at.

"Eraranat?" The constable gave Seg a closer inspection. "I've never heard of that Line."

"I am from the south. Visiting for the Sky Ceremony."

"Where in…the south?" the constable squinted and he glanced back at his partners.

"Am I being interrogated?" Seg stood as straight as he could manage, and tucked his chin indignantly.

"You will be if you don't answer," the constable said. "Could be you're just a Kenda, dressed up. One of their tricks, in the Block."

"You insulting little…" Seg raised an accusing finger.

"Take him," the constable ordered his cohorts. They rounded on Seg, each grabbing an arm. Seg sputtered impotently, which the constable ignored. "Take him to Correction and find out who he really is."

"Lord Eraranat?" A voice called from nearby. A woman's voice.

Every head turned at once. Seg felt a rush, first of relief, then of indignation. Ama stood a short distance away; one hand casually resting behind her back, where he knew her knife was sheathed. Aside from her usual wariness, she was unharmed and in no danger he could see. Unlike himself.

"Captain," Seg said, the word clipped.

The constable turned to Ama, "Is he with you?"

"Yes," Ama said and paused for a moment, then continued, "Yes… and he's not well."

"Thanks to you," Seg snapped, as he strained against the men holding him.

The constable took a few steps closer, now sizing up Ama. "He's your partner?"

"My passenger," Ama answered, hand still behind her back.

The constable smirked, raised his weapon and pointed it at Ama's chest, "You expect me to believe you're a boat Captain?"

"I am," Ama said.

"She is," Seg added, a second behind her. "Among other things." He steadied his head long enough to give her a disdainful glare.

"I think you'll come with us too. We can all have a nice long chat." With the gun, he motioned for Ama to start walking.

"Please!" Ama raised both her hands, looked to Seg, then back at the constable. "I wasn't lying. Lord Eraranat isn't well. He caught borefly fever while hunting at his uncle's estate in M'eridia. He's come here for the Sky Ceremony, for a miracle to cure him. His family hired me as his guide but he slipped away while I was registering with the Port Captain. He has these...delusions, hallucinations. He forgets where he is. Please don't send him to Correction for my mistake. He's the primary inheritor of the Eraranat Line and his family will be furious if anything..." she paused the breathless rant and turned to Seg, "if anything *terrible* happens to him."

Seg didn't miss the significance of the look or the emphasis on the word. His eyes darted between her and the constables as he gathered his thoughts. "Is my uncle here?" he looked left and right, with a giddy smile.

Ama pointed to Seg's head. "Oh no, he's been injured!" When the constable looked away, she rushed to Seg's side. One hand raised to the swelling lump on his head, while the other discreetly tugged down on the sleeve of his coat that had risen up, exposing part of the stunner hidden below.

He picked up on her ruse. "It was nothing. You should see the others. A dozen of them, there were. They took your name for ill, but I took their honor and sent their manhood fleeing." He waved his arm in a grand gesture for the benefit of the constable. "Fleeing!" He stopped and studied the man intently. "Who are you?"

"Shhh," Ama said, smoothing her hand over Seg's hair. "Has he done something wrong constable? He really needs to get back and rest."

The constable frowned; it was clear he wasn't completely convinced.

Just then a loud smash echoed from the Port House, followed by a scream and the retort of a gun. The men holding Seg gave their leader a questioning look. The constable hesitated a moment then gestured toward the Port House; the men released Seg and hurried inside.

"Keep him away from the Block. I see either of you here again, you'll be locked up." More screams drew away his threatening stare and he left Seg and Ama behind, to see to the trouble inside.

"I will, thank you. Blessings of the Shasir upon you!" Ama called to the constable's back, then raised Seg's arm, draped it over her shoulder and led him away. When they were a good distance from the Port House, she hissed, "What in the name of the gods were you thinking?"

"Trying to find you." Accusation crept into his tone. "What did you do to me?"

"I just saved you from Correction, that's what I did."

"You drugged me."

"You really are delirious. You were exhausted. One minute you were talking, the next you were asleep in my arms," Ama said. Then she added, "You think I enjoyed carrying you below deck?"

"When I woke up, you were nowhere to be found." Like the constable, Seg was not entirely convinced.

"I had to register with the Port Captain, as always, then I ran into my cousin, Brin, who invited me for dinner. He lives out of the city, on the river, which is why I'm so late. I thought you'd still be sleeping."

Seg let out a small, *hmpf*, but the exhaustion Ama spoke of was real and was draining the fight from him. "All of this—brawls, con men, whores drugging me," he waved his free arm wildly, "your people are barbarians."

Ama's step faltered. "Whores drugging you?"

"Old trick. She had it on her lips," he mumbled as he ambled at her side. He waved a dismissive hand. "Let's get back to the *Naida* before I fall on my face."

"*Her lips?*" Ama said, her steps dragging as she shouldered Seg's weight. "Never mind, I don't want to know. Just don't wander off like that again, you could have gotten yourself killed."

The pitch of her voice rose and Seg detected a genuine note of concern. As if Ama had realized this as well, she added hastily, "And we have a deal. So don't expect me to help you if you're going to go looking for trouble."

They wandered through the maze of streets back to the dock, where the *Naida* beckoned, like an old friend.

"My girl," Ama muttered, as they tottered down the ramp and along the dock.

"Water craft are not alive," Seg said as they made their way up to the deck of the boat. "Wood and metal, there is no spirit within."

Or was there? He rested a hand on the wood rail and wondered what small amounts of vita her dedication to the craft may have imbued it with. Interesting theoretical question for when he didn't feel as though his head were coming apart at the seams.

"She's more than wood and metal. She's my home, and my companion," Ama said, slowing her pace as they approached the hatch. "When I'm at the helm, guiding her, I become a part of her. In that way, she's alive. You can learn the mechanics of sailing, you can learn about wind and tides and current, but you'll never be a true sailor until you put yourself into your boat, until you love her. No matter what your science says."

He grunted in dismissal of her romantic nonsense as he climbed down below. He was far more interested in his auto-med and his bed than her strange relationship with a large piece of wood.

Ama watched Seg make his unsteady descent. All his weight was to one side, he gripped the stair rail and half-slid to the bottom. "Crazy drexla," she muttered. She would hook up the boarding bell then join him below. A blanket over Manatu's bunk would do well enough for a bed.

"All just stupid rumors? Is that so?"

Ama spun at the sound of Geras's voice, and nearly lost her balance. He stepped from behind the helm, red faced, fists clenched.

"Were you…spying on me?" Her mouth hung open.

"I was coming back from the Terithe estate, saw this piece of garbage tied up here and thought perhaps my crazy sister had come to T'ueve for something important. I should drag you back to the Banks by your hair. Who's that Damiar that was draped all over you?"

He bulled forward as if he would go below, after Seg; Ama blocked his path.

"Leave it Geras!" She waited a moment for him to settle. "We'll talk another time, I'm too murked for this tonight."

As she climbed down the stairs, she heard Geras's footsteps behind her. Her molars came together. Why couldn't he leave her alone?

"I'm getting tired of people trespassing on my boat," she said, her back to her brother. "I have a charter," she sighed, and rotated to face him. "He's my paying passenger."

"Oh I'll bet he's paying." Geras strained to look past her.

"Then that would make two of us whoring to the Dammies."

Seg stepped out from his quarters, bleary eyed, "What is thi—"

Geras's open hand connected with Ama's face. The high-pitched WHAP reverberated through the small space; Ama let out a sharp gasp as she stumbled into the galley.

Without a word Seg sprung forward, rushed Geras into the bulkhead, seized him by the collar and slammed his head back.

"Seg! No!" Ama yelled.

Geras raised his fist, "Keep your dirty hands off my sister!"

"You're the savage who struck her," Seg spat back.

"Geras stop!" Ama sprung up from the floor and grabbed her brother's arm to stop his swing.

"Get him off this boat," Geras growled.

Ama kept her eyes on her brother and wedged herself between the two men. "Leave. Now."

"I want him out of here," Geras growled.

"You don't give orders on my boat." Ama pushed her hands against his chest. "Go, before you do something else you'll regret." She knew, from the way the corners of his mouth twitched, he could see the red mark on her cheek where he had slapped her. "Please," Ama added, her tone pleading. It wasn't her brother's fault; he didn't know what was at stake here.

Geras shrugged away from his sister. "You're turning your back on your family. I don't know you anymore."

"I don't think you ever did," she said.

"You're coming home."

"You don't control me Geras."

"Someone obviously has to," his eyes burned in Seg's direction. "I'll be back tomorrow. You'll pull anchor and set a course for the Banks or I'll tie you below and do it myself."

"I'm not going anywhere," Ama replied, her jaw clenched.

"We'll see about that." Geras straightened his coat, opened his mouth to speak to Seg, then shook his head, "Cloud sniffers, think you own everything." He thudded up the stairs and off the boat.

Ama waited until she was certain he was gone, then let out a breath, "I'm so sorry, my brother is—"

Seg's hands grasped her shoulders, his knees gave way and they both tilted back into the bulkhead as his weight transferred to her.

"Come on," Ama grunted, pushing him up, "you need sleep."

"Is he going to be a problem? Do we need to be concerned?"

Seg's voice came out in a long slur Ama could barely comprehend, as she dragged him the short distance back to his quarters. She was out of breath by the time she managed to heave him up onto the bed, and flopped down on her back beside him.

"Geras is all bluster," she panted, her arm draped over her forehead. "We've been fighting with each other since I was old enough to talk. Anyway, thank you for the misguided defense."

Seg's response was a rumbling snore.

"Well, that's settled." Ama's eyelids grew heavy, she let them close. Her chest rose and fell in time with Seg's, the effect was hypnotic. *Just rest here a moment,* she thought. *Just a moment.*

CHAPTER 9

Morning air brought a shiver to Seg's exposed skin. He moved closer to the warm body whose limbs were intertwined with his own, and nestled his face into the silky hair spread out around him. The body shifted and murmured and, though not fully awake, Seg was washed in a blissful calm. Even lost in the land that existed somewhere between dreaming and consciousness, he recognized this moment as rare and squeezed the body as if to prevent it from slipping away.

A low moan brought him a step closer to reality. The pain radiating out from his head, another step.

He opened his eyes. A set of pale grey eyes, only a nose length away, opened a moment behind his. Both sets of eyes blinked.

"This is…" Ama began.

She tried to roll away but Seg's arms held her tight.

"I didn't…"

He released his grip and rolled in the opposite direction.

"Must have passed out after moving you." Ama bolted upright.

Seg sat up with equal speed and groaned.

"My head." He raised his hand to the swollen lump on the side, sucking air through his teeth at the pain. "Auto-med…" he leaned forward, to push himself off the bed. "Water."

"I'll get… Rutting hell!"

"What?" Seg turned to see her squinting against the beam of light razoring through the porthole.

"We slept late!" She tripped out of the quarters, calling out instructions as she crashed her way through the belly of the boat. "We have to get ready for the temple. Get up. Get washed. I'll pick out your clothes. Fix your hair so that lump doesn't show. Where's that magic arm thing? The cartul and porters will be here soon…"

"The temple," Seg murmured, as Ama continued to chatter too loudly. He worked up some saliva and swallowed with a frown. His mouth tasted as if a small animal had crawled inside it and died. "Water…" He wished Ama would stop talking so she could hear his request.

What would he need for today's recon? VIU, digifilm, some small, concealable weaponry. They hadn't discussed protocols. How was he supposed to address her? Transportation? Ama had arranged that, he hoped. What else? Water, he needed water.

"Karg," he muttered, as he shuffled to his pack to find the auto-med among the spilled contents.

I'm about to embark on one of the most dangerous infiltrations executed in a generation and I can barely keep a single coherent thought in my head.

"Here," Ama appeared in the hatchway, cup in hand.

He chugged the water down, with an uncustomary feeling of gratitude.

"You look terrible." Ama snatched the cup back and disappeared again.

"Thank you," Seg said, and would have rolled his eyes if the motion weren't so painful.

As Jarin and his assistant approached, a pair of tattooed caj swung the large doors of House Haffset's Raid Planning Chamber inward, bowing low as they passed. Gleaming, burnished grafts nestled in the back of the men's shaven heads, fresh tattoo patterns swirled around the metal. Jarin spared the men a glance, out of professional curiosity, noting that the new patterns did not correspond well with the patterns that ran across their bare backs and torsos. Apparently Haffset was not of the naturalist persuasion.

The room was large and spacious horizontally, and was one of the few in the estate that bore a window to the outside, a strip of thick, hardened glass that ran nearly the length of the rear wall. Beneath the window, seats had been set up as an observer's gallery. The chairs could be pivoted for a view of either the perimeter of the shielded city or of the large, circular table below and the various substations around it provided for data recorders, assistants and the like. Major movements of the House were conducted here — the raids and petty internecine House conflicts that were the lifeblood and entertainment of a stagnant world. The appointments of the room were luxurious, designed to impress upon the visitor the growing wealth and power of the Haffsets. A sizable contingent of serving caj waited silently in the wings at refreshment stations, to provide any manner of food, drink, and mild intoxicants. At present, they stood at rigid attention, awaiting orders.

An ostentatious display, designed for public consumption. When actual militancy was required, the House had a similarly sized martial chamber without all the decoration, stripped to function. Jarin took that as a point in their favor, along with the lack of dancers and other distractions that some of the more decadent Houses favored. Haffset was a young and hungry House, formed within the past two centuries, and they were worthy of being held a House Ascendant. This raid would take them into the status of Major House, should it succeed. Should it fail...

He looked around once more.

Should it fail, the CWA would most likely leap in to assume the debt and seize House assets The House Accountancy gestured everyone to their seats. "Theorist Jarin Svestil and aide Mar Gelad," he announced. Jarin nodded to the assembled House and raider representatives as he made his way to his seat. Behind him, Gelad followed silently. Silver haired, with dark eyes that looked out from a pronounced brow, sweeping across the room and back, the practiced observation marked

Gelad as more than assistant. The large man was a former raider himself, a long-service veteran who now used his experience for a different kind of service to the Guild.

Jarin sat and accepted his digifilm from Gelad. "I believe everyone is here," he started.

"Apologies Theorist," the House Master interrupted, "as this entire process has been somewhat unortho, the CWA has requested to send a representative to sit on the pre-raid planning."

Jarin nodded and pretended to scroll through his digifilm as he processed this new piece of information. While the CWA was traditionally kept abreast of raids and raid planning, due to their control of warp gate access, it was unheard of for them to formally sit in on planning sessions.

"I see," he said as he paused the film and idled his presentation. "I do expect that they are curious as to what we are considering here."

"Director Adirante Fi Costk," the Accountancy announced as the door cycled open. Jarin's head snapped up before he composed himself and turned to look at the newcomer.

Five Directors comprised the Central Well Authority Trust Board, the top layer of management for the gargantuan agency. Each was a power in their own right, equivalent to the head of a Major House or conglomerate. For one of those Directors to deign to arrive at a planning meeting for a raid, one of a dozen raids in the Consideration and Planning phase at any given time, was more than unprecedented, it was a seismic event. Jarin pivoted his chair toward the newcomer as the man entered. Adirante Fi Costk, as always, made a production of his entry. In the sleek black dress uniform of the CWA, trimmed with silver to denote Director status, he cut a sharp figure against the sea of grey and beige. The well-built man offered a polite nod to the assembled.

"Citizens, thank you for this opportunity." He turned directly to look into Jarin's eyes and nodded once more, a more formal and deeper nod. "Jarin."

"Adi," Jarin answered, pivoting back in his chair.

Whatever the game had come to, the stakes were now significantly higher. Apparently the CWA was not content to simply watch and wait for their next target; Haffset was their unwitting and oblivious prey.

"If I could take some time, Theorist," Fi Costk said as Jarin ambled to the door at the close of the meeting. Jarin nodded to Gelad, who proceeded past him.

The Director had sat mute during the entire discussion, his expression sober and attentive. House Haffset was undoubtedly already privately calculating the losses they were going to take in the amount of unregistered material they would now be unable to bring back. Skimming goods from raids was a routine gambit, universally overlooked by the CWA. But with the Director of External Affairs now scrutinizing the proceedings, there was no way the Haffsets could take the risk. Though they had no idea what the true risk was here, yet.

"Interesting," Fi Costk said, "that your prize pupil's first mission lands on such a vita-rich world, while contracted to an ambitious House with a high risk tolerance."

Jarin nodded. "Fortuitous for him. His initial exercise could establish his career beyond reproach."

"Or destroy it. Though I doubt he finds many obstacles in his path. In the political sense," Fi Costk said.

Jarin turned a frosty gaze on him. "You should know me better than that, Adi. I smooth the path for no student. Coddling the weak does not serve the Guild or society."

"Coddle? No Jarin, I don't expect you've ever coddled anyone in your life," he tugged at one of his sleeves, then added, "other than the Outer."

Jarin gripped the edge of the table behind him, refusing to allow the jab of memory to show. "Then what was your implication, Director?"

"I imagine that events will flow smoothly as long as Eraranat carries out your vision," Fi Costk said as he turned to the door, "and when he doesn't, you will dispose of him as you have so many other tools. After all, his purpose here is to allow you to leverage more power for the Guild."

"And what is your purpose here, Adi?"

Fi Costk leveled his eyes on Jarin without blinking, "I'm here to make sure that you don't steal more than you can carry."

The door cycled behind Fi Costk. Jarin pulled his hand away from the table and stared at his fingers as he flexed them to restore circulation to his fingertips.

So, the stalemate was over. To be expected, he supposed, though in his grand scheme he had not foreseen his student participating in a venture worthy of Director Fi Costk's firsthand scrutiny so soon. As he had guided Segkel here, Jarin would have to carry out his part of the design as well.

Segkel had no idea just how complicated his mad vision was going to make things.

The *Naida* had never felt cramped to Ama until this morning. As she rushed through her preparations, she bumped into Seg at every turn. Each collision prompted either an awkward, mumbled explanation or an equally awkward silence.

Once she had chosen a set of appropriate clothes for Seg, from his wardrobe, and plucked out objects suitable for the expected offering, she set about the task she loathed most: taming her hair. Certainly, she would never pass for a real Lady but she managed to comb, twist and pin the locks into submission and something resembling a style.

Hair, as it turned out, was the least of her concerns. A good portion of her body was bruised and marked from the events of the past few days, most noticeably her face, thanks to Geras. Their plan relied on passing through the temple unnoticed; her battered body wasn't going to help with that.

Choice was not a consideration when it came to her attire. She owned only one set of fluffery.

She tugged the layers of silky fabric over her aching flesh. Luckily, the dress was long, which covered her legs, torso and part of her arms. The wide, silver nove she wore for formal occasions hid her dathe. Before leaving, she would be careful to hang her leather nove on the hook next to her mother's likeness. This still left her face and arms exposed.

Some sort of cover was needed; Ama frowned as she picked through a pile of charts, tools and rope.

"No time," she muttered, then looked down at the dress. She lifted the top layer, grabbed her knife and hacked off one of the lacy under layers. This she cut and fiddled with until she had something resembling a shawl and veil.

Up close, Stevan might notice the marks beneath the gauzy layer but it wasn't anything new to him to see his sister busted up from one of her crazy misadventures or Port House brawls. Hopefully, this homemade shift would make her somewhat less conspicuous.

She placed her knife on the stern bunk, then picked it up again. *Best to be prepared*, she thought, lifted her dress and strapped the weapon to her calf. She rolled her eyes as she picked up her dress shoes and squeezed her feet into them.

Last of all, she draped a silver chain around her neck. Dangling from the chain was a pendant. Inside the ornate cylinder was the furien she would use to knock out her brother, should she need to.

Ama picked her way through the boat, her steps made necessarily small by the restrictive garb. She started up the stairs then paused to double check that the padlocks were secured on the cargo locker. T'ueve wasn't some seedy northern port town crawling with thieves but Seg's mechanisms were too valuable to leave completely unprotected. Satisfied, she climbed to the upper deck.

In the distance, she spotted the cartul and porters waiting. Seg was at the bow, looking every bit the Lord. Ama gave him the formal bow of a Kenda to her future husband, almost tipping over in the process.

Seg smoothed a hand over his hair. Ama looked ridiculous in the fanciful dress of the planet. He had grown accustomed to her usual, more rough and ready appearance.

A sheer layer of fabric, covering her face, was lifted by the wind, revealing a red welt. His own wounds he had cleared up using the same device that had sealed the cuts on his arm and shoulder. He had not considered her various bumps and scrapes or the spectacle they would present, but then he had never needed to worry about the needs of another. And she had done well to look after herself and not jeopardize their cover.

"You return the bow like this," Ama said, then bent forward, hand open, palm facing upward, right forearm across the stomach, left arm mimicking the same motion, in reverse, behind her back. "Always keep your eyes on me, never lower them."

Seg performed the motion. The auto-med and a stim dose had cleared his head significantly. However, he would have to avoid any future brawls. Recon auto-meds were small, designed for short-term emergencies, and his was nearly depleted.

"Good," Ama said, once he was upright. "At the temple, with the Shasir, you bow like this." She repeated the motion but with both hands held in front, palms up, as if she were holding a platter, eyes directed to the ground.

"Level of gaze indicates relative status," he said, mostly to himself, then performed the bow. "Very common. And in a patriarchal society, such as this, a man would never lower his eyes from a woman, particularly one who is of a lower caste."

"If you mean I'm not as important as you because I'm a woman and a Kenda, yes. That's the general idea. And that means you'll have to deal with the driver and porters," she nodded in the direction of the waiting servants. "That part will be easy. The sky spooks have a lot more rules – I'll fill you in on the ride up." She stood back to appraise his appearance. "You've got the cavich backwards, hold still."

She leaned in to adjust the decorative band that hung over his left shoulder and his eyes moved to the silver neckpiece she wore.

"Do all of your kind have gills?"

Ama's fingers stopped. She spoke in a low voice, "You mean dathe? No. I've only known of one other Kenda who had them and…" she resumed her fussing. "They're very rare now, I may be the last to have them, for all I know."

"Unique," Seg said, his tone matter-of-fact.

"You can't speak of them," she warned, "to anyone."

"Are they…" A figure stalking down the dock caught his eye. "Your brother has returned," he said, his muscles tensed.

"Stupid, stubborn gresher," Ama grumbled, hiked up the dress and charged down to the dock to intercept Geras. Seg noticed the knife strapped to her calf; the corners of his mouth pulled up for a brief second as he followed behind her.

"What in the…" Geras stopped short, his eyes jumped between Ama and Seg, then settled on his sister. "What are you trying to pull now? I told you you're going home, putting on some fluffery isn't going to change that."

"And I told you not to give me orders," Ama crossed her arms over her chest.

Geras pointed to the *Naida*, "Go change out of that ridiculous dress and pull anchor."

"Or what?"

The two faced each other in silence, the wind plucking at the loose edges of Ama's dress and veil. Seg stood a pace behind Ama. It wasn't his concern but, by the Storm, this familial squabble was taking up a great deal of time.

"Move aside," Seg said to Geras, as he walked past him, his Damiar persona firmly in play. When he was on the other side of the man, he extended his hand. "Ama, we're leaving."

Ama hesitated a breath, then placed her hand in Seg's and let him draw her to his side.

Geras spun to face his sister. "You leave this dock, and I'm taking the *Naida* home myself. The minute I'm back at the Banks, I'll sell her for scrap."

Ama's mouth opened, she lunged forward but Seg held her back.

"Do so and I will see you sent to Correction for theft of my property," Seg said, his voice calm.

"Your property?" Geras looked from Seg to the boat, then laughed. "You expect me to believe you bought this junk heap?"

"Hardly. No, I expect you to believe I bought the captain of this junk heap. Your sister and I have an arrangement." He let go of Ama's hand and tugged down on the cuffs of his overcoat.

"You're lying." Geras's shoulders rose.

"He's not," Ama hooked her arm through Seg's. "I told him about the problems with my license and my family's threats. Lord Eraranat agreed to purchase the *Naida* and transfer ownership to his name, leaving me on as captain. And I agreed to be his wife."

"Wife?" The anger in Geras's eyes was overlaid with shock, and then suspicion. He spoke to Seg in a growl, "What do you want with her? She's only a Kenda."

"Who is soon to be the sister of a Shasir'threa." Seg paused to allow for the Outer's next outburst. When none occurred he continued. "The connection suits my needs, as a man of business. It also suits me to have a wife who is indebted to me, whose family has no power and therefore no authority over me, and who understands that I, as her better, will know absolute freedom within our union. Your sister, for all her shortcomings, is pragmatic and not prone to the sort of romantic nonsense that infects so many of your class."

Seg's words showed on Geras's face as if he had been lashed.

"You can't do this," Geras said to Ama, but there was no authority in his tone.

"Why not?" Ama's words were choked. "You sent Wirch Jorrett to me with the same proposal. Lord Eraranat's offer was simply a better one."

"Ama, I know you're angry but…"

"You all wanted me on a leash," she spat out the words. "You're only angry because I've chosen who will hold that leash."

Geras was reduced to silence once more.

"We have to leave," Ama said, eyes on the boards of the dock. She slid her arm out from Seg's and walked to the waiting cartul.

"I won't let you take her from her family," Geras said to Seg, once they were alone. "I don't care who you are."

Seg surveyed the overly emotional man in front of him and wondered if all the Kenda were as irrationally devoted and passionate as the specimens he had encountered so far. "You are very loyal," he commented and dissected Geras with his gaze. A seed of an idea planted itself inside him. "Under different circumstances, this would be useful."

Consumed by new possibilities, Seg ambled away.

The temple came into view long before they arrived at the front gates. High stone walls surrounded the temple grounds on three sides. On the fourth side was nothing but cliff, where the river plummeted down to a large, frothy pool below.

Through the cartul window, Seg watched the temple grow larger. Impressive. The People didn't go in for grand, inspiring architecture. The inhabited portions of the World were largely functional, etched in stone and built from the recycled materials of nearly a thousand years and more of careful re-use. Defense against the Storm was a must, as well as from those who had gone rogue to the wasteland, and roaming bands of escaped caj. Precious water was not allowed to flow down cliffs, uncollected.

He didn't look forward to the next part of the journey, to his deferential act before these lowly Outers who thought themselves kings, but he was a pragmatic man, and this was his best opportunity for a very well-targeted raid.

He covertly checked the micro-chack concealed beneath his overcoat and turned his eyes to the tactical aspects of the area. Though he was not schooled in military theory as a raider, a Theorist had to be versed enough to be able to select attainable targets.

The first thing that struck him was the Shasir's misguided confidence in their ability to control the vertical dimension. The walls were formidable, but only designed to hold off raging peasant mobs or reasonably well-organized foot soldiers. A vertical attack played to the strengths of raider organization, which operated heavily through the use of vertical take-off/landing craft and could bypass the defenses to be in amidst the Outers before they even knew what was happening. A single squadron of fighters could make short work of Shasir airpower, and aerial drones could handle local fire support.

The Welf attendants would make good caj, those who survived. The Shasir would probably fetch a pretty price as well – many Houses collected such pampered creatures to delight in the pompous mighty brought low. His only concern was vita, but sponsors expected reports on all aspects of a raid.

Those were details to consider once all the mission data had been collected. Right now, he allowed himself to be led to the gates of the temple. He analyzed the structure before him.

In a pinch, the wall could be brought down with sufficiently powerful demolition charges. A direct approach would be costly but those were details for more military minded men than himself.

As he considered his tactical options, he maintained a light chatter with Ama.

Storm but he felt alive at this moment. He glanced at her, his one companion on a hostile world; the corners of his mouth pulled upward.

The lacquered wood floor in the office of T'ueve's Port Captain was worn thin from the daily passage of boots over its surface. Today the office was unnaturally silent, the heavy door closed for the first time since Port Captain Priot could remember. Head Constable Dagga's imposing frame, along with two local constables, filled much of the space. As the Port Captain passed the main manifest to Dagga, he studied the man's face.

He had never seen Dagga in person before today, but his story had been whispered in every Port House from the Rift Tribu to the tip of Malvid. The scars on his head weren't nearly as gruesome as Priot had heard told. However, he had witnessed the execution of one of the six Kenda who had given Dagga those scars—a man relentlessly hunted by the constable for over two years—and that man's suffering needed no exaggeration.

"Registered yesterday?" Dagga asked, not raising his eyes from the list of names in his hands.

"Yes, Head Constable, I registered her myself. I only received the Notice of Correction this morning or I would have summoned the constables earlier." He was telling the truth; he didn't need any grief from the authorities, he already got plenty of that as it was.

"And now?" Dagga raised his eyes to meet those of the wizened Port Captain, his meaning clear. He knew very well that the man kept ears and eyes on the docks at all time.

"She hired a cartul and driver; she and her passenger are on their way to the Sky Temple."

Dagga pulled his blade from its sheath and turned to the constable on his left, "I want a squad ready to leave for the Sky Temple, heavily armed. Set a guard detail on that boat. Now!"

The Port Captain blanched.

Dagga shoved the manifest back into the man's hand and pointed the tip of the blade between his eyes. "I hear one word of this on the docks, you'll be strung up and torn along with the traitors. Same for any water rat that helps 'em."

Port Captain Priot didn't reply and knew he wasn't expected to. When Dagga was gone, his eyes dropped down to the manifest. He read and re-read the entry.

Vessel: Naida

Captain: Amadahy Kalder

Crew: None

Passengers: One

He said a silent prayer to Nen, though he knew, with Dagga hunting her, Captain Kalder's life was already ended.

The cartul slowed to a stop as it pulled up to the front gate of the temple entrance. Ama straightened her dress and the veil covering her face.

Seg offered her a polite smile. In return, she gave a smile and nod of her own.

Four armed guards were stationed out front. The porters carried the trunk, containing their offering, to the guards for inspection. Because it would be an insult to look through the offering before their eyes, Seg and Ama remained in the cartul. When the contents were cleared, the driver dismounted and opened the cartul door. Ama waited for Seg to offer his hand, then descended to the earth.

Even without formal shoes on, she didn't figure she could ever get used to living on a surface that didn't move beneath her.

Rigid and unmoving, the Temple Keeper could have passed for one of the stone statues that adorned the temple entrance. Seg approached him, gave the formal bow she had shown him, raised his palms skyward in respect and made their request for an audience with Stevan. Ama waited next to the cartul, holding her breath.

If the Temple Keeper raised his right arm, they were in. If his left arm went up, they would be trekking back to the *Naida* empty handed.

This would be her only opportunity to get her brother away to safety.

Please let Seg be convincing.

Ama had told him this would be the first real test of their disguises. Seg steeled himself for it and reasoned that a certain amount of nervousness would be expected in one used to being deferred to but who now had to defer to the highest authority.

The Temple Keeper was draped in layer upon layer of blue robes, which made him look like a miniature ocean. Atop his head, a heavy, bell-shaped hat reached toward the sky. His movements were slow and methodical, which to believers must have appeared regal but, in reality, were obviously necessitated by the cumbersome wardrobe.

This was Seg's first dealing with the Shasir apart from the one the squad had captured. Useless creatures. If he were following an ortho path, he would never have excluded the Kenda from his target profile; they were clearly the most worthy Outers of the bunch. But caj were secondary to vita, and the Welf would make adequate labor stock.

He was careful not to show any contempt on his face and strove to appear humble. There was a long, long moment, before the Temple Keeper gave his answer. Seg was tempted to simply shoot him. At last, the man raised his right arm.

Seg relaxed ever so slightly and made the proper sign of deference before he turned and gestured to Ama to come to his side.

One test passed. He didn't even pause to relish it as he applied his mind to the next trial.

The trunk was hefted by the porters and carried off in a separate direction. As they walked along the neatly trimmed paths, Ama's fingers dug into his offered arm. He glanced down and saw her eyes surveying the geography in a methodical sweep. *Scouting, as any good navigator would,* he mused.

The temple was a sprawling structure. Three levels high, with spires that stretched further skyward, Stevan's sanctuary, according to Ama, would be on the second level. Their Shasir escort led them up a set of smooth, stone stairs and along a covered walkway, facing the cliff. Over the edge of the cliff, above the waterfall, was a long, curved platform, which he recognized, from the Shasir data he had read, as a stage used for various ceremonies. He couldn't help comparing it to the Killing Cliff of Alisir and wondered if any unfortunate souls had met their end by being herded over the steep drop. The wind was picking up; he could smell the water of the falls.

They were taken to a small library and offered seats to relax in while Stevan—or Shasir'dua Kalder, as he would have to be addressed—received word of their arrival and prepared for the blessing.

As Seg helped her into her chair, Ama flashed him a brief look, a shared message he understood clearly: *I despise these old men and their ceremony.*

Then they waited. As she had warned him, nothing happened quickly in the world of the Shasir.

Seg had plenty to occupy him. The books around him, for starters. He understood that many societies regarded paper as a disposable trifle, but it boggled his mind to be surrounded by such a casual display of splendor. During his training, he hadn't been allowed to use paper for anything until his final year. Those final projects and reports, written on the crudest of rough processed huchack fiber, became a part of the graduate record of a Theorist, forming the beginnings of their documented careers.

His own small collection of paper books was perhaps his only treasured possession. But his pitiful collection was nothing compared to the wealth on the three walls around him, a mere grain of sand in a windstorm. Someday, though, his collection would be large, larger even than this one.

More importantly, however, there were the vita readings to consider.

He arranged his hands so he could stare at the digifilm in his palm, to ensure the readings were being gathered properly. He had a deep desire to physically follow the readings, as he had at the Welf temple, but his movements here were controlled and observed. He would have to content himself with this until he and Ama made their break.

So far, though, he didn't like what he was seeing. The readings were surprisingly low for being in such a 'holy place'.

Vita levels increased both with the significance of the object or person, and the number of worshippers/admirers. It was not unheard of for cynical religious manipulators to produce disappointing crops of vita, but he had hoped here that the residuals from outside devotees would raise the levels into sufficiency.

Then again, a negative result could be just as useful as a positive. It was also important to remember that the results were only disappointing for this overly rich world; on other worlds, such readings would indicate a prime target.

He had to admit that part of his eagerness stemmed from a desire to grind the Shasir down, but if they weren't the ideal target he couldn't allow such emotional considerations into the equation. Besides, they would suffer enough in the raid, even if their prime temple didn't make the cut as a target.

Ama's elbow, nudging his, broke Seg away from his thoughts. When he turned his eyes to her, she gestured to a light fixture on the wall. "How does that magic work?" she whispered.

The glowing bulb was covered by a globe of intricately designed glass laid out in a mosaic; all shades of blue, reflecting the Shasir's reverence for their sky. "Electricity," Seg muttered, under his breath.

"What's that?" she whispered.

He paused to consider an easy explanation. She might understand the theory if he explained it in detail, she wasn't stupid, but now was neither the time nor place to give such a lengthy lesson.

"You know the lightning bolts in thunderstorms?"

"Yes."

"Well, electricity is just a scientific means by which you can control and contain the lightning."

"There's lightning inside of that?" she nodded to the light again.

"In a manner of speaking."

"How does it—"

Ama's whispered question was interrupted by the reappearance of their escort. "The Shasir'dua is ready for you."

After the requisite bows and gestures were exchanged, they walked down a long hall. A series of ornately carved wooden doors dotted the length of both sides, interrupted by the occasional nondescript door that almost blended in with the wall. Ama was struck by the silence. She knew, from Stevan's descriptions, that hundreds of Shasir lived here, with an army of Welf to serve them, but the temple was so quiet it felt deserted. The escort stopped in front of a door, opened it and gestured for Ama and Seg to enter.

Stevan's sanctuary was larger than she had imagined. It was basically one square, open room, with a series of wide pillars on either side and a heavy curtain across the end, covering his sleeping and bathing area. Furniture was sparse, though tables held bits of Shasir 'magic' and there were shelves full of books. Her brother Stevan stood in the center of it all, dressed in ceremonial robes and a tall hat that seemed to swallow his head. She was seized with an urge to run and tackle him, swipe the silly hat off his head and make him chase her to get it back, as she might have done when they were children.

They were not children anymore.

Seg bowed first, palms upward, eyes down, as he had been shown; Stevan returned the gesture, then it was Ama's turn. When Stevan reciprocated, they walked to the holy man, as their escort slipped away silently. This was the first time she had seen Stevan in this environment and Ama found his emotionless stare and cool demeanor disturbing.

"Lord Eraranat, you have effectively dispelled a myth too long held by the Kalder family," Stevan said, not casting so much as a sideways glance to Ama.

"Your holiness?" Seg asked – with the perfect amount of humility in his voice.

Stevan held his hands out in front of him, fingers spread and tips pressed together to form a wide triangle. "We have long assumed that Amadahy refused her many suitable offers of marriage due to a flaw in her character, an unwillingness to conform, if you will."

Ama felt her molars grind at Stevan's pompous speech and the way he spoke as if she weren't standing right in front of him.

"However, by her agreement to form a union with yourself, a Damiar Lord, we must now concede that her perceived selfishness was, in reality, a choice to save herself for a more worthy mate. In this instance, I am most grateful to be proved incorrect." He inclined his head slightly at Seg, then raised both palms skyward and added, "Praise to the Shasir'kia, our most revered Sky Fathers."

"Unfortunately, as joyful as I am regarding this union," he continued, "I must request your patience somewhat further and ask you, Lord Erananat, to return to the waiting hall, temporarily. There are important family matters I must relate to my sister before the blessing can proceed."

What could Stevan be talking about? Ama wondered. *Important family matters?*

This was definitely not normal. It was, however, the opportunity they needed. Stevan's lectures were infamously drawn out and Ama knew how to provoke him into even longer discourse, if necessary.

Seg bowed and agreed to step out of the room. When he was almost at the door, Ama said, "Excuse me, Shasir'dua," walked quickly to Seg's side, placed a hand on his arm and kissed his cheek, through her veil. Before she pulled away, she brushed her lips close to his ear and whispered, "Go now, I'll keep him busy."

The nearly imperceptible shift in Seg's gaze, told her he had understood.

Her action had been risky but Stevan would hardly be surprised at his sister behaving rudely. She dipped her head and shuffled back to her place, feigning embarrassment.

Seg exited and she steeled herself for the volumes of lectures she was about to have heaped upon her. Explicit directions on how a Damiar wife should behave and stern warnings regarding the consequences, for herself and Stevan, should she fail to uphold her wifely duties.

Stevan looked at the door, then around the room, and when he was satisfied they were alone, he grabbed the flesh of Ama's arm, just above the elbow and dragged her to the far corner, behind the heavy curtain.

She gasped as he gripped her by the shoulders, locked a set of angry eyes on hers and hissed in a barely contained whisper, "What in the name of Nen do you think you're doing?" She was too shocked by her brother's use of the Kenda title *Nen*, to answer. "Do you have any idea how dangerous that man is?"

Behind her veil, her mouth fell open.

Stealth, Seg understood, was in large part of a matter of mindset. Even the conspicuous can be hidden in plain sight with the proper motions and mentality. Look unobtrusive. Look as though one belongs.

As he walked down the corridor, Seg lowered his shoulders, decreasing his profile. He added briskness to his pace that suggested he had somewhere to be. Where appropriate, with the lower orders, he met gazes and immediately gave them a visual brush-off, as if to suggest that he was in a hurry and merely marking his path against obstacles. When he encountered Shasir functionaries, he made way politely and slowed down in order to respect his betters.

It wasn't the gilded bowls and statues that the Shasir treasured. While the artifacts had measurable quantities of vita, the readings were not in keeping with a holy place. But Seg knew that, at the very least, the Shasir the troopers had captured believed large portions of the nonsense they delivered to the masses. As such, there would be wellsprings somewhere within.

A technoshamanic society, one that believed their technology was, at some level, magical. He had to find their technobaubles, or get into their vicinity. Armory? Perhaps, but their weaponry wasn't very compelling. Hangars for the airships? Probably. Most certainly their communications arrays.

The airships would be easy enough, and plausible enough, to search for. After all, mastery of the sky would impress the nobility, and serve as a clear caste demarcation between Shasir and Damiar. Better still, it would involve a clearing from which he could likely locate the communications arrays.

He pulled a servant aside to make a quick inquiry and proceeded on his way.

The landing strip was busy. Garish, ornamental airships were tied-off at various moorings and as he watched another one was guided in.

Yes, these were better readings. The airships themselves were worthy objects, though a more comprehensive calculation was needed to ensure that the volume of material sent through the warp would justify the expenditure of the intrans.

He was only allowed within about two hundred meters of the landing area but it was close enough. Reaching into his left sleeve, he extended the spidered directional antenna for the VIU, then raised a hand as if to shield his eyes from the sun.

He blinked. The directional antenna had, by necessity, an extremely tight range of focus, and something had blipped it prior to being pointed at the airship. He tilted his head down, self-consciously wondering if he looked the fool, as he tried to pick up whatever gave the blip.

The blip came again; he narrowed his eyes and studied what seemed to be the source.

The airship mooring posts. The battered, old, un-ornamented mooring posts. Something about them was producing vita in an up-funnel effect.

He closed the antenna and maneuvered for a better look.

Each post had a basket in front of it. There was something significant there. Maybe when they extracted Ama's brother, he could explain their origins and meanings.

He made a thorough circuit of the field, playing the tourist, then proceeded toward the communication arrays.

Ama gaped at her brother. Dangerous? What did Stevan know about Seg? Had his cover been blown somewhere in his travels?

"Stevan, he's just a Damiar, from the—"

"Just a *Damiar*, exactly. You don't find anything strange in that?"

Stevan was as agitated as she had ever seen him. His controlled manner of speaking, his usual verbosity, were gone.

"You need to calm down," Ama said, hoping her measured tone might do the trick, "and explain why you're panicking just because I've chosen to marry above my class."

Puzzled, she watched her brother pace in a small circle, then pull the ridiculous hat off his head. "These are dangerous days, Tadpole," he said, in a low voice, as he drew close to her.

He hadn't called her Tadpole since... She couldn't remember that he had ever called her by her nickname.

"Stevan," she placed a gentle hand on his shoulder, "talk to me. I'm your sister. You can trust me."

"They have spies everywhere," he answered, casting his eyes skyward to indicate the Shasir'threa that lived aboard the skyships. "Looking for treason. It's no coincidence you were courted by a Damiar. One of the Shasir'threa has gone missing from the Ymira valley; they suspect he was kidnapped or even murdered. His guards were found dead, without a mark on their bodies. No one had access to the man except the guards and other Shasir, so naturally—"

"They suspect someone on the inside," Ama nodded, "and of course they'll look at all the members of the order who are Kenda."

Stevan smiled, "You should have stayed in the Lesson House, you know. You're too smart to spend your life ferrying Dammies around."

"I know Seg's not a spy," she said, even though it wasn't technically true. "But even if he were, what do you have to worry about? You've always been an ideal student and a loyal Shasir."

Stevan lowered his eyes and took a deep breath. He pressed his face close to Ama's and whispered in her ear, in the secret language of the Kenda, "Blood for water".

When they parted, Ama was speechless. Those were the long-dead words of the Kenda Resistance.

Her brother was a traitor.

As Seg had suspected, the communications arrays were covered with gaudy bric a brac and devotional offerings. Fortunately, that made access easier than it might have been otherwise. These Outers thought of their comms as conduits to the gods and treated them with appropriate reverence.

He wouldn't be at all surprised to find that the 'communing with the gods' they claimed to do was in reality only their interpretation of random static intercepted from the radio frequencies. It would be in keeping with their ignorance of their own technology and with their mystic bent.

He couldn't be too critical in that regard, though. Much of the People's technology, such as the chatterers that let them translate other languages, was barely understood, if comprehended at all. Where the principles and the equipment could be assimilated they were, but oftentimes only the raw technology itself could be stolen away. Sometimes, as with the chatterers, the technologists could figure out how to effectively and efficiently replicate it and the technology would proliferate. Other times, they could duplicate items but only at prohibitive expense, and such ventures were abandoned to avoid waste. Finally, there were times when they simply had to write off captured material as unusable, unsalvageable, or worst of all, with indiscernible purposes. Their own pace of invention was haltingly slow, and almost always derived from technology acquired during raids.

But at least the People were pragmatic about the wonders of science.

He resumed sweeping.

All that existed between Ama and her brother was the weight of Stevan's words. When at last Ama found her voice, it was colored with both awe and fear. "How long?" was all she said.

"Always," he answered, looking suddenly tired and small beneath his robes.

"I don't understand..." she pulled off the veil and shawl covering her, as if doing so might give her thoughts clarity.

"By Nen!" Stevan gasped, "What happened to you? Did that Damiar...?"

She had grown so used to the sensation of the welt that she had forgotten how alarming it would appear to her brother. Calling forth her best 'Are you kidding?' expression, she waved off Stevan's concern. "A small tussle, nothing to worry about. You know how things can get in the Port House."

He did know. She had counted on that and thanked her wild ways for the cover.

"Tell me about...everything," Ama continued, out of genuine concern for her brother but also to give Seg as much time as she could.

In hushed tones and with frequent looks to the door, Stevan told her his hidden history. The resistance had never died; it had been broken, scattered and pushed into far corners but remnants survived. Lacking numbers and Shasir magic, they had used their intellect; devised plans to span generations. A gradual infiltration of the Shasir, the acquisition of their magic and secrets, the formation of a complex network of communications and transportation, all leading to the eventual overthrow of the Shasir ruling class.

Stevan's sharp mind and sober nature had caught the attention of the Lesson House instructor, himself a member of the resistance. From there, it was only a matter of moving the boy up the chain. No Kenda had yet made Shasir'threa. Stevan was their great hope.

"I didn't lecture you all those times because I disapproved of your life," Stevan said, taking Ama's hand in his. "We need my ascension. I couldn't risk expulsion because my sister likes to get into..." he rubbed one of the bruises on her forearm, "*tussles*."

Lectures, yes. Stevan had given her a fair share of those, as had her father lately.

"Fa!" Ama's knees weakened and she nearly fell backwards as she sat against the edge of a table, "Oh Stevan, did Fa know?"

"Not until recently. I arranged for Brin to pass a message for me. It was necessary; there were discussions of my family among my superiors. Your name was mentioned. Repeatedly." He knelt down in front of her, taking up her hands again, "I'm sorry Ama, I'm sure he was hard on you but it was for a higher cause."

"And our brothers? Did they know?"

"Only Geras. And telling him and Fa was risk enough," Stevan answered.

She bit down on her lower lip. "If I didn't marry, I was told I had to sell my *Naida* and move home. Fa threatened to cut me from the family if I didn't obey him. And Geras..." she let out a sharp gust of air, "I think he may never speak to me again."

"Tell me you're not marrying this Lord Eraranat out of desperation?" Stevan asked, squeezing Ama's hands.

"No, it's my choice to be with him," she said, tempted to explain she wasn't marrying him at all.

Stevan didn't answer, merely hung his head.

"I've been so selfish," Ama said, placing her hands on either side of Stevan's head and tilting it back up to face her. "Stevan..." What could she tell him? That all his years of struggle and sacrifice were now for naught? That there was a greater threat out there, one not even he could conceive of? "The Shasir will fall, I believe that."

"As did I, once," he answered, standing again. "They've started sniffing us out, though. And now, since this Shasir'threa has gone missing..."

"Leave with me," she blurted out. "Seg and I will get you out of here."

"Leave?" The word was uttered with disbelief but followed by an affectionate laugh. "Of course. My sister, who charges headlong into everything, of course that is what you would do. I've always envied that about you." He sighed. "A Shasir'dua, privy to the secrets of the order, can't just walk out the door."

Ama grabbed him by both wrists and squeezed, her eyes locked with his, "Seg isn't a Damiar. His people have magic that make the

Shasir look as backward as the Welf. There's no time to explain, but if you stay here you'll die, along with the rest of the spooks. The Shasir will fall. Not in some far away future. *Soon*. You have to leave. Now."

Her eyes repeated the warning, her hands refused to let him pull away. A metallic chime came from somewhere outside the walls, the vibration added to the electricity in the room.

"You're serious." His voice was hushed. "There's..." he dipped his chin in thought, "there's a passage, it's on the other side of the grounds, beneath the meditation chambers. I can go through but you..."

The chime sounded again and Stevan tugged away from Ama to peer out the small window overlooking the grounds.

"What is it?" Ama asked.

"A warning," he answered. "The chime is an order for all Dua to stay in their sanctuary. It means—"

"Bad trouble," Ama said, now at the window, next to her brother. One hand absently gripped his robe as she watched a squadron of constables piling through the gates. "I have to get you out of here."

Stevan shook his head, "No, no. They wouldn't send constables for me. The Order has their own methods, their own enforcers. They must be after someone—" He turned his face slowly to Ama.

Her hand dropped from his robe.

Seg had made a good circuit of what he could access readily. Deeper penetration at this point would risk compromising the data he had already acquired. The target plan could be revised, while keeping the Sky Temple in it. With the lower than expected vita readings, the temple wouldn't be assigned the same priority as before but he could incorporate it as a bluff because most of the items that required lifting were man-portable, and he could easily arrange a heavy coverage raid that would lure whatever constituted the Shasir ready defense. Then they would make the real hauls elsewhere.

Visions whirled in his mind, as his planned strike grew more ornate and complex.

He knew well that the House would likely try to cut back or not implement the totality of his vision. If it went wrong, madness. House Haffset would be broken and swept away.

He had to hope they had enough gamblers' impulse to pursue this.

Shoes off, dress hauled up, Ama ran through the empty corridor beside her brother. Muted footballs from behind spurred them forward.

"The skyship platform, the offering hall, the room of communing…" Stevan breathlessly rattled off areas of worship or importance within the temple grounds as he ran. "There are dozens, your Seg could be anywhere."

The distant footfalls were getting louder.

"You get to the passage," Stevan huffed, "it's at the far east corner, beneath the fourth chamber. Look for…" he paused for air, "two diagonal scratches on the floor, that board lifts up and there's a handle beneath."

"I'm not leaving Seg behind."

"And I'm not leaving you to the authorities. I'll find him, I'll get him out."

They skidded around a corner, into a wide, round atrium, both stopping at once. Before them, Dagga stood, flanked by four armed constables. Ama looked behind her but two more constables moved together to block their only exit.

"Rats always run. Lucky I know how to herd 'em." Dagga said, with a smirk that possessed no good humour. He pointed his blade at Ama, "Murdering a Lord, that's bold, even for a Kalder."

Stevan raised his hands and reassumed his stately air, even though his face was beaded with sweat, "Constable, I assure you, my sister is no criminal. Whatever you believe she has—"

"Where's your partner?" Dagga ignored Stevan. He strode forward until he stood less than an arm's length from Ama.

She snapped her mouth closed, forcing her gasping breaths through her nose.

"Don't matter, I'll find out soon enough," Dagga said, then raised his arm and drove the heavy knife into Stevan's shoulder.

"Stevan!" Ama reached for her brother as he staggered backward, a long scream tearing from his throat. Stevan clutched at the protruding hilt while blood darkened his robes. Ama's fingers pressed uselessly against the wound, in seconds they were slick and red.

"Where's your partner?" Dagga repeated.

"I don't know!" Ama wailed.

Dagga, his face unmoved by the spectacle, studied Ama dispassionately then nodded. "Not lying, are you?" He turned sharply and marched back to the constables. "Bring them both. Leave the Dua with his own, tie the water rat up somewhere this Eraranat can hear her screams."

A guttural cry sounded from Stevan as he lunged at Dagga's back.

The moment unfolded for Ama in a series of sounds: the sharp retort of the banger, Stevan's body thudding to the stone floor, the clatter of the boots that rushed to where she stood, and her own primal scream as she pulled her knife from its sheath and slashed at the first body in her path.

"NO!" she yelled, as she ran to her brother's side. A second banger shot cracked open the air. She felt a hard, hot blow to her shoulder and her feet slid out from under her.

Only her rage kept her conscious.

As Seg was about to round a corner and re-enter the building that housed Stevan's sanctuary, a loud BANG ruptured the silence of the temple. He knew the sound. Weapons familiarization included primitive Outer weapons, such as burning-powder projectile implements. Around the corner, he spied two men in the blue and white uniforms of the local enforcers. Then he heard Ama scream.

This was different from the night with Uval and his goons, when he was tired, half-worn out and in a stimulant-induced stupor. His blood iced as he considered his options.

Retreat? He could. His equipment, left aboard Ama's boat, was the only complication.

This was why Theorists weren't supposed to infiltrate without support. It would have been nice to have Kerbin and her squad of cutthroats ready to rain the Storm down upon these Outers. A Theorist was too valuable to risk in a foolhardy venture. This was a job for an expendable trooper, such as Manatu.

As he produced the micro-chack from his coat pocket, he decided he would just have to not die. One of the enforcers saw him coming and opened his mouth for some pompous proclamation, likely an order for him to halt or surrender.

The fool should have simply shot him, or at least covered him with a weapon.

The micro-chack was near silent, its electromagnetic impeller inducing a slight whir as thousands of small venom-laced huchack slivers tore into and through the man's body.

The gurgling screams were not so quiet. Seg turned and unleashed another stream, cutting down a second enforcer before the man could raise his weapon.

The outside presence was eliminated. He dipped his hand into the pocket again and pulled out two micro-grenades. Now to see what waited for him behind the door.

If they've killed her, I'll burn every last hole on this planet.

CHAPTER 10

The pain, spreading from her shoulder outward, was like none Ama imagined possible. Smoke choked her and the infernal dress allowed her no freedom to maneuver. The sight of her brother, lying in a quickly spreading pool of crimson, kept her moving as she shuffled across the slippery floor to escape her attackers.

One of the constables grabbed a handful of her hair and pulled. With her good arm, Ama swung her knife up into the man's groin. She twisted the blade, felt the resistance of his flesh before yanking it back out, and savored the man's scream and the hot blood that sprayed her hand.

These men who hurt Stevan; they were going to pay.

Before she could make another move, ear-piercing bangs and flickering strobes of harsh, actinic light filled the room.

"Ama!" she heard above the din, and turned to see Seg standing inside the door. "Out!"

She hesitated. Seg fired a small, strange looking banger at one of the constables and ducked behind a pillar.

"NOW!" he yelled.

Ama scrambled to her feet, ducked forward and headed in the direction of the door. An explosion followed close enough behind to lift the bottom of her dress.

She pressed her back to the wall outside of the atrium, to hold herself up and to watch for more constables.

Seg appeared momentarily then charged back inside. Shortly after, she heard banger fire, the crash of glass and several screams. She prayed one of those screams belonged to Dagga.

With her left hand, weakened by the shot to her shoulder, she held the material of her dress while with her right hand she hacked the dress off at the waist. One problem solved.

Then she heard voices from another direction. And the heavy approach of boots. Lots of boots.

Bad trouble.

They had to get out of the temple. But then what?

The front gates would now be locked and guarded. There was the secret passage at the east end. But if anything went wrong, if they couldn't find it, if the authorities followed too quickly, they would be penned in. Trapped.

They had to run for the passage, there was no other way.

"Seg!" she yelled through the open door, "We've got company!"

He appeared out of the smoke and confusion, tattered overcoat flapping behind him, the strange weapon clutched in his hands.

With one hand, he pulled a black disk from the device, threw it to the floor and replaced it with another. "How many?"

"Too many," Ama answered, breathing heavily as she split her attention between Seg and the distant voices. "There's a hidden passage," she said, fixed her eyes on his and hoped he understood the message behind them. "Follow me!" she ordered and took off across the open walkway at a sprint.

He followed, seeding the area behind them with more of his devices, which bellowed clouds of smoke.

At the top of a set of stairs leading below, he caught up with her.

"Wait!" she shouted, as he was about to overtake her. She pointed to the lowest level, where more armed constables filled the stairwell.

Her head swiveled left then right. "This way," she ordered, backtracking.

She zigged left abruptly, before the entrance to the atrium, coughing at the smoke that filled the air.

At a nondescript door, similar to those she had noted during their escorted walk, she slid to a stop.

She tugged at the handle. Locked. Damn. The smokey cover gave them some time and she bolted to the next plain door. She hoped Stevan's detailed description of the temple had been accurate.

Stevan. She wiped his name from her mind.

At full speed, she almost missed her target and skidded to a halt just past it.

Please, please, please, she prayed as she reached for the handle. The door stuck fast, then there was a small *click* and it gave way and swung open. At that same moment there was another sound, from the walkway.

"Halt!" A constable barked.

She and Seg ducked inside a half second before another banger blast ricocheted behind them. The staircase was tight and steep, no need for grandeur for the Welf servants who traveled these hidden corridors.

Gravity helped speed their escape. Ama had no idea where they would come out, she would deal with that when they got there. All she knew was they would never make it to the meditation chambers.

Behind them, one of the constables shouted, "They're heading for the main level."

The stairs ended, a short pathway led to another door and she charged toward it, Seg right on her heels.

A group of Welf leapt up in surprise as the fugitives burst into their midst. This was obviously a service area, dishes and linens were stacked on shelves, servants were scattered about the room.

Ama scanned the area. There was a door leading outside. She ignored the servants, bolted for the exit and flung it open. Fresh air on her face was a relief.

One quick circle gave Ama her bearings and she pointed to a narrow path, leading to a high hedge. "This way," she called to Seg, panting from exertion, and ran.

By the time they reached the hedge, the voices of the authorities were behind them again. More shots rang out from the bangers. One tore up a patch of earth just behind them.

Ama turned around in time to see a klip curve through the air. "Duck!" she yelled at Seg and squatted down. A second later the weapon whizzed through the space their heads had just occupied, before it circled back to its owner.

Nen's death, that was too close!

Only once they were in front of it, was the small passage through the hedge visible, a clever optical illusion she had noticed on their walk in. They hurried through the gap and the grounds opened up before them.

There was a long stretch of emptiness between them and the ceremonial platform perched over the falls. They were wide open and exposed Keenly feeling their vulnerability, the two dug in and raced for the platform jutting out over the cliff edge. Shouts and banger fire continued in their wake. Ama's shoulder sent stabbing pains through her body with every step.

At the short flight of stairs that led up to the large, stone structure, Ama and Seg bounded up, two steps at a time, and ran.

Ahead of her, Seg slowed his momentum just before the apex of the curve. He looked around him, then back at Ama, "Where's the hidden passage?"

"Behind us," she panted, not slowing her pace.

Another banger shot behind them.

Seg's mouth opened. He looked over the perilous drop, to the churning pool of water below. "No, we can't—"

Her hand latched onto his coat collar as she tackled him.

Seg screamed as the water rushed toward him.

His stomach remained behind on the platform, or so it felt, as his body submitted to the demands of gravity. When at last he connected with the water, the element lost all of its soft and fluid qualities – it felt as if he had been thrown against a wall and the wind knocked from him. Beneath, the torment did not let up; water pressed on him from all sides, squeezed out what dregs of air remained in his lungs. His feet instinctively lunged out for something solid but, as before, found nothing; likewise, his arms clawed uselessly in every direction. Sound was muted; the only noise a relentless, gurgling thrum, like a monstrous heart beat.

When he was finally spit back up to the surface, panic set in. He thrashed in every direction, desperate for something solid to hold on to.

Ama's hand connected with his face. A direct strike, hard and immediate. The jar of it shook him out of his panic as she worked to keep him afloat. He shook his head and looked into her eyes, his fear and his loss of composure evident.

"*Hang on!*" she shouted above the roar of the falls, grabbed Seg's hands, one at a time, and repositioned them – one on each strap of her bodice. With her good hand she tore the silver nove off her neck, then her second eyelids flipped up.

She tugged him close, took a deep breath, pressed her lips against his, forced his mouth open, and pulled them both underwater. As much as he struggled, her grip held him firm – lips tightly sealed to his, both of their mouths open slightly

Seg kicked and writhed, then drove his fist into Ama's injured shoulder, but he was out of his element and eventually succumbed to her direction.

And then, somehow, there was air. He was breathing. Pressed so close, his vision blurred by water, he could only guess. Her dathe; she was breathing for both of them.

In a pause that stretched for what felt like a lifetime, Seg's eyes moved skyward. Above them, distorted by water, he saw the cliff wall, rays of sunlight, green. Then they were moving, the force of Ama's kicks transferred to him through the dense element. Her element.

Down and forward, caught now by the river's flow, they bumped and twisted along the bottom as they clung to each other. Several silvery bodies flashed by, small fish perhaps. *What else is in here with us?*

Seg closed his eyes, crawled inside his mind and willed his thoughts to shield him from the current reality.

Focus.

"Segkel doesn't care for family dinners," eldest sister said, with a wicked smile. "He's more the bookish type. I wouldn't think he'd want to go on such a trip."

Focus.

"Fitness!" the drillmaster screamed. "You think those Outers will care if you're tired? They're chasing you with sticks and knives and want to EAT YOUR LIVER, you lazy bastards! RUN!"

Focus.

When they surfaced, the shock of air, taken in without Ama's assistance, woke him out of the self-induced trance. The river had leveled out, shore was not far away but the temple, thankfully, was.

Ama's head swiveled left and right; he heard her gasping for breath. Before he could speak a word, she pulled him in again.

Don't worry, I'm not enjoying this either, her eyes told him.

Under again, back to the world of muted sight and sound, where creatures with poisonous spines and razor teeth hunted. He had no control here; he could not even summon the illusion. Ama directed his body and his fate. The distance between life and death was only the distance between his lips and hers.

Then he felt her kick again. Kick and turn. *She's heading to shore,* he thought. The relief that followed the realization slowed his panicked breath at last.

With a final burst of energy she dragged him to shore, then clawed her way up the riverbank.

Seg sloshed his way out of the few remaining inches of water, senses returning to normal.

The micro-chack was lost behind them, somewhere in the river. The Outers would probably recover it someday and reverse-engineer it in anticipation of the next raid. That was why the rules were in place. Once the People came, they didn't return. No matter how advanced their technology might be compared to many of the worlds they raided, their greatest weapon was surprise – and that only worked once.

For now, the lost weapon, even if discovered, would do these Outers no good, and he still had two pistols hidden away. He pulled one out, to have at the ready, then tossed off his sodden outer garments. Clad only in undershirt and trousers, he opened his mouth to call to Ama but she was gone.

His eyes moved across the landscape until he found her, not far ahead, face down in the mud.

"No," he murmured and crawled across the riverbank to her side.

He wasn't going to lose her now, not after that performance. He rolled her onto her back and cleared the mud from her mouth and nose; his fingers instinctively moved to the location where a pulse would be on a Person.

Something rustled nearby. He reached for the pistol, looked around and waited. Nothing. *Probably an animal.*

He returned his attention to Ama, pleased to find a pulse but without any idea where to move her or how to get back to the boat for his auto-med.

"You there, get away from that woman!"

Seg looked up to see a towering man, a short distance away. He lifted his pistol, then raised it further and took aim. The man brandished a weapon identical to the one Ama had used against him on the boat and, by his appearance, he was obviously Kenda. Beneath his fingers, Ama's artery pumped weakly. Was it possible she had chosen this point of exit deliberately?

He lowered the pistol. Her cousin, she had spoken of her cousin who lived on the river.

"Brin? Put that silly piece of metal down and help me," he ordered, a snap of steel in his tone.

The man reacted to his name, lowered the blade, then raised it again, took a few steps closer and examined the face of the limp body.

"Ama?" He dropped the weapon and rushed to Seg's side. In one stroke he scooped her up in his arms, "Come with me."

Seg slogged behind the Kenda, on legs chilled and rubbery. So, Ama *had* chosen this spot purposefully; a fact that gave him some measure of relief.

The Kenda led the way into the house, carrying Ama through the kitchen, answering his family's rapt stares with instructions to bring blankets, cloths, and clean water. As soon as he had her laid on a small bed, his wife grabbed a cloth and wiped away the dirt around the wound on her shoulder.

"Dalit, Nixie, go close the doors and all the shutters," the man ordered his children. With forced restraint, he spoke, "What happened to her?"

"The constables," Seg said, "killed Stevan and wounded her. We got out. My name is—"

"Seg," the Kenda said, his face grim.

The name halted the frantic tumble of words spilling from Seg's mouth. "Yes, that is my name."

"I'm Brin, Ama is—"

"Your cousin," Seg finished.

"They killed Stevan?" Brin asked, after his own pause, and exchanged a look of concern with his wife. When Seg nodded, Brin tightened his hands into fists.

"Brin!" Perla gasped, and directed his eyes to Ama's neck, now clear of mud and debris.

"Dathe?" he asked, in a hushed, awed whisper, and leaned closer as if he could not trust his own eyes.

"If you can stabilize her," Seg interrupted his eyes on Ama as he spoke to Brin, "I can help her – if we can get to her boat and extract some things."

Brin forced himself away from his cousin and pulled Seg aside to talk out of earshot of his young. "Get on that boat? Impossible. There's been constables crawling the docks since high sun. Whatever you've mixed Ama up in, the *Naida* will be locked up tighter than a virgin on the offering day." He ran a large hand through his mane of hair. "How is she?" he asked his wife.

"Breathing but weak," she answered, as she sponged clean the wounded shoulder. "I'll do my best but we need a healer."

"And the authorities will know that. Can your magic…the device you used on her leg after the drexla attack, can it help her?" Brin asked Seg, his tone unapologetically desperate.

Again, Seg flinched. His secret had been shared. As he continued to stare at Ama, to his surprise, no anger rose in him despite her betrayal. "Yes, but my…devices are hidden on Ama's boat. Get me on there and I can save her."

"Tonight," Brin said to Seg, coming to a sudden decision. "We'll wait for darkness, it's the only way, but we should hide her in case…" he paused, then turned to his offspring. "Children, fetch our guest some food and drink," he ordered, then waited for them to leave the room before speaking again.

"I've got a safe room beneath this cottage; we'll move her there. I have no time to vet you, and no reason to trust you, but it seems you've saved my cousin, so for that I am indebted." He made the admission grudgingly. "We have lost Stevan, we mustn't lose Ama. But you should know that if you speak on what you see here, your life is forfeit."

Seg nodded.

"The authorities will be on the prowl. You need to hide. I have matters to attend to but I will return before sunset."

"Wait," Seg said. "If you can get me a head count on who is securing the boat—an accurate count—as well as their positions, I can handle the rest."

Brin almost laughed. Given how ridiculous he must have appeared—dripping and shivering, in nothing but an undershirt and trousers, half the width of the man before him, announcing he would handle a boatload of armed constables by himself—Seg lauded the man's restraint.

"Leave this to those who have experience in these matters," Brin said.

"I will make my way onto that boat with or without your assistance. I won't let her die because of your ignorance."

"Ignorance?" Brin stepped closer to Seg, eclipsing him. Seg stood his ground against the mountainous Kenda.

"Brin!" the man's wife snapped in a forceful whisper, then directed her gaze to Ama, deathly still on the bed.

Brin stepped back and Seg had the distinct impression that he was being assessed.

"I don't need fighters," Seg continued, "I just need eyes and a head count. Ama's spoken of me; you have some idea of what I am capable of."

Once more, Brin looked to Ama, pale as a corpse, then back at Seg.

"Very well," he said, "you can wait for me to return with the information or you can come with me once we've moved my cousin to safety. I can outfit you in something less conspicuous, try to pass you off as one of my workers, or hide you in the cartul. Your choice."

"I am not Kenda, as you know, and could not pass well for one. You can hide me, and if need be you can signal me." He reached out and laid his hand on Brin's forearm, aware, once more, of the ridiculous contrast between his skinny forearm and that of the burly Kenda's. "Because if it comes to it Ama is..." he hesitated, looked down, looked away, then back at Brin, "I have killed to protect her. You are hers and you are protecting her, and I will protect you. And—" he paused, "and I want those bastards to bleed."

Brin smiled but not in jest. "Then let's make them bleed, my friend."

"You'll put on some dry clothes before you leave this house," Brin's wife ordered Seg, as the children returned with a pitcher and some bread. "Unless you want to fall ill from chills before you die at the hands of the authorities."

Seg opened his mouth but Brin raised a hand, "You won't argue with Perla, if you have a drop of sense in your head."

"Of course, I'd be glad to—" The bang of the front door opening silenced Seg. All sets of eyes moved in the same direction at once. Perla waved the children over to her. Seg's hand moved to the pistol hidden in his pocket.

"Brin?"

Geras's voice; Perla let out a held breath, Seg tensed.

"I'll handle this," Brin said, and stepped to the doorway just in time to block Geras from entering.

"Cousin?" Geras asked, head cocked, craning to see past him. "I just came from the docks, there's constables all over the *Naida*, what's..." His eyes found Seg, his nostrils flared and he tried to push past Brin. "What's he doing here? Where's Ama?"

"She's alive," Brin told him, both hands on his shoulders. "And you'll stay civil until the explanations are given."

Geras continued to fume but he nodded and Brin swung sideways to let him enter. He crossed the room in three loping steps, then knelt at his sister's side. "Tadpole," he whispered.

"She was at the temple, with Stevan," Brin began, pacing his words, keeping his tone low and even. "I don't know the full story yet, I will learn it. But..." he took a breath, "the authorities were there, Stevan was killed, Ama was shot and Seg brought her here."

Geras bowed his head, grasped Ama's limp hand in his and pressed it to his forehead.

"We're going to get Seg on the *Naida*, he has a healing device hidden there that can save her."

Geras laid Ama's hand back at her side, stood and faced his cousin. "And you believe him?"

"Ama showed me the marks from drexla spines that opened her skin; healed by his device," Brin answered.

"No one survives drexla poison," Geras shifted his attention to Seg.

"The auto-med is designed to formulate antivenom, as long as the toxin isn't too complex," Seg explained, a wary eye on Ama's brother.

"And your device can heal a banger wound?" Geras asked.

"We'll have to remove the projectile," he said and looked to Ama, "but the auto-med will provide a detailed picture of—"

Geras's fist caught Seg on the chin. His jaw slung to one side, his legs gave way and he stumbled backward into the wall. Brin was between the two of them before Geras could strike again.

"We don't have time for this." Brin's voice was low but firm.

"He's the reason she's lying here," Geras growled.

"Perhaps," Brin answered, his voice calm.

"Stevan's death could be his doing."

"Possibly."

"But you defend him?"

"I do what's best for my people." Brin darted a glance at Seg, who was righting himself and recovering from the blow.

"If my sister dies, he dies," Geras jabbed a finger at Seg.

"That's enough!" Perla piped up. The children hovered behind her, eyes wide and fearful. At the sight, Geras lowered his arm and backed away a step.

"Move Ama to the safe room," Brin ordered Geras. "You'll stay here to watch over everyone until I return. I'll leave my seft for you. If there's trouble, you know where to go."

Geras grumbled and nodded reluctantly.

Brin turned to Seg, "You'll help me hitch the cartul while Perla fetches you some dry clothes." Orders delivered, he strode out of the room.

Once out of the cottage, Seg lengthened his stride, to catch up to Brin.

Brin nodded to the pocket that held Seg's pistol; the pocket Seg had dipped his hand into after Geras's punch. "Thank you for not killing my cousin in front of my children."

"You could have let him finish me off before I had a chance," Seg replied.

"I promised Ama no one would harm you, and I'll keep that promise as long as she lives."

Seg was silent for a moment, "I could say the same."

Brin nodded. "Then we'd best not let her die, if we are to remain allies."

CHAPTER 11

Seg wasn't the first person or object to be smuggled through the city in Brin's cartul - he had made that clear. This time, however, the eyes of the constables were on alert and Seg imagined their stares as he was bounced through the city. In front of the compartment in which he had stowed Seg, Brin had loaded tools and pieces of lumber for cover. The rattles and bangs of the tools did little to ease Seg's concern. Nor did the many stops Brin made along the way, though he had warned Seg about this in advance. Brin was well known in this city and any deviation from his usual routine would cast suspicion. As well, the social stops and pauses to exchange hellos, trade a joke or some innocuous gossip, were opportunities for Brin to pass along information in the code his people used. With some of the men, he slipped a Kenda word, whistle or gesture into the conversation that ensured he would have eyes and ears of his own, watching his back, a precaution Seg could appreciate.

Luckily, Brin had to pass by the *Naida* to reach the boat works, their final destination, so his path could not be considered unusual. There was a brief moment of concern when a passing constable signaled him to stop but, from a crack in the wood of his hiding spot, Seg saw the man give only a cursory glance inside the cartul before waving Brin on.

The cartul slowed ever so slightly as they passed by Ama's boat. Seg's vision was limited, he could only hope Brin's information would be accurate.

At length, they reached the boat works. Around the back of the building, out of sight, Brin climbed off the driver's seat, and cleared the way for Seg to exit the hidden compartment.

"I counted seven men but there could be more aboard," Brin said, his voice covered by the dull thuds of hammering. He knelt down and drew a quick map with his finger in the sawdust covering the ground. "Three are stationed on the upper road, here. Two men are at the ramp leading to the dock. One is on the dock, at the end of the slip, near the stern. And one is onboard the *Naida*."

Seg stretched his cramped muscles as he examined the map. One against seven, not the best odds.

"At least three of them have bangers," Brin pointed to three of the indents in the sawdust. Seg's eyes were focused on the map, calculating. "I don't claim to know your business but these are Haitha odds."

Haitha, Seg recalled the name from his brief study prior to breaking off from the squad. The location of the Kenda's last stand against the Shasir. A slaughter.

"I have men eager to spill blood—if you ask, they're yours—but no matter, I'm at your service. Tell me what you need," Brin said.

Seg studied the map with a practiced eye and his thoughts went back to the grizzled old trooper who had taught the Combat Maneuvers class back in Guild training.

Know your Outers. Learn to read 'em.

She had preached that.

Most places, people don't look for a fight. Most places, they're looking to survive first. Most places, they aren't expecting a shock attack, and by the time they figure out what's going on, you're halfway through their asses and on the other kargin' side. Sometimes we'll run across real fighters, but most of the time the ones picked for guard duty are the slackers who wanted to get out of real work.

"On the eleventh hour," he told Brin, "I'll need a distraction for my entry, and then I'll make my own exit. Your people pull back and, when the time comes, I move. Either here," he dotted on the sawdust map, "or here, or here, depending on what comes to respond to my entry, and which direction they come from. None of your people should have to fight tonight. I'll do all the blood spilling."

He rubbed his face, which was smooth compared to that of his companion, and remembered that his razor was onboard as well. A good enough reason to return in and of itself. In a World all but drained of natural resources, articles as enduring and functional as a simple, reusable blade, held great value. And this blade moreso than others, being a gift from his father. In fact, it was the only gift he had ever received from the man. He would be damned if some Outer was going to prance about shaving his legs with it.

"One more thing," he said. "You don't need to be directly involved with this. I need you to stay clean, because if this doesn't work—"

He paused.

"If this doesn't work, it will be your responsibility to get Ama to safety, and I will hold you to that." From some vague, nebulous and probably non-existent afterlife, of course. "You and your men can decide among yourselves how many you want to commit to this." He eyed Brin for a long moment, thoughtful. "Just get my distraction and then be ready to pull me in and hide me when I come out."

"Distraction," Brin nodded, "I think we can arrange that. Don't worry about Ama, she will be cared for; Kenda look after their own."

Seg had already seen this was true. Had the Kenda possessed weapons and technology equal to the Shasir's, he was sure they would not have lost their war. True solidarity was rare, and potent.

"I think a runaway cartul full of fosfol, stove fuel, could start some believable panic. Light that cart, aim it at the right target and you have a very distracting fireball. That should give you plenty of time to move around. Now there's just the matter of choosing a target," Brin smiled, "but that will be the fun part, especially with so many lovely, luxe Dammie cruisers in port for the upcoming ceremonies. A plausible accident."

"Indeed," Seg stretched again.

"I'll go and see to my business then. A covered cartul will be waiting for you, when you're finished with yours – with my most trusted man to see to your escape. You'll see a blue and yellow flag hanging from the side. No flag means there's trouble and you should keep moving. If there's anything else you require, tell me now." With Seg's indication that nothing further was required, he turned to leave, then paused, pulled up one of the boards in the back of the cartul and retrieved a long blade nearly identical to the one he had brandished earlier that day. "You might find this useful," he said, pressing the seft into Seg's hand. Then he placed his hand on Seg's shoulder, "We Kenda look after our own."

Seg nodded as he received the weapon and examined it closely – a long curved blade with a handle that would enable the user to slice or jab with equal ease.

When Brin was gone, he put the primitive blade aside and studied what remained of his equipment. The stunner still worked. He had two pistols with full loads of ammo, three grenades, his VIU and his digifilm. The grenades would be crucial to getting away with this, especially if there were more Outers in the boat to deal with.

This was insanity. By all rights, he should make his way out on the next available boat. Even if he had some sort of revenge impetus, he could call Kerbin and the squad in to do the dirty work at a more opportune time. He didn't want anyone else to do the dirty work, though. For one, it was his mess. For another, he didn't want any dependencies, debts, or the embarrassment of having his botched reconnaissance spoken of.

Finally, these Outers had hurt Ama, and for that they would suffer. Them and their entire rotten primitive band. This wasn't about sense or justice, it was about pride and revenge.

He wished he knew how to swim, the way Ama did. That would have made the entire business so much easier. Again, he wondered at how her kind lost the war when they had such an advantage.

Weak.

But she had saved his life in the heat of the action. She was not weak.

The day was waning. Seg pulled on the extra set of ragged clothes that Brin's wife had provided him, tugging the hat down low over his face. He had smudged his face with soot and dirt, darkening his skin to blend with the lowest orders of the lowest class. It would work to his advantage that he would strike at night. The old drillmaster would approve of his preparation, if not what he was preparing for.

Once again, he re-checked his weaponry. Ready, as it had been five minutes before.

Everything was ready.

Seg had seen the scavengers moving about the docks late at night and, as with everything, he had filed away their patterns and their movements. No eye contact. Deferential. Wide personal spacing. Feet stayed close to the ground in dragging steps. Head swung side to side, looking for usable refuse.

Most human forms ignored such people, part of evolutionary winnowing. Easily understandable why people would shun failures, but also highly useful. Especially now.

As he moved along the dock, Seg towed a small cart behind him and used a stick to hobble. Ahead, the boat sat placidly on the water. The guards noted his presence with disdainful negligence.

Perfect. Surprise and speed.

His earpiece chimed. Eleventh hour, local time, and, of course, no explosion. Why had he even dreamed he could depend on these Outers? Should he abort? The incompetence of the Kenda aside, it was suicide to take the guards head-on.

Just then, a boat several slips over exploded in a spectacular ball of fire that lit the starless sky.

Seg brought up the pistol concealed in his sleeve. The three guards on the upper level had run for cover at the explosion. The guards on the dock had turned toward the conflagration, two of them standing in profile.

Seg's thumb clicked over to 'repeat fire' and held the trigger down, emptying the entire cassette in one protracted burst.

The first man was virtually sawn in half, falling down with the same look of surprise he had worn when the boat had exploded. The other man took a load of huchack spines to the stomach and torso and stood there, shocked. The spines were low-impact weapons; they didn't punch targets, they sliced through them.

Blood poured from the man's chest and he looked over toward the others, opening his mouth to speak. Seg accelerated as the man made a gurgling cry before he slumped to the ground.

The guard at the end of the dock raised his gun as Seg lifted the other pistol. He fired a quick, silent burst, driving spines into the man's shoulder. A hasty snapshot from the banger whizzed by Seg's left side.

The guard on the boat raised his gun and took more deliberate aim, but Seg had reached the cover of a post as he slid a stunner grenade from his pocket. He dropped low and moved back instead of forward, gambling that the guard would aim ahead instead of behind. He won the bet long enough to throw the grenade, then tracked back into cover.

The grenade detonated – far more effective in the darkness as the strobing light flashed insistently and the deafening noise echoed through the hull.

Now was his best chance; Seg broke cover up the stairs.

The guard was nowhere to be seen. He had obviously gone to cover while shaking off the effect of the grenade. Dangerous man.

There were now two enemies on the boat that he knew of, with at least one projectile weapon between them. They also had the close quarters to make other weapons useful. Seg shifted the pistol to his off-hand, reached behind his back and drew the curved Kenda blade from its hidden sheath.

Time to make it personal.

As Seg gripped the seft, the drill instructor's voice haunted him again.

Stabbing does not bring the quick kill. Stabbing makes them karging mad enough to stab you back. And they're better with knives than you are, pup.

No time for subtlety. He tried the latch and then shoved open the hatch to the lower deck, leading with his last fragmentation grenade. He regretted the damage he was doing to the boat, but it would be past the point of recovery when he was done anyway.

He stepped from behind the shield of the hatchway after the grenade detonated, and dove into the belly of the boat. One down, permanently. The other? There was a blood trail leading further down.

Wounded animals are easier to kill than healthy ones. If you have a choice, let 'em bleed out.

Unfortunately, he didn't have the time. He crouched low at the corner and stuck his head and hand out, ready to hose the area with huchack spines.

The waiting Welf kicked his hand, spines streamed off the wall with a muted clatter. Seg lost his grip on the pistol and scuttled backwards as the Welf came roaring around the corner, in time to meet Seg coming to his feet.

A strange, curved hammer crashed down on his shoulder as his blade flew upward. Seg fell backwards, his arm, shoulder, and back screaming with pain. The Kenda blade he had driven into the Outer tore free and left a gaping wound. A fatal wound.

Blood fountained from the man's midsection and he slumped to his knees, his hands grasping at his stomach. Seg lay on his back, grimacing. He pressed his hand down on his injured shoulder as he watched the Outer topple.

Storm but that was it. If there was another one onboard, he was meat.

He waited a long moment for the next guard to come around and finish him. When none did, he began the painful process of righting himself. He felt the grind of broken bones. The nature of the injury he recognized from the time his instructors had demonstrated such a thing by snapping his forearm. His collarbone was surely broken but he could function and he had one good arm left.

Now he was going to have to count on the Kenda to cover him out. He stumbled around the corner and gathered up his pistol.

A third of a cassette of ammo left and more in the storage locker. Half falling, he moved forward. He couldn't haul everything. Even with two functional arms, it would have been impossible but now he would be restricted to one or two items only.

He reached the cargo locker and for a moment all he could do was stare blankly at the heavy lock Ama had used to keep his belongings safe. The key was somewhere at the bottom of the river. A moment later he remembered the pistol in his hand; pain numbed his thoughts but he needed to finish this.

One burst took care of the lock. He opened the door, opened his bags and Manatu's and peered inside. Most of the extraneous cover items were gone, gifted to the unholy Shasir. His articles, those from the World, lay in plain view.

There was the auto-med, which was required to save Ama; the field warpgen, warp gate and warp comm unit, his emergency exit home and only means to communicate with the World; weapons and ammunition, it was a safe bet he would need those. Anything he couldn't carry would have to be destroyed.

He tried to replenish his pistol one-handed, but it didn't work. Finally he settled on yet another one of Manatu's spare micro-chacks and shoved the depleted one into a bag.

No time for debate. Seg grabbed the auto-med, wrestling with the bag and the unit to stuff it inside. Next he dug through the remaining weapons in Manatu's bag and tossed them in as well. Almost ready. He sorted through the surprises in Manatu's luggage and punched up the sequence that would self-destruct the gear.

He gave himself two minutes to escape. The explosion wouldn't be overly dramatic, but it would be enough to finish the gear and ignite the boat.

He slung the bag over his good shoulder; that effort alone nearly toppled him.

At the stairs, he paused, looked back at his quarters, then swung back and stepped inside as quickly as he could move. He couldn't speak to what possessed him.

Ama's leather nove hung on the wall, next to the image of her mother. He tore it from the wall and ran. Pain shot up his left leg, pain that corresponded to the damage to his shoulder and back. The auto-med was going to get a workout tonight.

He staggered down the street, blood-soaked and battered, until he reached the covered cartul. At the sight of the blue and yellow flag hanging from the side, he allowed himself a sigh of relief.

"I'm ready," he panted, threw his bag inside the open door, and turned his face to the driver. "You!" he gasped, his suffering too great for a more elaborate response.

Viren Hult tipped his hat. "Lord Eraranat, what a welcome surprise."

"You're Brin's most trusted man?" Seg panted.

"A scandalous rumor, I assure you. Now, toss yourself inside before our banger-toting friends show up to spoil our happy reunion."

"This is a trick," Seg swayed where he stood.

"Get in or I leave you for the authorities."

"Again," Seg grumbled. From behind, he could hear whistles and shouts as the commotion escalated around the burning boats. His broken collarbone delivered a fresh stab of pain. He jumped inside, rolled poorly and landed on the wounded shoulder. The subsequent jolt of agony was enough to put him out.

Unconsciousness wasn't always a nice, peaceful oblivion. Sometimes it was a painful, discordant business full of noises, bumps, and terrible pain. Seg enjoyed the latter. As the cartul rattled its way across the cobblestone streets, he moaned, slowly rousing. Across from him, Brin looked on. He reached for his bag and withdrew the auto-med, heedless of the Kenda's prying eyes.

He wrapped the sleeve on his arm, then punched the button and waited for the diagnostic.

First matters first, the unit injected him with an anti-inflammatory and an analgesic; enough to stabilize him, then pumped him with stimulants.

As his mind sharpened, he assessed the pain. It was very, very painful.

Unfortunately, between Manatu's injury, Ama's drexla encounter, and his own previous wounds, the auto-med's supply of anesthetic and painkillers was all but depleted. Ideally, he would save the scant remainder for Ama's surgery but without some chemical assistance Seg knew he would be in danger of passing out again. He needed to stay awake and focused. A press of the button delivered the final dose of anesthetic to his shoulder; enough to take more edge off, but not enough to make him fuzzy. The bone was broken but thankfully not protruding. The auto-med recommended full immobilization, which was not possible at the moment, but at least he could numb the pain a bit.

As the cartul pulled up to Brin's home, Seg shifted his body and pulled the auto-med sleeve loose. He re-packed the unit while Brin watched in silence. "I'll tell you more about things once we're inside," he promised. At Brin's nod, he added, "Your driver is an undesirable character."

"Whose loyalty is without question," Brin replied.

Seg stared at Brin, unblinking. *Loyalty* – there was that word again.

Distracted by larger concerns, Seg hadn't paid much attention to the safe room below the cottage earlier. Now he could see it was big enough to hide several men in relative comfort for a short period of time. There were shelves stacked with books, maps, food supplies and, in the corner, a stash of weapons. Against one wall, was a small bed, where Ama laid, the light of the lantern painting her with a golden hue.

Geras met the two men as they entered, seft in hand. He stepped aside only far enough to allow Seg to pass by and shadowed him to his Ama's side.

Seg sat down next to Ama and wrapped the sleeve on her arm before starting the auto-med unit.

Shock, naturally. The imager projected a three dimensional depiction of the wound above her shoulder, as well as the suggested primitive implements and local tonics for treatment.

"I'll need…genga root," he read off, "slivee leaves, a sharp knife, alcohol, and heat. Your hands steady, Outer?" His cool mask dropped for the slightest moment as he looked down at Ama.

Brin stood and stared, then eventually forced himself to look away from Seg's magic. When he spoke, it was as if he were in a trance. "I… yes," he shook his head.

Seg looked up at Geras's hovering frame, "You have to leave this room."

"I'm not going anywhere."

"Go upstairs, cousin," Brin said, riffling through a small chest of herbs.

"My sister…" Geras protested.

"Exactly," Brin said. "This is difficult enough as it is without your eyes on my every move. Unless you'd like to be the one to cut her open?"

Convinced, Brin led Geras away and returned with the rest of the items. "What now?" Brin asked.

Seg took the slivee, a natural topical anesthetic, and rubbed it around the wound. Ama stirred, he grimaced and settled himself on her legs. "Hold her down." As Brin complied, he continued the vigorous rubbing. – according to the auto-med, the more saturated the area was with the slivee, the more effective the 'freezing'.

"Now," he said, eyes on the readout. "This is going to be tricky. First order of business is to remove the projectile. I will pin her down. You will make the cut. I would have it the other way around but…" he gestured to his wounded arm. "Tie her good arm to the bed; I'll hold the legs and the other arm."

Seg's eyes flicked to the auto-med again. Removing the projectile wouldn't be so bad, as long as they avoided the artery, and the vein, and, well, Brin had best have very steady hands

Once Ama was immobilized, Seg guided Brin through the preparation. He was no coward and had obviously done similar rough-and-ready first aid, though nothing of this sophistication. There was a moment of hesitation, however, this being his precious cousin and not one of his fellow resistors. Brin soaked the blade in the alcohol as ordered, then readied himself.

"When we go in, you can't hold back," Seg informed him. "Your movements must be deft and sure. I will direct you."

Brin made the first cut. Unfortunately, they had nothing to generate suction, which made for a mess and slowed their work. Ama squirmed unconsciously but thankfully was still weakened by her ordeal. Seg grunted, as she jarred his bad arm, but maintained the pressure on her limbs. "Keep moving!"

Brin had some difficulty grasping the projectile but, once he did, it came out with relative ease. It was a round, silvery ball. A primitive construct. Seg had Brin continue to poke at the wound and pick out any obvious scraps of clothing or other foreign debris.

The auto-med had enough antiseptic for a few days and would direct treatment to that region so long as it was attached. Seg would make sure it stayed attached as long as needed. Also, it would direct her immune system to aggressively attack any signs of infection and stimulate rapid tissue regeneration.

Seg sat back and mopped the sweat from his brow with his good hand. She would survive and, with proper care, regain full use of her arm.

Now to get his arm properly immobilized, and then talk to Brin further. The idea that had come to him only that morning, during his run-in with Geras, had taken hold in his latest dealings with Brin and even the scoundrel Viren.

Then something struck him, "Parentless son of a—" he swore, cutting himself off before finishing. Brin looked at him quizzically. "Never mind," Seg said. He had forgotten his damn razor on the boat. "I need a razor. For shaving."

Brin's mouth fell open and then, for the first time since finding Seg on the riverbank, he laughed.

Amazingly enough, Seg found himself chuckling along with Brin, then actually laughing. It was a release from the stress, a reaction to the pressure. But also, there was something infectious about Brin, a sort of easy-going affability.

He could see how the man could easily attract followers. Furthermore, he had seen some evidence that he could competently manage them as well. The two skills were often far enough apart to seem mutually exclusive.

"I thought I'd met every person there is to know; you've proven me wrong. You will have a razor," Brin said. He eyed Seg for a long moment, then pointed to the auto-med sleeve on his cousin's arm, "But you also promised me an explanation."

"I should ask, first, which secrets of mine did Ama not share with you? And I'll assume she drugged me before we arrived in port, despite her assurance to the contrary?" Seg asked.

"Would you have done any differently?" Brin asked but didn't wait for a response before he recounted all Ama had told him.

When Brin finished, Seg cast his eyes to the floor. He had known from the moment he made the arrangement with Ama that it was treasonous, but hearing it verbalized for the first time, from the lips of another, brought forward the implications of his action. Even so, he was about to take that treason a step further.

He raised the cup of grint Perla had left for him and took a long drink before speaking. "What you already know, regarding my arrangement with Ama, could easily have me killed were it to go wrong. Or worse. Much worse." Seg looked aside, staring at the jumping shadows on the wall, "But I've faced death here. I know where I stand on the concept."

"As do I," Brin said. "What passes between these walls, friend, is only for the people in this room. You have my solemn oath on that. My oath on the lives of my family."

He swallowed, stood up, and checked once to ensure the trap door was closed and all was quiet, then he turned back to Seg. The lantern light cast harsh shadows on Brin's bearded face.

"Ama's brother Stevan was a member of the Kenda resistance. I am the leader of that resistance. I will tell you more but that alone is enough to see me hanging from a rope, or worse. That is your insurance."

One corner of Seg's mouth tweaked up and he let out a short, forceful breath. "Your petty overlords are nothing. Pretentious, ignorant fools who use pageantry and fakery to deceive those willing to accept their pomposity, and terror to subdue those who will not." He finished the grint with a hearty swallow. "They have no idea just how ripe they are for a fall. A regime such as theirs typically succumbs completely within two to four generations at this stage, and sooner if an inspirational leader comes along to rally the fighters to their side. Their functional bulwarks are the Welf and Damiar. The Welf are ruled through sham and superstition; a proper rediversion of Welf belief can undermine the entire structure. The Damiar represent a larger problem, but their loyalty to the Shasir is not so blind and thus they can be turned, with the proper motivation."

He slammed the cup down and immediately winced as the shock transmitted to his bad arm. "Brin of the Kenda, I am extending to you a courtesy that is normally reserved for the—for those of my blood, as it were. I will treat you as an equal."

Whatever Brin was feeling at that moment was not revealed on his face and he gestured for Seg to continue.

"My People will come here, take what I have identified, leave and never return. My arrangement, with Ama, was that I would ensure the attacks were directed away from the Kenda."

He drummed his fingers on the table and took a deep breath. He glanced at Ama and the line of his mouth spread outward and around.

"Were any of this to come to light with my People, I would be, well..." Seg paused, his wince a product of both real and imagined pain, "the consequences would be beyond any penalties your self-proclaimed overlords could devise. We are not, as you might have gathered, a merciful or gentle People."

Brin nodded, then wordlessly gestured for him to continue.

"I would expand this arrangement," Seg said, "and extend it to you."

"You might find it more difficult to pass me off as your wife," Brin said, with a smile that didn't reach his eyes.

Again, Seg felt compelled to share the mirth. His lips twisted wryly. "Indeed. But..." He rose to his feet, moved instinctively to clasp his hands behind his back and winced again as the effort jarred his shoulder. "But I am one man, one of my People. I am not a soldier. If anything, I'm a scholar."

He stared at his hand – his mind slid back to the skirmish on the *Naida.*

"A scholar with a certain amount of training but no warrior." He flexed his fingers. "What comes after I return the information to my people, what comes then will be the warriors. And there isn't an army on your world that can stand against them. I do not exaggerate when I say that ten soldiers of my People could stand against a thousand of yours, given the right circumstances. We are experienced, well trained, and we will have complete and total surprise."

Brin glanced up at the trap door. "So long as you don't go burning any more boats or fighting your way out of temples."

"Aberrational," Seg said, stopping his hand before the instinctual, dismissive wave. "The Shasir's tension will rise somewhat, but they won't be expecting a full military assault. And when it comes—"

"You'll burn anything that's in your way," Brin finished for him.

Seg glanced at him sharply. It was his own habit to impatiently finish sentences, and he wasn't delighted to have that turned back toward him. "As you say. And so I offer you a bargain. An addition to the planned raid, separate from that of my People's forces, organized and financed by me, solely designed to shatter the Shasir. If you provide me with targets, I can destroy their air fleets, dislocate their Welf defenders, and clear a path for your people to rise up and take power."

Brin folded his arms across his chest. "At what price?"

"I need fifty of your men. Warriors," even as the words left his mouth, Seg could hardly believe he was saying them, "to accompany me back to my World."

"But you've just told me that ten of yours could handle a thousand of ours."

"Not ten of *mine*," Seg said, putting a hard emphasis on the final word. "Ten of ours. Ten warriors of my People."

Brin rubbed his hand over his jaw, "You want your own army."

"In a manner of speaking, yes."

"You can't find soldiers on your world?"

"The soldiers on my World are loyal to the Houses or organizations they serve, and those bodies are loyal, above all, to orthodoxy, rules, protocol. Tell me, would you rather captain a vessel crewed by men loyal to the Shasir or loyal to you?"

"You know the answer to that already," Brin said, as he looked around the hidden room.

"The next world I cross to, I will have my own crew, loyal to me. I want dedicated, creative men, willing and capable of shedding blood, able to improvise, and who know how to follow orders. *My* orders. I want no deception in this, Brin of the Kenda. I want fifty men who understand that I will burn the Shasir to the ground and so thoroughly weaken them that your people can rise, successfully this time, and supplant them. And, in exchange for their people's liberty, I will take them to my land, and others, and they will live under my command."

He turned toward Brin and rested his hand on the back of a chair. "Those I take with me will never return home. They will live the harsh life of soldiers, and all I offer them is the freedom of their people and my pledge to see that their service will be rewarded as it is due."

"I won't send you slaves," Brin said, his voice low.

"They will not be slaves. I will only take men willing to give and stand by their oaths."

Brin shook his head and rose to his feet. "I'll need to think about this, Segkel of the people whose name I don't even know."

"We are the People," Seg said. "We need no names."

Brin looked aside for a moment, his eyes drifting over the knives lying on the table before returning to Seg.

"I'll need to think about this," he said again.

CHAPTER 12

U pon waking, Ama found the world half-blurred. As consciousness crept toward her, she realized that her second eyelids were still partially up, which meant she was either very sick or...

"Uhhhg," she groaned when she tried to move her head.

Seriously injured.

She blinked her eyelids back into position and licked her lips. "Seg?" she called, her voice raspy and weak.

Where am I? The room was dark, illuminated only by the low flicker of a lantern. Her shoulder throbbed painfully. She remembered the riverbank and then...nothing.

"Seg?" she called again, this time with more urgency.

"Shhh," a familiar face came into view, "he's resting, as you should be."

"Brin," Ama smiled and then coughed. "Help me up a little."

With a gentleness not in keeping with his appearance, Brin helped Ama shift in the bed, mindful of her shoulder, until she was almost sitting. He passed her a cup of water and she sipped gratefully. Then he motioned to Seg, sleeping in the corner, on top of a mound of rags and linen. His forehead was covered with a sheen of sweat, his face was locked in a grimace, and Ama saw one of his arms was bound with a bandage.

"What...?"

"It is a long, strange tale but the end is happy – you are alive," Brin brushed away the hair that was matted to her face. "Geras had business to finish but he will be by later to visit with you."

He looked strangely older since she had last seen her cousin. How many hours had she been asleep?

Brin related the events of her arrival right up to the surgery on her shoulder, with breaks to offer her water and make sure she was comfortable. When he was done, Ama was silent for a long spell.

"Why would he do that?" she asked, at last. She looked over at Seg, who twitched and moaned. "If he was able to get onboard the *Naida*, he could have used his machine to go home, he could have escaped, he…why did he come back here?"

"Ama," Brin smiled softly at his cousin, "if you had seen the look on his face, when we first brought you here and we thought we might lose you…" Brin leaned in closer to her, "Even if there had been a hundred guards on that boat, he would have fought his way through them. Whatever he has told you and whatever he pretends to, that man is bound to you."

Ama opened her mouth to speak but no words came out.

Brin lowered his voice even further, "Cousin, can I trust this man?"

The question surprised her. How was she to answer? Not very long ago, she would have answered no. A firm no.

He could have left her, but he had stayed. He had risked everything for her.

"Why do you ask?"

Brin took a deep breath, his brow furrowed into deep lines, "He's made me an offer."

Now it was Ama who looked concerned. "What has he asked?"

Brin explained the terms of Seg's deal.

"I know, it's a great sacrifice, but the truth is I could likely find a thousand Kenda men willing to lay down their lives to see the Shasir toppled for good if it could be guaranteed. If it weren't for Perla and the children, I would volunteer myself."

"I trust him," Ama said, surprised to find that she did. "It's strange," she continued, staring at Seg, as he slept, "I find myself wanting to know more about him, about his world."

"Well, I guess your father was right all along. He always said no man in the world would satisfy you. Leave it to Tadpole to find a man from another world." Ama's cheeks burned at the implication; Brin's smile rose and fell. "He's dangerous, isn't he?"

"As dangerous as the Big Water."

"Then you are meant to be with him as surely as Nen is your true father," Brin raised his fingers and placed them just below Ama's dathe. "Perhaps this is your destiny? *Kiera Nen*."

"Don't call me that," Ama said, heat rising to the rest of her face.

"*Nen's chosen one?* Why not? Why could it not be you?"

"Because…" her voice failed her. She stared away, past her cousin, "Because the Kiera Nen is a hero, a savior for our people. I'm just a selfish, stubborn girl." Her eyes brimmed with tears and her throat grew hot. *Stevan.* She couldn't say his name aloud but she sensed Brin understood.

"No, you're not," he wiped a stray tear from her cheek, and looked toward Seg, asleep in the corner. "Now," Brin patted her hand, "you get some more rest. Perla will be stuffing you full of food soon enough." She nodded and he climbed back out of the room, closing the trap door behind him.

Ama looked at Seg. *That man is bound to you.*

He had every reason in the world to return to his people when he had the chance, but he had come back here. For her.

With a grunt, Ama forced herself upright. She used her good shoulder for support and swung her legs around until her feet were flat on the floor. It took several minutes but she managed to get off the bed, and onto floor. On all fours, she crawled to Seg's side and fit herself along his body, inhaled and savored his scent. It was tinged with blood and dirt and sweat, as she imagined it would often be.

As she breathed him in, she drifted off to sleep again.

Seg watched his hand twitch without trying to restrain it. The tremors were mild, within acceptable parameters, and the hand was secured to his breastbone by a bandage wrapped in a figure eight around his shoulders.

He was functional again, and comfortably warm. Ama was curled into him. He made no attempt to pull away but, instead, studied her in her sleep. Pale, drawn, still worn, but according to the auto-med she was weathering well.

He reached into the bag at his side and his fingers fumbled past the weaponry he had recovered. For some strange reason, he didn't want to wake her and took care not to disturb her. He dug out the nove and laid it next to her face, then settled back as he contemplated what to do with his new bodyguard of troops, when and if he acquired them.

Jarin often chided him for looking too far beyond the moment, wasting precious time and resources on the tenth step rather than focusing on the first.

Well, Jarin wasn't here.

Ama moaned and stirred. As she shifted her body slightly, she reached out with her good hand and picked up the nove. Fingers curled around the soft leather, she held the collar to her face. "You're a crazy drexla," she said, and turned to look up at him.

"You're welcome," he said.

"I still hate you."

Their faces were close. Not touching, but close enough to feel the heat rising from each. Seg brushed a stray lock of hair from her face. What a pair they made, similarly useless. He shifted slightly; sharp pains from his shoulder stabbed him as he moved and he cried out.

Ama moved to help him, then let out a cry at her own injury.

They exchanged a glance and Ama broke into low laughter, her body rocking against his. Then the laughter stopped, and once more it was as if they were back in the squall. The veneer of civility fell away, Seg's eyes ripped into her, Ama's lips parted.

The trap door flew open and Perla sailed down the stairs with a platter full of food.

"You two must be hungry by…"

She stared at the empty bed, then turned her head to see her two wounded guests huddled together in the corner. Perla turned her head to the side, though not in time to hide the smile that crept onto her face. "I'll just leave this for you," Perla said, depositing the tray on the table.

"Thank you, Perla," Ama said, inching away from Seg, her cheeks red, "for everything."

"Just rest and get better. Both of you. And I'll find you some clothes, cousin."

Ama looked down at the tattered bodice of the dress. She opened her mouth to speak but Perla was already on her way up the ladder.

"I could eat an entire gresher right now," Ama said, then pushed up from Seg and moved as quickly as her broken body would allow. Just as she reached the tray, loud beeps sounded from the auto-med sleeve.

"Stop," Seg ordered.

Ama froze in place, eyes darting to the sleeve.

Seg had hoisted himself up and was making his own slow progress to her side. He glanced at the readout then pointed to the bed. "You're over-exerting. Lie down and rest."

Ama took a longing look at the tray of food then lowered herself to the bed, and settled in. When she was in place, Seg checked the readout once more and frowned.

"Is it bad?" Ama craned her neck to try and see what he was looking at.

"It will be if you do not do as you are ordered. For once," he answered with a pointed stare.

Seg sat down on the bed, broke off a small piece of cake and held it to her lips. Ama swallowed the bite of food quickly.

According to everything he had been raised to believe, his life was more valuable than hers. Nevertheless, "You performed well in getting us away from the temple." To cover for the awkwardness of praising an Outer, he fed her another bite.

"It was my fault, the trouble. One of Uval's men must have survived. We're wanted for his murder." She looked up at him with genuine regret, "I'm sorry."

"It wasn't your fault," he said, took another bite and chewed mechanically. "When I disposed of the bodies, I didn't ensure they were all dead."

For a moment, they ate in silence. Seg took care to feed Ama only small bites, offering her water as well, with occasional glances to the auto-med.

"The situation has changed," he said, breaking the quiet intimacy, "I must return to my People. I have no way to communicate with them." He silently cursed himself for leaving the digipad behind. It had been stored in his quarters, not far below the nove he had been so set on retrieving in the moment. "If I am not at the designated rendezvous point in fifteen days, they will return to the World without me."

Ama nodded and then raised her head suddenly. "If you don't make it back…"

"I will be stranded here and the Kenda will know no protection when my People return to attack your world. And they *will* return."

"Your people!" She sat up abruptly, "I need to talk to Brin, I've made a huge mistake."

He felt his heart shudder as he stared at her. "What did you do?"

"I didn't understand, I didn't know if I could trust you," Ama began, her voice catching in her throat. "On the globe you showed me, I saw where your team was headed. Brin's sent men to hunt them down and capture them."

He froze in place. "You've killed Brin's men, very likely."

Ama deflated before his eyes. "Brin can stop them, he can send runners, call them back."

"If Kerbin hasn't killed them already."

"I was only trying to protect my people."

Seg slumped back and stared at the ceiling for a moment. "My mission. My responsibility. I tried to do too much."

"Once we speak with Brin, we'll figure out how to get back onboard the Naida. It'll be tricky slipping past the authorities and we'll have to travel at night, but it can be done. I can have you back at the Banks in three days if the sky's clear and the wind's in our favor."

"Your vessel is no longer functional." Seg picked a piece of cheese off the platter, looked at it, then held it out to Ama. His appetite had vanished.

"No longer functional? What does that mean? What did they do to my girl?"

"I destroyed your boat."

"You?" Ama pushed Seg's hand away from her face. "Why? Why would you do that?"

"Necessity," Seg said. Then, seeing her confusion and shock, he added, "The risk of others discovering the items I left behind was unacceptable. Now eat, you need it. The auto-med tissue regeneration requires a high caloric intake."

Ama took the cheese, her brows drawn together.

"I would suggest another boat, something Brin could arrange to have us smuggled out on, but the authorities will have every port sealed up and down the coast, and I can't ask anyone else to risk running at night. Any boat coming or going will be torn apart. So, there's no chance of that. We'll have to go over land; that won't be easy. I wonder..." she turned her head to the stack of shelves that held supplies. "Help me up," she said, shifted to one side and extended her good hand.

"I ordered you to rest."

"We need to plan. We don't have much time," Ama said, and grunted as she tried to stand again.

Seg offered his good hand, "You won't be any use to me if you don't heal."

"And you won't be any use to me if you don't find your people," she said as he helped her over to the shelves. Her eyes skipped across each of the items. "Good," she said, when she located a stack of maps and charts. With her able hand, she thumbed through the pile, pulled out three maps and, with Seg's help, carried them back to the table where Perla had set the platter of food.

With awkward movements, the two of them wrestled the tray to the ground. Together they bent over the maps, unfolded each one and lined them up on the small table, to form a complete picture of the land from T'ueve to the Banks. "Where are you supposed to meet your people?" Ama asked.

Seg gave the maps a quick appraisal; they were primitive but well detailed. "Assuming they are still alive…here," he said, and touched his finger to the spot he and Kerbin had pre-arranged for the meeting.

She knew the place, a small valley, with a sparse and widely scattered population of Welf, on the south side of the Humish mountain range.

"Is it feasible?" Seg asked. He leaned closer, searching for the scale of the drawing, then noted the distance between where they were and where they needed to be. "Can we make it?"

"Maybe," Ama said, and pulled out a chair for Seg. "The distance isn't a problem so much as the terrain. Mountains, rivers, gorges…" she traced her finger across the various obstacles on the map. "Let's just say it's a good thing our legs weren't injured; we have a long walk ahead of us."

Seg refused to rest. Sleep eluded Ama as well. Perla hadn't returned, nor had Geras paid the visit Brin had warned him to expect. There was no way to know what was happening above and leaving the safe room was out of the question.

They had passed much of the time poring over the maps and the possible routes, calculating distances, considering alternatives, relentlessly scrutinizing every detail as Seg transferred the information to his digifilm. Eventually, though, even the planning was exhausted and they had sunk into a tense silence.

A noise behind the far wall startled them out of their brooding. Ama reached for her knife. The wall slid open; she stepped in front of Seg and held the blade outward, as the figure of a man appeared.

"Stay where you are," Ama warned. He spoke something in the Kenda tongue, and Seg rose.

"Hult," Seg said, and pulled Ama gently to one side. "Where's Brin?"

"Ah!" Viren said, his eyes moving between Seg and Ama. "You found her. See, just like I told you." He brushed past Seg to the half eaten platter of food, where he scooped up a piece of trettle cake and swallowed it in one bite. "You kids have the authorities hopping faster than cold drops of water on a hot skillet, I'll say that for you. Brin is having a friendly chat with our good friend Head Constable Dagga," he said, wiping crumbs from his beard.

Ama's legs gave way; she stumbled to the bed to sit.

"Will he give us up? Do we need to move?" Seg turned to the small pile of equipment he now possessed.

"Easy now, your Lordship," Viren raised a hand for Seg to stop. "Your secrets are safe. Brin knew this would happen. He's a Kalder, after all."

"What about Perla? And the kids? Geras?" Ama gripped the edge of the bed.

"Don't worry little Captain, they're all safe. Now, as to your leaving, that will happen tonight, which is why I am here. Not that the company of a pretty girl isn't reason enough for the visit. My name's Viren, by the way." He sat down next to Ama. His weight created a small well and she tilted in his direction.

Seg sat on the other side of Ama; he gave Viren a stern glare to warn him away. "So what is the plan?"

"You know, I have a banger wound too," Viren said, ignoring him and shining his scoundrel charm on Ama as he nodded to her bandaged shoulder.

"From fighting in the resistance?" Ama asked.

"No," Viren shook his head, "no, from a woman. Two, actually. Very long story." He rubbed his chin and squinted, "Three women, I suppose, if you want to get technical about it. And the wound is on my left buttock. Now where was I?"

"You were failing to impress anyone with your competence," Seg said, his voice tart. "We have an urgent matter to consider. Brin sent some men after my people. Unless you want your people quite dead, you need to call them off."

"Sorry," Viren said, standing, "that's the boss's call. I'll make sure to pass along the message though."

Seg leaned forward, "Listen, my people are trained soldiers. They can see in the dark, they can hear heartbeats, and they will kill your people without mercy if they detect them."

"Is he always this high strung?" Viren asked Ama, as he wandered to the table where the maps were spread out.

"Seg is right. But it's not just those men who are in danger, it's all of the Kenda," Ama said.

Viren gave them both a serious, and appraising glance. Then nodded his agreement. "Fair enough. Now, come gather round," he waved Ama and Seg to the maps, "and let me show you how you might escape being torn and hung before you reach your destination."

"Thank you," Ama said. "I know I've caused a lot of trouble for everyone."

"Oh, I excel at trouble," Viren said, with another swipe of charm. "Now, on to your daring escape. Brin's sent runners ahead. You'll have shelter as often as we can give it. Which won't be much, I'm afraid, but you'll find safe houses here," taking up a pencil, he drew circles on the map, "here, here and here. Anyone who displays the blue and yellow signal flag will give you food and shelter. They'll also expect to hear the code from both of you."

"What's the code?" Seg asked.

"*Blood for water*," Ama said, in Kenda, then repeated it for Seg in S'ora, the common tongue. "I'll teach you some of our language. Only the Kenda speak it, which can be useful for passing messages."

"Or for cheating at cards," Viren added, with a wink.

Seg rested his hand on the table edge, and faced Viren, "Has your *friend* replaced his deck? I expect you had to lift some coin off another mark to afford it."

"Don't think of them as marks, think of them as patrons of the resistance," Viren said.

Ama's right eyebrow rose as she looked between Seg and Viren. "Have I missed something? Do you two know each other?"

"Brin's lackey tried to drug and rob me," Seg said. He knew that he should have been more cooperative, but something about the man set him on edge and he didn't particularly trust him.

"Is that true?" Ama asked Viren

"Sadly, I am every bit the scoundrel he paints me," Viren said, hanging his head in mock remorse. "But not his Lordship here. No. A paragon of virtue he is." He moved to Seg and placed a hand on his good shoulder. "You would have been astounded. Not only did he outsmart my devious assistant and lay low one of the very unsavory men who attacked us, but he was beyond loyal when it came to you. *Ama, I only want Ama. I must find her!* He would touch no other woman and, believe me, the beauties I threw in his path are immensely touchable. The poor fellow is either insane or completely smitten with you."

He offered Ama another toothy smile, then removed his hand from Seg and pointed to a stack of weapons in the corner. "Have a suspicion we'll need these soon," he said, and gathered up an armload of crossbows. "Oh! And that," he added and bent down to scoop up a small barrel. "Shasir's 'magic' black powder, took years to pilfer it. And now, I'd best return to the gutter, lest I be missed. You leave tonight, pack those bags!"

Seg busied himself with their paltry stock of equipment. He felt a flush creep up his cheeks and wondered why this Outer's needling got to him. Ridiculous.

Loaded with weapons, Viren stepped into the tunnel, grasped the tether that pulled the 'wall' closed, and winked once more, "Until we meet again!"

Ama set to work gathering the meager supplies Brin and Perla had left behind. Seg snuck a glance in her direction and considered providing an explanation of what had occurred at the Port House that evening to counter Viren's absurd assertions.

Just then, Ama stopped in place, the wooden plates she had gathered slipped out of her grip and dropped to the floor, bouncing and clattering around her feet. "What have I done?"

"What is it now?" Seg asked.

Ama's face lost whatever color remained. "Dagga... He went after Brin because Brin's a Kalder. My brothers, he'll go after them too. And my father. Fa..." she ran to the false wall, the auto-med beeped continuously as she tried to pry the wall open.

"Wait!" Seg ran behind her, wrapped his free arm around her waist and pulled her back. He grunted as the motion jarred him; the painkillers had worn off some time earlier. "You can't do anything for them right now. Except be captured."

"You don't understand, I have to—" she relaxed against his grip, obviously surrendering to the futility of the situation. "I feel sick." she wavered, and Seg did his best to steady her. She turned her face to his, worry hemorrhaging from her eyes, "You don't know what this man is like, you don't know what he'll do."

"I have some idea. But there's nothing we can do right now."

She stared at his hands around her waist. "I wish you'd never come to our world."

"I could wish I didn't have to," he said, with a scowl, as he released her and turned away, "but it wouldn't change anything."

Hours had passed. Seg had slept briefly and woken groggy and stiff with pain. Ama had paced, worried her nove, and checked the contents of her pack four or five times, he had lost count. Now her ear was pressed to the false wall. With a fist, she hammered against the wall, then drew in a sharp breath and raised her hand to the wounded shoulder.

Seg rolled his head to look over at her. "You won't make it go any faster. Settle down."

"Your family isn't out there being hunted," she snapped.

"And I'm sure yours will be relieved by your banging on the wall and panicking," he retorted, his tone thick with sarcasm. "For my own part, I'm cut off and wounded and the closest thing I have to kin on this world are out of contact and may or may not show up for the rendezvous that I may or may not show up for myself. Shall I join in the futile bleating?"

Ama opened her mouth, ready to fire back a reply then stopped and crumpled to the bed, where she sat and stared at her pack.

"My father," she swallowed, then lowered her head, "I wish those weren't the last words he heard from me."

"What words?"

Ama turned to face him and shook her head, "What do you care?"

"If you don't wish to talk, then you can remain silent," he said, waving his hand at her.

She pressed her lips together, as if she would not respond, then: "My mother died when I was very young. Since then, my father—we're very close. We argued, not even a week ago. He told me I had to marry or give up my boat, or he would shun me. I thought he was just being like every other man on this world, telling me what to do." She paused and steadied herself, "But it was because of Stevan, because of Stevan's role in the resistance. They needed him to ascend and my life, my behaviour, threatened that." At the mention of her brother's name, her face faltered, "I didn't know. I—"

"Taking the blame for matters you were held ignorant of is pointless." Seg shifted with a grunt. "If anything, your family are to blame for keeping you unapprised of the situation. Now, retaining important information can be a necessity, but if one does so they should assume responsibility for control of the situation."

He let that settle in, then wondered if he had tried to articulate a too-complex notion. "I'm saying it's not your fault," he concluded.

"What's your father like?" Ama asked.

That was a simple answer. "He's a hard worker."

"Your mother?"

His lip twisted. "She was a hard worker as well."

Ama cocked her head. "Do you have—" her question was interrupted by the grate of the wall sliding open. Ama jumped to her feet, the auto-med chirped a warning.

In the dim light, a stooped figure could be seen, unrecognizable as Ama's cousin until he limped further into the room.

"Brin!" Ama cried.

Brin stumbled forward, with a pronounced limp. One side of his face was purple and swollen, and he cradled his right hand, which was wrapped in a hasty bandage, stained with blood that had already turned from red to brown.

Off balance, he crashed into the small table and tipped it to one side. Seg rescued a cup of water as everything else tumbled to the floor. Ama flew to Brin's side to support him.

Seg righted the table and shook his head, "There was no need to try it for yourself. We could have told you this was unpleasant."

One side of Brin's mouth rose in a weak smile. He placed his unbandaged hand on Ama's head to calm her, "It seems Constable Dagga was in need of an extra finger. I try to do my part for the authorities."

Ama tried to lead Brin to a chair but he refused. She raised her hand to the auto-med sleeve on her arm and struggled to pry it off. "We can put this on you. Seg, help me. Get this on Brin."

He shook his head. "If we shift it now, it will lose the work it's doing, waste its charge and capacities, and then we'll have to start over again. It's nearly depleted as it is." He levered himself up and looked over Brin carefully. "What happened?"

"Nothing." The look Brin returned told him he knew his fears, and had kept his tongue. "I was lucky, very lucky. Viren's army of doxies are old hands at passing and acquiring secrets. And when it comes to the Judicia, whose power supersedes Dagga's, those secrets were enough to ensure my release. Nevertheless, we'll have to get you both moving."

"There is another matter," Seg said."The people you sent after my squad. You need to recall them before my People kill them."

"I sent two runners to do just that," Brin said, "right after I left you at the boat works."

"Your man Viren—"

"Was instructed to keep silent on the matter. Whether they will reach them in time..." his brow furrowed.

Ama grasped Brin's bicep and squeezed, "My father, my brothers. If Dagga went after you, you know he'll go after them."

The half of Brin's face that could move, clouded. "Ama," he said, then let out a long gust of air, "Dagga sent an order from Alisir, before he reached T'ueve, your brothers are safe but your father...Odrell has been taken."

"No, no," Ama grabbed her pack off the floor. "I have to go, I have to get back to the Banks!"

"Which is what Dagga wants," Seg said without heat. "For you to obligingly walk into his trap."

"That is exactly his intention." Brin's frown dug in deeper. "He announced that Odrell will be locked in the Secat until you both turn yourselves in or are handed over." He rested his hand on Ama's shoulder, "Dagga knows how much you love your father; he's counting on you to be irrational."

"The *Secat*?" Seg asked.

"The As'Cata Corrective House for Purification and Cleansing," Brin said, his voice laced with sarcasm. "It's a prison, a Shasir prison for those whose souls cannot be redeemed. In our language, *Secat* means an absence of all water, a place reserved for those shunned by Nen."

"You know what Dagga will do to him in there," Ama said, eyes on Brin's bandaged hand. "I have to do something. I have to—"

"Ama," Brin said, his voice equal parts authority and compassion, "you're part of the resistance now, whether you realize it or not. You have to trust we'll get him out. I can't have you within fifty miles of the Secat, it's too dangerous."

"No one has ever escaped the Secat. No one," Ama said, her words coming out in forceful bursts. "I won't leave him in there. This is my doing; I'll turn myself in."

"No," Brin's eyes flared, he shook his head. "No."

"He's my father."

"And you believe that once Dagga has you, he'll just let him walk free?"

"It's better than hoping for some impossible rescue."

"Don't be stupid. He'll kill both of you!"

"Just like he'll kill your men if—"

"Wait," Seg cut in, loud enough to break through the storm between the two cousins, now inches apart and red-faced. "Don't send any of your men," he said to Brin. Then he turned to Ama, "Your emotion is muddying your judgment. The objective is to free your father and this will not be achieved by your sacrifice. Dagga will be prepared for anything either of you do. But when my People come …" his eyes moved to the far wall as he considered possibilities. "When they come, then you will have surprise. And opportunity."

"My father could be dead by then," Ama protested.

"He could be dead already," Brin said, his tone grave.

"Don't say that," Ama said, her stance shifting as if preparing for a brawl.

"We will operate on the assumption he's alive," Seg said to Brin, but for Ama's benefit. "Get my fifty and get them ready. You'll provide me with details of the prison; I will arrange an air strike and weapons the Damiar guards cannot defend against. When I return to this world, we will retrieve the man," he fixed his eyes on Ama, "and kill this Dagga."

"If your people are capable of all you say, your plan has merit," Brin said, scratching his beard.

"Swear to it," Ama said to Seg. "Give me your oath you'll do what you promise."

Seg raised his open palm, "I could manufacture some god or force that my people swear by, but we don't have such things. You have my word."

Ama studied his face, then her eyes moved down to his bandaged shoulder. That seemed to satisfy her. "Your word. Very well."

Despite his injuries, Brin straightened to his full height, his head nearly brushing the ceiling, "About the matter of your fifty men." His one good eye was fixed squarely on Seg as he drew his blade from its sheath.

"Yes," Seg said, "I'll understand if you haven't had time to assemble them yet." He watched the blade, ready to move in case Brin had been faking the extent of his injuries and had decided to collect a bounty.

Brin shifted the knife awkwardly to his bandaged hand. He could barely grip the hilt but, even so, he held his uninjured hand aloft and drew the tip of the blade across his palm, opening a long, thin cut. He motioned for Seg to hold up his right hand.

Seg recognized the significance of a blood exchange ritual and hoped his vaccinations and preparatory treatments were up to whatever strange pathogens the Outer might have as Brin drew the blade across his own hand. The blade was sharp and parted the skin with only the slightest of stings, which intensified as Seg unconsciously flexed his palm.

Brin returned the knife to its sheath, then leaned over the table and held his hand above the cup of water there. He allowed a single drop of blood to fall, then held the cup out to Seg. After collecting a drop of Seg's blood, he swished the contents of the cup, took a hefty drink and passed it off.

Seg's stomach churned. The ritual served as a reminder that even though he felt an instinctive kinship to this Outer, the other was still a primitive barbarian, one of the entrail-eating cannibals he had been warned about.

He lifted the cup to his lips and took a drink. The water was almost flavorless, but he could swear that there was a faint salty tang to it. He smacked the cup back down on the table and repeated the words to Brin that he had learned in the Kenda tongue. "Blood for water."

"Blood for water," Brin repeated, after a pause, then added, "brother." He wiped his bloodied hand on his trousers, "Now, Segkel

Eraranat, of the nameless people, you are Kenda. Yes, I will give you your fifty men. Fifty *brothers*."

"I—" Seg began, with a throat suddenly dry. He stared at the cup, the only source of fluid available, then swallowed and cleared his throat, surprised to find his voice hoarse with emotion. "Thank you, brother. I will care for them as my own."

"I know you will," Brin said. "And Ama, you have a mission of your own." He turned to face his cousin, "Get him to his people. Everything depends on that."

"I will," Ama answered.

"Once he's safely away, keep moving east through the Humish Valley, until you come to the Milabek River." Both Brin and Ama touched their index and middle fingers to their lips at the mention of the river's name. "There's a small cottage just beyond the ferry crossing. You'll see the signal flag; it's a safe house. When your father is freed, we'll bring him there." He tilted his head down to fix her with a stern look. "No sudden heroics or crazy schemes. If you don't make it to the cottage, we'll assume the worst and plan the rescue without the aide of our brother Seg."

"I'll make it," Ama said, then turned to Seg. "We'll save him."

"We will," Seg affirmed, full of conviction.

She stepped forward, as if she would embrace him, then stopped herself. Instead, she wrapped her arms around her cousin, who folded her into his wide chest and held her tightly.

"Come on then, we should hurry." Brin kissed the top of Ama's head, scooped up both packs in his one hand, and gestured toward the open wall. "I have a cartul rigged to smuggle you out of the city while it's still dark. I'll take you as far as I can, then you'll have to walk." He lifted his face to Seg, "When we are out of the city, we will talk more of your plans."

Ama was the last to enter the tunnel. When she pulled the wall closed, they were encased in blackness. Blind, she groped her way forward. Seg felt her hand brush his leg. His hand found hers and guided her forward through the darkness, a thin line of blood slick against their joined palms.

CHAPTER 13

The ride out of T'ueve had been long, bumpy, and punctuated by stifled cries of pain from the two fugitives hidden in the cartul's secret compartment. Once free, Seg and Ama had paused only long enough to work out the details of their plans for the raid with Brin before resuming their journey on foot. Avoiding the authorities meant avoiding the main roads, sleeping in the woods or wherever they could find enough cover, and never letting down their guard. Injured, hunted and exposed to the elements, every day was a test and yet, to Seg's surprise, the unending hardship was compensated by the camaraderie that developed between he and Ama. Along the way, she began teaching him the language, stories, history and customs of the Kenda and, in return, he explained the fundamentals of such wonders as electricity and radio waves. Both were as eager to teach as to learn, and in those moments they could almost forget their aching wounds and empty stomachs.

Then, seven days into their new life on the run, luck finally chose to smile on them. In the Largent Valley, a Kenda family offered to hide them for the night.

After a week sleeping on the damp ground, huddled together under the cover of brush, surviving on whatever morsels of food they could steal or forage, Seg thought the Kenda boathouse might as well have been a House estate for all its luxury. Tonight, warm, dry boat skins would be their bed; smoked fish, cream and kembleberries their dinner. The family hiding them—a husband and wife, their child and the boy's grandfather—had even provided a lantern. Light, shelter, food – in a very short time he had developed a new appreciation for these most primitive necessities.

Ama, sitting cross-legged beside him, held up one of the few remaining pieces of fish between her fingers. When he reached for it, she pulled it away and cocked her head questioningly. Seg frowned and dug into his memory.

"*Larula*," Seg said, the Kenda word for fish.

"Not bad." Ama smiled and held the morsel to his lips. "The r sound is softer, though, almost like an l."

He ate, though not with the ferocity they had both attacked the food at first.

"This method of language acquisition is difficult," he said, and rubbed the back of his neck.

"Yes, but if the Shasir or the Damiar had those—" Ama paused, waving her hand in a circle as she searched for the word.

"Chatterers," Seg supplied. "And, yes, it is fortuitous that your enemies do not possess such technology. Given the history, your people's determination to ensure the survival of your native tongue was clever and likely risk—" he stopped, winced and drew in a sharp breath.

"Your shoulder?" Ama asked, and pushed the plate aside before Seg could answer.

He raised his one free hand, as if to stop her, but in their travels he had learned that when Ama set her mind on something all arguments were useless.

She lifted the right side of his shirt, looked underneath, and let out a murmur of disapproval. "I'll get the slivee," she said, then hopped off the stack of skins to fetch her pack, and the healing leaves she made a point of collecting as they traveled.

"It appears worse than it is," he said, a blatant lie. Forced to carry his pack on one side, it had come down to a competition of which shoulder was most miserable. The left pained constantly from the broken collarbone, the right was chafed raw from the strap and the weight of his pack.

"Here, let's get this off," Ama said, as she undid the first three buttons of his shirt and pulled the collar down. When his shoulder was bare, she mashed the leaves between her hands, working them to a pulp. "At least we'll be dry tonight, maybe it will heal a bit."

As she laid her hand, with the leaf pulp, over the burning wound on his shoulder, Seg could not help closing his eyes and letting out a relieved breath. Ama's hand was cool, soothing, and the mild tingling promised a reprieve from the ache.

"We were lucky to find this place," she said, her voice low as she worked the pulp into the wound. "The family told me the Shasir have ordered all of the Kenda out of the valley, most have gone already. They're doing something to the Largent River."

"A dam?" Seg asked, recalling the unusual stacks of rocks and timber they had passed when they had crossed the bridge over the river.

"Perhaps. Not for us to know."

"Even if that's the case, mass relocation seems impractical. I doubt the flooding would be significant enough to necessitate such measures."

"They don't care about that. The spooks don't like eyes on their... magic." She said the last word with emphasis, knowing his distaste for it. "Whatever it is, the Kenda who've lived here for generations, fishing and harvesting praffa grass, are moving out; Welf workers are moving in. There's been some trouble downriver, Kenda who resisted. Constables burned some shops and houses. Boats and nets too, of course."

"Of course. That would explain the deserted homes and empty roads we passed."

These had made Ama wary and she had suggested pushing straight through the valley, even if it meant walking all night. Trusting her judgment, he had agreed, but then the rain had started. By the time they had spotted the cottage with the blue and yellow signal flag, the thought of a dry sleep and a real meal made their fears seem suddenly trivial.

"Unfortunate for your people, but at least we may sleep somewhat easier this evening," he said.

"Small mercies." Ama gently lifted her hand from his shoulder. "Better?"

"Yes." He opened his eyes to see her face inches from his, her lips stained red from the berries. "Thank you."

The words seemed laughably minuscule. Without her, he could not have hoped to make it this far alive. Against all instincts, he had to admit that Ama was as resourceful, clever, courageous and as deserving of the title 'Person' as anyone on the World. The implications of this thought disturbed him.

"Is something wrong?" she asked, head tilted.

"No," he answered, shaking off the thoughts and the question with a wave of his hand. "Aside from fatigue."

"I'm dead on my feet, too," she agreed, pulled away and reached for the lantern. "I asked the family to—"

A loud bang on the boathouse door stopped her.

"Authorities!" the voice of the grandfather warned them as the door flung open and revealed his black outline. "The authorities are on their way, you have to leave."

Ama and Seg leapt to their feet and scrambled to grab their packs and the clothes they had hung to dry.

"Hurry, hurry," the grandfather urged. "Riders were spotted on the bridge and th—"

The air cracked open, another loud bang cut short his warning. The man rocked forward, stumbled and dropped to the floor in a cloud of smoke.

Ama gasped as blood spread from the fallen man's torso. Seg cursed their failure to survey exit points and keep their weapons close at hand. If there was another way out, he could not see it. There were two small windows, both far too high to reach; a wall of uniformed constables blocked the only escape. His pistols and stunner were in his pack. He lunged for it but a familiar voice halted him.

"One twitch and I open this one up," Dagga said, and pushed a small boy into the boathouse, his blade pressed to the delicate throat. The boy's bright blue eyes darted down to his grandfather. Above him, Dagga loomed like a giant, the lantern light reflecting off his bald head and its web of scars.

Seg and Ama halted, their bodies locked in place. Two constables rushed inside. Seg felt the hard, cold metal of a gun muzzle against his temple; a gun was raised to Ama's head, as well.

"Tie him up and bring in the rest," Dagga ordered as he shoved the boy to one side. "Don't want any of 'em sneaking around."

The boy whimpered as he fell onto the lifeless body of his grandfather but was quickly yanked upright, his hands bound with rope behind his back.

Dagga stalked toward Seg. Obviously the encounter at the temple had instilled new wariness. When he was an arm's length away, he looked Seg up and down, then pressed the tip of his knife against his stomach. "Should gut you right here," he pulled the knife away, "but there's others want you breathing. For now."

Dagga turned to one of the constables that waited at the doorway, and waved his knife at Seg and Ama's packs, lying on the ground. "Dump 'em out. Don't touch nothing."

The constable complied. As he set to work, emptying both packs on the dirt floor, others brought the Kenda family inside. The husband and wife, hands tied, tried to offer some comfort to their boy as they bunched together under the guards's weapons.

"Surprised?" Dagga asked Ama. He slid a hand inside his coat and pulled out a scrap of paper, which fell open to reveal part of the map Seg and Ama had used to plot their route. "Left this in the rat nest."

The circles around places of possible shelter—including the Kenda village in this valley—might as well have been drawn in blood. Seg's mind flashed back to that last night in the safe room and an injured Brin stumbling and knocking everything off the table – including the maps. In all the drama of the moment, they had forgotten about such damning evidence.

Dagga let the map fall from his fingers. "Think no one knows about your filthy little Kenda secrets? Nests and tunnels, whistles and code words, and…" he turned, walked to the door and tugged a blue and yellow flag from the hands of one of the constables. He walked back to Ama and stuffed the flag down the front of her shirt, where it jutted out like some absurd flower, "Signals."

Seg pressed his lips together and reminded himself there was nothing he could say now that wouldn't make things worse. As if sensing Seg's thoughts, Dagga turned to him and rested the flat edge of the blade under his chin.

"Shasir call you a demon. Gonna send you up to T'ueve. Gods'll rain your blood from the sky." His eyes wandered over Seg and, as they lingered on his bandaged arm and shoulder, his lips curled into a sneer of contempt.

Dagga pulled the knife away and moved it to Ama, tracing it down her cheek, "Got a long list of them that want your blood, Kalder, but I'm a loyal man. Corrus gets you first. Don't think there'll be no friendly chat this time."

Outside there was a sound like thunder, which grew steadily louder. Hoof beats. Horses and armed riders, Seg guessed. Dagga backed away a few steps, admiring the scene with obvious satisfaction. With the toe of his boot, he pushed at the items from Seg's pack. Spotting Seg's knife, he sheathed his own and picked up this latest trophy. He raised a surprised eyebrow as he weighed the light weapon in his hand, then ran a finger along the blade's edge.

"Sharp," he muttered, approvingly. He walked back to Seg, paused in contemplation, then dug the tip of the knife into a section of exposed skin on the upper part of Seg's bandaged arm. With a flick, he tore open a piece of flesh, wiped the blade off on Seg's bandage, and slipped the knife into his belt.

Seg had managed to keep quiet despite a flush of panic. Though not immediately lethal, his blade contained enough toxin to warrant concern. Without an auto-med to counteract it, the huchack venom in the blade would kill the skin tissue around the wound, which would fester and ultimately lead to blood poisoning.

I'll be dead long before that happens, he thought. Grim consolation.

Dagga reached inside his coat once more and this time he withdrew a single huchack spine, wrapped in a piece of rough fabric. He displayed it for Seg, handling the spine with care. In contrast to the knife blade, these spines were deadly.

"Know what these are, don't you? Found a bunch of 'em in the men at the temple and on the boat. Any that weren't killed outright died quick. Died hard." He bent down and picked up the pistol with as much care as he had handled the spine. "This what shoots 'em?"

Seg sealed his lips tightly together and stared straight ahead.

Dagga nodded, then moved to the huddled family, hooked his hand into the crook of the wife's arm and yanked her away from the others. She shrieked as he pointed the pistol at her leg.

"Seg..." Ama pled.

"Yes! Yes, it's a huchack pistol," Seg blurted. When Dagga paused, he continued spitting the words out, "Huchacks are a kind of swamp dwelling slug from...from the islands where I come from. Their spines are poisonous. I crafted a weapon to fire them. Leave the woman alone and I'll tell you more."

Dagga pursed his lips and nodded. The woman sobbed. Then there was a whir and several clicks as Dagga pulled the trigger. The shot lacked the noise of a burning powder weapon but the effect was no less severe, as the spines sliced through the woman's leg. A red bloom spread out across her dress and she screamed, lost her balance and fell to the ground.

"NO!" Ama yelled.

Seg's muscles tightened; his free hand curled into a fist as he watched, unable to stop the torture. He felt Ama's weight hit his shoulder as the constable pushed the gun harder against her head to silence her.

Dagga ignored Ama's pleas, and the woman's wails of pain, as he inspected his handiwork. Then he turned the pistol on Seg, "Care about the water rats, do ya, Lord Whatsyername?"

Seg's mouth went suddenly dry; Dagga growled out a laugh.

"Bring all the rest to the Shasir," Dagga ordered a constable, who hurried to re-pack Seg's gear with a fearful eye to the strange instruments. Dagga nodded to the pistol. "Judicia'll want this."

Seg felt the slight weight of the digifilm in his pants pocket. Dagga had not stolen everything from his World, though Seg could find no satisfaction in the knowledge.

The Kenda husband bent down awkwardly to comfort his wife, who writhed on the ground. The venom was in her system. If the wound itself didn't kill her, the poison would take care of the job.

Dagga waved the pistol at Seg and Ama, "Load these two up, get 'em on their way, lock the rest inside."

The guards shoved Seg and Ama forward, out of the boathouse and into the dark. The rain had stopped but the ground was slick and puddled. At least sixty men, mounted on horseback, surrounded the property; any flicker of hope was extinguished at the sight.

Seg turned his head to see uniformed men barricading the boathouse door. Dagga snatched a lantern from one of the constables, strode to the side of the building, and hurled it up through the small window with a *crash*.

Seconds later the smoke started, as the flame hit the tinder-dry goods stored inside.

"Move it!" the guard behind ordered as he directed Seg to an open cartul.

Muffled shouts and banging rose from inside the boathouse, echoed seconds later by Ama's long cry of rage and despair.

Seg felt as if someone were filling his stomach with molten lead. Even when Ama had dragged him under the water at T'ueve he had not felt so helpless.

"Seg! No!" Ama screamed as they were dragged apart. She dug her feet into the mud, trying desperately to stop the guards as they pulled her away, slapped shackles on her wrists and ankles, and tossed her in the back of the waiting cartul. Hers was fully enclosed, the windows barred.

Seg was shoved into the other cartul, where his one free wrist was locked in a metal shackle, connected to the rough wood wall of the cartul by a length of heavy chain. He strained forward but the chain allowed him no more than a few inches of free movement.

"Secured," the guard shouted.

Dagga marched across the muck, his boots made a heavy suctioning noise with each step. He stopped next to the driver. "Largent Temple. Stop for nothing. Get him on that skyship. I'll be in Alisir three days from now. I expect a dispatch."

"Yes, Head Constable," the driver answered, the respect in his tone underlaid with fear.

As he walked away, Dagga paused, leaned in close to Seg and stated flatly, "She'll die slow."

Seconds later the cartul creaked and rumbled forward. Ama's cartul rolled in the opposite direction. Seg caught only a glimpse of her face before his cartul passed behind the boathouse. Flames licked out the window, lighting up the night, and black smoke poured out between cracks in the wood. Over the sounds of the horses, cartuls and the shouts of the constables, he heard the screams of those trapped inside the inferno.

Seg stared at the scene, numb. He didn't smell the smoke, didn't feel the chill of the night or the metal shackle digging into his wrist, didn't notice the blood leaking from the cut Dagga had given him, or think about how long it would be before the venom started to rot the skin and turn his blood toxic.

He only heard Ama, calling his name.

Viren spat out a mouthful of benga juice and tucked the stick into the pocket of his coat. Beneath him, his horse whickered, as he shifted his crossbow to his right hand.

Prow's horse snorted. "This is crazy," Prow whispered. To which Viren had no answer.

This *was* crazy. Twenty Kenda, with only crossbows and sefts, hoping to take out six squadrons of trained Damiar constables armed with bangers. Nothing this bold, or stupid, had been tried in generations. Succeed or fail, tonight's ambush might as well be a declaration of war.

But Brin had been adamant: stop Dagga and save Ama and her mysterious companion, Seg. Just as Brin had predicted, Dagga had torn T'ueve inside out in search of his prey. Then, with his small army, he had set off on the trail of the fugitives. Viren, with his much smaller band of rebels, had followed close behind.

Just before sunset, two events had roused Viren's suspicions. First, a skyship had landed at the Largent Temple. Then, shortly after, Dagga had taken his army and two cartuls, one a prison transport, and headed south. With most of the valley empty, the only likely destination would be the few cottages where Seg and Ama might have taken shelter.

Prow let out a low whistle and Viren returned the same. In the distance, there was a rumble. The copse of trees on either side of the road was good cover but meant the Kenda wouldn't be able to see the convoy until it was right on them.

He heard the whistled signal pass down the line, all the way to the bridge. Under the bridge, one of the men waited to light the fuse on their precious store of Shasir black powder. Dagga's men might anticipate an ambush but they would never expect their own tricks in the hands of Kenda. The explosion would create useful chaos and dropping the bridge would cut off this road to the temple. After that, their only hope was to hit hard and fast, free the prisoners and run.

The rumble grew louder, the thunder of hooves. Viren's heart kept time with the pounding. He gripped the reins tighter, turned his head toward the bridge and let out another set of whistles to pass along to the bridge man.

Soon the ground began to tremble. The convoy, perhaps sensing their vulnerability as they entered the woods, was picking up speed. He heard the sounds of the men urging on their horses. The first rider appeared, the white and blue uniform obvious even in the dark. Viren held his horse in place, raised his crossbow, and waited for the cue to attack.

More riders passed, sending up waves of muddy water as they splashed through puddles. Then there was the familiar creak of a cartul. Viren turned to Prow, his question apparent even in the dark. Why hadn't the bridge blown yet?

Through the trees, Viren could see a single figure in the back of the open cartul. Lord Eraranat was getting a rough ride tonight. It would get rougher if the convoy crossed the bridge. Then the cartul passed. The first riders would be arriving at the bridge. Viren shook his head. What had happened? Was the powder wet? Had the man lost his nerve? The window for rescue was closing. Once Dagga had Seg and Ama on that skyship, they were lost.

"Bilge sucking son of a—"

An earsplitting BOOM echoed through the trees.

Viren's horse skittered sideways at the noise. "Come on," Viren said to Prow, and turned his horse toward the bridge, weaving through the trees at a fast trot.

The bridge came in sight, intact for the moment, though it sagged and creaked ominously in the middle. Stunned by the blast, the riders on the bridge remained there as the structure gave way. Those at the front-edge of the column tried to outrace the spreading collapse; the others were pitched off the bridge and into the river. A few, no more than four, made it safely to the opposite side.

The screams of men and horses echoed in the damp night air, while those still on land reeled and goggled at the disaster. A few moved toward the shattered bridge, and leapt down from their horses to help the men who had fallen into the river.

"Form up!" a constable shouted. The order came too late. Crossbow bolts whizzed into the disorganized cluster. Exposed and unprepared, guards fell without firing off a single shot.

The air was ripe with the sweet and metallic smell of gunpowder, the ground littered with the dead or dying, parts of bodies and debris from the explosion. Horses kicked up mud, red with blood. Fragments of the bridge continued to creak and break, dropping into the rushing water. Screams of pain and panicked shouts heightened the swelling fear.

In the confusion, the Damiar guards pulled together. The first banger shots cracked out as they struck back blindly at their tormenters.

"NOW!" Viren yelled, though the Kenda rebels were already charging from the trees, bearing down on the terrified and disoriented jumble of guards.

More smoke and shouts filled the air, dying men wailed and fallen horses littered the road or ran in riderless panic. Through the disorder, Viren saw how close they had come to failure –

the open cartul was right at the bank of the river where the jagged remnants of the bridge stuck out from the earth like accusing fingers. The driver was trying to turn the cartul away from the edge but was slowed by the knot of men and horses around him.

"HEYYUP!" Viren shouted, and dug his heels into the horse's belly. Head low and crossbow raised, he charged for the open cartul and driver.

A constable was headed right for him. Viren tugged the reins to one side, the horse swerved. On his left, Prow overtook him, seft held out in front. The constable tried to correct but he was in Prow's path now. The seft caught the constable on one shoulder, tore it open and launched him from his horse.

Viren arced around the constables who had closed ranks. He slowed slightly as he sighted the cartul driver. The hefty man stood in the driver's box, grasping the reins with both hands and shouting at the others to clear a path. Seg, chained in the back of the cartul, crouched as low as he could to avoid banger fire and stray bolts.

With a sharp pull, Viren halted his horse and squeezed the trigger of the crossbow. There was a soft *thwep*, as the bolt released. The driver stiffened in place. One hand reached up to the bolt in his neck, then he dropped, his upper body dangling out of the box.

Once more, Viren spurred his horse forward and leapt onto the driver's box, while the battle raged around him.

"You!" Seg shouted over the din.

"Where's Ama?" Viren shouted back, as he pulled the cartul reins from the dead man's fingers.

"Dagga's taking her to Alisir. We have to get her!"

"Get down!" Viren shouted, and ducked as he spotted a constable raising a banger. The shot rang out but whizzed by harmlessly. He yanked the dead driver upright and patted him down quickly until he felt hard metal. "Have to get you out of here first," Viren yelled as he passed the key to Seg.

Beside them, a horse reared and fell, smashing into the side of the cartul.

"HEYYUP!" Viren called as he slapped the reins down and guided the cartul to the left and the road that led downriver.

Viren looked over his shoulder to make sure Prow and his other man, Ruch, were following. Seg had one end of the key in his mouth, the other jammed in the lock, head tilted to one side as he struggled to free himself.

"Hang on!" Viren yelled as he veered the cartul to one side to avoid a low hanging limb. He heard a *thud* and looked back to see Seg, loose from the shackle, had been thrown against the cartul wall. Well, he *had* warned him.

Now on a clear path, Viren put the four-horse team to work as they galloped ahead. He would need to put some distance between himself and the constables. Prow and Ruch soon flanked him, keeping pace and ducking branches that hung over the narrow riverside road.

"Where's Kalder?" Prow shouted.

"Other direction," Viren answered, bouncing up out of the seat as the cartul hit a rock.

"More Dammies coming!" Ruch yelled.

To his dismay, but not his surprise, Viren heard the shouts of reinforcements arriving from the north. Across the riverbank, more riders approached. Though the bridge was gone, those on the north side had bangers and it looked as if they were setting up to use them.

For now, those constables following the cartul on the road were being slowed by the rebels.

"Ruch, pull up," Viren ordered. He pulled back on the reins and called over his shoulder to Seg. "Get up here, time to go."

Seg gave Viren a look that questioned his sanity, but climbed up to the driver's box, waving his free hand as he wobbled precariously. As the cartul slowed, Ruch rode up closer to the side where Seg waited, and shifted forward in his saddle.

"Watch your step," Viren said, transferred the reins to his left hand and grabbed Seg by the collar of his shirt with the right hand, then maneuvered him toward the waiting rider.

"Storm!" Seg shouted as he balanced on the driver's box. His free hand stretched toward Ruch, clawing the air.

Viren kept one eye on Seg and one on the road as the sounds of hoof beats grew louder. "GO!" he shouted, shifted his grip, grasped Seg by the waist of his trousers and pushed.

Seg lurched forward and dropped, legs spread, onto the saddle behind Ruch. He slid sideways, feet kicking wildly, but Ruch reached a hand behind and held him in place until Seg wrapped his hand around the man's waist. Banger shots cracked through the air, ineffectual scattered fire from the frustrated constables on the other side of the river.

"Get him to his people," Viren called to Ruch, as Prow leapt from his horse and into the back of the cartul to act as decoy. "See you on the other side!" The road curved south, away from the water, and the cartul followed.

"Blood for water," Ruch answered, then veered right, closer to the river's edge.

"WE'VE GOT HIM! THIS WAY, MEN!" Viren shouted, to draw the constables away from Seg.

To both his chagrin and pleasure, they took the bait, leaving Ruch and Seg to follow the narrow footpath west, along the riverbank.

Seg clung to Ruch, feeling like a rag doll as they bounced along the path.

"We're gonna follow the river as far as we can. There's some old homesteads further down, we'll cut south there. Hide out if we need to," Ruch explained.

"We need to find Ama, " Seg said, as forcefully as he could muster.

"Too dangerous, there's constables," Ruch swayed slightly, "constables all over this valley."

As Ruch swayed, Seg felt something hot and wet between his fingers, which gripped the man's coat at the waist. "Are you wounded?"

"Just a graze," Ruch answered but his labored breathing spoke otherwise.

Seg swore softly but nodded. Every jounce of the fast-moving horse delivered spasms of pain, which narrowed his vision to a black tunnel that threatened to close over him. The terrain sloped downward as it followed the river gradient, beside them the churn from the water increased with the growing rapids. The rain, earlier that evening, had left the ground slick and made the going difficult. Ruch fought to control the horse's gait; the effort obviously cost him and he let out the occasional grunt.

"Might have to..." Ruch's hand loosened and the reins slipped through.

"No, don't!" Seg snapped, as the horse, sensing its freedom, picked up speed. "Stay awake. You have to control this animal!" Seg ordered and watched the reins fall from Ruch's grasp. His hand, at Ruch's waist, was soaked in blood. "At least get us stopped so I can help you."

Ruch let out a gasping breath and started a slow slide from the saddle, pulling Seg down with him as he fell.

Darkness. Pain radiated in lightning waves from his damaged shoulder as Seg came to from the momentary blackness. He wiped dirt from his eyes and saw the horse trotting away, growing smaller on the path as he lay there, helpless. He rolled to his side; Ruch was face down in the mud.

"Come on," he said, and levered himself upright into a sitting position. "Come on, you," he ordered Ruch, grasped the man's collar and rolled him over. "We have to keep moving."

Ruch didn't respond. His body was limp, unmoving, his torso wet with blood, his face plastered with mud.

"Fan out!" came a shout from above, followed by the sound of constables riding through the trees, not far in the distance.

Not all had followed Viren, it seemed. From the sound of it they were closing in, fencing him against the river. Seg looked at Ruch for a moment longer, then gave him one more shake. His head lolled from side to side. Gone.

Leaning to one side, he pushed himself up and off the ground, staggering slightly as he found his footing. One more quick glance to Ruch's body confirmed the worst, and he bent down to remove the knife and sheath from his belt.

The snap of branches told him the riders were getting closer; he could not hope to outrun them. He glanced back at the river, his only means of escape. But this time there was no Ama to help him, to breathe for him or keep him afloat. He could kick his legs and pull with his one arm, for a few moments, but in that rushing water he would be dragged under and drowned before anyone even had a chance to shoot him.

"Down here! Over here!" The shouts were louder now.

Debris was still floating down from the shattered bridge. His eyes moved to a large chunk of timber as it bobbed and raced through the waves.

"There!" A shot pinged off a rock; a constable on the opposite bank had spotted him.

Seg jammed the sheathed knife into his boot. He took a couple of deep breaths, set his timing, then ran. At the water's edge he leapt, soaring for a second before splashing down. The current seized him and he kicked madly, head tilted up, as the wooden beam floated just out of reach. His fingers brushed the surface, the beam rolled, then he finally gripped a splintered section.

With a grunt he pulled himself to the beam and wrapped his arm around it.

More shots spattered the water as the river dropped again, picking up speed and tossing rider and beam over white liquid haystacks. The foam created by the turbulence offered no support and Seg, clutching the wood as if he were choking the life out of it, slipped under. At least he had learned to close his mouth, to time his breaths.

The water spit him up to the surface again. He gasped a quick breath before another set of waves pulled him down. He had no way of knowing if the constables could still see him, but he knew that he was moving faster than any horse.

Down, under, cling. Up, surface, breathe. The motion played over and over, allowing him not a second of rest. All heat leached out of him, sucked into the water. There was no thought, only the instinct to hang on and steal air whenever the bucking whitewater allowed it.

The ride lasted an eternity. At points it seemed that simply letting go would be best, but he did not. At last, the river flattened, slowed, quieted. The beam drifted to one side and Seg could see shore and a beach, its sandy soil black in the moonlight.

When he felt he was close enough, he forced his hand and arm to release the beam. With numb legs, he kicked the short distance to shore, grasping at the thick stalks of praffa grass that dotted the shallows, to pull himself along.

Land. He had made it.

Once he had dragged his body out of the river, he curled up on the sand and shivered. He couldn't stay here but he was too spent to move yet.

At least he could breathe freely now. *Small mercies.* Ama had said that.

He closed his eyes, clenched his chattering teeth and dug his hand into the sand to pull himself up. To his left, he saw a short, sagging pier extended out over the water, to which no boats were tied. Small droplets of moisture assailed him as a cold drizzle pattered down again.

"Water," he muttered, with a grunt. Everything hurt, though the systemic ache damped out individual complaints. With a pained wheeze, he lifted himself to his knees.

"Move," he ordered himself.

Using his hand for balance, he thrust one leg out in front, then pushed up. In the soft sand, he staggered left, then right, stumbled forward a few steps and fell to his knees again.

"Karg!" he swore and hammered a weak fist into the sand.

The second attempt was better but he was moving too slowly. If any of the riders came after him, he would not be hard to catch.

To his right, in the tall, bushy praffa grass, he spotted a mound of fishing nets. It was better than wandering around in a daze, waiting for capture. With leaden, laborious movements, he crossed the short expanse to the nets, taking the time to erase each boot mark from the sand as he went.

The pile was heavier than he imagined and it took every remaining drop of his will to lift the nets and squeeze himself beneath it. Once underneath, the weight threatened to crush him. Luckily the soft soil let him dig out a nook. The air was putrid and stifling but he had shelter from the rain and some measure of warmth.

Between the pain that enveloped him and the knowledge that his hunters were out there, searching, his eyes remained open through the night.

At intervals, there were some distant shouts and muted hoof beats that jolted him back to alertness and stopped his heart, but none of the riders lingered or noticed his hiding spot. Eventually there was nothing but silence and Seg allowed himself a ration of hope.

Seg stifled a cough as he surveyed the landscape in the grey morning light.

Not far down the beach from the net mound that had sheltered him through the night, he spied a battered wooden building. The door hung open on broken hinges. A short walk, he could make it. Ruch's knife hung from his belt, pitiful defense.

Evade contact. Gather survival materials. Either get into a safe position for extrans, or return to extrans point. Basic training dogma. He swayed where he stood, then stumbled forward with as much speed as possible.

The shack was decrepit, but reasonably watertight. He peered in cautiously. It appeared to be a Kenda Port House, though significantly more primitive than the one he had visited in T'ueve. The smell wafted out of the room, a horrid stench of rotting fish, old sweat, smoke, mildew and something much worse than all of those together. A bar dominated one half of the main room, the bottles smashed on the racks, the tables and chairs overturned or broken. In the back, behind the bar, he could see a door, possibly to a storage room or the Port House keeper's lodgings, probably both.

Bar. Alcohol, he was going to need that. He glanced at his arm, where Dagga had cut him. The skin had already puckered from the touch of the huchack venom. Tissue was lost, dead, and the effect would spread until the gangrene poisoned his blood and killed him.

Now that he had avoided death at the hands of the Shasir, the need to tend to the small wound was paramount.

Assuring himself the Port House was deserted, he stepped in further. Broken glass crunched under his boots, along with some soggy, flour-like material scattered on the wood. Inside, he glanced up and noticed the wall decoration for the first time – a large, dusty skeleton with an unmistakable serpentine shape. The drexla's empty eye sockets stared out at him, challenged him.

Water was death.

He sifted through the debris, wary of the sharp-edged glass that lurked in the muck. Even though the windows were uncovered, the murky morning provided little light with which to work.

Most of the bottles had been smashed during whatever upset had befallen the place. But in the corner, behind the bar, he found a crate that had been set aside for refilling. Many of them had a few dregs left, and he took an experimental sip from one. The taste of raw alcohol hammered his senses and made his eyes swim.

"Good," he muttered, and set the bottle aside. The rawest of spirits was what he needed. He continued through the case, with sips from each bottle. When he found a bottle of proper potency, he poured the small quantities into the first. The lips of the bottles clinked together as he tapped them to make sure every drop was extracted.

The rain picked up in intensity as he worked, fatter drops spattering against the windows. Every few moments he glanced at the open doorway. In this rain, anyone could simply walk up to the door and he wouldn't hear a hint of their presence until it was too late. Knife or not, an Outer child could overwhelm him right now.

He lifted the first bottle and swilled it around, then peered through the dark glass. Perhaps a cup's worth. It would have to do. Beside the precious bottle of alcohol, he set a small bottle of lantern oil he had found under the bar.

Next, he needed something with which to strike a fire. The local techbase was advanced enough to use matches, which they kept in small leather packets with a sewn-on striking surface. The dead lanterns in the room offered him hope. Finally, under the bar, near the shattered jar that had likely held money from the patrons, his search was successful.

He fixed the match packet in his mouth, then gathered the two bottles carefully under his good arm. Last, he grasped the knife. There was no place to sit in the main room, but perhaps somewhere behind the door?

He nudged the door open with his foot and he coughed as a fresh wave of stench washed over him. With a look to the floor, he discovered the source of the rotten odor.

Her cheeks sagged inward and it appeared that the woman had been dead at least a couple of days. Too-red hair was speckled with strands and clumps of silver and grey, the results of a poorly done dye-job. What remained of her clothing was taut and suggestive, and it was easy to deduce what employment she found in the back room of this fisherman's tavern. Her throat had been cut, as had some of her clothing. She lay on the floor, hollow eyes staring at the ceiling.

An act of savagery, nothing less, likely from the Damiar constables. The realization jolted him. The authorities were engaging in general reprisals now. Stevan's death, the shoot-out at the temple, those actions had sparked a fresh wave of oppression.

He sat down on her bed with a weary groan. This world felt as if it were bearing down on his shoulders.

This woman had suffered and died from his actions. It was one thing to cause death when it directly affected his mission, another entirely when it was simply spillover. Needless, incidental waste.

"Evade contact," he repeated aloud, to pull himself back into focus. "Gather materials. Move to extrans."

The room was, as suspected, used half for storage, half as living space. A curtain had once partitioned the two; it hung by one corner now, likely torn off by whoever had murdered the whore. Likewise, the stores had been ransacked.

He took a deep breath, lifted the bottle of alcohol and allowed himself one small swallow, then carefully set it on the nightstand, along with the bottle of lantern fuel. His boots rubbed against the body and he frowned, then tried to nudge it away. Every push lifted it slightly, then saw it fall back onto his foot. Finally he braced himself with his good arm and pushed her away, turned those accusing eyes toward the floor. He scooted along the bed toward the nightstand. Lifting his knife, he looked at his arm.

"Focus", he whispered. If he did not hold still he would botch the job and end up worse than he started. With another deep breath, he checked the edge of the weapon. Ruch, the man who had died saving him, had kept a sharp blade.

"Good man." Would he have been one of the men Brin recruited for him?

"Focus," he reminded himself. He placed the blade on the proximal side of his wound and angled it carefully. Then he stopped as a thought occurred to him. Laying the blade aside, he grabbed the filthy sheet from the bed, balled it up, then bit down on it. The taste was greasy, tangy and he put it out of his mind as he applied the blade to his skin once more. Mentally he counted down from three, then pushed. He screamed into the improvised gag as he sliced the flesh away. Likely he took far more skin than he needed to but the risk in taking too little was greater. At the end of his cut, he squinted as he pinched the shaved skin with his thumb and forced the blade through.

Done. He hurled the blade away and beat his good hand down on his leg as he continued to groan into the sheet. Blood oozed down his arm from the fresh wound. Finally, he spit the sheet out, then held it on the wound to soak up the blood until the flow ebbed.

"Damn." His eyes watered. "Oh damn. Damn."

Not finished yet. He had to make sure the toxin was completely eliminated. He lifted the bottle and emptied all of the contents on to the wound, then spun the cap on the lantern oil and did the same. He writhed and nearly fell backwards as the sting of the alcohol and the oily fuel met the sliced flesh.

Gasping for air, he fumbled for the matches and drew one with a shaky hand. He couldn't strike against the striker with one hand, and he had to squirm around to position his immobilized arm at the base of the small packet. Fighting the pain, he struck the match, watched it flare to life in front of him. He had to move quickly; the flame was already guttering. With a panted whimper, he jabbed the match into the wound. It ignited with a blue flame that didn't hurt at first. The heat came as the oozing blood sizzled and blackened, then the meat began to char and singe underneath.

Though nearly unbearable, he let the fuel burn as long as he could stand. But it was not long before he slapped down the flame and smothered it with the greasy sheet. His breath came too fast, too ragged. He fell back in a haze of throbbing pain and fatigue.

He had no idea of how long he had laid there. Despite the discomfort, he had dozed off. Now, pain shivered up and down his body like a web of fire. He felt something tickle his cheek and turned slowly. The insect was easily half the size of his thumb, its antennae twitching inquisitively. Its forelegs ended in vicious pinchers that it waved at him, as if to warn him away.

It worked. He lurched from the bed, away from the creature, upending the bottle on the nightstand, which fell with a soft thud onto the body that he nearly tripped over as he backed away. He staggered forward and grabbed the knife. Distractedly, he wiped it clean on his pant leg as the insect meandered over his newly vacated kingdom.

Seg caught his breath, steadied himself, and walked back into the main room. By the light, he knew he must have slept the better part of the day. There were only a few hours of daylight remaining and he would have to be on the move when they were gone. He took a long look around; the enormity of what lay ahead threatened to paralyze him.

Gather materials.

Bandage, he would need a bandage for his wound. He started his search.

Outside the Port House, Seg shouldered the grimy, half-rotted knapsack he had found in the back room. The pack contained only the few supplies he had scrounged but even so it weighed on him and he knew it wouldn't be long before the wound on his shoulder flared and ached.

He oriented himself in the dim light of early evening, turning a slow circle. The surrounding village had been mostly burned, the ashes now washing away in the rain. Ahead of him, the dark forest lurked, with all the dangers he had already encountered on this savage world and doubtless hundreds more besides. His enemies were spread throughout the region, hunting him.

His digifilm had survived intact. If nothing else, he had a map and a compass. He needed to get to the rendezvous. He needed to get to Alisir and rescue Ama, or die trying. Both destinations were south. Both impossibly far away, unreachable.

"Move."

He could sort the rest out later.

Behind him, he heard wood cracking and shifting. Men's voices drifted through the rain. Looters? Constables? It didn't matter. He was prey to everyone on this world at the moment. All he could do was run.

Ama's chains rattled as she was pulled from the prison cartul. Around her, the river port of Alisir mirrored her defeat. A pall had fallen over the city. Smoke rose in grey tendrils from Kenda boats the authorities had torched, their black skeletons a warning to the masses. In spite of this, business went on in the city but the sound and color had been drained away. Surrounded by constables, she hung her head and trudged down the ramp, with a sidelong glance to the other boats anchored nearby. Her fellow mariners were well aware of her presence, but kept their eyes deliberately averted as she was hustled along the dock, toward a waiting cruiser.

Dagga led the procession. From his elevated shoulders, Ama could tell he was agitated.

Her pace was restricted by the shackles on her ankles, which were joined by a heavy chain just longer than the width of her shoulders. Her wrists were shackled in front, with barely an inch between them. Another chain ran from a ring between her hands to the guard that dragged her forward.

At the stairs to the cruiser, Judicia Serval waited. His smile of greeting drooped as Dagga approached.

"No checkpoints outside the city. No patrols," Dagga spat as he approached, barking out his displeasure. "I sent a dispatch with orders."

Serval spread his hands, "Head Constable, you have to understand, there have been uprisings. The Sky Ceremony is underway at the temple. We need the—"

"*You* understand this," Dagga growled, jabbing his finger at the Judicia, "we got traitors infesting our cities. Get those men and lock this scum pond down. Now!"

"Watch your tongue with me, Head Constable," Serval fired back. "I am still your superior and Alisir is not your jurisdiction."

"Orders come from the Shasir, not me. You gonna disobey them?"

"Never, Head Constable," Serval acquiesced. His eyes stole to Ama as she was herded past him, to the stairs. What did she catch in that fleeting look? Fear?

"Got my dispatch from Largent?" Dagga asked.

"The Shasir'dua sent a runner from the Alisir Temple this morning." Serval passed Dagga a folded piece of paper. Ama tried to keep her eyes on Dagga as he read but the constable leading her yanked on the chain. She stumbled forward, barely catching herself from falling.

There was a moment of silence but it was soon shattered.

"Escaped?" Dagga roared, from behind.

A wind blew through Ama's heart as she stepped onto the deck. Below, Dagga raged at the Judicia, at the constables, at the absent Kenda rebels, but Ama only heard that one word.

Escaped.

From Dagga's reaction, it could only be Seg. He was alive.

Careful not to betray her joy, she kept her head low and scouted the boat. Too many guards, no allies here. She was being led to the hatch that would take her below deck, where a cell waited to hold her for the voyage to the Banks. If they locked her up, it was over. Now was the only chance she had.

Dagga was shouting orders, the men were distracted. Purposefully, she slowed her step and let the constable pull her forward again. This time she was ready. When he tugged, she used the momentum to cover her charge.

Both arms swung up as she tackled the constable. She wrapped the loose length of chain around his neck and cinched it tight, choking him as she hopped to the port gunwale.

"Halt!" one of the guards yelled, and raised a banger. But Ama kept the choking constable in front of her as a shield, while she backed up against the rail.

Dagga charged up the stairs, his hand pulling the knife from its sheath as he ran. Ama leaned back, using the weight of her hostage to help push her overboard The man's arms flailed as they fell. Her back hit the water with a *smack* and the man's weight drove her down deep. Her second eyelids flipped up.

The guard thrashed to free himself but Ama held tight as the current pushed them downriver and into the hull of the neighbouring boat. Banger shots pierced the water, out of range. Ama and her human cargo were pinned against the hull. At last, the struggling ceased. She loosened the chain and pushed the dead weight away.

Her nove – she needed to get it off so she could breathe. Hands raised, she strained to reach the laces in the back but the shackles held her wrists too close together. Her lungs burned. She craned her neck and tugged down on the leather with her fingers until one side gave way a little.

On her left side, part of her dathe were exposed. Enough to buy some time. Bit by bit she worked the collar down until most of both sides were free. She gave herself a few seconds to suck in oxygen and sound the underwater landscape.

Swimming against the current was impossible, even without the shackles. But Dagga would have every constable in Alisir spread out downriver to fish her out if she tried to make it to shore. No one knew about her dathe. For now, the safest place was right here under their noses. But she couldn't stay under forever.

With her hands, she pulled herself along the hull, to the stern, and the rudder that jutted downward. She held onto the rudder and waited for what felt like hours, her mind racing as she imagined a map of Alisir, of the Gwai River, of all the possible escape routes. If it came to it, she could drift out to the big water. But then what? With these shackles, she couldn't swim for any distance. She would be at the mercy of the tides and the currents.

A school of rukefish swam by, heading upriver, chased by a spinner. The scene reminded Ama of simpler times, of her midnight swims and dreams of escaping from the Banks.

The reminiscence halted suddenly. A spinner.

It was a long-shot, but she let go of the rudder, pushed off and down. Arms tight to her body, shackles against her navel, she brought her legs together and pumped, the same way the spinner used its long, wide tail.

With her dathe to help her, she saw the shape of her water brother turn from the hunt and head in her direction. The noise of the shackle chains would naturally appeal to the spinner's curiosity.

That's it, Ama thought, *let's play, my brother.*

Despite her effort, the current was pulling her downriver, as the spinner circled around her. With its stubby snout, it nosed at the dangling chain, taking it into its mouth once or twice, jerking Ama's hands from side to side, before spitting the chain out. When it passed under her, and rolled, Ama took a moment to stroke the slick fur of the spinner's belly.

Please, help your sister.

The animal circled once more then jetted away, distracted. Just as Ama was contemplating the ride to the river mouth, the spinner appeared again. With determined tail pumps, it dove down, then bolted to the surface for one of the spinning jumps it had been named for. After it splashed back down, the playful animal, which was almost twice as long as Ama, slid beneath her.

Nen praise you! she thought, as she stretched her bound hands out and slipped them over the spinner's head.

Together, they plowed against the current, upriver, past the docks, past the city. The spinner corkscrewed and twisted, dove down and rose up. A smile locked on Ama's face for the entire ride.

Escaped.

From her hiding spot in a thicket alongside the road, Ama watched the comings and goings of the Welf village. Travel through the woods had been excruciatingly slow, thanks to her shackled hands and feet.

At every noise, she had been ready to dive for cover. When, at last, the village had come in sight, she had been faced with a dilemma.

She could trust her fellow Kenda to help her, or to at least not to betray her to the authorities. Welf? They were another matter. Blindly loyal and obedient to the Shasir, she could count on most to turn her in. The rest could only be bribed, and her coin was long gone. But she needed to free herself from the shackles; there was no way around it.

Night. She would have to wait for darkness, creep into the village and try to find something either to smash the chain or pick the locks. And hope she wasn't found out.

She rolled to her back and armed the sweat from her forehead, the loose length of chain wrapped securely in her left hand. Wherever Seg was, she hoped he was faring better than she was. As soon as she dealt with her restraints, she would head for the rendezvous site. That would be Seg's destination; he had made clear the importance of returning to his people, and his world. And if he didn't make the rendezvous, she would have to convince his people to find him. Assuming they didn't kill her on sight.

"He'll make it," she whispered.

Behind her, on the road, she heard a Welf singing above the rattle and groan of a push-cart. Probably returning home from a happy day of groveling beneath the boots of the Dammies. She couldn't decide who angered her more — the cloud sniffers who used these backward people as their pawns, or the naïve Welf who let them.

Eyes closed, she laid motionless and listened as the singing grew louder. The tune was simple, nonsense rhymes and endless repetition. Her eyes flew open suddenly. The song, the voice, they both were familiar.

Ama rolled to her elbows and squinted out to the road. It was impossible to tell for certain, but the cart and the Welf's height and build were the same. Could this be the boy, Tev, who had helped her gather provisions during her last visit to the Alisir docks?

Hope banished caution. Ama snatched a small stone from the ground, hauled back with both hands and tossed it. It dropped just short of the Welf. She scrabbled in the dirt and found another, cocked her arms back further this time and let it fly. The stone bounced off the boy's hindquarters. He stopped, looked around and scratched his head in bewilderment.

Ama gave a short whistle. His head swiveled, searching for the source of the noise. She whistled again, louder this time and rose up just enough for him to see.

There was no one else on this stretch of road at the moment but she was pleased to see he did not call out or draw too much attention. He turned the cart and pushed it across the road, stopping right in front of the spot where she was crouched. His face scrunched and then burst open, a surprised smile lighting up his face.

"Captain Ama?" he asked, wise enough to keep his voice low.

She nodded and raised a finger to her lips.

"You're in big trouble, everyone's looking for you. First they says you killed Lord Uval, then they says you killed one of the Sky Fathers," he whispered, his face narrowing with concern.

"I know, and I don't have time to explain the truth. Look, I don't want to get you in trouble, but I need some help. I promise there'll be some coin for you if—"

"Don't want your coin," Tev shook his head emphatically.

Ama's face fell.

"Don't know about t'other part, but Lord Uval was a bad man," Tev continued. At another time, Ama might have laughed at his exaggerated expressions – the broad, guileless smile, switching rapidly to the childlike scowl. "I knows he sent men to kill Jibri. Killed him they did, and stole the extra coin you tipped. I saw it, saw it clear as air."

"Killed Jibri?" her voice dropped away as she fit the pieces together. Jibri, the dock runner who had run her creds to the Port Captain, hadn't been killed for his coin; he had been killed because he knew too much. "Tev," she said, then raised her arms to display the shackles, "I need to get these off. Will you help me?"

Tev looked up and down the road, then nodded at her with his lips pushed together in another exaggerated expression of determination. "Yup, stay put."

He backed up the cart, until it was alongside the tangle of brush. He lifted the empty sacks inside and gestured for Ama to climb under. When she did, he covered her up carefully and patted her shoulder.

"Best others don't know 'bout this," he said, lifted the handles, and walked the most wanted woman from M'eridia to Malvid into his village.

Inside the shelter of Tev's tiny cottage, Ama examined her wrists. The skin was red and raw but it would heal and, for the moment, the pain was dwarfed by the overwhelming relief and gratitude she felt. If she still had the coin Seg had paid her, she would have happily given it all to Tev. As it was, he brushed away her thanks and praise, which seemed to make him uncomfortable.

"You keep this," he said, passing her the lengths of metal he had used to pick the locks, "might need 'em again, yup."

"You may be right about that," she said, and thanked him once more as she dropped them into the small sack he had found for her.

His cottage was no more than a one-room shack, with furs on the floor for a bed, a small stove, table and washbasin. Despite his poverty, Tev had shared a meager dinner then packed up extra bread and a hunk of cheese, for her journey. They sat on the furs, waiting to be sure the villagers were asleep before Ama headed out again.

"I'm sorry about Jibri," Ama said, quietly.

Tev sniffed and wiped a tear from his eye, "Was a good friend and true. Lost my da when I was a sprout, never knew my ma. Jibri kept care of me, helped me find a living, yup. He's in the Cloud Temple sure as rain, though. And he's smiling to knows I helped you."

"I hope so," Ama said. She had her doubts about the Cloud Temple but she hoped that Jibri had found peace in death wherever he went.

"You be careful out there, now. Ever since word comes that you be hunted, the Kenda been doing all kind of fightin' and such. Word come out that they was taking away any Kenda shows the blue and yellow flag. Next day those flags be everywhere, every house and boat and shop. The blue coats be mad as haffsa's, yup."

"I'll be careful, believe me," Ama said. She did not share her elation at that news with her host. The Kenda were finally making a stand. How long had she wished and prayed for this? And the timing couldn't have worked more in her favor. If her people were keeping the authorities busy, that meant less attention on her and Seg. For this rebellion to succeed, Seg had to return to his people and his world.

Ama and Tev listened for a moment and heard nothing but the ocassional animal noise. Tev brushed his hands together, and both he and Ama stood. She collected the small sack, then laid a hand on his forearm.

"Tev I want you to listen carefully to me. I can't tell you why, but your people are in danger from…from powerful demons, sent by the O'scuri. If you see any trouble around here, big fighting or fires, I want you to run and hide. Even if the blue coats tell you to fight, promise me you won't. Go to the mountains, to the woods, take anyone who will listen and hide until it's quiet. Swear you'll do that."

Tev was busy making elaborate gestures with his hands, petitions for protection from the Lords of the Sky, but when he finished he raised both hands, palms up, and said, "I swear, Captain Ama."

She grabbed him in a rough embrace and kissed him on the forehead, then slipped outside, into the dark.

Four days left to make the rendezvous. She looked up at the moon and offered a quick prayer to father Nen and mother Min, then jogged out of the village.

The cartul was dilapidated but covered, pulled by a hulking gresher and driven by an old, stooped Welf, with a small girl seated beside him. To an untrained eye, the clothes they wore were little more than rags, but Seg could see the small embellishments—the colored ribbons in the child's hair, the man's buttoned shirt—that signified some special occasion.

He limped toward them, part cover, part genuine; his feet were badly blistered and the knapsack rubbing against his shoulder forced him to move slowly.

"Blessings of the Sky Gods upon you, children of the soil," Seg said, his voice grave but infused with the lilting tones of the Welf. He held up a grimy hand, palm skyward, in greeting and was careful to stand downwind.

This was his first contact since the Largent Valley. A risk, but necessary if he was going to find Ama and escape to the rendezvous in time. He had just finished a long hike, through the night. But as hard as he was pushing himself, his destination stretched too far in the distance, and exhaustion and hunger were starting to slow his progress. He needed rest, and he needed to move; the cartul held the answer to this conundrum.

"Blessings on you," the old man returned, stopped the cart and raised his palm in return. He swung to face Seg, his eyes white and clouded, his gaze guided solely by sound. The girl, who was perhaps six or seven years old, sat silent beside him, clutching his sleeve. "Is it a fellow pilgrim we meet?"

"Not a pilgrim this day, wise one," Seg said, adding the referential. Age and wisdom were as one to the Welf. "But I'll take the journey soon enough. Making my way to Y'idvaris, to collect my ma. She's sickly and would make one last pilgrimage before she ascends to the Above, yup."

"Ahh, good boy," the blind Welf raised a hand and laid it on the girl's head, almost as seamlessly as if he possessed sight. "First year for the grandbaby, properly blessed by our sacred fathers now, she is."

The gresher stamped the ground and bucked its head.

"Must keep a-rollin'. Need to make it home in time for the fires." He gestured roughly toward the back of the cartul. "Got a fine load of the blessed wood to burn for the Sky Ceremony. Abundance of the mother to you."

With a rattling *Ayup*, the old man slapped the reins and the gresher resumed its amble.

"Was wondering, wise one," Seg said, limping faster to keep up with the cartul, "if I could trouble you for a ride, since you be heading toward Alisir. I need to get passage to see my ma, soon as can be. Got no coin to spare but I won't be a bother. Been walking day and night, got a bad case of footsores."

"Not going as far as Alisir," the old man answered, smacking his lips together then opening them wide to reveal a mouth missing all but a few teeth. He slowed the cartul, leaned down and whispered something in his granddaughter's ear. She, in turn, whispered something back at him. He nodded and turned in Seg's direction, "Come, come closer then, boy."

Seg hobbled closer. He thought about the knife tucked into his pack and hoped he would not have to decide between two lives and his own survival. Even Outer lives such as these. As the man beckoned, he reached for the rail on the side of the cartul and climbed up on the step next to the driver's box, then waited.

The man's hand reached forward with practiced motions, found Seg's hand, then his forearm. He pinched and squeezed. "Work the fields?" he asked.

"My Lord's game collector, I am," he answered, letting a note of pride enter his voice. "A huntsman."

"Ahh, well and true on that," the elder Welf nodded his approval. "Thought you too scrawny for a farmer." His didn't withdraw his hand, but moved it upward, along Seg's arm, over his face, then stretched up to the top of his head. "Grandbaby says you're strange tall and bright-eyed."

Seg was quiet for a moment. He had already considered the answer but it was one that required the proper amount of hesitation.

"My da's no Welf," he said, with a cough to indicate his embarrassment.

The old man nodded and when he spoke his voice was softened, "Go on then. Not sure as the ride will be as fine as suits you, but there should be room enough. Move the wood aside if you likes. Few morsels in the bucket back there, don't be shy."

"Thank you, wise one," Seg said, as he scrambled into the cart. "A child of the soil who keeps his eyes on the skies above needs no soft bed to sleep," he quoted. He grunted as he tried to shift the heavy logs. They were embossed with some sort of Shasir runes he couldn't translate, likely an old tongue. Perhaps they had some vita infusion in them, but without his VIU he would never know.

Unable to shift the weight, he simply curled up in the side of the cartul, well out of sight of passersby. He wedged the knapsack against the wall to at least provide his head with some padding. The rumble of the cartul was hypnotic; sleep claimed him within moments.

Twelve days.

In his small teaching office, Jarin sat and watched the amber flash from his comm, alerting him to urgent messages. However urgent, none of those messages contained the news he wanted. For once, he was content to hide from the World.

Twelve days since Segkel's last contact. The raider lieutenant, Kerbin, had checked in at the scheduled times, but Segkel had failed to make contact. No word to the World, no word to the squad. He had vanished.

Theorists died on recon missions. Entire squads had been lost. It was singularly dangerous work, among the most hazardous duties People exposed themselves to, without the use of slave, proxy caj.

"He's not coming back," Jarin muttered, as he stared at the blank screen of his digipad. To accept the fact now would allow him to move on. Throughout his career, he had always worked with fallback plans and contingencies, but the CWA's recent maneuvers constituted a new threat and left them with precariously little room for error.

Jarin considered the Guild students who were still in training, and the young, recently graduated Theorists. So few possessed the vital and defiant spark that would be necessary to spearhead change on the World. None possessed it in the quantity of Segkel Eraranat.

The boy had come to him in possession of all the necessary qualities; Jarin had only to shape and direct them. These others? He would have to breathe defiance and rebellion into them, along with a host of other traits.

"More difficult, but the work must be done."

He reached across his desk, to the seldom used tumbler of thin liquor, to take a drink. His hand—wrinkles gathered at the knuckles, veins protruding, spots of age appearing like tiny islands—flashed its own warning. Time, another enemy.

He glanced at the comm again. Soon he would return to those important matters but, for now, he needed to choose the next young minds to mold and harness. Even if the fight was lost, it was not within the People to simply concede. He would find another to carry his hopes, and look for ways to reverse the course of history.

Twelve days.

His hand shook slightly as it traced across the digipad and queued up the student rolls.

CHAPTER 14

Sansin – Seg could scarcely believe he had arrived. A trading city, Ama had explained, with a mix of Welf, Kenda, and Damiar alike. Rundown hovels rimmed the outskirts to the north; Damiar estates spread across the south; in the center a cluster of markets, inn's, shops and cottages. But for Seg, Sansin was the crossroads.

Crouched behind a towering statue of a Shasir priest, Seg lifted his bottle of water from his pack with trembling hands.

He had waited for sunset to pass through the city, adopting the half-Welf persona he had used to secure his cartul ride. With his two weeks growth of beard, threadbare clothes, tanned skin, affected stoop, and layers of dirt, he was close enough to pass for one of the lowest caste. Even so, he had believed every eye was on him, every footstep that of the authorities coming to seize him. By the time he had reached the far side, his mouth and throat were parched and his heart was beating so quickly his chest hurt.

The water was nearly gone but he guzzled it anyway. Water, at least, was never hard to find on this world.

The lantern lights of the city cast a glow by which he read the marker signs. Pointing one way, the sign to Alisir. That road would take him to the riverport city. From there, he still had to find Ama and free her, one-armed and his only weapon a knife. He leaned back against the cool stone and let the bottle hang loose in his hand.

She'll die slow.

Dagga's voice clouded his thoughts; he forced himself to focus. The other road marker pointed in the opposite direction, to Ymira. That path would take him to the Humish Valley and the rendezvous, which he had to make before sundown of the next day or be left behind on this world forever.

The mission was his priority, that was undeniable. But the vita readings he had collected from the Welf settlement at Ymira and the Alisir temple alone would be enough for House Haffset to plan a strike and reap a profit, not to mention any additional vita readings from Kerbin's people. He had given Haffset a target and if he did not return to coordinate the raid they could make a success of it.

On the other hand, he had compromised the mission in one vital area: Ama. Because of him, she knew too much about the impending raid, and now she was in the hands of people who could actually use that knowledge to damage or thwart it. No one, not the most disciplined troopers, could stay silent indefinitely under torture. He and the rest of the recon squad had kill pills embedded in one of their molars for exactly those circumstances.

Ama had no such escape. Dagga could brutalize her endlessly – to make her talk. And he would.

The neck of the bottle was in a chokehold in Seg's hand, he pounded the bottom against the dirt, then lowered his head and took in a deep breath of the hot, humid night air. His path was clear. *For the good of the mission,* he assured himself.

He replaced the stopper in the bottle, stuffed it in his knapsack, then brushed off his pants with his one hand. Knapsack cinched closed, he turned toward Alisir, the wisdom of his choice becoming clearer. The World would never know the reason for his sacrifice, his glorious career ended here, on a dirt road, but that did not detract from the importance of this moment.

He raised his chin, a hot breeze blew over him and his various aches and complaints all vanished. Ahead, the road was empty, a promising beginning. A twig snapped somewhere beyond the veil of trees, but he did not jump as he once might have. He was growing used to forest noises.

He started to rise. A hand slapped over his mouth and another latched onto his pack and tugged him backwards. His free hand released the pack as he shouted into the flesh. Fingers clasping the hilt of Ruch's knife, he yanked it from his belt and spun to face his attacker. The knife came up in a wild swing, then he stopped as he looked into the eyes of his assailant. Chest heaving, the knife dropped from his fingers and he could do nothing but stare. Was he hallucinating?

"Ama?"

She raised a finger to her lip to silence him, then glanced at the thin slice across her arm and shook her head to fend off any concern he might have.

There was no thought in that moment. With his free hand, he grasped the back of her head, pulled her to him and pressed his lips to hers. A searing heat rushed through his body and with it the sum of his desires and fears. This was a new language, instantly learned. She wrapped her arms around him and dug her fingers into his back; her lips yielded completely to the force of his. The Bliss, which had overwhelmed him crossing to this world, had not come close to this moment of perfect fusion.

When they parted, he could not speak. His lips were open, her taste lingering there; he heard only the synchronicity of their breathing.

Around them, as if summoned by the moment, the hot summer wind blew more intensely, plucking at the edges of their clothing. Ama tugged on his sleeve and gestured for him to flatten against the statue with her. Seconds after they did, two constables walked past, only a few feet from the fugitives they sought. When the men were a safe distance past, Ama grabbed Seg's hand and led him away, onto a narrow footpath and down to a creek.

"Where were you going?" she asked in a whisper that clearly conveyed disapproval.

The words snapped him back to reality and he blinked as if to clear his vision, hardly able to believe what had just happened between them.

"I…" he shook his head slightly, "I was coming to find you."

"You have to get to the rendezvous!"

"Your knowledge of the mission could have jeopardized it," he explained, uncomfortably aware of both the defensiveness and lack of conviction in his tone.

"You…" Ama's rant halted, her expression softened. She opened her mouth to speak just as thunder cracked and rolled through the valley. "That road is a trap," she said, and pointed toward the path Seg had been about to follow. "There are constables hidden all along it, waiting for you." Any foolishness he felt was allayed when she added, "I've had the eyes and ears of my people helping me."

Lighting forked down on the opposite side of the city, illuminating them both for one vulnerable second.

"Storm," Ama whispered.

Seg's body tensed instinctively at the word, and as if Ama had spoken a magic incantation the skies opened and rain poured down in torrential sheets.

"Come on," she said, the noise of the tempest requiring her to raise her voice almost to a shout. "We better get to shelter!"

She scooped up both his pack and her own and jogged along the creek, away from Dagga's trap. Seg followed, as the cold drops lashed his skin.

There was no space between the thunder and lightning any longer. Small rivers ran down the dirt roads, and the driving rain made it impossible to see more than a few feet ahead. Ama ran with purpose. Seg was equally anxious to find shelter, but when the next flash of lightning showed the sprawling mansion ahead, he latched his hand onto one of the packs she carried, to slow her.

"Are you insane? That's a Damiar estate!" he shouted over the howl of the wind and rain.

"It's deserted. The family's left Sansin," she shouted back.

"How do you know there are no constables in there?"

"Do you see any lights? Besides, it's the last place they'd expect us to hide."

With that, she resumed her run. Soaked through and shivering, Seg followed.

As they got closer, Seg could see statues that had been knocked over and smashed, a half-burned luxury cartul, and, most notably, a blue and yellow signal flag nailed to the front door.

It was that defiled, ornate door that Ama stood in front of now, body shaking and teeth chattering uncontrollably. She dropped both packs, dug through hers, then pulled out two long, slender pieces of metal. These she fit into the keyhole of the door, cursing at her quaking hands as she attempted to circumvent the lock.

Seg did his best to wait patiently, while the rain slashed sideways against him, chilling him to the bone.

At last there was a *click*. Ama grabbed the handle but the wind took the door, flinging it open with a *bang* that was barely masked by thunder. They both hurried inside, any concern for potential occupants driven away by the summer storm. Ama closed the door and Seg leaned against it to help keep it shut while she re-engaged the lock.

"Th-th-is way," Ama stuttered, as she turned from the sprawling entryway and walked down a wide passage.

The interior of the house was dark. And cold. His teeth chattered as he dripped his way across the smooth stone floor. As his eyes adjusted to the dim space, he followed her into what must have been the main sitting room – a cavernous, sterile place, with a fireplace a man could stand inside and several loungers and chairs not designed for comfort, the only item of warmth, a wide, plush rug. The inhabitants had not been gone long; the furniture covers had not even gathered dust.

Ama slid one of these covers off, shook it out, and eyed it appraisingly. "We'll have to leave as soon as the storm passes." All business now, she tossed the cover to Seg, and pulled off another one for herself. "I'll light a fire if there's wood, no one will notice it in this storm. And we can use these to keep warm while our clothes dry."

She faced away from him as she pulled off and discarded her sodden shirt. His hand rose to the buttons of his shirt, but paused at the sight of her bare back.

"Ah," he said, then forced his eyes away from her, "yes, yes." He tried to follow her example, but with one arm the going was difficult; the clothing stuck to his skin tenaciously. The water pressed upon him, oozed tracks down his body and dripped from his hair. He shook his head, droplets of water flew everywhere.

Ama stepped forward, holding her wrap together as she worked at the buttons of his shirt.

"You should have seen Dagga when he found out you'd escaped," she said, grinning and moving awkwardly to slide his sleeve off as Seg shivered.

He twisted as she pulled the soggy clothing from his body. "And you? Did your people free you as well?"

"They couldn't. So I took one of the constables for a swim. Turns out he couldn't hold his breath as long as me." She gestured for him to use her shoulder for balance, as she tugged off his boots. "How did you make it this far alone?"

"Apparently I was dirty enough to pass for a Welf, and they are invisible on your world."

He became suddenly aware of her presence as she pulled his trousers away. He lifted his leg awkwardly, nearly overbalancing. The cover had slid away from her as she knelt, and once more he stared at her flesh.

Awkward electricity filled the air, which Seg did his best to ignore.

Ama stood before she realized she was exposed, then quickly pulled the material up to cover herself.

As she helped him wrap the cover around his shoulders, cinching it with a loose knot, her hand brushed his bare skin.

"I should light a fire," she said, but didn't move.

"That would be good," he agreed, staring down at her.

She opened her mouth as if to speak, then backed away and pattered, barefooted, to the wood box. "Son of whore!" she cursed, as she tossed a few skinny sticks into the fireplace.

She looked around the room, her eyes lit on a picture hanging on the wall and she smiled. "Aha!" she pulled down the picture, tossed it into the fireplace, then struck a match from the box on the mantle. The stern face of a Damiar Lord ignited and Ama immediately set to finding more burnables.

"Help me," she said to Seg. "Anything that will burn, toss it in."

"Yes," he agreed, looking around. He pulled down another picture, an image of a dour-looking matriarch and crossed the room to deposit it into the fireplace. He saw her about to heft a book into the flames and shook his head. "Wait!"

"What?" She paused, her gaze curious; she glanced from the book to Seg. "It's just a book."

He snatched it from her hand. "Just a book? Are you insane?" He turned away from her and pulled the book close as if to protect it from her barbaric impulses.

"You sound like Stevan," she said. The comparison had rolled off her tongue naturally, but a moment after the words were out Ama's face clouded.

She pushed her way past him, ripped another picture off the wall, a Damiar family, safe and happy, surrounded by luxury. She smashed the frame against the stone floor and hurled it into the fire, where the now crackling flames devoured it, as she muttered curses in Kenda.

Seg put the book on a table, and used the edge of his cover to wipe the wet handprints away from the front of it. Stupid to be so sentimental about such things, perhaps, but in its way the book was a treasure.

The fire, now fed with some pieces of furniture, burned with reassuring strength. He stepped past Ama and opened the heavy cover slightly, letting the warmth seep in against his chilled skin.

The fire was burning well but the fire inside of Ama was only beginning to catch, he could see. A fire that demanded fuel. She hurled everything she could lay her hands on into the flame, smashing what was smashable, until the cover was most of the way off her body and the flames threatened to burst from their cage.

She raised her hand to throw in a chair leg and Seg grasped her wrist. "Ama, enough. The fire is burning sufficiently."

She struggled against him and he braced himself for the argument. To his surprise, she simply let the chair leg drop and the cover along with it.

Lightning flashed, silhouetting her. He pulled her wrist and they crashed together just ahead of the thunder.

Then they were falling, a slow twisting motion that took them to the floor, legs entertwined. She ground against him, biting down on his lip hard enough to draw blood.

He pulled away, wiped his lip, then snaked his hand around her neck, tugged and fumbled at the strings on her nove, until they pulled free. He yanked the collar loose and tossed it aside, glaring a challenge down at her.

She looked up at him, dathe exposed, naked in a way that transcended lack of clothing. Her eyes were a deep amber, desire on their surface, answering his challenge with one of her own.

He traced his fingers over the tiny slits on her neck, stretching the moment out as she shivered. Her back arched, her head tilted back, revealing even more of her neck. He dropped down and pressed her to the floor, the pent-up frustrations and exertions of the entire expedition burning in him.

Each low, animal rumble that reverberated from him was echoed back from her; they attacked more than caressed. Seg clamped his mouth down on Ama's neck, the edge of his teeth just grazing her dathe, as determined and ferocious as the drexla who had stalked her. She let out a savage howl, bucking at the sensation but at the same time opening herself to him.

Behind them, the fire cracked and spit, hissing as it found knots in the wood. He was lost in her in a way that he had never been before, pushing against her as she pushed against him, feeling her fight, yield, then come back and fight again.

She raised a hand as if to strike him; he caught her wrist and pinned it to the ground, above her head. A series of shudders rippled across her body and his responded, driving into her while the fingers of her free hand gripped his skin and urged him deeper.

And then he was gone, surrendering to the storm.

His mouth was open, lips pressed against her dathe; she quivered as they lay tangled, in each other and the covers.

"I thought I'd lost you," she said, voice husky.

Seg raised his mouth to her ear, "I wouldn't let that happen."

Judicia Serval examined his fingernails. Not that they were in any need of grooming, but the task gave him something to focus on. Something other than the muted screams from behind the door. As eager as he was, as everyone was, to see the recent waves of rebellion and resistance cease, he was equally eager to see the back of Head Constable Dagga.

His fingers curled as another long shriek echoed through his office. There were rooms for this sort of questioning but Dagga didn't care. He had dragged the Kenda rebel into the detention room, lashed him to a chair, slammed the door shut and locked it without a pause to ask permission or offer a polite word.

With a scrape, Serval pushed out his chair, pulled his glasses from his breast pocket, slipped them on and strolled to the far side of the office. An elaborately painted map covered one wall. It was to this he turned his attention.

His eyes followed the path of the Gwai River. Constables had been stationed at every possible point the Kalder woman could have exited. Word had been spread concerning the reward for her capture and the punishment for aiding her, or withholding information.

No one had come forward.

Ama Kalder was dead. Doubtless they would find her body washed up soon enough. But Dagga refused to listen to reason; he was convinced of some larger conspiracy. Unfortunately, the Shasir in T'ueve agreed with him and had bestowed temporary, and wide ranging, powers to the belligerent little despot.

He realized, absently, that the screaming had stopped. Perhaps, once the mess was cleaned up, he could get on with his many pressing, legitimate duties.

The door flung open, Dagga marched out of the detention room.

"She's alive," he proclaimed.

"Are you certain?" Serval asked, adjusting his glasses.

Ignoring the question, Dagga shoved Serval to one side and drove his knife into the map. "Get me every available man, armed and ready to ride. And send a message to the temple."

"What shall I say?" Serval inquired.

"Say I know where to find them," Dagga said, and removed the knife with a victorious yank. "Tell 'em this time I kill the traitors on sight."

In that moment, Serval got his wish. He watched Dagga's back, as he strode out of the office, and let out a relieved breath.

He turned to the map, to the point where Dagga's blade had entered. A river of blood now ran through the Humish Valley.

On the rug, cover puddled around his feet, Seg sat with his back against one the few chairs that had not been fed to the fire. They kept wary ears open for intruders and their knives and packs close at hand. But as long as the rain fell, they were content to stay inside where it was dry.

He leaned his head back and stared at the skipping shadows on the wall as the fire popped and crackled. From there, his eyes moved around the room. Whoever had lived here, theirs was a life of privilege, near the top of the social strata on Ama's world. Wealth, power, and all the trappings that went with that. Exactly what he had always dreamed of.

And yet, the only life in this room came from him and Ama. Particularly Ama. On her boat, in the squall, he had felt alive in a way he had never imagined possible. Even being on the run with her, despite the very real dangers and trials they had endured, was exhilarating. This wasn't the dry and regimented cultural infiltration he had been schooled in, this was exploration in its purest form. And it was intoxicating.

His eyes moved to Ama and he tried to see her as his People would, tried to imagine her as caj. His fist clenched at the thought.

"What is it?" Ama asked, stirring him out of his reverie.

"Hm?"

"You were staring at me."

"Oh," he glanced away, "I was just picturing you on my World."

Ama stretched, her limbs syrupy in the warmth of the fire. "What's it like? Your world?"

"Boring," he said, and tilted his head back. "Dusty, dry, and full of self-important, feeble-minded, unimaginative fools. But I'm going to change that."

"You're going to change your world?" Ama asked, now perking up, a smile dancing at the edges of her mouth.

"Indirectly, yes. My People are pragmatic, disciplined, thorough, but they've strangled themselves with their own rigidity. I've always known it, I suppose, but seeing your world, your people, has solidified the notion for me."

"I have studied cultures and civilizations, across the dimensions, at every stage of imagined development, and one fact is clear: stagnation is the precursor to collapse. For all its brilliance, the Theorist's Guild, the cultural light of our World, is run by old men and women who care more for upholding tradition than searching out creative solutions to the challenges we face." He stopped at the realization that she was the first person he had ever spoken to about his ambitions.

"Is that why you want Brin's men? To help you change your world?" Ama's face was serious now, almost studious.

"Yes," he answered, without hesitation, happy to have another soul to share this with. "I haven't worked through all the...specifics, yet, but yes. The recon squad that escorted me to your world, and others of their kind, function well in a military capacity, but I need more than that to achieve my goals." He sat upright, buoyed by the thoughts rolling through him. "I need what no training or schooling can teach: I need recon teams that don't care about the rules and protocols, who come to the task without prejudice, who live with passion, creativity and loyalty."

"A rebel?" Ama took his hand in hers, turned it over and traced her fingers over the red line Brin had cut into his palm. "Perhaps you truly are Kenda."

"Your code, *blood for water*, where does it come from?" he asked.

"From the old Kenda resistance, from the war with the Shasir. It means we are willing to kill or die for what we love."

"Blood for water," he repeated, in the Kenda tongue this time.

When she lifted her face to his, they were only inches apart.

I want you. I want you to stay with me. The words were trapped behind his eyes.

She cocked her head, then stood abruptly. "The storm's passed. We have to go."

They dressed in silence, shouldered their packs and headed to the door.

"Wait," Ama said, spun on her heel and jogged back to the fire. Seg followed her back in, a question on his lips as she poked her hand into the fireplace and pulled out a chair leg that was half burned. Wordlessly, she held the glowing end to the bottom of the heavy drapes and handed the torch to Seg.

He watched the flames play up the curtain before he lowered the improvised torch beneath a highly decorative chair. Smoke billowed up from beneath the chair and continued to pour out as he pulled the torch away. Foolish action, perhaps, but they were not the first to vandalize this estate and by the time anyone noticed the fire he and Ama would be long gone. Satisfied, he put down the torch long enough to re-shoulder his pack, then stood for a long moment and watched the beginning of the conflagration.

There was enough fuel left for the blaze to take hold and burn the estate to the ground.

"There," Ama said, leading him away by his pack, "now we're rebels."

By the light of the full moon, they walked through the woods. The trees were well spaced and Ama passed by a number of suitable spots to camp out for the evening. She didn't explain her reason for pushing forward to Seg; there was no need. He understood, as she did, it would be prudent to put as much distance as possible between them and the burning Damiar estate.

At a stack of rocks, however, she stopped. "Here," she said, turned an abrupt ninety degrees and led Seg through a tangle of brush.

"Here?" he asked, frowning as he pushed aside the damp, clingy vegetation.

He had his answer soon enough, as the greenery gave way to a cleared area. The spot was well disguised, he would have walked right past it on his own, but it had obviously been some sort of dwelling or meeting place years, perhaps centuries, earlier. A skeleton of a structure, made of stone and wood, was slowly being swallowed by the forest.

Ama dropped her pack and made preparations for the evening. "It's no feast but at least they're fresh," she said, and held up two apples.

Seg plucked one from her hand, bit down and let the sweetness flood his mouth. "It is a feast."

"Viren and his men stocked me up as well as they could."

"Hult?" Seg asked, pausing mid-bite. "You found him?"

"It wasn't difficult, once I managed to get word out to the Kenda that I was alive. He wasn't very happy about me coming after you.

Word's spread that the men Brin sent after your people are dead. He said if I tried to talk to your people without you, they'd kill me too."

"They would have," Seg dropped down to his haunches beside her, his legs weakening at the thought of what would have happened if Ama had approached Kerbin. "Listen to me, whatever happens, do not go near my People without me."

Ama looked uncertain but nodded.

"I've got a shortcut that will take us over the mountain tomorrow. It'll be hard going but it will keep us away from the roads where Dagga's men might be, and you should make the meeting with your people with time to spare," she said.

"And you?"

"Brin's men will be waiting for me at the safe house. They'll make sure I'm protected until after the raid."

"Good," he said, but his voice was flat. It was strange to even consider returning to that life. And as for leaving Ama... He took another bite of the apple but his appetite had deserted him.

"Oh, I almost forgot," she dug in her pack again, this time producing a familiar slim, rectangular object.

"Where did you get this?" Seg asked, eagerly pulling the VIU from her hand, as he set the half-eaten apple to one side.

"Your pack was in the cartul Viren stole. I couldn't carry all of it but I remembered you said this piece was important. I brought your banger too," she said, withdrawing Seg's last remaining pistol

Ignoring the weapon, Seg slid open a cover on the back of the VIU and pressed on the small dimple. A faint, green icon appeared and he tapped it to light up the display screen. He waited for the self-diagnostics to complete and the menu to appear.

As the reading lights flashed, Seg frowned at the mechanism, smacked it against his leg, then powered it down and restarted it. The People's equipment was built for much harsher conditions than the VIU had been exposed to, but who knew what treatment it had received in Hult's care. Once powered up, the flashing resumed, displaying the same readings.

He was about to shut it down when a thought struck him.

"What is this place?" he asked Ama, as he stood and walked to one of the stone pillars.

"Oh, it's just an old Welf grovel pit."

"A what?"

"A grovel pit, a place that Welf used to come to—back before the spooks—and pray to rocks and stuff. This one's in pretty good shape, I figured it would be a good place to hide and," she spread out a bedroll, "the ground is dry."

Intricate carvings were revealed, as he pulled aside the vines. He looked down at the VIU, amazed at what he saw. The readings weren't anywhere near those he had taken at the temple in Alisir but they were substantial. This 'grovel pit', this crumbling Welf holy place, had more vita than T'ueve.

It wasn't possible that he would have missed something this promising as a potential target. To be sure, he tucked the VIU under his arm, dug into his pocket and pulled out the digifilm, with the stored locations. A scroll through the list made no mention of any sites near Sansin. Strange.

"Do others know about these 'grovel pits'? Would the Shasir know of them?"

Ama shrugged, "Maybe. Pre-Unification gods are forbidden, though. They aren't even to be spoken of. The spooks don't like competition."

That could explain it. The Welf had no written history prior to the arrival of the Damiar and if the Shasir forbade their religion, it would have been abandoned and forgotten. "And yet you know of them?"

"Anyone who's spent time in the forest knows about them."

"Are there many more?"

"Lots, especially in the Ymira Valley; that's an old, old Welf settlement."

"Why did you not tell me of this?" His voice was stern, as he gestured to the vita-rich site around them.

"I thought you were looking for important places, big temples, fancy…stuff. Grovel pits are just old dirt piles nobody even uses. All the dots on the globe you showed me were on Shasir holy sites, I thought that's what you wanted."

His flash of annoyance subsided. She was so competent in her world, he sometimes forgot she could know nothing of his. And even a normal Person might have missed the relevance. This was, after all, what Theorists trained for and why native contact was essential to missions

"I should have been more explicit," he conceded, returning his attention to the readouts and his new, expanded plans for the raid.

This site was not as rich as Alisir but it did have ample vita and was about as easy a target as his People could ask for — undefended, easily penetrated. While the larger raids were under way, a single squad could make away with enough vita from a half dozen of these sacred sites to make the entire raid break even, likely without a single casualty. Ideal.

He raised his eyes from the screen to look at Ama, who was busy carving slices of the apple that was her dinner. "Can you show me, on the map, where more of these grovel pits are?"

With a smile, she knifed a slice into her mouth and took the digifilm from his hands, "How many would you like?"

It'll be tough going. If he were not half delirious and ready to pass out, Seg would have laughed at Ama's description of their journey. The last portion of the ascent had been the worst: baking hot, steep and at points treacherous, the air so dense and humid it could almost be chewed.

Even the short descent to the banks of the river had been difficult. There were swarms of insects, and the heat was relentless. By the time they made it to the riverbank, they both collapsed in silent heaps and panted in a patch of shade. But there was no relief, even there. Summer had arrived with a vengeance, the numbing cold of the previous night's storm a delicious and taunting memory.

By the map on his digifilm, they had not much further to travel. However grueling, the route *had* been a shortcut and there was ample daylight ahead of them.

When she had recovered a bit, Ama left Seg and set out to find the cable crossing over the river.

He was sitting up when she returned, guzzling the last of the tepid water from his bottle. He had removed his shirt; his skin was slick with dirt and sweat.

"We need to talk," she said, then stripped off her shirt and trousers until she was down to her waterwear, "I need to teach you to swim."

"This is hardly the time for humor. We'll use the cable crossing."

"Gone. A flood most likely, took out part of the bank on the far side and the cable tower with it. We have to swim."

"Swim? In water?" he shook his head, "No. You'll have to come up with another solution."

"There is no other solution, believe me."

"Impossible."

"OK, then here are your options: One, you let me teach you how to swim, to float, actually—just the basics, you don't even have to put your head underneath—so that I can help you across the river. Or two, I drag you under the water and breathe for you, just like I did back in T'ueve. I know how much you enjoyed that. The choice is yours." She put her hands on her hips, cocked her head and waited for his reply.

He stepped toward her. "Do not give me ultimatums."

"I've been charged with getting you to your people and you're the only hope I have to save my father. If that means giving ultimatums, I'll damn well give them. Unless you have a better solution?"

"It is not the options that are an issue, it is the attitude and disrespect you've become too accustomed to delivering."

"Because I'm an *Outer*?"

Seg opened his mouth then slapped it shut, they had visited this argument more than once already, in their short time together. It never ended well.

Ama turned on her heels, and headed upriver. "I know you're scared," she called out, without looking back.

"I am not scared," Seg protested, striding to catch up with her.

"You've had three experiences with water and they were all pretty terrifying."

"I hunted rigla, as part of field training. Rigla! Do you have any idea how frightening a rigla is? Your silly water is nothing compared to that."

"You nearly got eaten by a drexla…"

"Which was your fault."

"…then you fell off a cliff and traveled to Brin's house underwater…"

"Necessary, but also your doing."

"…and finally ended up riding the Largent, which is some serious whitewater…"

"Of my own design, clearly demonstrating a lack of fear."

"…so no one would blame you for being nervous but…"

"I am not nervous!" He stepped over a log then stopped mid-stride. Ama stood at the edge of a pool of water.

"I'm going to show you that water isn't always dangerous and frightening." She backed a few steps into the water and everything about her softened. "So, *please*, will you let me teach you how to swim?"

He turned sideways, his fists clenched and unclenched.

"Eighteen…Fortitude in the face of adversity," he muttered.

"What?"

"The 47 Virtues of a Citizen. I'll explain some other time." He sighed, "Fine. Show me."

Ama smiled, and beckoned him to her. The water was deep but not over his head, calm and clear.

"Most important rule: control your breath." She placed her hand on his chest, fingers spread wide, "This is how you stay afloat. When you breathe in, your lungs fill with air, and you rise up, when you breathe out, you lose air and you sink. Control your breathing."

She backed in further, up to her knees and held out her hand, "Ready?"

"Simple physics," Seg said, gruffly, as he trod into the water. His first, unexpected, lesson concerned the difference in perspective inherent in looking through clear water, as he stumbled and nearly lost his balance. He grabbed her arm and righted himself as he stared at the untrustworthy liquid rippling around him. "How do you get used to this?"

"I've been swimming since I was a baby; I never had to get used to it. Don't fight it, the water will help you if you let it."

Ama guided him in deeper, until he was nearly to his waist.

"You're going to have to trust me, now," she said. He dug his fingers into her arm. "I'm going to hold you, support you. All you have to do is lean back."

With a deep breath in, then out, he mastered himself and forced himself to lean backwards. He had already trusted her with a blade and his life. What more was there?

Filthy, stinking water.

As he slowly lowered himself into the water, Ama stepped behind him and slid her hands under his back to steady him.

"Good. Feel that? Feel how the water supports you? Now, take a deep breath in and hold it."

He did as she instructed, his chest and thighs rose up out of the water.

"Let all the air out slowly. Perfect. Now repeat that, except this time don't let all the air out. Practice letting out just enough air to breathe without letting your body sink all the way below the water."

Breathe in, breathe out; his body rose and fell. It took some time but he eventually found a rhythm, a way of breathing that kept him afloat. In, out. Up, down.

"It's all you now. I'm not even holding you," she informed him, and he realized she had slipped her hands away while he was focused on his breath.

Floating was a wobbly, precarious state. He understood the physical principles of buoyancy, he had learned that at a much younger age. As so often occurred, though, understanding the theory and being comfortable with the practice were entirely different things. Guild training consisted of a large variety of physical requirements. The many worlds and environments they visited necessitated this. But swimming was not among the disciplines, primarily for lack of facilities and qualified instruction. Cadets received theoretical instruction and one, half day, land-based session of training that everyone had understood was mere technicality. He thought back to that day – standing on one leg while he kicked with the other and paddled with his arms. His training struck him as even more ridiculous now that he was actually in the element.

The water could take him where it willed. He couldn't guide himself. And if he gave up control of his breath he would plummet under. All very unnerving. But at the same time, floating had a strangely relaxing feature to it. It was comfortable in a way that no bed he had ever lain in had been. He had weight, but no weight.

Floating.

The word had an entirely new and visceral meaning to him now.

And as much as he hated to admit it, he felt fully refreshed now that he was cool.

"When we cross the river," Ama said, "you're going to be on your back, just like this. I'm going to tow you; that's the easiest, safest way—especially with your shoulder as it is—but you're going to have to help me. We'll have current to deal with. All you have to do is kick your legs," she mimicked the action with her fingers. "Don't bend your knees, keep your legs straight – think of a pair of scissors, like the ones Perla used to cut the cloth she bound your arm with."

She ducked down, moved her body beneath his, slid her hands under his arms, taking extra care with his injury, and hooked onto him.

"We'll try crossing to the far end of the pool," she said, then tilted her head back and kicked with an easy motion as she directed them to their goal.

He experimented with the movement, overdoing it in the fashion of the complete novice. He realized he wasn't making efficient motions and corrected his strokes. Legs straight, despite the instinct to bend. Fluid motions, not choppy. Power does not equal success.

Ama directed them in a circle and made another pass across the pool. After a few more laps, she stopped and helped him back to a standing position. She swam around in front of him, beaming, "Wow, I didn't expect you to be so good on your first try. Would you like to try swimming on your own? I can show you a way that won't hurt your shoulder."

He stared dubiously at the water. Honestly, he would prefer to just get out of the filthy stuff. But this, he forced himself to concede, was a method of maintaining control of his environment and not being at its mercy – something that might prove invaluable in the future.

"Yes," he said reluctantly. "Show me."

"You're going to lie on your back like you just were, but with your good arm over your head, like this," Ama rolled onto her back. "You'll kick just like you were doing, and stroke with your arm like so." Ama demonstrated the moves for him out of the water first and then in, moving slowly so Seg could see.

The movements come so naturally to her, he mused. *She belongs in the water.* A ridiculous notion. All humanoid evolutionary paths, across the dimensions, led out of the element not back into it.

"The good thing about swimming this way is your head is always out of the water. You try and I'll stay close to help." She dove under, brushed his leg as she swam by, and popped up behind him. Hands on his shoulders to guide him into position, she waited.

He frowned; he would need a thorough cleaning after paddling around like some sort of sea creature. The thought struck him suddenly. "Is there anything in this water with us? Anything potentially dangerous?"

"You mean like drexla?" Ama asked with a stifled laugh. "No, nothing like that. The only dangers are water hazards – sweepers, holes, pour-overs, that sort of thing. But I scouted and all we've got is a few bumps, so no need to worry." She dove under again and came up in front of him. "Besides, I would never let anything harm you. Never."

The last came out forcefully, more forcefully than she had intended he guessed, as she immediately looked away.

"Well," he glanced down and cleared his throat, "I'll give this a try and then we should keep moving."

"Yes," Ama agreed, still facing away from him, "we have to get you home."

Seg stood on the bank of the river, next to Ama as she surveyed their path one last time. Their clothes were packed in their kits. Since his knapsack was only cloth, she had packed it into hers, which was Kenda-made, soaked in a mixture of oil and wax to waterproof it. The bag was closed in such a way as to trap air inside, to keep it buoyant, and tied around Ama's waist.

She pointed to the water, moving her finger downriver slowly, "With this current, we can expect to make it to the other side near that widgewood tree hanging over the water but don't worry if we drift further. I'll get in first and set you up with me before I push off. It'll be over before you know it."

She waded into the water and extended her hand. To his surprise, he stepped forward with no hesitation and let her guide him into place. His swimming skills, he knew, were hardly enough to warrant confidence. It was his trust in her that made him face this threat so willingly.

"Ready?" she asked.

He nodded. This time, he was ready.

CHAPTER 15

As the crush of trees opened to the Humish Valley, Dagga brought the thundering procession to a halt. Before him, a grassy plain, dotted with a few cottages, wide pastures and the occasional barn presented a scene of pastoral tranquility. But he knew otherwise.

He raised his spyglass and swept the landscape. His prey would be coming from the north, avoiding the main roads, which left only a few viable routes over the mountain.

Collapsing the glass, he swung his horse in a tight circle to face his men.

"First and second squad, with me. Dismount at the base of the mountain, spread out on foot and lay low."

He spurred his horse and rode further down the line of men. "Third and fourth squad, get around the south side of the valley. Stay covered." He gestured in a semi-circle, to indicate the desired formation.

"Gonna set a net around this valley. No one makes a move 'till the rats are inside." He turned left, to face the first two squads, "Soon as they pass by us, we close in. If we miss 'em…" he turned right, to the third and fourth squads, "they'll run right to you."

He rode up and down the line. Men and horses were huffing and sweating from the hard journey. "No way out this time. Gonna drag their carcasses back to Alisir."

Up and down the line, the men nodded and muttered their assent.

"Now move!" Dagga shouted, and headed north to set his trap.

A bright purple jinje fruit hung heavy from a branch, Ama jogged ahead to pick it, then stopped and sliced it open—careful to avoid splitting the sac of bitter juice in the center—while she waited for Seg to catch up. The oppressive heat had not subsided but there was shade to be found and, under cover of the trees, Ama had felt safe enough to remove her nove and tuck it into her pocket. The river crossing had been smooth and the last leg of their journey was downhill.

"This is a good omen," she said, passing Seg a slice. "Jinje are only perfectly ripe for a day before the sac bursts and spoils the meat of the fruit. It was my favourite treat when I was growing up; my brothers and me would fight over it. Do you have fruit like this on your world?"

"Mmm, similar. Not free-growing, and usually reserved for the very wealthy, grown in private gardens. Graduated Theorists get such as befitting our place in society."

She cut him off another slice and he ate silently. In fact, he had been silent since they had crossed the river and though she could guess why, instead of quiet, she felt the need to fill the awkward space between them with words.

"What is your place in so—"

"Ama," he interrupted, the angles of his face sharpened by sun and shadows. He stopped in place; Ama walked a few paces forward then stopped when she realized Seg was no longer beside her.

She turned to face him, he lowered his pack and stared at the ground.

"Is it your shoulder?" she asked, reaching out a hand.

"No, no," he waved her off, but then said nothing more.

A flock of birds took flight nearby, shaking the trees.

It wasn't like Seg to hesitate, he was a man who knew his mind and spoke it. Ama waited for him with growing unease. Just as she opened her mouth to ask what the trouble was, he broke the silence.

"I need to speak to you about a…about a personal matter. What I am about to suggest is

unortho, at best, even for me."

As she faced him, a glint in the trees above and behind Seg caught her eyes.

"Ama, I want—"

She leapt forward, covered his mouth with her hand and pulled him to the ground. As they ducked, a banger shot whizzed by, cracking open the quiet of the forest. A widgewood tree splintered as the musket ball found purchase.

Ama raised her head; now she saw a flash of blue and an unmistakable figure charging toward them.

"Dagga," she hissed, eyes locked on Seg's.

"Nowhere to hide, water rats," Dagga called out, his voice echoing through the forest.

Whether Dagga's words were true or not, surrender meant death. "Run!" She whispered to Seg. "Run!"

She dropped her own pack, grabbed Seg's, and took off through the trees at a sprint.

"Take them!" Dagga shouted, just ahead of a hail of banger fire.

The slope of the hill helped their descent but took away any control they had over their path. Ama's foot hit a section of loose rock and she slid into a tree. The impact threw her off balance, but Seg was right behind her. With his free hand, he helped haul her up as he passed and they continued to hurtle blindly to the valley below.

Dagga and his men were closing the distance, boots crashing louder and closer. Ahead of them, the forest that offered their only protection from the banger shots was beginning to thin.

A branch lashed Seg across the face, opening a cut on his cheek. Ama leapt over rocks and roots, ducked beneath low hanging branches. With only one arm for balance, Seg did his best to keep pace.

A musket ball passed by Ama's head close enough to lift her hair. She jigged left and bounced off an unyielding bonewood tree. In seconds they would be exposed. She looked down on the approaching valley, a wide grassy pasture punctuated with a few rows of crops, a small barn and some grazing greshers. And nothing else.

"Where are your people?" Ama shouted, frantic, as they burst out of the cover.

"I don't kn—"

Ama turned to see Seg's leg buckle, a streak of red marking the graze of a musket ball across his thigh. She reached out a hand but he launched forward, hit the ground, flipped over and kept rolling. His path was clear of trees but too steep to stop his momentum; he bounced and tumbled down the slope.

Ama sprinted to catch him, heedless of the weapons fire that sliced through the air around her.

Hooking her arm under his, she pulled him to his feet. "Keep… moving," she panted.

They would have to cross the open valley and hope to find some shelter on the opposite side, where there was more tree cover. At least the ground was flat now. If she could find water, get them to a river, they might have a chance.

"Ama!" Seg yelled.

Ahead of them, more constables were pouring out of the woods on horseback, closing in a circle. They were right in the middle. Trapped.

Ama's head whipped left and right.

"There!" she pointed to the small barn. It wouldn't protect them for long but it was the only cover they could hope to reach.

She turned to run, her foot dropped into a deep rut left by a gresher and she fell forward onto her face. Seg's pack flew from her hand, as the air was driven from her lungs.

She raised her head. Seg was at her side but it was too late, the constables were closing the net around them.

"Get down!" Seg said. He dropped to his knees, grabbed his pack, dug in for his pistol, then wrapped himself on top of Ama. Even as he clutched the weapon, he understood it was a futile gesture against so many. He could only hope to shield her now.

Then, from above, there was a shrill hiss of air followed by a ball of fire. A small explosion rocked the ground, sending a shockwave through Seg and Ama as they huddled together. The fireball hit a cluster of constables. Men screamed as they were engulfed in flame. Others backed away or stopped in their tracks as heat and smoke filled the air.

Seg raised his head. Through one of the shutters in the loft of the barn, the barrel of a weapon was just visible. He heard a sharp *pop*, another hiss, then a scream and knew that a huchack rifle shot had found home.

"Kerbin," he said.

"What?" Ama gasped.

"Inside!" He pulled Ama up, then snagged the straps of his pack and tossed it over his shoulder.

Dodging gresher ruts, they ran to the barn, which had now come alive with superheated bursts of heavy needler fire and the deadly spines of huchack rifles.

As Seg charged through the open entryway, he heard the heavy needler fire again. He surged through the stalls and directly into the butt of a weapon that cracked him on the jaw. His feet flew out from under him and he landed on his back with a loud THUD, only to stare down the barrel of a huchack carbine wielded by Kerbin. Her eyes were hidden behind her visor, but he could see her teeth as her mouth skinned back in a grimace.

"SEG!" Ama ran to his side, sliding to a stop as one of Seg's people pointed a weapon at her chest.

Kerbin glanced sideways at Ama, then back to Seg. "So it is you. Couldn't quite tell, the way you're done up."

She pressed her boot down on his chest as she listened for the reports from her comm. From the tiny twitches at the corners of her mouth, Seg saw that Kerbin had known it was him all along.

Outside, the weapons fire continued but it was obvious the constables were being steadily eliminated.

"Okay, keep watch for more of 'em, we'll get the warp gate set up. We got our Theorist, I'll make sure we're taking him back with us,"

Kerbin said into the comm. She nodded at the pistol Seg's fingers were seeking, "Wouldn't do that if I was you." She pulled her boot off him and stepped away. "It's beyond karged out there. If Haffset's got half a brain, they'll pull an abort on this whole karg-up raid and ship you to the basement."

"What are you talking about?" Seg said as he rolled to his knees, then rose up. His jaw ached and his entire body felt as though it had been hammered.

"We've had locals on us for days now. First some bunch of raggedies. De-pop'd all but one of 'em. Kept him alive long enough to pry the intel out. Said some local named Brin sent 'em. Then the wardens, or whatever they're called around here, started sniffing around. Been dogging us ever since. Thing I want to know is, how in the name of the Storm did anybody know we were here?"

Seg shook his head, careful to avoid looking at Ama. "I have no idea, Kerbin. Were you indiscreet?"

She glared at him. "My ass. We ghosted this whole mission. No slips!"

Behind them, other members of the squad were assembling the warp gate. Both Seg and Kerbin ignored the feverish work, focusing on each other.

"None?" Seg demanded, his eyes narrowing. "You're lying."

"Hey, we didn't have time to bag the bodies of the first group of Outers, but that was after they knew we were here," she said, bracing up toward him.

"So you made the one mistake, you likely made others. Obviously so."

"Karg you. We got your job done, even with the hassles. We weren't wasting our time collecting pets."

"I'm no one's pet," Ama said, still held in place by the banger. "And I'm helping Seg, so tell your man not to shoot me."

"Pets that think they can talk back to People." The lines around Kerbin's mouth deepened, then she moved closer and squinted at Ama's dathe. She nodded to the trooper whose rifle was aimed at Ama, "Go ahead. Shoot the freak."

"No!" Seg yelled to the trooper then whipped his head around to face Kerbin. "Do it and I'll have you…" he stabbed his finger at the trooper, "and you," he looked around to the rest of squad who were visible, "all of you, I'll have you all broken and reduced and grafted."

Kerbin's answer was to raise her rifle.

Seg raised his pistol as well. "Go back without me and you're already karged," he told her. "This is shaping for the biggest raid in history, and the Guild will not forgive my loss."

They glared at each other over the sights of their weapons.

"I'm taking this up-chain when we get back," Kerbin said, tone thick with menace. She lowered her rifle. "We'll see who gets grafted over this."

"Do what you're told and you'll be rich. We're almost there. Don't ruin it now."

"More coming!" came the call from over their heads. "Twenty hostiles, maybe more."

Kerbin turned toward the assembled warp gate and glanced at her wrist. "We're in warp window. Get that gate opened and let's get out of here. Storm take these Outers." Then she looked back at Seg, "We're not done with this yet."

Seg moved to Ama's side and pulled her away from the troopers. "You have to come with me," he whispered

"My father…"

"Ama," Seg lowered his voice but spoke more forcefully, "this isn't the time to be stubborn."

"Your people want to kill me," she hissed back, with a darting glance to Kerbin.

"The people outside want to kill you too. And they will if you stay here. At least I can protect you from these ones" he said, nodding to the troopers. He pocketed his pistol and grasped her elbow. "Come on!"

"Promise you'll get me back here. Promise." Her fingers latched onto Seg's arm, silently pleading as they twisted the fabric of his shirt.

"I swear it."

"I don't trust her," Ama whispered, her eyes flashing at Kerbin.

"You have excellent instincts," he whispered, as he ushered her toward the gate.

Kerbin grabbed the back of his shirt and shoved him toward the shimmering circle. He tripped and plunged in, pulling Ama with him. Ama looked back at her world one last time as she fell. Her last sight was Kerbin's eyes, staring at her as if she were looking at an animal being led to slaughter.

CHAPTER 16

A
s she fell through the warp gate, Ama took a deep breath and held it. Foolish but instinctual. Inside the warp, it was as if she were being stretched taut, her insides twisted, and there were voices, thousands, scratching against her eardrums like fingernails on the hull of the *Naida*. Then it was over and she felt ill. All she wanted was to lie down until her head and stomach settled but this notion was doomed.

Lights. Noise. Hands. Everything was too bright; it stung her eyes. Her second eyelids flipped up but did little good. Beasts, bigger than men, grabbed her and she screamed in spite of herself.

She held tight to Seg's hand but the beasts pulled them apart.

"Fear no," Seg called out to her, in the broken Kenda he had learned, then he spoke in his own tongue to his people.

Their language was discordant, broken glass noise. Ama covered her ears with her hands but the beasts yanked them away and talked more loudly at her.

They're only men, in strange clothes, she told herself but they terrified her, especially when they started pulling off her clothes. Again she fought, again they ignored her, overwhelmed her. "Seg!" she called, but he was busy talking back to the suit-men, in their broken glass language. Soon she stood naked, uselessly struggling to cover herself.

Then they reached for the shell bracelet on her wrist and she screamed. "NO! That was my mother's!" She might as well have not existed; they did what they wanted, took what they wanted.

One of the suit-men motioned to her to spread her arms and legs but she shook her head and refused. Another suit-man joined him and they forced her into position, while a third raised a hose and sprayed her with a foul-smelling liquid that stung the many scratches covering her arms and face. While she coughed, they turned her to face the other way and sprayed her back side. Next she felt the scratch of brushes against her skin. The suit-men scrubbed everywhere, even the delicate spot between her legs but she couldn't scream for the coughing.

The foul smelling liquid was in her dathe and it choked her.

When they rotated her back to face the suit-men with the brushes, the process was repeated. No part of her body was neglected.

They kept talking at her, even though she couldn't understand a word. Then they pushed her forward until she was standing over a drain. A blast of liquid hit her and nearly flayed the skin from her bones. As she squeezed her eyes shut, she prayed to Nen to make it stop.

More hands, this time they pulled at her, then pointed some kind of device at her midsection as they chattered to each other. At least they seemed to be ignoring her for a minute; she crouched forward, covering her body with her arms and hands.

The respite was short lived. They pushed her through a doorway of sorts, though not like any doorway she had ever seen; this one opened up like a mouth.

Nothing was like anything she had ever seen.

She looked back, relieved to see Seg walking in the same direction. If she lost him, what would she do?

Were their eyes weak? Was that why everything was so bright?

They pushed her toward a glaring white table as they continued to talk at her.

"Seg," she said, coughing the taste of the liquid out of her dathe, "what's going on?"

He answered in broken Kenda, his voice clipped and low. "Clean you they. Sick...yes, no. No talk me." His eyes were like two stones, "Danger. No talk, Ama."

Shortly after she was settled on the table, Ama watched the suit-men leave; they were replaced by men and women who wore plain, white robes. No, not exactly robes, more like coats. They attached something to her arm, much like the sleeve Seg had put on her for her shoulder. An image appeared out of the sleeve, she recognized it as a body but with all the inside parts visible. One of the men reached a hand toward her dathe and Ama gasped. His hands were white and the flesh on them was abnormally smooth. Two other men held her as he prodded her dathe.

It didn't feel the same as when Seg touched her there. It felt like a violation. But then, Seg was gentle with her dathe, this man pulled and poked at them. "Careful!" she spat out as he pinched one of the folds of skin between his fingers.

He ignored her. They all ignored her. She looked to Seg again but he was talking in his language to two men dressed in plain grey coats and trousers. Seg had a similar sleeve on his arm but the white-handed men weren't interested in poking at him. He wasn't a freak, like her. He had also been given a robe to cover himself. She tried to understand what the men were saying to Seg but everyone's face just looked hard and angry.

The two uniformed men stood at the door, waiting; the white-handed man spoke something at Seg who then stood and followed the other men out. Ama waited for him to return, to come back and take her away with him, but the doors he passed through never opened again.

He's left me.

"Can I have my clothes back now?" she asked the men, after a lengthy wait. They didn't answer her, didn't even glance in her direction. She studied the room to see if there was something to cover herself with but found nothing.

"I want to talk to Seg," she demanded after another stretch of silence. "If someone doesn't talk to me, I'm going to go find him myself."

She waited for a response; there was none.

Well, I warned them.

When the white-handed men turned their backs, she leapt off the table and ran out the door.

Jarin entered the corridor leading to the secondary quarantine room, his face set in a frown. His instructions had been specific: immediate notification upon the recon squad's intrans. Not only had he not been informed, someone had deliberately misled him regarding the time of the scheduled intrans window. Given the rigorous attention he had paid to this mission, the responsible party had gone to great lengths to keep him away from Segkel, who he had only just learned was returned and alive.

Though he was positive Director Fi Costk's hand was all over this misdirection, he had yet to discern the purpose.

From around the corner, he heard a series of shouts and stopped in place.

"Stop! Get back here! Security!"

A moment later, a woman charged around the corner. She was running for her life, obviously an Outer, and completely bare. Her eyes skipped over Jarin. "SEG!" she yelled, head moving left and right as she ran.

Segkel, what have you done now? Jarin sighed.

Around the corner, two intrans medicals labored after her, no match for the girl's well-toned muscles and youth. "Stop her!" they called to Jarin.

He raised a hand to speak to the Outer but she barreled past him. He rotated where he stood. At the other end of the corridor, two security personnel appeared, stunners drawn.

The escapee skidded to a stop, body folding from the halt in momentum. Her fingertips brushed the floor; she pushed up and off, then reversed her course. The two Security ran after her. The net would close shortly.

"STOP!" Jarin bellowed in his language. Then repeated the order in the Outer language.

The girl's head whipped around in his direction.

"Come here and do everything I say," he told her. She paused, mouth open, chest heaving, then ran to his side.

"You speak my language?' she panted.

"Yes. Quiet," he ordered as the medicals and security arrived together.

"Theorist Svestil, thank you," one of the medicals huffed, hunching forward to catch his breath. "Theorist Eraranat left the Outer behind, he's been taken to in-processing." He coughed and stood upright. "Stun it and take it for processing and grafting," he added to Security.

"Did Theorist Eraranat give the order to have her processed and grafted?" Jarin asked the medical.

"The Outer is dangerous, it escaped from decon," the second medical answered.

"I will assume the answer is no," Jarin said. He regarded the young woman, "And dangerous? This girl?"

"Dangerous and unstable," the medical affirmed.

"Outer! On your knees before People!" Jarin bellowed at the woman in his language. She stared, uncomprehending. "No chatterer yet?" he asked the Medicals.

"That order wasn't given," one of the men explained.

"And neither of you bothered to upload the lingua forms from the recon to your own chatterers?" The medicals offered embarrassed head shakes. "I see." He faced her again, "Girl! I am shouting for the benefit of these men. Get on your knees and bow your head, pretend to be afraid! Quickly."

She did as ordered.

"Quite docile, once she understands her orders," Jarin said to the medicals. "Fetch her clothing. I would prefer not to walk these halls with a naked primitive." He waved away security. "The Outer is my responsibility until Theorist Eraranat is done with in-processing."

The men hesitated then went in their separate directions.

"You may stand now," Jarin said, when the four were out of sight.

Now that the chase was ended, the woman colored at her lack of clothing and positioned her hands and arms to cover herself.

"That was very reckless behaviour," Jarin chastened her, "but of course Segkel made no province for your reception. Typical. My name is Jarin Svestil, Senior Theorist of the Cultural Theorist's Guild. Welcome to the World." He waved his hand around the corridor, with a wry smile. "Your clothing will be returned to you shortly. Segkel will be detained for some time longer for in-processing."

The boy had no idea what he was in for. It was fortunate that the Council vote had been taken well early into his escapades, because the Guild was buzzing with consternation over his actions and proposed plans, and now the CWA was nosing into the mission as well. If the episode that had just occurred was any indication, Segkel had managed to find even more trouble than he had let on over the comms.

Well, the in-processing had begun, he had missed the opportunity to speak with his student alone, but Segkel was his own man now, and he would have to face whatever awaited him on his own. All the same, Jarin hoped, fervently, that Segkel would show a modicum of restraint.

Seg walked down the long corridor toward the in-processing room, struck for the first time by how lifeless the facility was, how devoid of color or identity. The People prided themselves on functionality and practicality; the color of the World was provided by captured trophies and Outers taken in raids. This was something he always belived set them above the Outers they conquered, but now the absence of decoration did not feel as much evolved as it felt empty. He briefly considered the fact that there was no sensation of Bliss in returning to the World, but the thought did not occupy him for long, as he found himself standing in front of the door for in-processing.

He had a complicated raid to coordinate and oversee, a terrified woman anxious to return to her home world, and no patience for the maze of bureaucracy the Guild expected him to run.

"Theorist Eraranat," the processor said, as Seg stepped inside the small room, "please have a seat."

"I believe that medical issues take priority over in-processing," he said as he continued to stand.

"Under normal circumstances this is true. These are not normal circumstances. At present, the Contract House for your venture has assembled in excess of two thousand infantry troops, four detachments of armor, six detachments of combat skimmers, nine air detachments, and is currently negotiating for fourteen special service detachments. At this point, your raid will go through as designed simply because the forces have been assembled and dissolution of the various contracts would bankrupt the House. However, this means that you cannot be allowed any spare time away from in-processing and preparation. Tell me, honestly, will your physical situation deteriorate in the next two days?"

"No," Seg admitted, grudgingly, then settled into the hard chair. "They will need more than nine air detachments."

"You aren't financing this raid, Theorist Eraranat," the man said curtly. "Now then, you're familiar with the basic action review process. To repeat the formula—"

"To repeat the formula, the basic action review process is vital to gathering first impressions before the details are altered by basic memory process—"

The processor waved an impatient hand. "Yes Theorist, you can quote the book at length. I'd heard that about you."

"Good, then you know that I know the process. My final raw recordings are in my digifilm and available for upload. I am aware that my action review would normally be completed by this point, but this raid is proceeding, as you have pointed out, under extraordinary circumstances and I will complete the review as soon as I am treated for my wounds. I recorded my findings with one arm bound from the broken bone I am going to be treated for, and I've had enough of working under that constraint."

"Theorist Eraranat," the man said, "any number of your actions have been cast as unortho. It would behoove you to stay and attend these matters before they become a larger issue."

"My validation will come with the mission," Seg said as he pushed himself out of the chair. "I killed nearly a dozen Outers on the extrans, I am in severe pain, and I am feeling quite cranky at the moment. I will have my injury tended to, complete my action review, then return here when I am ready. You will perform your recordkeeping duty and enter the information you received."

He turned and started out the door.

"Theorist Eraranat!" the man shouted as he rose to his feet. "You can't just walk out on a in-processing brief!"

"I remind you, Processor, that I am a Theorist of the Guild, and you are a functionary," Seg said. His words came out in barely constrained bursts. "Press this matter and I'll see you in an amp chair before the day is done."

He stalked down the hallway, fuming. He was on the verge of completing the most thorough observation of such a rich target in possibly the history of the Guild. Yes, he had been unortho, not once or twice but with incredible regularity, but he had also produced results, as the raid would show.

At the infirmary door, he stomped inside, shoved aside a curtain and nodded to the medical on duty, "I have an injury that needs to be tended to."

After the raid was done, he planned to sleep for a week.

Jarin spoke her language! Not perfectly, not as well as Seg, but at least now Ama could communicate. And he wasn't a barbarian, as all the others seemed to be. She pulled on her clothes, happy to finally know some modesty.

Jarin was old, very old perhaps. His hair hung down like sea moss, and his face was weathered. Not in the way Kenda faces weathered, from sun and wind and salt, but simply from the passage of time. His eyes reminded her of Stevan's, as if this man carried the weight of a thousand secrets. He was the first of Seg's kind that didn't scare her.

"My name is Captain Amadahy Kalder," she said, when she was dressed. "And I need to get back home."

"I am afraid that is impossible. Warp gate access is strictly controlled and you, I am sorry to say, will not be allowed to pass through."

"Seg promised to return me home."

"Did my student teach you about our World?"

"A little. He said it was boring and…" her eyes moved to the far left as she drew up the memory, "full of self-important, feeble-minded, unimaginative fools."

"Yes, that sounds like a lesson Segkel might deliver," Jarin said, "and one you would be wise not to repeat. Here, if you come from another world you are considered an—"

"Outer. I'm an Outer, I know that."

"Then you should also know there are no free Outers on the World. In practical terms, this means you have no rights, you cannot come and go as you please."

"You don't understand, I have to get back. There are people waiting for me and—"

Jarin raised a hand to stop the onslaught of words. "We will have to wait for Segkel to discuss that matter. If he has made a promise, be assured he has every intention of keeping it…no matter how ill-thought out the gesture" He leaned closer to her, "And regardless of how Segkel allows you to address him, when referring to him in the presence of others I would advise that you call him 'my master' or 'Master Eraranat'. There are forms that are expected here. Segkel has obviously given you some measure of respect, but do not expect it from any others."

"Master?" The sick feeling from the warp returned.

"Come child," Jarin said, and ushered her down the corridor, "the intrans process will keep Segkel busy for some time and there is nothing for us to do but wait. We may as well do so in the comfort of my quarters, where we can speak openly."

His collarbone properly set and healing, along with a dose of stimulants, Seg was energized and ready to get to work.

Ama, he had been informed, had been collected by Jarin. At least he could be sure of her safety in his mentor's care. Nevertheless, the sooner he dealt with his business here, the sooner he could share his plans with her, to see her back home. Doubtless she would be frantic by now.

He rolled his shoulder as he walked, overjoyed to be free of the confining bandage at last. For the next three days he would have to wear a healing grid on the skin over the break but it was thin and barely noticeable. From the infirmary, he moved with long, sure strides to the Debriefing Room, where he would complete his action review by collating and prioritizing the targets.

"So it's true, what they are saying about you," a woman's voice sounded behind Seg's back.

He stopped and looked back, to assess the threat. She didn't look to be armed and her posture was not aggressive, though she tried to project an air of dominance and authority that the unschooled might find convincing.

"I doubt it," he said. "Common wisdom is rarely wise."

"You've just proved my point, Theorist Eraranat." She smiled and held her hand up, palm open to Seg, "Jul Akbas, Efectuary of the Political Interactions Sector, Central Well Authority."

If there were a word to describe the woman, Seg mused, it would be 'contained'. Thin, hair pulled tight, immaculately groomed, and with facial features of perfect size and symmetry, Jul Akbas was as crisp as a finger snap.

He touched his palm to hers to make the fleeting contact of a formal greeting between those of high social rank.

"You're not known for your patience either, so I'll make this succinct," she continued. "We've been following your recon. We're impressed. We have a proposal we think you'll want to hear."

"Proposal?" he asked, as his face twisted. "For what?" He had expected a great many things following the recon mission, but to be confronted with the CWA bearing some sort of offer was not one of them. Beyond the delivery of vita, why would they even care what he did?

"We're putting together a new division, a means by which we can become more involved in the raid process, increase efficiency, decrease errors and loss. The current system, we feel, is flawed. We're looking for individuals to address this." She passed him a digifilm, "The Cultural Research Division will examine raids in greater depth and enact changes to our outdated procedures."

She was silent for less than a heartbeat as she watched Seg study the film.

"As second in command of this division, and eventually first if you perform to expectations, you would design and direct the nature of raids for all Theorists. Without the Guild Council setting your terms."

"From a desk," he said, and passed the film back as if it burned his hand to hold it. "The work is done out there," he waved his hand toward the intrans chamber, "not from meeting rooms. This is simply the verification process."

"The Division is still in the planning stages, Theorist. There's nothing to say that your observations couldn't be done in the field, working with existing missions." She leveled her gaze on him, her ice blue eyes hinting at something beyond a mere job offer. "Think on this very carefully. We don't make many offers of this nature. With us, you will control and direct your path. Tell me, can the Guild offer you that? Or do they question your every move? Unortho, that's what they say about you. We say you're simply a man who sees more clearly than others."

Seg rasped his hand through his unkempt beard as he considered the woman before him. "Among the attributes that Guild Theorists are trained for is the ability to perceive the mendacity in others. You are the sort that will say anything to get your way. This could be commendable if you worked toward higher goals, but it's entirely about the personal enrichment of…" he scratched the beard once more, "what did you say your name was again?"

"Akbas. Efectuary Akbas," she said, chopping every syllable.

"I expect I'll be hearing it again, though likely not in connection with any worthy ventures," he said before he turned away.

"Congratulations on your first mission," she called to his back, her voice an octave lower. "We expect we'll be hearing your name again too, Segkel Eraranat. Though not in connection with any ventures. Worthy or otherwise."

The click of her boots marked her departure.

Seg dismissed her presence with a shrug. He knew that, despite her rosy picture, the CWA was so hidebound as to make the Guild look revolutionary. He had paid that much attention in Fundamentals of World Affairs, even if the class had been a dreadful bore.

Combined with her obviously devious and underhanded nature, he was better quit of her as soon as possible. But no sooner had he resumed his course when someone else called his name. Would he ever get out of here?

"Unless this is urgent, it can wait. I'm on my way to debriefing," he said to the House Accountancy now at his side.

"Your debriefing has been postponed. An emergency meeting has been scheduled, Theorist."

"On whose orders and with whom?"

"I'm sorry, I was told it's classified. This way, Theorist." The man directed him down the corridor, past the Debriefing Room, to an unmarked door. With a nod, he ushered Seg inside.

This intrans process was becoming increasingly unconventional.

He entered the room, surprised at the occupants. The Master and Marshal of House Haffset, attended by six serving caj and their Handler, stood near a long projection table. First the CWA, now this? He glanced over his shoulder; the door cycled closed in front of the House Accountancy.

Affairs had just turned even more unortho.

Although Jarin told Ama the name of the building they were in, there was no direct translation to the language she spoke. The 'Intrans Facility', Jarin explained, was like a very sophisticated 'dock' for people returning from other worlds but nothing she had seen compared to any dock she knew of – even those for the Shasir skyships.

Now, as they walked toward the exit, it was difficult for Ama to keep her head down as Jarin had instructed her to do. The building was constructed simply, largely from stone, and composed of sharp, unforgiving angles. The walls were bare except for the long hallway they walked down, which was covered with art and other objects, (plundered from other worlds, she guessed, judging by the wide variances in form and color). When they reached the door, it irised open and Ama let out a gasp as Jarin led her out into the wider world.

He paused as she stepped out, then positioned himself to shield her from the sight of others and allow her a moment to take in the view. The sky was coppery and shimmered over their heads. Beyond that, dark clouds lurked, firing bolts of electricity among themselves; occasionally a bolt hurled down into the copper, where it sizzled and dissipated.

"Don't fear the Storm," Jarin said. "We are in a shielded city, where there is no need to shelter from it. Did Segkel tell you of the Storm?"

"No," she whispered, as she stared at the sky. "I didn't know…" her voice trailed away. As a veteran of storms, Ama was perplexed by what she saw. The dark clouds were unreadable, lacked connection to weather patterns. They were, in short, unnatural.

"Your world is *malfut*," she said.

Jarin tilted his head, "Say that last word again."

"*Malfut*," Ama repeated, "It's a Kenda word. It has a special meaning; sick, broken, unbalanced, abandoned by Nen, all of those together."

"Have a care of how you speak when you are away from me, child. For one thing, all responsibility is levied from property to master. Therefore, your errors belong to Segkel. This is the way of things. As for our World," he glanced up at the Storm, "you are very perceptive.

Though I would not recommend sharing that with anyone else, either. Come along."

He beckoned her to follow him across a bustling marketplace. Seg's people, dressed in their drab clothing, jabbered at each other. A line of shackled men, strange barbarians with pale skin and muscular builds, were chivvied along by bellowing overseers, who prodded at them with sticks that arced lightning at the end. There was a crowd, and Jarin took her arm to guide her through the throng. "Stay silent," he ordered, close to her ear, "and do not look anyone in the eye. Just follow me."

As Ama walked, she compared Seg's world to her own. The sounds on this world matched the language his people spoke: hard, metallic, unnatural. No birdcalls, no crash of surf, no rustle of leaves, nothing familiar. Likewise, the smells were unnatural too, as metallic as the language, one particularly that she couldn't define. This scent permeated everything, almost as if something were burning but not quite, and not wood. And everywhere a fine dust hovered in the air, irritating her dathe.

Not a speck of green was visible. Not a single plant or tree. There was light, coming from somewhere beyond the shield, but the storm clouds blocked out much of it and the shimmering shield above muted what remained. *How do these people live without seeing the sun?*

Malfut. Dry, sharp, hard and, with the exception of the people, lifeless. So, this is where Seg had been born and raised, this is the world that formed him.

No wonder.

CHAPTER 17

fter thirty minutes, the meeting with Rethelt and Haffset had begun to feel less like a discussion and more like an interrogation to Seg. In effect, he had been forced to complete his action review under their scrutiny, and now he waited as the men reviewed the preliminary data and proposed targets.

The air in the room was dry. Had the air here always been this dry or was this some side effect of the medical treatment for his shoulder? Seg scooped his glass off the table, turned as if to go fill it, then stopped as one of the serving caj rushed to his side with a pitcher of water. He had forgotten about them during his time extrans, the faceless, nameless Outers that waited, against the wall, to serve the People.

The service of caj was a fact of life on the World. To question this was to question the innate superiority of the People. But Seg's time on Ama's world had often demanded his self-reliance in matters that, on his world, were relegated to the lower orders. He had not just grown accustomed to such tasks as fetching his own water, he had grown to enjoy them. Petty as they were, the chores imbued him with a feeling of independence and, oddly enough, strength.

Seg looked at the man, as he poured the water. Had he ever 'looked' at a caj before?

The man, if he were to stand fully upright, would barely reach Seg's chest. He was very small and thin. His hair, grey and sparse, showed the brown age spots on his head. The backs of his hands were covered in red markings that ran up under the sleeve of his uniform.

Xlny'xt. Seg remembered the name of that race of Outers from his studies. A civilization carved in stone, literally. They had built their cities into the sides of mountains, painstakingly chiseled over thousands of years.

From his position Seg could see the control graft, on the back of the caj's neck, which delivered instant correction and kept him temporarily mute.

Just as Seg's glass was nearly full, the caj teetered, slightly off balance, then knocked the pitcher into the glass and sent it crashing to the floor. Immediately the man moved to clean the mess but, before he could, he dropped to his knees, back curved in a painful arch, mouth stretched wide in a silent scream.

Seg tensed, ready to move torward the man, before he realized what was happening. He glanced up and spotted the Handler, his thumb on the button that administered correction via the control graft as he approached. "Apologies," the Handler said, and Seg watched him press his thumb down again, sending the old caj into a round of convulsions that spilled the contents of the pitcher on himself and the floor. Air hissed from the man's open mouth and tears ran from the corner of his eyes. "Third warning. One more and this one's off to the recycler," the Handler muttered, as three other caj arrived to clean the mess and haul their comrade away.

Marshal Rethelt flicked his eyes over the scene impatiently then turned back to the holographic display that stretched out in front of them, nearly half as wide as the room. "Theorist?" He cleared his throat, "Theorist?"

When Seg looked back at him and nodded, Rethelt continued. "I understand targets Malvid, Alisir and T'ueve, but these other primaries of yours – Ol'cania, L'albor, and Myan'as? They're strictly military targets, with no vita worth recovering. Even assuming they're diversionary or disorganizational strikes, they exceed necessary mission parameters."

Every raid came down to this, the balance of the cost of force commitment against the return of vita, tech, and caj. The vita paid out directly in exchange with the CWA, the Central Well Authority, that directly oversaw the mitigation of the warp and minimization of the effects of the Storm. Tech, caj and materials were property of the sponsoring House or corporation, and sold or dispersed as those entities saw fit.

Like all Theorists, Seg had taken his own swing at deciphering the complex algorithms by which the CWA assessed the relative value of vita in the current market. However, he was frustrated, as others were, by the classified portions of the calculations, namely the variant hunger of the warps and, closely linked, the strength of the Storm. He had a gut suspicion that the CWA's algorithm was deliberately made to be obtuse and impenetrable, to underpin an unsustainable situation.

He had a feeling that was the situation in general. He lacked hard proof, but he felt that no matter how much vita they fed to the Storm, sooner or later it would consume them all.

But then death came for everyone, and that didn't mean that one simply accepted it and lay down. That was not the way of the People. They had withstood the Storm for generations, it was likely they would withstand it for generations to come.

"There are additional targets that I am commissioning personal strikes on," Seg said, "the purpose of which is my own business."

Rethelt studied him. "Personal? Are you carrying a vendetta into this, Theorist?"

Seg's head snapped up, "Are you accusing me of compromising my bond with your House to satisfy my personal grudges, Commander Rethelt? Because I assure you the targets that you have been given for collection are the best available targets to maximize the return for your investment. As with all assignments, my assessment will be subject to a thorough professional review, both by the Guild and by the CWA."

Rethelt raised a placating hand, "I don't doubt your target assignments but there's something deeper here, Theorist. You have your own agenda, by your own admission."

"An agenda I am also paying for."

"From your potential profit share," Rethelt pointed out.

"Which means that I have as much at stake in this as the House does. Failure of this raid will lead to both our ruins. In the event of failure, at best we'll be sent to the Storm. At worst, we'll both be working for my father in the recycler."

"You have a point," Commander Rethelt agreed. His brows drew together at the mention of the recycler. "But this will be the subject of much discussion during the planning sessions. This proposed raid is ambitious to the point of megalomania."

"I respect your opinion," Seg said. He kept his hands tucked behind his back, to conceal their twitching. For a moment, he stared down at his legs and willed his hands to steady before departing. Before him, the caj parted from his path. "And of course I respect your rights of oversight over all mission priorities. With that in mind, I need to dress and get to work."

"Of course," the House Master said, then stepped forward and grasped Seg's elbow – a gesture of shocking intimacy. The mere contact sent a jolt through Seg's body. It was everything he could do not to recoil away from the touch. The House Master gave him a warm smile, reading the discomfort in Seg's eyes plainly.

These were dangerous men. As dangerous as any he had encountered on Ama's world. He was in just as much danger among his allies, his People, as he had been during the entire mission.

One battlefield to another.

Jarin guided Ama through the streets, into a narrow pathway, then stopped before a plain building front. He pressed his palm against a glowing panel on the wall. A door opened soundlessly, he stepped through and pulled her in with him.

The quarters were claustrophobic. If Jarin were wealthy, he was not one for ostentatious displays of it. What he obviously did enjoy was visual imagery. His walls were festooned with likenesses of a hundred different worlds, some of which featured Jarin at various stages of his life, dressed in native clothing, or in the sort of battle gear Kerbin and her squad wore.

He led Ama into the common area and gestured toward four old, heavy and well-padded chairs, each wide enough to seat two people. "Be seated," he said. "Make yourself comfortable."

Ama sat but her gaze drifted, as it always did. When Jarin's back was turned, she walked to the likenesses on the wall. Here was a world made of sand, another with skies of purple; in one, a likeness of Jarin stood up to his thighs in cloud. So many worlds, who could have ever imagined?

Jarin returned with two steaming cups. He held one out for her and smiled wistfully at the likenesses. "Most of those were from a lifetime ago. A different time, that was. So, tell me of your world, Amadahy," Jarin said, taking a sip. "Oceans, I understand? Oceans and mountains and forests. A seagoer you are," he nodded toward her neck and exposed dathe, "with a most interesting adaptation."

Unconsciously, she raised a hand to cover her dathe, then lowered it. There was nothing to fear about showing her dathe on this world, after all.

"My world…" she pointed to a likeness, "is much like this, but with more mountains. Water is what I know, what my people know. We came from beneath the Big Water; we all had dathe then." She touched her neck, tilting for Jarin to have a better look. "When the Kenda moved permanently to land, they lost their dathe. I've only known of one other of my kind that had them but she's dead now. Not that it matters; even on land, our hearts remained in the Big Water. It's sacred to us."

Jarin smiled slightly and his eyes were warm and welcoming; she felt an instant kinship with him.

"Your people don't swim, do they?" she asked. Jarin shook his head. "That's a shame. Water humbles you. There's no more demanding and benevolent master. Nen will feed you, carry you on his back, cool you in the heat, but if you fail to respect him…" she raised her open palm and snapped it into a closed fist.

Jarin imitated the gesture, "Yes, the powerful can be like that. Those of us who travel through the warp often make the acquaintance of water. Few get used to it."

"Have you been to all these worlds?" Ama asked as she gestured to the likenesses on the wall.

"Most of them, not all. We do not revisit worlds we have already plundered. Cruel math dictates our operations, as Segkel will soon be reminded." He took another sip of his drink, then looked at her dathe again. "We all came from the water, as well as we can figure. Children, in the womb, have vestigial gills like these. They are soon lost. There are aquatic mammals with fully developed bones for digits they no longer use. The evolutionary process is a wonder."

Ama took another sip. She raised her fingers to a likeness of a wide, marshy valley where thousands of brightly colored birds filled the ground and the sky. "Beautiful," she whispered, then swept her gaze over the small space Jarin called home. "Why do your people stay here? You can travel to any of these places but you stay on this dead world, I don't understand."

He tapped his fingers against the side of his mug and forced a smile, "That question marks you as more of an outsider than your gills." For a long moment he stared into the liquid in his cup, in contemplation. When he raised his head, once more Ama was reminded of Stevan in those final moments she had spent with him. "The reasons are many. Foremost, of course, is simple mathematics. We do not possess the vita needed to extrans even a third of our population."

"But some of you could leave?"

"Some, yes. Though the act would drain the vita stocks and leave the rest to be devoured by the Storm. I cannot imagine any who would choose to relocate under those conditions."

"I understand, I wouldn't leave my people that way either," Ama said and winced as she thought of Brin's men, waiting for word from her.

"Not all of our reasons for staying put are so...noble, however," Jarin continued. "The People are clever, but our cleverness has also bred arrogance, and with it a kind of willful ignorance. A lie told often enough, and with sufficient conviction, becomes truth. For centuries we have held off the Storm, and we have convinced ourselves that this act makes us great. Greater than all others. The People find comfort in this, as they also do in permanence and orthodoxy. To suggest we leave our World is to suggest we are imperfect; the People will not have that.

"And it is important to understand that the world you see now has been shaped over millennia, not weeks. Across the dimensions, humanoid populations share several common traits, the greatest of which is our adaptability. And the slower changes occur, the more easily we adapt. To the People, our world, our way of life is, well, normal."

"But there must be others that think like you?"

Jarin's eyes flicked away from her for a moment, "Very few. And none that will speak aloud." He opened his mouth to speak then shook his head.

"What is it?"

"Only that I have spoken on this subject to a mere handful of people in my lifetime, and to only one person have my thoughts on the matter been unguarded. I do not know what possessed me to speak so frankly with you."

"I won't tell anyone," Ama said, laying a hand on his arm. "Not that they'd listen to me if I did. Well, Seg would but..." her hand fell from his arm.

She dropped the cup on a side table, with a heavy thump. The liquid sloshed over the side.

"How long is this going to take?" she asked, pacing across the small room. "I need to see Seg. Why can't I see him?"

Jarin sighed and retrieved a cleaning rag to wipe up the liquid. "You cannot see him because he is no doubt embroiled in the massive controversy he has created with his highly unorthodox actions on your world. In order to assist him, and therefore you, I would be best served by knowing more about what occurred over there." He lifted a hand, "I am not asking you to compromise any confidences. But Segkel is brilliant, ambitious, and under the youthful assumption that being supremely intelligent and competent will allow him to reorder the world to his own vision. He is going to learn very soon that this is not so."

Ama reached her fingers to her absent nove, then lowered her hand and faced away from Jarin, feigning interest in one of the likenesses. "There was some trouble."

"Such as?" he asked. He stepped around to the side and studied her face carefully. "You care for him greatly, obviously."

"I—" she felt her face grow hot. "I had some trouble with the authorities. Seg got involved." She turned to Jarin, her face hardened, "You've been very kind but I don't know you, which means I can't trust you. I don't know anyone on this world." She pressed her lips together and swallowed. Just then her stomach growled.

"Your caution does you credit." Jarin's face softened, "As does your stoicism. When was your last meal?"

"We've been on the run, food's been thin."

"Let's get you something to eat then." Jarin waved an inviting hand.

Ama followed him, her stomach aching as much with worry as with hunger. They stepped into a small kitchen, or what Ama assumed was a kitchen as it resembled none she had ever seen. A dark haired woman spun to face her, dropping into a low bow.

"Master Svestil," the woman said, her voice honeyed, "I thought you were gone."

"Lissil," he said, offering her a polite bow, "this is Captain Amadahy Kalder. You do not have to call me 'master' in front of her. Amadahy, this is Lissil a-Das of the Welf. She was, ah, sent through earlier."

"A Welf?" the words spilled from Ama's mouth. "I'm sorry," she corrected, "it's just—" She tilted her head, "When did you come here?"

The Welf's eyes passed over Ama's body, appraising. Where most people walked, Lissil seemed to glide, which she did to Ama's side and, just as gracefully, slipped her hand into Ama's, fingers interlocking as she pulled her close.

"You are of the seafarers?" Lissil asked.

"I'm Kenda," Ama answered, stiffening, "if that's what you mean." She had met this breed of Welf before, in the Port House, well schooled in seduction and trickery. She darted a glance to Jarin, who appeared as uncomfortable as she felt.

"Yes, I could tell," Lissil said, squeezing Ama's hand. "Did Lord Eraranat send you through as well? The household will need servants."

"Servant? I'm not a servant." The word sat in Ama's mouth like rotten Jinje fruit. "Did he send you here to be his servant?" Ama asked Lissil, then flashed an accusing glare at Jarin. "Is she Seg's slave?"

"Yes," Jarin answered, after a pause, "she is. Registered to his name and awaiting final transaction from his share of the raid profits."

"Caj," Lissil corrected Ama. "Their word is 'caj', not slave. So you belong to him as well?" Her voice arched as she released Ama's hand.

"I don't *belong* to anyone," Ama said.

Seg had a slave. A Welf. He had never even mentioned the girl. Ama looked at the dish of food sitting on the counter—foreign by appearance but inviting by smell—and frowned. "I've lost my appetite," she muttered, and backed out of the room, unable to move her eyes from Lissil.

I put my father's life in the hands of a liar.

Behind her, Jarin murmured something to Lissil. Moments later, he followed Ama into the main chamber.

"I realize this is all traumatic for you," he began.

"Send me home," Ama interrupted. She stabbed a hand in the direction of the outside world. "Take me back to the machine. Now!"

"I told you that is not possible."

"Fine, I'll go myself. I'll make them send me back." Ama charged toward the door.

"They will kill you," Jarin said, his tone level. Ama stopped inches from the exit. "My People will kill you, or worse, much worse, if you try to leave."

Her chest rose and fell as if she were summoning courage, but her body remained in place.

"Segkel will come for you."

"He didn't tell me about this Welf slave," she said, her voice choked. "How can I trust him now?"

"He does not give his word lightly. For that matter, he does not give his word at all unless he is ready to fight for it. To the death, I believe."

She flipped around and pounded her back and fists against the door with a frustrated cry.

"Amadahy…" Jarin stood in front of her reaching out a hand from a safe distance, "I do not know of all that has passed between you two, but I need to know. For him, for you, and apparently for your father."

The edges of Ama's her jaw tensed. "Get him here. I can't say any more."

"Oh, I will bring him here," Jarin assured her. "He has a great many questions to answer."

CHAPTER 18

Seg pressed the chime on the door to Jarin's residence, a modest unit in the C Block of the Guild compound. Given his mentor's success and talent, he often wondered why he chose such a small existence. Every corner of the world, but for the wealthiest and most powerful of its citizens, was crowded, as the Storm ate away at the remaining habitable land. While Jarin lacked the resources of Senior CWA members or the prominent Houses, he could easily afford a detached living space, or at least a larger unit within the A block.

The door slid open. "Segkel," Jarin said, with the slightest of nods.

"Mentor," Seg answered. "I'm not here for dinner, though your invitation was gracious. I'll speak with Ama, then I must return to my office."

"The meal is prepared and you know well the First Virtue of a Citizen: Allow no waste. Unless you would prefer I create a charitable institution for those incapable of providing their own sustenance."

"I'm in no mood for games, Jarin. I have pressing matters to attend to. House Haffset has insisted—"

"You have pressing matters here," Jarin stepped aside; Ama stood in the entryway.

He stepped inside at the sight of her and the worry carved on her features. Worry and something else.

"Ama, I would have come earlier but..." His attention was drawn away as another woman appeared behind Ama. The woman was obviously caj by her dress and demeanor; had his mentor changed his views since he had been gone?

Before he had time to ask, the strange woman squealed, "Master!" and threw herself to the floor in front of him. She knelt prostrate, her forehead pressed to the floor, fists against her head knuckle-first near her temples. A picture-perfect rendering of the *retyel*, the posture of obeisance offered by a caj to its owner. He stared at the strange, crazy woman with a questioning look that he then passed between Jarin and Ama.

Then realization. He had completely forgotten about the Welf he had sent back over. Things had taken on a whole new tone over on Ama's world after the night they had killed Uval, and it was as if the entire episode had come in a before and after chapter.

"Oh," he said, staring blankly.

He knew what was expected of him, the formal words of release. There were protocols for owners, as well as caj. But he found himself muttering, "Get up. That's enough."

The girl hesitated and there was a strained moment, as Seg felt Ama and Jarin's eyes on him. Then, at last, she rose.

"I await your pleasure, Master." The words dripped from her tongue like nectar.

He had barely looked at the Welf the day she had been taken, had never noticed that her lips seemed to pout and smile at once. She reminded him of the whore who had drugged him with her painted lips; the resemblance, down to the pinched waist and ample hips, was uncanny.

"There's no need for all the..." Seg's hands fluttered to indicate the retyel and general protocol. "If we're to eat, let's be quick about it." he said, then to the girl: "Join us for the meal."

"You do this caj great honor, my Lord." Her cheeks dimpled as she smiled.

"When do we leave?" Ama asked, her voice icy.

"There is work to be done before the raid goes through," Seg said, turning quickly from the Welf.

"The raid?" Ama stepped up closer to him, eyes boring holes through his. "I have to get back now. You said—"

"I said I would get you back," Seg's voice dropped until it was nearly a whisper. "And I will."

Ama launched into a diatribe in her native tongue. Seg could pick out only a few words – father, promise, death, lie, slave – though her agitation and unhappiness required no translation.

Jarin placed himself between Seg and Ama, raising his hands for silence. "As I said, dinner awaits. We have much to talk about, so let us all proceed to the table where we may discuss the raid." After a brief pause he added, "And what came before."

Seg's head whipped back toward Ama. She had told Jarin about his alliance with her people. Obviously.

Head bowed, the Welf girl led the group to the small dining area. She dished out generous helpings of food to Seg and Jarin, then paused, regarding Ama. The question of Ama's position was written on her face.

"Everyone is to be served," Jarin said.

"Yes, of course," Seg added, a touch of irritation at edge of his words. Did the old man think he would make the Welf kneel on the floor? "What is your name?" he asked her.

"This caj is known as Lissil, my Lord," she answered, a rosy blush rising to her cheeks as she retrieved two plates and dished out much smaller portions for Ama and herself.

"I wonder what they're serving in the Secat this evening," Ama asked, eyes on Seg.

He clenched his fork and glanced sidelong at Jarin. "Don't," he warned her.

"Enough of this," Jarin said. "There are matters which concern us all here. Segkel, this raid of yours is perilously close to the precipice."

"My raid is assigned, it is in the process of being tabulated and tasked. Once the Council votes, it will proceed," Seg said, then added quickly, "and it will succeed."

"The CWA is directly involving itself with the process," Jarin said, "and if they detect any breaches of protocol and orthodoxy, they can make matters very difficult for you. To the point of potentially aborting the raid."

"I've met them already. A representative." He straightened up to look Jarin in the eye. "I dealt with her."

Jarin paused, his fork before his lips. "With your usual diplomacy and grace, I am sure."

Seg bristled visibly. "I accorded her the respect she was due."

"This is not training, pupil," Jarin said. "You cannot expect to simply awe People with your brilliance and prove your theorem correct. There are ramifications to your actions that extend throughout the World."

Seg slammed his fist on the table, making the plates jump. "I know this raid will affect the World. That is the point. Do you support it or not?"

Jarin lowered his fork. "More than you know, Segkel. But you need to at least appear to be working within the boundaries of orthodoxy. The People need conformity and respect of the traditions and virtues."

"But they worship results, and I will give them results. Is there anything else?" He glared a dark challenge at Jarin.

"No," Jarin said, at length. "But we need to discuss the planning and interactions further. You can expect the Question for this raid to be thorough."

"Then I'll answer to that," Seg said.

"I am certain of your confidence in the process but will you answer to me now?" Jarin placed both palms on the table and leaned in toward Seg, "What occurred on your extrans, after your comm to me, and beyond the sanitized report you turned in?"

Seg pressed his lips together and drew a breath in through his nose; his eyes darted to Ama then back to Jarin. He rose to his feet, threw his fork on his plate, then nodded curtly. "Thank you for the meal, teacher."

"Segkel!" Jarin called to Seg's back as he stormed out of the room.

Ama kicked out her chair and ran after him. "Hey!" she yelled, both her fists clenched. "We're not finished yet." He was already outside the residence and, heedless of Jarin's warnings, she followed him.

Seg spun on his heels, reached past Ama, and cycled the door closed to give them some modicum of privacy.

"You have a slave? A Welf?" Ama spat the words at him.

"There is more to the situation than you are aware of. I've had no time to explain anything to you. If you'll—"

"And now you say I can't return until the raid? You know what's going to happen. Brin's people will tell him I didn't show, he'll think we're dead. He'll send his men into the Secat and they'll die. His men will die because of me. Again. And who knows what Dagga will do to my father. You need to get me through that gate, you need…."

"Stop. For once, stop talking and listen!" he placed his hands on Ama's shoulders and gripped tightly. "We can't change what has happened. I brought you here to save your life, I would do the same again no matter the consequences on your world. I am moving the raid planning forward as fast as possible and when my People extrans I will bring you with me. We will free your father."

Ama held his gaze for a moment before she glanced over her shoulder to the door, behind which the scene with Lissil had unfolded. "Is that what will be expected of Brin's men? To grovel at your feet like animals?"

"I see that I haven't earned one particle of trust from you," he said and dropped his hands from her shoulders. "This is a complicated world."

"Which I didn't ask to come to!"

They both turned silent but the argument continued in their eyes.

"I didn't want to send that girl here. I did so to spare her a worse fate," Seg explained.

"And now you own her," Ama leaned back against the door and looked to one side. "This is my own fault. I got swept up in being with you and I forgot who you are. I thought—" she shook her head. "That doesn't matter. Dagga is probably torturing my father. Right now. And I'm stuck here. And there's nothing I can do about it."

"We will go back to rescue him," Seg said. He took a step closer to her and lowered his voice, "I promised you that, and I carry out my promises. And no, your people will not be using the retyel." At her confused look, he gestured toward the door. "The posture of caj. Brin's men are not to be caj."

"Caj." She looked into his eyes, searching, or so it seemed to him. "You have a slave, Seg. How can I believe in a man who treats a person like property?"

At her words, his face hardened, "All worlds, all cultures, have their own customs. Every society finds its own way. This is ours. Whether I agree with it or—"

"It's barbaric."

"On your world, are women allowed to hold positions of power? Are they considered equals to men? Were you encouraged to seek out independence and freedom?"

"No, but—"

"The People of my World consider that barbaric. And yet your kind consider this both normal and necessary."

"Not all of us."

"And not all of us keep caj," he gave a significant glance at Jarin's residence. "There are outliers in every social group, on every world. This does not alter the facts of the matter."

"So…you're going to keep her? Your caj?"

"She's been registered," Seg answered, then added, "which means she must stay on my World, forever."

"I'm not…registered, am I?"

"Only with the Guild. Not formally, not as property of the World and the People, no."

"I can leave."

Seg's jaw tensed slightly, "It will be difficult, but not impossible, yes."

"Good."

As if a cord had been cut, Seg backed away from her, a cold mask of indifference dropped over his face. "Yes, as you should," he said, straightening his coat. "You don't belong here. I must return to my work, Jarin will see to your needs until it is time to return to your world."

With that, he took a few more backward steps, then whirled around and walked away.

Ama walked a few paces after Seg then halted, watching until he turned a corner and vanished. She lingered there long after he was out of sight. Eventually the door slid open and Jarin stood silhouetted in the entrance.

"Come in, Amadahy," Jarin said. "He won't be coming back." He placed a hand on her elbow and pulled her inside.

She raised her head and caught a glimpse of movement from inside. Dark hair, disappearing behind a corner. Lissil, watching and listening. Spying.

"Thank you," Ama said, and pried her elbow away from Jarin, "but I can look after myself."

"Not here. It is not possible," he said. "Here, the People will kill you if you do not present the public appearance of compliance."

Ama saw in his eyes that this was no threat, merely a statement of fact. She nodded, "I'll do what I need to do." She paused, still seeing Seg walking away from her. "It will happen though, won't it? The raid?"

Jarin hesitated. "We will do everything we can to make it happen, yes. And I will do everything I can to see you returned to your world safely. You have my word on this."

"I hope so," she said, eyes on the closed door. "I hope so."

On a thin mat, back to the Welf, Ama stared at a bare wall. Jarin had apologized for the sleeping arrangements. He kept no caj himself and had only recently cleared out a small storage room for Lissil, and now Ama, to call a bedroom. Behind her, she heard the rasp of the brush Lissil pulled through her long, silken hair in methodical strokes.

"Lord Eraranat's very handsome," Lissil mused in a singsong voice.

Ama didn't bother to answer.

"He's only just starting in his career, too," she continued. "Master Svestil says he is poised to become a great man. And, when that happens, I will be at his side."

"As his property," Ama muttered.

Lissil let out a throaty laugh. "And you believe that is so terrible?"

"Don't you?" Ama asked, turning to face Lissil.

"I consider it an honor."

"To be a slave?"

"To be claimed by a man of such power."

The old antipathy she felt toward the Welf surfaced. Had they not rolled over so easily for the Shasir, the spooks wouldn't be sitting in power today, and her people would be free. "I'd rather die than live as a slave."

"Then you're a fool and he's better off without you." Lissil tilted her head to one side, but paused the brush mid-stroke as she scrutinized Ama's face. "Ah, now I understand." Her full lips split into a smile. "You're in love with him." She nodded and resumed her grooming.

"I am not. I…you don't know anything." Ama turned her face away so that Lissil couldn't read it any longer, though she suspected she was too late.

"I know men," Lissil purred. "Who knows, he might have some feelings for you, though certainly not because of your looks. Maybe you thought he might ask you to be his mate? Let me spare you the heartache because it can never happen, not on this world. You aren't one of the People and they would never accept you. You're caj or nothing here."

"Not to Seg," Ama's fingers dug into the mat beneath her. She didn't know why she bothered to argue but something about Lissil's taunts dug at a tender spot.

Lissil lowered the brush and leaned forward, both palms flat on her mat. "Does it matter? No matter how much affection he may feel for you, he can't take you out among his people as an equal. Outside of these walls, he can't take your hand and talk with you; you can't look him in the eyes or call him by his name. He'd grow tired of the hiding, you'd become frustrated and anger him. One day he would simply put you aside."

Ama turned her head away from Lissil. "It doesn't matter what you think would happen. Once I return to our world, I won't come back here."

Lissil gasped dramatically, "But he'll be heartbroken!" She laughed again. "So much better for me," she continued, collecting herself. "He'll be easier to guide without the distraction of some ill mannered Kenda demanding his attention."

"*Guide?*"

"You really are the stupidest woman I've ever met," Lissil said, shaking her head. "Yes, guide. What? You think all slaves are powerless? On our world, Damiar and Shasir did my bidding, brought me gifts, moved me into a position of power among my people. This world is no different; Seg is no different. I'll figure out what he needs, I always do. Give a man everything he wants and needs, surrender yourself completely, and you'd be surprised what he'll do to keep you. Of course, that would be below you, wouldn't it? You Kenda, so noble, so proud," she glanced at Ama's exposed dathe, "so secretive. You think the only way to get what you want is to fight, even when the fight isn't winnable."

"And you wouldn't leave here if you had the chance?"

Lissil looked at Ama as if she had sprouted a second head. "And return to the dirt?"

"You'd be free," Ama said, spreading her hands to indicate the world outside their tiny prison.

"Free?" She set the brush down and gave Ama her full attention. "Here, the crops never fail. If I get sick or injured, they wrap a magic sleeve on my arm and I'm cured. There's no wood to cut because there's no fire to burn. No freezing winters, no scalding summers, no animals to slaughter or milk, no insects lurking in the grass or buzzing around my head, no river to overflow the bank, and for that matter, no water to collect — it comes from a tap at the press of a button. Every night I sleep in safety, warm and dry. I hope I never see our backward world again. I don't think you know what 'free' means."

Ama turned her back on Lissil again, this time lying on her side and wrapping the thin blanket around her. "I don't care what you think or what you do. Just let me sleep."

"But you do care." She felt Lissil's breath on her ear. "It's going to kill you, handing me the keys to your pathetic little kingdom, knowing your man's hands will be on my flesh, his lips calling my name. Good. Go home Kenda. You don't belong here."

She pressed her lips to Ama's ear, then rolled away and shut off the lights. *You don't belong here*, just what Seg had said. Ama let out her breath, though she knew sleep would be slow to come. Behind her she could hear Lissil stretching on her mat, and couldn't help wondering what she would do once she had Seg in her clutches.

It's not your problem. Let it go.

"Sleep well, sister," Lissil whispered, her voice the hiss of a serpent.

Once the women were tucked away in their room, Jarin left his quarters and returned to the intrans facility to consult with his peers. In the matter of the mission, he had expected Seg to be brash, arrogant and unortho—as his behavior over the meal had proved—but this business with the CWA was troubling, as was whatever was going on between him and Amadahy.

Ansin and Maryel were livid when he passed along the news that Segkel was overlooking Kenda targets and personally financing military strikes unconnected to the raid.

"This is insanity. He has to have worked out some sort of arrangement with the Outers, which means the entire operation is potentially compromised. The House could be shattered in this, and we would have to step up our quota by thirty-eight percent in order to compensate for the losses. And I mean quota overall!" Ansin slapped a hand on the table. His slight frame was rigid.

Maryel paced the meeting room, hands clasped behind her back. Her grey hair swayed as she walked. "We can forcibly alter the parameters of the raid. We supported him at your instigation," she said as she gestured to Shyl and Jarin, "if he goes down, he takes us with him. This will be worse than Lannit."

Shyl tapped her stylus against the table. "We could redesignate, draw down the force parameters, and bankrupt the House by forcing default on their assembled contracts. The singular target option, at best, delivers a break-even if they scoop every last dram of vita out, and if the creditors are forgiving with the defaults." Her tone was light and hinted of sarcasm, which belied the blunt seriousness of her words.

Jarin sat silent. He had worked hard over the years to assemble this small contingent of the Guild Council and arrange for their secret meetings. Together, this bloc had proved a powerful force within the Council and he had gradually used his influence to steer them in the direction he knew was necessary. But his guidance had been subtle and slow, so much so that he could not reasonably be accused of any guidance at all. This was the key, ensuring that his agenda, beliefs and personal feelings were left out of his dealings with the bloc. If he bent them to his will here, it would demonstrate blatant favoritism for his star pupil. This would shatter their trust. Maryel, though, would have nothing of his silence.

"Speak, Jarin. Justify this madness. You've always been the talker," she urged.

Jarin took a sip of water, the classic gambit to give time to assemble and order unspoken priorities. He considered his odd discussion with Amadahy. Truth? A dangerous proposition. But perhaps the time had come for danger. "None of us want to admit this," he said, finally, "but our world is doomed."

"Clarify," Ansin demanded.

"What was the increase in the vita tithe after the last assessment?" Jarin asked, as he set his cup on the table.

"Seven percent," Ansin answered.

"And that was actually a low increase. We've had to progressively step up operations for over a century now. The Storm hungers," Jarin said, "and it will consume us all."

Shyl nodded. Her face always projected a somber air but tonight her voice aligned with her features. "This is true," she said.

Again she surprised him. Jarin raised an eyebrow at her, then looked at Maryel, who shook her head. "You are my colleagues because you represent the broad cross-section of the Guild," he said, "and I knew that eventually we must all face this, and I would need your help to lay the groundwork."

"The CWA has raised tithes consistently as a political ploy," Maryel said.

"There is some element of truth to that," Jarin said, "but there is independent corroborating data. Storm intensity has increased by nearly forty percent over the past two centuries." He looked at his colleagues, "One hundred and fifty years ago, this city was unshielded. Unshielded! When was the last time any of you saw our natural sky?"

There was a heavy silence.

"The fact is that the increase in demand is going to continue," Shyl said. "By my calculations, within the next ten years our current mode of operation will be unsustainable. Single targets and conservative strikes can no longer be our policy. Young Eraranat is showing us the future here. What the future will have to be, if we wish to sustain our survival."

Ansin looked at her across the table, "And if the hunger continues to grow? If you're right—" he took up a stylus and tapped furiously on his digipad. "The increase has been more geometric than linear, which is the current prevailing assumption."

Let them say it. Jarin watched as Ansin ran the numbers.

Maryel watched his calculations, then looked up, "The CWA has been underfeeding the warps. They know it and they have been keeping it to themselves."

Another, more profound, silence descended upon the room. Even Shyl looked disturbed at the notion, so obvious once brought forth.

Ansin sat back in his chair, stared at his hasty calculations, then ran a hand across the smooth patch of skin on the top of his head. "Are they attempting to avoid public panic?"

Jarin shrugged. "Their security is on par with ours, and we have no reasonable level of penetration in the departments that account for quotas and feeding of the Storm. I make no effort to guess at their motivation without further data. What little I've been able to gather— some data on the increase in Storm force—cost us dearly in terms of what few assets we do have there."

"Regardless of motivation, the fact is that even at the current rate of tithe-growth," Shyl said, "our mode of operation will fail shortly. And if you are correct," she gestured to Jarin and Ansin, "then the situation is worse than I knew. As such, what Theorist Eraranat is doing will, *must*, at some point become the norm. His model must become orthodox."

Ansin glanced over at her, then at Jarin. "How long until the Storm consumes us altogether? Can it have a peak hunger? A satiation point?"

"Perhaps the CWA knows. Perhaps not. Perhaps there is no way to know. Perhaps the Storm will grow and consume all reality," Jarin answered.

"Jarin," Ansin said, as he straightened in his seat, "you represent our educational facilties, and other resources. Knowing you," he tipped his head respectfully, "you're gearing your instruction with this in mind. Shyl, have you likewise been directing the Acquired Technology and Research division toward this end?"

"Yes and no," Shyl said. "I had been following these numbers, but I see now that we must not rely on the CWA as the sole authority on the nature and hunger of the Storm. I, apparently, reached my conclusion much more recently than Jarin."

Ansin tapped the pad. "Protocol must be altered. My area. Maryel, you can intervene on Eraranat's behalf during the Question, and see to shifting of the Field Operations and Review sector."

"No," Jarin said. Ansin looked back at him, surprised. He continued, "Segkel must face a truly intensive Question. His methods must be critically examined. He has done more than field a multi-strike, he has taken risks that may well have compromised the mission, or could have compromised the mission in the hands of someone less talented. Radicalism must be tempered. I have advocated on his behalf here and in the Council precisely because it will take a strong-willed, competent individual to be our standard bearer in this process, but we cannot give him a free pass to do whatever he wants. Please," he looked at Maryel, "by all means, challenge him. He will either prove worthy or not."

"You think he will," Maryel said.

Jarin favored her with a slight smile, "I think he will. He will also rage against all of us."

"The anger of a cub Theorist is something I think I can bear," Maryel answered. "I agree. We seem to have a consensus here."

She looked around the room, each head nodded in turn.

Jarin paused in the darkened hallway of the intrans facility. The setting was ridiculously atmospheric, in his opinion—darkened chambers, stone walls and deep shadows—but such places did make for good covert rendezvous. He leaned against the wall and waited. Shortly thereafter, the feminine figure approached. She held out her hands, and he took them in his.

"Shyl surprised you," Maryel said.

"Yes, somewhat. I thought that I was the only one who had this knowledge and carried it for so long," he admitted. "I did not know which way she would go. She has been advocating on my behalf enough lately that I quite expected another one of her reversals into a new position."

"Nevertheless, we have the consensus you wanted when you formed the group."

"Yes. We've achieved the first stage," he said.

"I have no duties tonight," Maryel said, a blatant and bold change of subject.

"Unfortunately, I have several. I will be reviewing Segkel's data. I was just notified that he has turned in his final assessment. Verification will be laborious, though at least I know he will have demonstrated all his calculations and attached exhaustingly copious notes and condescending asides. Also, there is the matter of his women."

"His *caj*," she teased. "You soft-hearted old fool."

He lifted his chin, "Soft-hearted is not an accusation I get often. Ever, actually."

"Other than from me," Maryel said. "I'll not wait, then."

They squeezed hands once, then went their separate ways.

Seg reviewed the digifilm once more and, with a frustrated growl, threw it across the planning room. The conservatism of the House and their military apparatus galled him. They were going to lose seventeen percent of their potential take with their current structure. He stared at the plan outline and what was left – a wide-range medley of targets, projected takes, force packages. He tapped a button on the table, which brought up the global projection. Glowing amber lights represented targets. Green icons representing various force commitments by type were shown at their projected locations. Special carats indicated his own chosen targets, the ones he had given over to the support of the Kenda uprising. It was merely a quirk of psychological projection, but he felt there was some special question, some insult in that differentiation.

I'm treading more dangerously here than I did there.

It had seemed so right to make the deal with Brin in the heat of the moment but now he considered abandoning the extra strikes altogether. The risk was incredible and if the mission was at all compromised the Question and subsequent punishment would be brutal. They would make an example of him for the next ten generations. Perhaps they would keep him in a cage, hooked to an amp to shock him, and put him out for the students to pelt with rotten food.

I gave Ama my word.

If he backed out now, the Question would come around to his instability and unreliability.

No, he had committed and, long-term, it was a worthy gamble.

His stomach churned as he typed out his final version of the force commitment.

I will be there. I will make this work.

CHAPTER 19

T he members of the bloc studied Seg's assessment in silence, each typing notes here and there next to the text on their digipads. At one point, Ansin emitted a low whistle, which caused everyone to look up.

"The young man is even more ambitious than we thought," he answered, before he scrolled through the pages of the assessment once more.

Shyl was the last to finish; she laid her digipad down but continued to stare at it.

"Well then," Maryel said.

"Yes," Ansin said.

"And this is what is going to become the norm?" Shyl said. "This?"

Maryel looked over at her. "This is what you and Jarin argued will have to become the norm. Now is hardly the time to balk. We're going to have to present this to the Guild Council with a straight face."

"I like it," Ansin said, which caused all heads to turn again. "I wish—" he glanced up at the ceiling. "I wish I'd had the courage to call a raid like this on a few targets that I'd surveyed."

"I believe that before long we will all have that particular regret," Jarin said.

"I hope so," said Shyl, "because that means your pupil will have achieved unprecedented success."

Ansin stood before the twenty-three assembled Guild Council members, his hands folded together. He could be quite the master of oratory, and Jarin waited with a calm demeanor that masked his nerves.

In the assembly room for the Guild Council, the only decoration of any note came in the form of the artifacts that adorned the walls. Jarin's eyes fell on a shield – bronze, an image of two moons stamped into the metal. The piece was not as worthy of notice as many of the others in the room but Jarin knew it intimately, down to the singed hole at the top right. His first extrans. He had been proud the day he surrendered his souvenir to grace the Council walls but now, looking at it, he saw the face of the man who had held it and was swept over with shame. When he was young, it was easy to write off the death and enslavement of so many souls as a necessary sacrifice. The man who had held that shield had died so that the People could prosper and thrive.

His other regrets about that first extrans he forced from his mind.

He moved his eyes from the shield to the grey walls, to the grey tables, to the greying Council members whose faces reminded him of corpses. *We do not prosper, we are not thriving.*

He needed Segkel to succeed, not only for the good of his People, but also to soothe his conscience, to make him believe the man, the 'Outer', with the shield had not fallen for nothing.

His decision to bring Shyl and Ansin into what had previously been his and Maryel's concern had been a gamble. Ansin was crucial to the next phase, because he more than any other could sway the conservative elements of the Guild (the predominate elements, naturally) toward his course.

"Many arguments have been made this night," Ansin began, "and, as always, the Guild moves with many minds, brilliant minds, but one purpose. We unite for the vital purpose of ensuring our continued existence in the most efficient and expeditious way possible."

Amazing. Jarin could speak those same words but, while his fellow Theorists might well agree with him, for Ansin the heads would nod and murmurs of agreement would come to the fore. Even after all these years, he still marveled at his compatriot's ability to sway the crowd.

One would think that those who studied the very essence of hyperbole, myth, and legend would be more inured to such theatrics. By and large they were, but Ansin had a rare and singular gift.

"It will not surprise any here for me to say that I am proud to be a devout defender of orthodoxy. The Guild, and indeed the People, have traditions laid down since the early times of struggle, traditions that have enabled us to survive and even prosper in the face of adversity. Adversity that would have crumbled those whom we rule over. Tradition is our strength."

Setup. Get them moving in the direction they expect to go.

"But tradition emerged from experimentation. The way of now was not the way of yesterday. While we must stand with what has made us successful, we must also make room for growth and development."

Reversal. Take them in an entirely new direction.

"We must study and analyze each new possibility, as we study and analyze each new world. We must test these theories. We must grow." Ansin was not an energetic speaker, but he was one who delivered his words with force, emphasis, and conviction. His voice, not loud but penetrating, carried through the room.

"Theorist Eraranat is young, yes." Now Ansin did pick up the tone, he lifted his volume slightly as he dissected the opposition arguments. "He is known to be brash, yes." Ansin circled between the tables at which sat perhaps the brightest minds in the World. "He could well be leading the way to disaster, yes!"

His eyes focused onto the distance, a trademark for Ansin's best speeches. It was the time when he would see further, normally into the past but today into the future. "But he could also be blazing a new path. Brothers and sisters, let us give this young man his lead. I, personally, will pledge a portion of my own estate to the recovery of this venture should it fail. I have faith! Faith in Theorist Eraranat and faith in one of our own illustrious brothers, his teacher and mentor, Theorist Svestil," he gestured to Jarin. "Faith enough to stake my own fortunes upon this. Tradition, yes, growth, yes! They are not mutually exclusive values."

He slowed his pace, moved back toward his table and brought his gaze back down to focus on his peers. Masterful. He slowly drained the energy he had raised in the room, his words having played the assembled Theorists like an instrument

"Thank you for listening, bothers and sisters," Ansin concluded and settled back in his seat. Jarin glanced around the room. Heads were still nodding, the odd hand raised in affirmation.

Let it be enough.

Seg entered the Raid Planning Chamber of House Haffset and noted that the principals were already assembled, albeit not yet all gathered at the table.

Jarin's appearance at his office, informing him that the raid had passed the Council vote, was the first moment, since he had gone extrans, that he had allowed himself to feel victorious. This was the second moment.

He was surrounded by luminaries, People of status and power, all awaiting his words on the raid to come. His work would enhance the fortunes of many, perhaps create shifts in the balance of power in the World, though that was not his concern. It was the process that enthralled him, and the crucial position he held within it. All the others were accessories to the important work: the location of functional vita sources that could be extracted with minimal cost.

He set his film down on the table, along with a rough huchack fiber notebook of hand-scribbled notes. A silence had descended upon the room as all eyes turned toward him.

Obviously they were waiting for him to commence the process. He nodded, taking in the occupants of the room. The House Master was present, along with the House Marshal. Standing next to them were representatives of a half dozen raiding contractors – the suppliers of men, material, and military expertise. The Guild was represented by two Recorders, recordkeeping attendants, clad in crimson robes.

Finally, his eyes settled on Adirante Fi Costk, the Director of External Affairs for the CWA, flanked by the woman who had come to him with the unexpected proposal, Efectuary of the PIS, Jul Akbas.

She gave him a cold smile, and he felt a flash of foreboding.

"Well then," he began, "the calculations have borne out my field observations thus far. This raid will easily be the most profitable of the century."

Better to start modest. The raid was going to be the most profitable not of the century, but of all time. However, setting the bar lower gave him an easier mark to aim for at the end.

He raised his eyes to the room. Only a few had taken their seats but all were staring at him. Staring and silent, not with admiration or professional vigilance but with perplexed discomfort. Clearing his throat, he looked down to his notes again. "If you will consul—"

"Theorist Eraranat," Efectuary Akbas stepped forward, "your enthusiasm is inspiring. However, you are aware that you are no longer a participant in this process?"

He pivoted to face her directly. "Explain yourself."

"You don't give orders here. Actually, you don't give orders anywhere anymore." She passed him a digifilm. "You've been suspended from this raid and from all professional activity pending investigation into a complaint filed by Lieutenant Kerbin. Please, take a moment to read, you'll find everything is in order."

He snatched the digifilm away from her. "So the personal dispute between two individuals outweighs the process of a record raid. Politics trumping success. Is that your aim, Efectuary Akbas? Petty vengeance?" When she opened her mouth, he continued. "I know you'll protest that you're simply following procedure. My refusal of your offer to breach my contract with the Guild and my low opinion of your character have nothing to do with the matter." He tossed the film at her feet. "This is not finished."

Blood roared in his ears. It was everything he could do not to leap out and attack her physically. She, who had never left the safety of the

World and her own little games, attempting to destroy the work of her betters.

Worst of all, Jarin had been right. He had crossed the CWA and now they were crossing him back. His feet refused to move, though he knew he was no longer welcome and that every set of eyes were focused on him, waiting for his retreat.

"Eraranat!" Akbas snapped, her booming voice incongruous with her slight frame. She pointed to the floor and a caj scurried over to retrieve the digifilm and return it to her hands. She looked Seg up and down, then fixed a sharp smile on him, "We hope you enjoyed that juvenile tantrum. Your mentor understands politics, it's a shame his protégé did not absorb that particular gift. But then, we are amazed that the son of a recycler overseer even made it into the Guild at all."

Seg's mouth twitched, triggering the corners of Akbas's smile to reach higher.

"You are right, this doesn't end here," she continued, loud enough for all present to hear. "You should consider sending your father a comm, to see if he might have a position for you. That may be the best you can hope for soon."

"That will be all, Efectuary Akbas," Director Fi Costk said, from his seat. "Theorist Eraranat, the matter is under consideration. Should the finding against you be shown as lacking merit, you will of course be restored to this deliberation. As such, I would recommend that everyone mind against statements which could later disrupt the function of this tasking."

"Lacking merit?" Seg fired back, with a derisive laugh.

"Theorist Eraranat, I have stated our position, this matter is closed," Fi Costk said, his voice deepening. "You may leave now."

Seg slapped his hand on the table. "I demand an immediate inquiry! Since when have the groundless accusations of a—"

"Security!" Fi Costk called. Two uniformed guards appeared immediately, both armed with huchack rifles. "Escort Theorist Eraranat out of the building and ensure he does not return."

The men reached for Seg's arms but he yanked free of their grasp. "I'll see myself out."

As he turned to leave, he caught his reflection in the gleaming visors of the guards, his humiliation clearly visible. To everyone. He stormed out as fast as his legs could carry him and didn't look back.

Jarin cycled the door open and gestured Seg inside. From his expression, it was clear he had received the news.

"Akbas," Seg said.

"So I understand," Jarin answered, as he guided him to a seat.

Ama hovered on one side of the room but burst forward as soon as she spotted Seg. "What's happened?"

"There has been a setback," Seg said. "Political. The CWA is trying to keep me out of my raid."

"What?" The word shot from Ama's mouth. "They can't do that. We have to get back. I have to get back." She turned to Jarin, "Can they do that?"

"They can." Jarin sat in the chair facing Seg and leaned in, forearms resting on his thighs, "I warned you that you needed to handle the CWA delicately. You have the expertise to scout a raid, you do not know all the permutations of the legal code, Segkel."

"But the Guild does," Seg said, sitting up, "and they have every reason to fight this."

Jarin let out a sharp breath of air through his nose. "Ah, so now you value the assistance of the Guild?"

"They have a role as well," Seg conceded.

Ama paced, stopping between the two men. "Whatever you need to do, do it. Quit sitting here and act!"

"That attitude is precisely what brings us to this juncture," Jarin said. "What we need to do is determine what can be done, if anything."

Seg avoided Ama. Her very presence, her hope, was like the water that had once suffocated him. He spoke instead to Jarin, "Is there a legal avenue?"

"If there is, be assured the CWA has considered it. And blocked it," Jarin answered. "What was the ostensible reason for your dismissal?"

Seg sat forward. "Lieutenant Kerbin brought a complaint against me."

"Is there any merit to the complaint?" Jarin asked, studying Seg's face.

"Depending on the interpretation of the events…"

"That is an affirmative, then," Jarin said, then raised a hand to stop further discussion. "The lieutenant can be dealt with."

Jarin stared through Seg for a moment, the severity of his expression betraying, in a brief flash, the darker side of his nature.

"You must understand," Jarin continued, leaning back in his chair and resuming an air of contemplation, "this is no petty feud, Segkel. this is strategic and deliberate. The CWA is moving to sabotage the raid and undermine House Haffset in order to move on the House when it defaults. So be aware that when you plot your moves, they are plotting to counter you."

Seg rubbed his hand over his face where his beard had been.

Ama stopped mid-pace and faced Jarin. "You're saying it's impossible? Seg can't go back to my world? I can't go back?" Her shoulders drooped, hope drained from her face.

"I wish it was not so," Jarin answered.

Seg was not so easily deterred. "Fi Costk stated in front of witnesses that I could return if Kerbin's complaint is removed. You said Kerbin can be dealt with. I can continue to plan for the raid as though I'm at the meetings and be ready to step in the moment I am reinstated."

"Do you believe Fi Costk would make it that simple for you? You are overlooking something rather important, Segkel," Jarin said. "Specifically, how do you intend to keep abreast of the latest planning developments and data interpretations while the legal obstacles for your return are cleared? That information is critical to the raid's success."

Seg shook his head. "I can model them independently."

Jarin lowered his head and pierced Seg's desperation with his stare.

"I can do it!" Seg argued but the slump of his shoulders spoke otherwise. He stood, wiped a hand across his face, and took Ama's place in the frantic pacing

"And you will fall on your face when that fails," Jarin said, "and destroy all remaining credibility you possess. You will be removed from the raid again, of your own doing. You need the first-hand data."

Seg rapped his knuckles on the back of the chair in which he had sat moments before. "The Guild Recorders. Simply suborn one of the Recorders and have them bring the data out."

Jarin shook his head. "Two complications there. First, the Recorders have to surrender all documentation to the safekeeping of the House Accountancy prior to exiting each day. Secondly, one of them is Fi Costk's man."

"What?" Seg's eyes widened and he leaned toward Jarin, "You know this and you haven't done anything about it? Why is the Recorder still alive?"

"Segkel, if you have an agent identified in your ranks, you can eliminate him and wonder who will take his place, or you can use him to feed false information to your enemy. Which would be preferable?"

Seg frowned, then nodded sharply and resumed pacing. "The CWA are making a move to cut the Guild away from our function. That is the work they were trying to offer me – their own Theorist division."

Jarin coughed. "Yes, Fi Costk has been trying to implement that for some time now. It will fail. Again. But this move does have critical ramifications. As for the Recorders—" he shook his head. "This brings us to another impediment engineered by Director Fi Costk. He knows we need raw data from the inside, which I, as an observer, do not have clearance to obtain and you will not have clearance for until this matter with Lieutenant Kerbin is cleared up. Even if the Lieutenant retracts her complaint today, there are any number of means by which the CWA can sabotage your return in the next five days."

"Let them, the raid won't launch for two weeks, I can be ready," Seg said, his hands clenching and unclenching.

"No," Jarin said, the word thudding from his mouth. "Director Fi Costk has pushed the timetable. The raid will launch in seven days. As I explained, he has foreseen your moves. And mine."

Seg opened his mouth and closed it, several times in succession, then sat again, sinking into the chair as if willing himself to disappear in it.

"I don't understand," Ama said, stepping forward after watching the discussion from the far side of the room. "I don't understand what any of this means."

Jarin waited for Seg to speak, when he didn't, he stood, spread his hands, and slipped naturally into the role of teacher he was so accustomed to.

"In the typical process, a House, which is a familial entity, much like your Damiar Lines, wins the bidding to sponsor a raid. They employ a recon unit and a Theorist to examine the world and determine the best vita sources for the raid," he said, "then the Theorist returns. After submitting his raid proposal, the Theorist turns over the data for processing—as it is not his property but that of the sponsor House—and sits in to help determine the single best vita source, based on risk and reward. A rich, but highly defended source may be passed up in lieu of more easily accessible sources, for example. This is a collaborative process, and it is refined as the Theorist works his information until very specific trade-offs can be made – 'If we select this target, we will use a hundred troops and expect to lose ten...'" he used his hand, as he talked, to aid her visualization of the process. "Even in a normal raid, this can be a very painstaking process. Every trooper moved back and forth, every ounce of material sent, every caj or piece of technology or raw vita source, they all have a cost. Everything must be accounted for as closely as possible and with a minimum of force used to achieve a maximum gain."

Jarin turned, resting his hand on his chair. "Then you take a supremely complex raid such as Segkel has proposed, as has been accepted by House Haffset. There will be no fine balance on this mission, at all. Even if given the full span of time, it would be a far more convoluted process than before. And because Segkel is not sitting present as they weigh and evaluate the prospective targets, he would have to guess at the allotments. He is somewhat above-average in this regard, but there are limits. In short, he has been shut out by the CWA, with the knowledge that without the raw data to help him prepare, and with the reduced time frame before launch, there is no way he can lead this raid."

"And this…raw data, there's no way to get it?" Ama asked, desperation coloring her question. "You couldn't steal it somehow?"

"No," Jarin said, allowing a faint smile at her brash suggestion. "Segkel is banned from entering the building, and interactions with the Recorders are closely monitored, mine particularly, I can assure you of that."

"So, it's over. It's hopeless."

The room was thick with silence. Ama backed away from Jarin, lost in thought, then stared at a wall as if she were staring through it. Jarin sat once more and rested his chin on his hand, absorbed in thoughts of his own.

"I can't fail" Seg said, eyes on the floor, voice hollow

"The failure is not yours," Jarin answered, his tone echoing Seg's. "You planned a brilliant raid."

"Plans are irrelevant if they are not executed."

"So are promises," Ama murmured, then drifted away from the wall and out of the room. Seg rose as if to follow but Jarin shook his head and gestured for him to sit.

"Do not make it worse."

"It can't get worse," Seg grumbled, sinking back in the seat.

Jarin's mouth twitched briefly into a smile, "The naivety of youth." He pushed himself up with a grunt, "Let me make some enquiries. We will at least clear your name as regards the good Lieutenant." He called Lissil into the room. "Please prepare a cup of greshk for Segkel," he said, "and also for Amadahy."

"Yes, Theorist Svestil," Lissil lowered her eyes and bowed before gliding out of the room.

Jarin looked down at Seg. "We will do our best to salvage your career. As for the rest…" he sighed and his eyes shifted to where Ama had stood, "some lessons cannot be learned in a classroom."

"It's true then, she told you everything?" Seg's face became even dourer. "Not that it's of any consequence now, I suppose."

Jarin placed his hands on the back of the chair. "No. Aside from one emotional and vague outburst of concern for her father's safety, and despite my repeated solicitation, she refused to tell me anything about your time together. Amadahy is unschooled and out of her element but she is, for whatever reason, loyal to you."

Even as Jarin spoke the words, Seg knew they were true. The knowledge didn't make the situation any better. It made it worse.

"The old man wants you to drink this," Lissil announced as she entered their small room, where Ama sat, arms wrapped tightly around her legs, face buried in her knees.

"Leave it," Ama said, without raising her head.

"Oh, by the Sky Fathers! Now she pouts and cries like a child. Stupid and petulant…he really is better off without you." Lissil took a sip of the drink and leaned against the doorframe. "Glare all you want, it won't change anything. Besides, fathers die all the time, you'll survive. Me, I would have paid someone to kill mine, though the bottle-loving bastard did me a favor the day he sold me off."

"Eavesdropping again?" Ama leaned back against the bare wall, clutching her knees.

"Collecting information. A trick you'd be wise to learn now that the mighty Lord Eraranat has been shoved off into the scrapheap. That is, if you hope to get anywhere in this life beyond fixing meals and scrubbing floors." Lissil examined the nails of her free hand and made a face.

Ama shook her head, remembering Judicia Corrus's offer. "I don't spy on people I care about."

Lissil laughed and stepped further into the room. "Care about your overlords all you want, you'll always be beneath them; they'll never care about you. You're in the mud with me now, sister. All we have are our eyes, our ears, our brains and the guts to use all three when it counts. I've collected a nice stack of secrets since the old man took me in; if I need to use them, they're there. See, one of the benefits of being in the mud is that you're invisible. You're beneath notice. These people are no different from the Shasir or the Damiar, too busy with their heads in the clouds to care about some caj milling around their feet like a field animal."

Pulling her hair back into a stiff knot, Ama frowned. "Maybe that's how your world works. I'm not an animal. I'm not invisible and…" her hands dropped and her hair tumbled from the knot she had been about to cinch. "That's it," she said, and rushed past Lissil, out of the room.

Seg was staring into his cup of greshk when Ama burst into the living area once more. He braced himself for her tirade; his forbearance of her emotional sputtering was at least some minor penance he could pay, though hardly compensation.

"The place, where the raid is planned, where the information you need is kept, can Jarin go in there?" she asked in a rapid staccato.

"Yes," he began, as Jarin appeared once more.

"Certainly I can," Jarin answered. "I can attend raid-planning meetings at will. However, as mentioned, I have no access to the data and I also cannot keep my own notes on the matter, as I would merely be an observer. Adi," he shook his head "has maneuvered this one quite nicely."

"Adi?" Seg asked.

"Adirante Fi Costk. We knew each other in another life. You should know, I have sent a comm to—"

"Can you take caj into the meetings with you?" Ama interrupted Jarin, her voice loud and insistent.

Jarin opened his mouth to reply, then shut it. Both men turned to look at her, then each other. "That could work," Jarin said after a moment.

Seg nodded. "Inobtrusive and overlooked, the key elements of infiltration. Invisible in plain sight."

Ama sat down next to Seg, her knee touching his. "You'll have to teach me what to do."

"No, there is a better teacher here," Jarin looked back and nodded to Lissil, who had just reentered the room.

Ama frowned but assented, "Of course."

"The House will be screening for leeching devices or any other means of stealing data," Seg said to Jarin, who nodded but was clearly already contemplating a solution.

"There is one leech that contains only a single component that could be read by the scanners…"

"Yes, but everyone gets scanned, even caj," Seg countered.

"I think I have a man who could get it through," Jarin said. "All that will be required is to maneuver Amadahy close enough to the Recorder to leech the data from his digipad, which I believe can be done. And, of course, she will need a chatterer installed, which will require some favors to be called in, given that she is unregistered. However, there is also the matter of your return. No one can know of it or suspect it or Adi will simply engineer another obstacle, but there is no possible way security will let you pass through into the Chamber without prior, CWA authorized clearance."

Seg's mouth slid into a smile, "I think I have someone who can get me through."

"Indeed?" Jarin's eyebrow rose.

"Yes, though I believe my mentor would caution me against divulging the name of an asset."

"Quite correct," Jarin said, with a slight nod to indicate approval. "Very well, but you should stay here until that moment, as your quarters are no doubt under surveillance. I will make room for you in my private chambers. You can play the part of the wounded young champion, mourning his failure under the care of his older…and much wiser mentor."

"*Much* older," Seg added. "The other portion is debatable."

"This can work?" Ama piped up, the drained hope returning.

"Possibly," Jarin said. "Very possibly."

Ama turned to Seg, "I almost don't want to ask this but—if I get caught?"

"They will hold me for what crimes you commit, and I will be penalized up to and including execution. You will be executed," Seg said, "so don't get caught."

"I'll do my best," Ama said, swallowing. "How long until we can get in there?" she asked Jarin.

"Today you train, tomorrow we begin attendance," Jarin said. "There is one other matter, though—" He reached up and tapped the back of his neck.

Seg rubbed his chin. "Can we rig some sort of prosthesis?"

Jarin nodded. "I believe that can be arranged."

"What are you talking about?" Ama craned around to try and see the back of Jarin's neck.

"Caj wear grafts," Seg said. "Usually. They're mechanical implants that serve as control devices."

Jarin frowned. "They are designed with a variety of functions, including pain, sedation, nerve immobilization—they can paralyze, that is—and also a destruct feature that kills the caj. They are used to prevent escapes and rebellions."

"You're not going to put one of them in me, are you?" she asked Seg, hand unconsciously gripping the sleeve of his coat.

"Never," Seg said, his voice emphatic. "We'll get you something that looks just like it, but doesn't actually go into your skin. A fake."

Ama let out a breath. "Good. I would wear it, if I had to. I'll do whatever it takes to get home. But I'm glad I won't have to. It sounds barbaric."

"Some feel that way," Jarin said, letting his words hang before Seg.

Seg turned to Lissil. "You have your duties. Ama needs to know the basic caj protocols by morning and I'm sure Jarin will provide clothing for a suitable disguise."

Lissil bowed. "Yes my Lord," she said, eyes artfully averted. She held out her hand to Ama, "Come, sister, I'll show you how you should behave."

Ama stood, though she refused the extended hand, and moved to follow Lissil out of the room. She paused at the threshold and looked back at Seg, her throat tight. "We'll make it work."

"Of course we will," he assured her. He looked back at Jarin. "This isn't over, this incident with the CWA. It won't be over."

"Segkel," Jarin said, with an enigmatic expression, "it never ends."

CHAPTER 20

Her idea had seemed brilliant, until this moment. Ama's palms were cold and slick with sweat, as she followed behind Jarin and his assistant, Gelad, to a large arch that marked the entrance to House Haffset's Central Raid Planning Chamber.

Eyes downcast, she waited for her turn to walk through the machine that Jarin explained could see through people, through their clothes and even their skin. On her neck, the high, thick collar Jarin had given her to wear, bejeweled and studded with ornaments, grew suddenly heavier and more obvious. Despite Jarin's assurance, she wondered if the machine would show the tiny device hidden inside, the means by which she would steal the raid data for Seg.

This is no worse than running and hiding from the authorities, she reminded herself, *you got through that, you'll get through this.*

On the run, however, the goal had been to remain inconspicuous. The disguise she wore now was as far from inconspicuous as she could imagine. Rich, red fabric wrapped her in crisscrossing patterns that she would never have managed without Lissil's help. Any visible skin was painted with intricate black swirls; even her face was covered with the designs. Her hair was coiled in black and red ribbons and her wrists and ankles sported thick bands, identical to the collar she wore. And although she had argued that the disguise would only draw attention to her, since she had stepped out of the cartul Seg's people called a 'trans', no one had paid her even a passing glance.

Gelad went ahead of her. The machine screeched and hissed, Ama's heart lurched. The man was pulled to one side where uniformed guards ran their hands over his body. Gelad was an old soldier, whose injuries were beyond counting, Jarin had explained. As impossible as it sounded, many of his body parts had been replaced or enhanced with metal; he would always set off the machines.

Gelad was waved through and Ama stepped up next. She stood statue-like, as the machine hummed, and waited for the dreaded noise.

"Clear," she heard one of the uniformed men say, realizing only then that she had shut her eyes.

The first obstacle passed, she allowed herself a relieved breath as she hurried to Gelad's side—her 'owner' for this undertaking—in front of a set of large, grey doors. Neither Jarin nor his man looked at her, something else she had been warned to expect. Caj are beneath the notice of People.

But the caj standing at the door was not invisible to Ama, even with the round, metal graft on the back of his neck that marked him as property. He wasn't much taller than her and he was lean, all sinew and muscle, where his skin showed. But what caught Ama's eye was his head. At first, she had thought the man wore a hat but a closer inspection revealed that the 'hat' was some kind of shell, which the man's skull had grown around. As much a part of his body as his fingernails or teeth.

His job, that she could see, was to open and close the large doors for those entering the room and he did so with haste. But, when no one was looking, he darted frequent glances to the tall, wide window inside the room, on the other side of the door.

He's too confined. Ama could feel his discomfort, the walls pressing in around him. Wherever he had come from, she imagined he must have roamed freely, in open spaces.

Jarin stepped to the door, and the man pushed it open. Ama's dread returned in a flood as she cast her eyes on the room. The only thing that kept her from turning to run was the thought of her father.

With a steadying breath, she followed Gelad inside.

There were two tables that comprised most of the sprawling space – a solid round, inner table, and another table that encircled the first on two sides. It was at the outer ring that Jarin took his seat. This was the consulting table; he could follow the proceedings but was not allowed to participate or interject unless directly questioned by a member at the inner table. Even so, Ama noticed that several of those seated at the center table greeted the elder Theorist with nods and gestures. Except for one man, who fastened a stoney and unmoving stare on Jarin from the moment he entered.

This man, Ama guessed, must be the Fi Costk Seg had spoken of.

Ama waited for Gelad to sit, then knelt down beside him as she had been instructed. When her position was first explained to her, she had reacted with disbelief. Surely people would not allow themselves to be treated like furniture but now she saw, with no small measure of disgust, that it was true. There were at least thirty men and women in the room and, with the exception of Jarin, each had a personal caj attending them. Some caj, as she did, sat obediently at their owner's knee; others tended to physical needs – massaging necks, hands, even feet: some seemed there only as an outlet for nervous energy, their owners absently running hands over their body or through their hair in the same way Ama used to fidget with her nove – which she did now with the heavy collar, though this time her movements were deliberate.

Another group of caj belonged solely to the House responsible for the raid; their primary function was to serve food and beverages or act as decoration. The caj from the front door was one of these and he was inside the room now, scurrying back and forth, tending to the needs of the various House members. Inside the room, with the door closed, the helmeted caj's claustrophobia was even more pronounced. Ama wondered how anyone could fail to see it, or fail to care about his distress.

At one point, the caj froze, his face turned to the large window, an obvious attempt to calm himself. A moment later, however, he was on his knees, back arched, mouth open as if he were screaming, but no sound emerged. Ama started to rise, her every instinct was to rush to the man's aid, but Gelad had surreptitiously hooked a finger into one of the rings on her collar and held her in place.

Eventually, the caj collapsed, panting for air as a woman stood over him, berating him. He recovered slowly, and rose to his feet. Ama's stomach twisted, as she watched him return to his chores.

She forced her eyes away from the scene, to the world beneath the level of the table and the other kneeling caj. Some were looking at the spot where the helmeted caj had dropped yet none regarded the scene with any particular degree of shock or dismay. They didn't speak aloud but Ama noticed these caj communicated between each other all the same, through looks, subtle gestures, finger taps. To her, they paid little attention, but there was a whole culture that lived below the table, below the eyes of the Lords and Ladies of Seg's world.

Lost in this discovery, Ama nearly jumped when Gelad nudged her with his boot.

On her knees, she turned her body and began to knead and massage Gelad's calves. This was part of her cover but that didn't make the act any less distasteful.

Above her, the proceedings were not going well. The raider leaders were bickering over the target assignments and priortization. The House accountants were contesting the projected vita yields from targets. Jul Akbas, the woman Seg had spoken of, was offending everyone she spoke to. The proceedings were in a fine state of roil, when the House Master called out to Jarin. "Theorist Svestil," he said "perhaps you could join us at the central table. We need Theorist representation at this venture."

"It would bring me nothing but pleasure to do so, House Master," Jarin answered. "But unfortunately I am bound by the rules of the Guild Charter, which states that a Theorist cannot be replaced upon his mission other than by reason of physical or mental incapacity, except by full deliberation of the Guild Council. The Council has called inquiry into this matter, but a proper inquiry will take in excess of the timeframe of this raid, what with the unfortunate compression of the timetable."

There was a pause after Jarin's words before the bickering resumed once more. As the voices above rose in pitch and strength, the world under the table grew more agitated. Caj traded fearful glances, some cowered, one petite young woman clutched her stomach as if she might be ill.

While Ama did not have to worry that her owner would take his frustrations out on her, she had more than enough concerns of her own. She left off massaging Gelad's legs and moved up to his forearm, moving her hands in quick strokes, probing with her fingers until she found the patch of false skin. With a darting glance to make sure she was unobserved, she scraped away the rubbery material, while shielding the motions with her other hand.

Her wet palms did little to speed the process and each tiny shift of Gelad's body sent paralyzing waves of fear down her spine. After an eternity, she had the small piece of metal palmed. Now the tricky part.

With a grunt from Gelad, she returned to her 'relaxed' position and fidgeted with the collar again. She had practiced the movement at least a hundred times, with the goal of making her fidgeting seem natural. But now, as she guided the small bit of metal into its holder—hidden within the collar—it seemed that every move was fake, an announcement of her disguise.

The metal slipped from her fingers, to the floor, with an audible *click*; Ama gasped.

I'm dead. I'm caught.

Just then, a woman launched into a loud, blustering diatribe and all heads below and above the table turned their attention to her. Ama scooped up the dropped bit as quickly and deftly as possible, then just as quickly, fastened it into place.

She closed her eyes and let her heartbeat settle. Too close. She placed her hand on Gelad's left knee and squeezed twice.

"Redress!" a man above shouted, and rose to his feet.

"I'll see you in the courtyard," the cold, female voice replied.

"Stop this!" the House Master shouted over them both. "We will take recess of this meeting for a time. Take refreshment, make talk and we will settle this discord without violence. Are we barbarians? Are we Outers? The Seventeenth Virtue is Unity of Purpose and Action, and I will see it practiced in my home! Is that clear?"

There were muttered apologies, then, here and there, People rose to their feet, stretched their legs, tried to make conversation and defuse the tension that had gripped the room.

Gelad was one of those who stood. "Gonna go talk to my old bud," he said, studying his fingernails. Then he rubbed his thigh and nodded to Jarin. "Works great. Good idea to get a tender for my battle aches, Theorist." He rapped the back of his hand against Ama's temple, the knuckles jarring her slightly as he jerked his head toward the center table, before he stepped through a gap and made his way toward the middle.

Once again, as she had been taught, Ama stood and followed just a step behind Gelad, hands clasped in front of her, eyes lowered. Around her, the other caj did the same. Their training demanded that they move as one with their owners, as if they were an extension of their body, but equally important was that they must never touch a Person unless ordered or invited. This made for an absurd and chaotic dance, as the owners moved freely and erratically, forcing their caj to be hyper-vigilant, even with their gazes toward the floor. There was more than one near collision, and the tension between the People was now transferring into their caj.

Ama stuck close to Gelad, thankful that his path was away from the main crush of bodies. He approached a silver-haired man whose skin was ashen and whose flesh hung from his face in loose folds. This was one of the Recorders; Jarin had showed her a likeness of the man. Gelad raised his palm in greeting. As soon as he stopped, Ama dropped to her knees at his side. Her hands once again rising to her collar, pulling and twisting at the baubles and rings protruding from its surface. With her thumb she pressed on a stud to start the device hidden within. As long as she stayed within five feet of the Recorder, all the information collected in his digipad, would transfer to the device she carried.

This part, however, was up to Gelad; she couldn't move without him. He had to keep the Recorder close.

"Voz," Gelad said, giving the Recorder a craggy smile, "been some time."

The other man squinted, then grunted. "Hunh. Sergeant Gelad. Heard you'd come over to work for Svestil. *Theorist* Svestil," he corrected himself. "Were the Orchara as bad as they said?" He nodded toward a pair of dusky-skinned caj garmented in gleaming, shiny-threaded clothing following one of the officers.

Gelad shrugged and held his hand out to accept a drink from a passing caj. "Had moments. Made a good deal off of that, sweetened the Service Termination Payment good."

The other man nodded as he rose to his feet, lifted the digipad off the table and then slid it into his robe. "If you'll excuse me, I've got urgent business here."

As he passed by, stepping toward the space Ama occupied, Gelad grasped his shoulder. "Listen, some of the old hands have a fourth-day game in the RQ, get together, have some drinks, tell some lies. You be interested in that still?"

The man went stiff at Gelad's grip. "No, I don't think so." With that, he stepped on, forcing Ama to scuttle awkwardly to the side as the Recorder made his way toward the cleanser. Gelad glanced down to confirm that she had acquired the data, then tensed at the sound of approaching footsteps and half pivoted as a stout woman called his name.

"Sergeant Gelad! You old rock!" Ama recognized the voice as one of the two whose arguments had brought the meeting to a pause.

The data successfully loaded into the device on her collar, thanks to the miracle of Seg's science, Ama wanted nothing more than to return to the table or, better yet, to leave. But the drawback of being invisible was that she was...invisible. And she had to stay that way. A feat made difficult by this newcomer who moved with exaggerated steps around Gelad. Ama was forced to shuffle in all directions to avoid both the loud woman and her nervous caj.

"Charter Commander Myrd. So, were you really going to clear holster on Mixis?" Gelad asked, leaning close to the woman.

"That old bastard? By the Storm I would," she said, then dropped her voice slightly. "Political officer. Can't plan an operation to save his life. I tell you, I hope we end up on different ends of a House war someday. That'd be some easy pay."

The woman turned to circulate with the rest of the crowd, boldly striding forward. Her own caj cleared the path, rising smoothly to follow, but Ama was a half second too slow and the large woman's foot clipped her calf. Charter Commander Myrd lurched forward, arms flailing as she tried to regain her balance. Gelad lunged after her, in vain, as the big woman tumbled to the floor, her head grazing a chair as she went down with a solid *thud*. The room went silent as Myrd groaned and pulled herself to her knees. A few titters spread through the crowd. Gelad helped her up. The woman's caj, kneeling at her side, shot a venomous glare at Ama. As Myrd rose up, she turned her own wrathful gaze to Ama, as well.

"You!" she howled, hand sliding toward a fortuitously empty holster. Finding no weapon at easy grasp, she advanced forward, her face darkened with rage, her hands clenching into beefy fists as she prepared to pummel the impudent caj.

Gelad stepped into her path, his face cold and blank. "My caj, Charter Commander," he said calmly, "my responsibility."

He whirled on Ama. "You clumsy, worthless piece of shit!" He grabbed one of the rings on her collar and jerked her head forward. "What's the matter with you, huh?" He dipped his hand into his pocket, then brandished a small square device before her. "This is what you get for your laziness."

Ama recognized concern in Gelad's eyes as he made an exaggerated motion, pressing his thumb on device. What was it? What did he want? Then she remembered the helmeted caj.

She dropped forward onto her hands, back arching painfully, mouth wide open to mimic a scream, though only a hiss of air escaped.

She shuddered and convulsed, and out of her very real fear, managed to shed a few tears.

Gelad stepped forward and stood with his legs splayed over her, looking down with the perfect mask of merciless anger. He pressed the button again and Ama took that as her cue to stop. "Don't do it again," he warned her. "I didn't pay for you anyway, wouldn't be nothin' to ship you to the huchack ponds." He stepped back and folded his arms, his expression expectant.

Ama's relief was genuine. Though not for the reasons others in the room would suppose. Her efforts, however, had momentarily driven all the lessons from her mind. She panted and feigned lingering pain to cover her pause as she scrambled to remember what to do in this situation, what Lissil had taught her. Lissil. Yes, the first meeting with Seg.

Without fuss, she lowered herself until her forehead touched the floor, her hands clenched in fists, next to her ears. The retyel. Basic pose of caj to owner.

Gelad stood over her for a long time and dragged the moment out. At length, he lifted his foot and placed his boot against the back of Ama's head, pressing it hard enough against the floor to make an audible *thonk*. "Your obedience is accepted. Rise caj."

"My apologies again, Charter Commander," Gelad said to the woman. "If this matter is not resolved to your satisfaction, I will take further measures to damage the caj."

Myrd brushed away her own attendant, pushing the caj back on his heels as she shook her head. "No, no. But she's got no art to her. Good thing you didn't pay for her."

"Art's all in the hands, Charter Commander," Gelad said, then added, "and other places." He gave her a small smile, to which Myrd responded with a guffaw and a backhanded slap to the chest that sent him back a step and forced Ama to dodge out of the way again.

"You old rigla," the woman said with a little snort. "Don't you change, even if you're only driving trans and shepherding one of the digis these days," she jerked her head in Jarin's direction.

With that she departed. Gelad fired a glance back at Ama, then made his way to his seat at Jarin's table.

Ama followed him, aware of the eyes on her, shocked to find that looks of disapproval came not only from People, but from other caj as well.

They sat for a span of time long enough to avoid suspicion but short enough to get Ama out of the room before she could make any more mistakes. Seg would be waiting anxiously for the data. For her part, she wanted to be done with this hall of horrors.

The helmeted caj opened the door for their exit. There would be no machine to pass through on the way out. Thankfully. Ama was busting out of her skin. *Why do Gelad and Jarin move so slowly?*

They passed out of the raid planning area and down the sprawling stairs toward the main exit. Free. Finally.

At the bottom of the stairs, a tall, thin woman fixed Jarin and Gelad with a smile that reminded Ama of icicles.

"Theorist Svestil, Sergeant Gelad, we're so pleased you've decided to grace these meetings with your presence. It is a shame young Eraranat cannot be here."

"Efectuary Akbas," Jarin said. "Segkel is similar to most of his age and ambition; he has much to learn. A pleasure to meet you." He raised his hand, palm facing inward, only inches from his chest, his eyes twinkling as he waited for her to respond.

Akbas raised a sculpted eyebrow a fraction, then slipped her palm against Jarin's. "We rarely see the traditional method of greeting anymore," she said, then pulled her hand away as if she had touched something scalding hot. "How...quaint. And Sergeant Gelad, we see you've acquired a pet. We were beginning to worry that some of Theorist Svestil's philosophy was wearing off on you."

"Didn't figure anybody'd be interested in my luggage," Gelad said with a shrug, holding his palm up for her to meet, though neither made contact.

"We are interested in *everything* that comes in and out of the raid planning room," Akbas said, raising a finger to her lips. Her heels clicked as she pounced, snagged Ama by one of the rings on her collar, and examined her closely. "This one seems fresh. Where did you get it?"

Ama's mouth went dry and she froze in the woman's grasp. Akbas's hand held her collar right at the spot where the leech was hidden.

Gelad's hand shot out, grasped Akbas's wrist then lifted her hand away and stepped between the two women. "Don't know how things go in Orhalze, but here we don't handle other people's property without asking nice first," he paused before concluding with, "Efectuary."

He released her wrist but stayed close.

Akbas smoothed a hand over her hair, though not a strand had moved out of place. "Yes, we always forget how touchy you in Cathind are about your property. We have such an abundance in Orhalze that there is no need for such petty protocol." She cast her eyes over Ama, then offered another cold smile, "Obviously not a pleasure-caj, but then you were never the type for decoration, were you Gelad?"

She didn't wait for an answer as she turned toward the stairs.

Gelad leaned over to Jarin. "Guess she knows more 'bout me than I do, eh?"

Aside from his eyes following Efectuary Akbas's departure, Jarin was the picture of perfect calm. "I've had enough of this for the day. Let's return to the compound, Gelad."

The second the door to Jarin's residence cycled closed behind her, Ama's hands darted to the back of the collar. "Stupid…thing," she grunted, as her trembling fingers fumbled with the intricate clasp.

"Here," Seg, who was waiting in the entranceway, extended his hands. He moved behind her and pushed her hands out of the way. "Hold still!"

Ama took a deep breath and rooted herself in place while Seg removed the collar.

"How did it go?" Seg asked, his voice tight.

"Well," was Jarin's reply.

"Didn't tell her about the amp," Gelad said to Jarin.

"Amp?" Seg asked, pausing as he released the collar from Ama's neck.

"Amadahy handled herself very well, despite our minor oversight," Jarin said.

Gelad pulled the graft control unit from his pocket and flashed it to Seg. "We had an incident. Forgot to tell her how to act if she got amp'd; we improvised." He pointed the unit at Ama, "You did good. You'd make a good agent...except for being an Outer and all." He turned to Jarin, "Boss, if it ever comes up to de-pop that Akbas, I want the job."

Ama smiled as she placed her hands over her dathe to soothe the skin, which was chafed and raw from the rub of the thick collar. Seg removed the disc from its hidden pocket and passed the collar back to her, their fingers brushing as he did.

"Thank you. This is what I needed. I will do what has to be done." He raised a hand to her dathe, "We should get an auto-med for that."

Jarin cleared his throat. "Yes, I'll have Lissil fetch it. Amadahy, you need your rest. Go on." He ushered her out of the room, and sent Gelad off to the dining area, then turned to Seg, "And you need to get to work." He let out a long, thin breath and headed to the main living area.

"Mentor..." Both Seg's hands were curled into tight balls, his mouth moved undecidedly.

"Segkel?" Jarin looked back over his shoulder, then turned at the sight of his student's agitation. "What has occurred?"

"Things got worse," Seg answered with a wry grin that immediately changed to an angry glare. "The CWA sent two collectors here today... for my caj."

Jarin nodded, "Trans costs unpaid for and, in Amadahy's case, unregistered. A bold move that assumes you will lose your portion of the raid profit. Or, at the very least, that the two will be grafted and processed by the time the payout is made and you reclaim ownership. We should have anticipated this."

"I sent them off. But if this doesn't work," Seg whispered, holding up the leech disc, "they'll be taken and auctioned. I have to get her away. I have to…" He dragged a hand through his hair and looked up at the ceiling.

"Amadahy is registered with the Guild. Not the required, formal registration, no, but as long as she remains within the Guild compound, I can stall any action to remove her for as long as possible. Lissil, as well." He placed his hand on Seg's forearm and nodded to the disc, "We have five days, let us not waste them."

Kerbin had prowled the Raider's Quarter with restless energy for the past day and a half. The deliberations attached to the raid had carried on, she had been told, but without Storm-cursed Eraranat. The cub had overreached, pushed too many unortho behaviors for the House and other parties to tolerate. At the very least, the legal proceedings would tie him up well beyond the actual conduct of the raid, which satisfied her to no end. Better yet, the CWA representative she had dealt with had said he could well lose his share of raid tithe.

Which meant that both of those worthless Outers he had gathered would go up for auction. Kerbin had already half-decided to put in a bid. Wouldn't it be too precious to parade his little toys in front of him, properly grafted and broken?

Then she would sell them off to the worst and most wretched recycler or huchack pond she could find, to rot away and die. Just for the spite of it.

She took another drink and assured herself that this was the best plan.

An old man slid up to the bar, next to her. Even in her semi-impaired state, she noticed he didn't fit in the place, even as a retiree. Old Raiders had a rough edge to them—the harshness of contained violence—that this man did not possess.

No, this man smelled altogether different. But he was inobtrusive enough to have some sort of experience. Which screamed Theorist.

"A moment of your time, lieutenant?" he asked, confirming her impression.

"Eraranat send you?" she asked, with no effort to disguise her bitterness. "Because I'm not letting him loose on that."

The old man laughed lightly. "No, he did not send me. My name is Jarin Svestil and, after a fashion, you could say that it was I who sent him."

"What's that mean to me?" she asked.

"Potentially a great deal, lieutenant," he said, then studied her for a moment the way the digis always did. The way she always hated.

"Stop dissecting me, Theorist," she said, then raised her fist to warn off the serving caj, who had come around selling amba sticks and other off-World hallucinogens.

"I was merely considering the similarities between yourself and Theorist Eraranat," Jarin said, and moved the caj along with a less hostile wave.

"Ha!" Kerbin barked out a laugh. "Me and him? That a joke?"

"You came from an unprivileged background, and entered military service at sixteen. At the bottom of a long chain, true, but an ambitious move for one so young. Three years of drudgery on-World, guarding ammunition stores or other equally mundane duties. At the—"

"Know my own history, thanks."

"At the age of nineteen," Jarin continued, unperturbed, "your persistent applications for a raider position paid off – a last minute opening on a mission, which you jumped at. That is where everything changed. You excelled and your superiors, recognizing your potential, moved you upchain with startling speed. You were a prodigy in your own right. First recon mission at the age of twenty-four. Impressive. Though, as I recall, that mission had some…challenges."

"Kargin' shit mess," Kerbin said, her eyes assenting as she dipped into memory.

"But you came through the experience. Wiser, I should think. As Theorist Eraranat will come through this mission."

"Cubs like Eraranat think extrans is some kind of vacation. Start letting Theorists run over recon squads the way he did over there and you're gonna have stacks of bodies piling up at the warp gate. There's a reason we run things tight. Like I said," she leaned back and crossed her arms, mug still clasped in one hand, "I'm not letting him off on this. So if there's any thing else you'd li—"

"I'd like to talk about your father," Jarin said, cutting her off.

Kerbin slammed her mug down on the bar with a warning growl, the liquor sloshing over the sides. "How do you want to die, old man?" she asked, voice low and barely restrained.

"I'd rather not see it coming," he said, as he pivoted to face her fully, "but it won't happen here. And now that I have your undivided attention," Jarin pulled a digifilm from his pocket, "let us discuss business."

CHAPTER 21

Seg leaned forward and rubbed his face in his hands. The patterns on the digipad blurred before his eyes. He had done the essential work, crafted the target priorities and made rough measurements as to the suggested manpower diversions based on the available troops. If need be he could go in and deliver his plan immediately.

But his planned raid wasn't perfect. It wasn't to the level of craft he would have turned in for an assignment. The lack of assistants didn't bother him, he preferred to trust his own calculations and only use others to check for errors. It was the insanely compressed timeframe that had made the journey so wearying. He took a deep breath, closed his eyes, and went through a simple mind-clearing mnemonic, as he prepared to wade back into the work.

"So I'm not the only one who talks to themselves," he heard Ama say. When he opened his eyes, he saw her looking down at him in the dim light.

"What?" he asked, then remembered that he had been repeating the mnemonic aloud. "Oh. At times, talking to one's self is the only way to ensure an intelligent conversation. Shouldn't you be resting?"

"Could you sleep right now?" she asked, but his hollowed eyes and dishevelled hair answered the question for him. "Tell me this is going to work."

Seg felt the urge to reach out to her, stopped himself momentarily, then lifted his hand. After everything, now was hardly the time to be timid. Still, he felt a measure of relief as she squeezed his hand and let him draw her next to him on the chair.

"I don't fail. I've never failed." He closed his eyes, taking in her scent and warmth. "I don't make many promises, Ama. But I keep those I do. One way or another."

Somewhere in the excitement, fear and work of the past five days, the anger between them had steadily burned itself out. She smoothed his hair from his face, letting her fingers linger on his skin.

"I want to show you something," he said, leaned forward and plucked the digipad off the center table. He tapped the screen in one corner then pushed a button, scrolled through a set of images, stopping at a photo of a gunship, bristling with arms. "There," he passed the digipad to Ama.

"What is it?"

"A skyship. In fact, it is a 739 M Tactical Raider Transport," he said. The 739 was an older model, lesser-equipped, but he was a man working with a budget. He recited the specifications the rental agent had told him from memory. "It has independently tracking twin solid-projectile multicannons, four mount-points for mission-specific weapon loadouts, rocket pods in this case, also side and rear-bay heavy needlers for fire suppression."

There were other features, but they involved technical minutiae such as countermeasures and other electronic arcana that didn't concern them and weren't necessary against opponents whose idea of high tech weaponry was burning powder.

"The raiders that will ride in it will be equipped as Kerbin's squad was," he said, digging again into his memory for the sales pitch. "A proper mix of antipersonnel weaponry ideal for deployment in a close combat environment against urban primitives." He turned his head to face Ama, who was entranced by the image on the screen, "And it's yours."

"Mine?" Ama's mouth opened as she pried her eyes away from the digipad.

"That's the gunship that's going to carry you, and me, and twenty-eight heavily armed raiders into the Secat in two days time. Dagga could have a hundred men guarding your father, it won't matter. With my troops and this rider, we'll have him free in less time than it takes to drink a mug of grint, with an onboard med-station ready to tend to any injuries he might have sustained."

Ama reached a hand out to the image of the gunship, trailing her fingers over the screen. "I don't know what to say. You make it sound so easy. Your people must win every battle."

"Not all but, yes, a great many. Our combat methods have been honed over centuries. There are two philosophies central to our success, even against opponents of equal or greater technology. One, we know exactly what we want before we go in, and we do not deviate from the objective – with the full knowledge that some sacrifice will be required. Two—and this is established as our most effective weapon—surprise. Catch your enemy off guard, even for a second and you gain the upper hand. Then you keep after them until you've gotten what you came to get. We don't fight to win, we don't fight for honor, we fight to achieve our objectives and nothing more. The thirteenth Virtue of a Citizen is efficiency – do no more or no less than what it takes to get the task accomplished."

Ama smiled as Seg finished his lesson with a long yawn. "You should sleep."

"So should you. There's another thing."

"More?"

"I've decided to take her back, no matter the consequences," he nodded toward the room where Lissil slept. "We can disguise her and hide her among the raiders. It will be a risk, and if she's caught before we extrans…what is it?"

Ama was shaking her head, "She doesn't want to leave."

"She told you this?"

"Yes."

Seg considered this for a moment. "Ama, if she stays, I can't place her anywhere else. She wouldn't be safe from the CWA, they would

KRISTENE PERRON & JOSHUA SIMPSON

take her, torture her for any information about me, then dispose of her."

"Then she'll have to stay with you."

"But not as caj," Seg countered, took Ama's hand and squeezed. "She'll be a free Outer, under my protection, just like Brin's men. I swear it."

Ama smiled at that. There was gratitude in the expression but also sadness.

"Do you miss…" she looked away. "Do you miss my world? I think you must. This world of yours it feels—it feels like a prison sometimes."

"This is my home. The World has to survive. The People must carry on, and they must learn to change," he whispered. "They need me."

"I need you, too," she blurted out.

His tired eyes brightened, he grasped her hand and squeezed. "Then stay with me. Go with me, where I go. You're an explorer, as I am. Why confine yourself to just one world? There may be no end to the worlds out there, across the dimenions. I want to see them all…with you." He wrapped his arm around her and pulled her closer, pushing the digipad to one side. "Trust me."

"That sounds like a dream. But…my family, my people, they need me."

"When we return to your world, we'll ensure that your family is safe. As for your people…" he lowered his voice. "After this raid, and the strikes I've commissioned against the Shasir, the Kenda will be free to determine their own future. And you will be free to choose your own path."

Ama folded her lips inward and lowered her eyes away from Seg. She took a deep breath. "I'm nothing on your world, Seg. In that room—all those people, on their knees. That's who I am here. That's who I would always be."

"Are you on your knees right now?" he asked. "In *our* world?"

She raised her eyes to his. Despite the worry and exhaustion, the familiar heat that existed between them flared.

"No," she said, then her mouth twisted into a smile, "Why? Do you think you could make me?"

His hand snaked up to the back of her head, fingers curling in her hair. "If I had the energy at the moment, certainly." He gave her head the slightest tug. "I never fail," he said, with an impish smile.

Her breathing became more pronounced, her muscles tensed. "We'll have to test that one day." Her tone was low and full of need. She swung herself around, legs straddling him, his hand still gripping her hair. "You know I'm a fighter."

He looked up at her, grasped the front of her nightshirt and bunched it around his fist to pull her closer. "Fighters don't win wars, thinkers do. The pattern of history cannot be denied."

The door cycled open and they both jumped.

Jarin struggled to keep a frown from his face at the sight of the two lovers so happily entwined.

"Am I interrupting?" he asked, loud enough to startle. "Good. Amadahy, to bed, you need your rest. Segkel. I have instructed you not to overthink your analysis in the past, and I'm sure that is exactly what you are doing now. Well," he allowed, "perhaps not at this precise moment. Regardless, you both need your rest. Go. Go," he said, waving his hands.

Ama slid away, avoiding eye contact with Jarin, her face flushed. She spoke something to Seg in her native tongue then disappeared down the corridor.

Jarin cycled the door closed behind her and took a seat. "Segkel, we need to talk."

"Reproductive Physiology covered the basics, Jarin," Seg said, his voice weary, as he rose to his feet and stretched. "I have some idea of what goes where."

Jarin looked away to hide a sad smile. Either it was the experience or it was the woman, but since his return from the mission Segkel had shown more and more hints of actually having a sense of humor, something the serious student had never done. That made what Jarin was about to do that much more tragic.

"You must let her go, Segkel." He watched the young man freeze, hands clenching instinctively, and braced himself.

"Why?" Seg asked, and pivoted to face Jarin, his eyes narrowed. The boy was in a dangerous place, ready for a fight.

"For her good, and yours. This is not her world. She will never be accepted here. She will always be lesser. Outer. Caj, whether grafted or not, in the eyes of your peers. Confined, the way the World has always confined you. If you care for her, take her back and set her free. Let her be with her people, let her find her own way, her own life. Her own love."

"What if she wants to be here with me?" Seg challenged.

"Then she's operating on the very same irrational, instinctive, hormonally-driven impulses that you yourself would mock in anyone else besides a woman who is triggering in you those very same impulses," Jarin said.

"Karg you," Seg cursed.

Jarin pushed himself up from his chair and turned on his former student the black look he reserved for those moments of utmost distaste and disappointment. "Graduated or not, I will not abide that in my home."

Just as he had done on their first meeting, Seg stared down the man before him. This time, however, he surrendered and looked away. But of course he didn't apologize.

"There is another matter," Jarin said, and sat once more. As Segkel reluctantly took his own seat, Jarin pressed his palms together. "As you are aware, I am not one for sentimentality. However, to let you proceed with this plan tomorrow, without offering you the truth, would be unjust." *And unkind*, he thought but could not say.

"I know the risks," Seg said, a defensive edge to his voice.

"Indeed. What you do not know, what I have not explained to you, is that you have another option. You stand at the decision point, Segkel. If you step back and accept a loss here, you can recover and move on. There will be some stigma, this is not the best way to launch a career. With your talents and considerable intelligence, however, I have every confidence you will be a successful Theorist over the long term."

"Behind a desk."

"For now, yes. Your goals will not be reached with the expediency you hoped for. Like all Theorists before you, you will be greying before you will attain a seat on the Council or are voted into the position you desire: Selectee for Field Research." He smiled, "Do not look so shocked, pupil, I have been aware of your ambitions for a good many years."

"And Ama? Fi Costk will kill the raid, you know that. How will she get home?"

"She won't. I am sorry. But I will ensure that she is placed in a position of minimal labour, with an owner who will not treat her unkindly. I cannot promise she will remain ungrafted but at least you will know no harm will come to her."

Seg lowered his head in thought. "No," he said after a pause. "No. I won't fail. I can do this, you know I can."

"I know you are capable, yes. But you have already experienced how easily even the best plans can be swept aside by the capriciousness of fate. If you pursue this path and fail, you will lose everything: your Theorist status, Ama, your freedom. Perhaps even your life."

"I'm aware of the consequences."

"Are you? Have you considered the consequences should you succeed? Because if this raid is a success, your struggles have only begun. You will face the eternal enmity of Adirante Fi Costk. As one of the single most powerful individuals on the World, he will make every mission a battle, turn public opinion against you, sow distrust among the Houses who would contract you, create obstacles to block your every move, and he will not stop until he has broken you and destroyed everything you care about. As a CWA target, your peers will never consider you for a Council seat, and a Selecteeship will be unthinkable. And if you also keep Amadahy with you..." Jarin looked away from Segkel and shook his head, "You will be privately ridiculed and publicly shunned."

"You're saying I should abandon everything we've been working for? Everything Ama has risked her life for at those meetings? Leave House Haffset to be broken by the CWA?"

"I am saying you have choices. That is all. It is not too late to save yourself."

Seg pressed his back into the chair, his eyes left Jarin and moved slowly across the room. For a very long time he sat silent before his mentor. When he spoke again, his voice was uncommonly pensive.

"Why don't you keep caj, Jarin?"

Jarin blinked, he rubbed his palms against the arms of the chair. "That is my affair."

"Because of a situation like mine? It would explain why you are so personally invested in the matter."

Jarin tilted his head back and took a deep breath, then he nodded.

"Did you keep her or send her back?" Seg asked.

"I kept her," Jarin said, prepared for the surprise on his former student's face. "It killed her. I speak from experience on the matter. That is all I will say. Now, go to bed, consider what I have told you. Decisions can wait until morning."

Jarin glanced at the wall crono in the Central Raid Planning Chamber, then silently chided himself for forgetting his oft-preached lesson to his students about the oppositional effect of watching the time when one wishes it to speed up or slow down.

As it had every day, the meeting opened with contention and devolved into outright conflict. *Your plan is working brilliantly Adi.*

He glanced briefly over at Amadahy, in her usual position at Gelad's knee. There would be no thievery today; all the data that could be collected had been collected. Her appearance today was simply to keep anyone from making the connection between Gelad's caj and the information leeched from the Recorder. Most would suspect Jarin of some kind of collusion but, as always, he took great pains to remove any evidence of his involvement.

In a momentary break with protocol, Amadahy raised her eyes to Jarin's and flashed a small, fleeting smile, which was at once nervous and hopeful, and which he did not return. Nevertheless, the gesture triggered a long-buried ache and all his old regrets filled the room like ghosts. They haunted him even as he turned his attention back to the argument of the moment.

The House Master stood and shouted over the combatants for silence. Then he turned his eyes to Director Fi Costk. "We have reached an impasse that cannot be bridged without the guidance of a Theorist. With respect Director, your agents are unable to provide us with satisfactory answers to guide the prioritization of resources."

Fi Costk nodded. "The next option is to disassemble the raid, House Master. Given the unusual circumstances, the CWA would be willing to lend you the funding to absorb the contracted standby costs you have incurred."

The House Master went pale as Fi Costk openly laid the gambit upon the table. It was a better option than the bankruptcy he faced in the present circumstances, but barely. When the CWA took a House under its program of recovery loans, it hollowed them out. The House would be converted into a functional extension of the CWA, their resources used for CWA purposes. Inevetiably, within a few generations, such Houses faded into the fold.

His was a choice between a slow, numb death and an immediate, painful death. Jarin did not envy the man.

"Theorist Segkel Eraranat," the Accountancy announced.

There was an audible gasp from all present. Jarin's face remained impassive but inside he was seized with unexpected and contradictory feelings: relief and pity.

Segkel blazed a trail through the entrance, the entry caj moved quickly to clear the door from his path before the determined Theorist barreled into it. At Segkel's side, a hulking security officer kept one hand on his needler, prompting even more gasps and exclamations. A step behind Segkel, Lissil followed on his heels – a not-so-subtle jab at Fi Costk, who had sent the collectors to intimidate the young Theorist with their threats of removal. The girl moved as naturally as if she had been trained from childhood. Beautiful, graceful, obedient; those who were not offended by her appearance would be covetous.

Predictably, Akbas was the first to rise, "What is the meaning of this?"

Segkel ignored her as he made his way to the inner table, to the vacant seat reserved for the raid's Theorist.

"Security!" Akbas roared, stabbing her finger toward the man standing next to Segkel. "Eraranat is barred from these proceedings, remove him at once!"

The guard lifted his visor and shrugged, "Sorry, can't do that."

Jarin feigned a cough to cover his laugh at the sight of Manatu Dibeld, the trooper Segkel had taken such pains to return to the World following his injury.

"House Master," Segkel said respectfully, as he nodded toward the older man, before he turned his head toward Fi Costk and nodded again. "Director."

Fi Costk's reply was a hateful glare.

"I believe that it is...ortho," Segkel continued, "for the assigned Theorist to attend the pre-raid planning sessions." He sat down at his chair and Lissil moved closer to his side.

"As you, and everyone in this room, are aware," Akbas spoke slowly, in an attempt to draw out the humiliation, "you are no longer the assigned theorist on this raid. We don't have time for your delusions."

Segkel turned to House Master Haffset. "Is everyone in the room aware?"

The House Master smiled. "Welcome back, Theorist Eraranat. Your presence has been badly missed."

Segkel nodded and looked back to Akbas. "Ah! You are referring to that silly matter of the foolish trooper."

Jarin winced at Segkel's description of the lieutenant.

Segkel held out his hand, Lissil slapped a digifilm into it. "As of this morning, Lieutenant Kerbin has withdrawn her charge against me. Moment of anger and all that. And as your superior stated, once that matter was resolved, I could return at will." He thrust the digifilm toward Akbas, and spoke in an obvious imitation of her voice, using the words she had used against him at his dismissal, "Please, take a moment to read, you'll find everything is in order."

Akbas stomped across the room and snatched the film from Segkel's hand, eyes scanning left to right furiously as the room waited in silence. During the pause, Jarin remained passive, though his eyes took in every detail of the moment: Segkel placing a hand on Lissil's head, his eyes on Fi Costk as he did; Lissil casting a stealthy, downward eye to Amadahy, as she enjoyed her master's attention, a territorial gesture; the House Master hovering on the edge of his seat, with his eyes fixed on Segkel, his salvation; and Fi Costk, Adi, who looked directly at Jarin, his pupils narrowed to pinpoints.

When she finished, Akbas hurled the film on the table and it slid across to the other side. "This does not address the matter of your security breach," she sputtered, pounded a fist on the table, then pointed at him. "You did not have clearance to enter this building! You...you..."

Segkel ignored the woman's tirade. "Director Fi Costk, does this woman have any relevance to this proceeding? If not, I would prefer she move to the outer table. With the timetable as it is, we can't afford to waste time on...juvenile tantrums."

Fi Costk continued to stare at his old rival for another moment.

Jarin inclined his head a degree. *A brilliant plan, Adi, but you underestimated the boy. You won't make that mistake again, will you?*

Fi Costk turned his head toward Segkel. "Yes," he said, "you are correct Theorist." He nodded, his eyes smoldering. He turned to Akbas. "Go."

She opened her mouth, ready to fire a volley of vitriol but the look from Fi Costk held her in check. Her lips came together in a thin, flat line and she took her time collecting her digifilms and straightening her coat. When she was composed she nodded to the general assembly, avoiding eye contact with Segkel. However, she directed her exit in such a way that she passed closely by him.

"Good luck with this mess," she hissed. "This will be your last raid, count on that."

"Unlike you," he said, his voice low, "I keep my word and can actually execute my designs. Now, go sit with the lessers."

Segkel turned back to the table, disregarding her presence altogether. "Now, on to the matter of raid assignments. I have worked out a profile based on the unit strengths and vita sources that I was aware of," Lissil handed him a stack of digifilms, which he passed down the line, "that we can review now. I believe it will be largely in line with your operational parameters and capabilities, though of course I defer to the raider leaders in their expertise on these matters."

Chatter resumed around the table but when Segkel spoke, all stopped to listen, completely engrossed and eager for every word. He had not just assumed control of his raid, his bold move had shown the crowd something they had not seen among Theorists in a very long time: passion.

Jarin leaned over to Gelad and whispered, "Look at that. Just look. Segkel has had one extrans mission and has never actually executed a raid, nevermind the most complicated raid in a century. Yet every head is turned to him for guidance, even the senior MRRC raiders. He could tell them to strike at a hundred targets and I believe they would follow him."

"Proud, Theorist?" Gelad whispered back.

Jarin gave a small shake of his head. "Frightened."

CHAPTER 22

Dagga rubbed a hand over his head; the tiny ridges of his scars spoke to him, reminded him about the virtues of patience. He had known and delivered his share of suffering, understood the art of torture, embraced its necessity. His failure to capture or kill his prey required penance, and so he had been called from Alisir to T'ueve, to face the Shasir'threa.

Outside the Sky Temple, this prison of stillness and solitude to which he was confined, was war. While the Assembly of Shasir'threa debated and meditated, consulted ancient texts and communed with the gods, the rats were on the move. His punishment? Inaction. He would sit here, *must* sit here, and wait for the Threa's decision.

No lash or blade could match this agony.

The waiting hall was windowless and dimly lit, another expression of the sky-worshipping Shasir's unhappiness. Dagga sat on one of the four intricately carved chairs. The other three were empty.

He respected the gods but he didn't fear them. Every man had his place and purpose, Dagga knew his well. He was not meant for the clouds; his place was below, with the filth.

The doors opened with the faintest sound and Dagga stood. A Shasir'dua stood flanked by two guards.

"Head Constable," the priest said, his voice sonorous, "the Assembly is ready for you."

Dagga followed the man down a long corridor to the doors of the Assembly Sanctuary. Servants opened them wide at the small party's approach and a bright blue light streamed out.

The Sanctuary stretched skyward, ending in a glass dome. The walls and floor were painted to give the illusion of walking among the clouds, tall windows of blue glass completed the effect. On a high dais, sat ten Shasir'threa, in full ceremonial robes. Below them, on a lower platform, was a table of Shasir'dua, and below them, in rows of chairs, was a gathering of Commissioners and Judicias.

Dagga was led to a table in the center of the room. On the table sat four objects: a piece of paper with a list of destinations – all holy sites, a knife, the strange weapon that shot poison spines, and a heap of melted metal. The last was all that had been discovered when Dagga and his men had finally entered the barn after the conflict in the Humish Valley.

"Head Constable," one of the Shasir'threa began, "we have considered all that you have brought before us.

The wizened, sallow faces looked to one another. Their fear was palpable, Dagga could almost smell the sweat beneath their robes.

"Before we render our decision, we would ask you one final time: Do you swear to all you have spoken of?"

Dagga cleared his throat, "Upon my honor, your holiness."

There were nods and murmurs all around. The Shasir'threa who had spoken raised his hands for silence.

"Be it known, by decree of the Assembly of Shasir'threa, voice of the Shasir'kia, gods and protectors of all S'orasa, that Spiritual War has been declared in these eastern territories. The people known as Kenda have proven to be in league with the O'scuri and demons of the Underneath, they have rejected the light and unification of their lords and fathers. Henceforth, the Kenda are to be purged from this land by whatever means necessary. As the hands of the Shasir, it is the duty of all Law Givers to carry out this decree. Rise and swear your oaths."

Dagga contained himself as the formalities droned on. When at last he was ushered out of the Sanctuary, he marched directly to Judicia Corrus.

"Well?" Dagga asked, striding beside the Judicia, their boots echoing in harmony through the stone corridors.

"The skyship fleet is to be outfitted for battle. They are preparing one specifically for us. We leave here tomorrow. Priority is to reinforce security around Shasir holy sites and temples. But I will send a dispatch to As'Cata; we begin executing the Kenda prisoners two days from now, at high sun," Corrus answered, staring straight ahead.

"Odrell Kalder's mine," Dagga said.

"Of course," Corrus nodded. "You have earned as much."

"Make sure word gets out to the water rats. Only need to tell one, word'll spread."

They rounded a corner. Corrus stopped, looked around to make sure they were alone, then spoke in a whisper. "You believe Ama Kalder will return from the Underneath?"

Dagga resisted the urge to frown. He knew what the holy men believed but he wasn't convinced these were demons they were dealing with. Still, Corrus was a believer, right to the core and Dagga had learned not to question matters of faith.

"To save the old man? She'll come back," Dagga said.

Corrus considered this, then raised his chin. "Then we must be prepared to welcome her."

As Shasir'threa Vintil As'kar took his walk along the perimeter wall of the Malvid temple, he listened to the *pips* and *chees* of morning bird song, convinced it was going to be a good day.

Certainly there were troubles. The perplexing infiltration of the T'ueve Sky Temple, the deception and death of a promising apprentice, and the resulting skirmish had caused much consternation. In the Humish Valley, over thirty constables had been mysteriously cut down. The survivor's tales were implausible and often conflicting – weapons that sprayed fire, a band of demons, the attackers vanishing from a locked barn. And now, Spiritual War.

As always, the trouble had started with the Kenda.

Below him, he could hear the bustle of newly doubled security forces, which was reassuring. Argument among the Threa continued but word had been sent across the Eastern Territories for an immediate tightening of security and soon the Kenda would be purged.

Already peace had begun to return. Despite the whisperings and panic, he had every faith that the mysteries would be solved, the demons rooted out, captured and destroyed. This was simply the repetition of a familiar cycle of rebellion among the Kenda. At last they would be dealt with, as he had always pushed for.

His fellow Threa had long considered his ideas too radical. Perhaps now they would recognize his wisdom? Perhaps a nomination for ascension was not beyond consideration?

As he stretched his arms wide, Vintil felt the warm rays of the sun reach out to touch him, and took a deep breath of moist morning air.

In the distance, a flock of birds was making its way toward him, and he nodded at the goodness of the omen. The katla bird was the totem of his order, and he was sure they were about to confer a fresh blessing upon him.

He turned away from the birds and looked over the grounds of the temple as he made his way back to his sanctuary. Today would be another fruitful day of finger pointing, contention, argument, and opportunity.

There was a strange hum behind him and he turned, wondering at the source. It sounded like one of the blessed o'rakla that conferred mystic energies to their relics but it seemed to be coming from the approaching birds.

Which, upon closer inspection, did not appear to be birds. He leaned forward and squinted at the strange devices that flew toward him from the north. His mouth opened as one of them suddenly accelerated, swooped toward him and a nozzle at the end discharged.

Shasir'threa Vintil As'kar opened his mouth to shout a warning but no sound escaped. The first casualty of the new war, he saw parts of his body fly away from him and then he saw nothing more.

Even without the Bliss, Seg came through the gate pleased at the precision and success of the raid as it was progressing. The first waves were in. The drones had done their job to neutralize the areas around the extrans, secure points and allow the troops to pour through the warp gates unmolested. The pathfinders had carved out bloody perimeters for the follow-on troops, who moved forward aggressively to secure their targets. Behind them, the support and command elements streamed in and moved efficiently, as they calculated and re-calculated the situation on the ground.

One of the most difficult aspects of any raid was the ability of the forces to take over structures without destroying the vita sources within. Preliminary data suggested thus far the balance between firepower and preservation was being maintained adequately.

As he stepped back into Ama's world, Seg was grabbed by one of the Tenders, who shoved him forward, "Keep moving, keep moving, we have equipment coming through!"

At his side, Ama had held her anxiousness in check until this moment. "Where do we go to..." Her mouth fell open and Seg didn't have to ask the cause. The T'ueve Sky Temple, an edifice symbolic of Shasir dominance, was in flames.

"There," Seg said, pointing to the temple. "That's where we're going."

They were chivvied along to the field headquarters that had been set up inside the perimeter of the temple. A massive hole had been blasted in the wall and, even as they passed through, engineer-extractors were busy clearing the rubble away. As they walked, he moved more and more quickly, forcing Ama to scramble to keep up with his long-legged strides.

Two priorities fueled his haste. First, he had to send a comm to Brin, who wouldn't be expecting his arrival for another week at the earliest. If he had received the air-dropped comm unit, that was. Second, he had a rider waiting—the gunship and his body of troops—to rescue Ama's father. Complicating both these tasks was their secrecy. No one from his World could know what he had planned; he would have to accomplish his goals while playing the part of an earnest Theorist whose only concern was the raid itself.

When he arrived at headquarters, he pulled on a comm helmet, plugged into the data network and scrolled through the channels to see how the attack was going – his interest at once genuine and mere show.

As he listened to the reports, he was distracted by the arrival of an officer.

"Theorist," the officer said, keeping his voice low, "your intrans warp gate has been placed at the specified location with the automatics for defense. Code's as specified to deek the turrents."

"Good," Seg replied, then immediately returned to the comm.

So far, the raid was unfolding near perfectly, though they were encountering heavy resistance from the Welf at the temple at Alisir, predictably enough. Both he and Brin had forseen this.

Brin had proposed that he gather Seg's fifty men near Alisir. There was a boat works along the river large enough to hide so many men, which also would serve well as the launch point of the Kenda revolution. Among Seg's personal expenses was a comm unit he had arranged, with his segment of the raiding troops, to have dropped at a specified location at the beginning of the raid. The location was known only to Brin and his inner circle who, according to their plan, would wait nearby to recover the comm unit. Ama had written instructions for its use in the Kenda language both for her cousin's benefit and to prevent any others on her world from deciphering its purpose, should it fall into the wrong hands.

Ideally, once Brin received word that Seg's People had finished their attack, Odrell had been freed, and the Shasir targets had fallen, he was to prepare the fifty for departure before his own men launched into a full-scale takeover of the Shasir and Damiar strongholds. The early launch of the raid, however, pushed everything out of the realm of ideal.

With a quick look around, Seg scrolled the comm to the secure channel he had arranged with Brin. "Kalder, Kalder, this is drexla," he said, as quietly as possible, into the comm, then waited.

No response. Ama stared, questioning, and he worked to hide his concern.

"Kalder, Kald—"

"Theorist Eraranat!" Marshal Rethelt called, from the opening of the command tent. "Get over here."

Seg's fingers quickly switched the comm channel and he indicated to Ama that she should follow him.

The tent was an open-sided structure where the Marshal processed data with haste while his aides moved in and out to bring him updates.

"Storm take me if this isn't the coup you promised," the Marshal said, without even a flinch as the sound of projectile weapons fire intensified down the avenue. The raiders were running things right at the edge of the combat zone, and the Damiar guards were fighting for all they were worth. Such resistance wouldn't change things, but the locals weren't simply rolling over.

Seg stood at the edge of a table where the battle schematic hovered, and noted the icons moving across the map as he pulled his helmet off. "Marshal," he said, rallying enthusiasm, "I see things are progressing well."

"Your plan, unortho as it may be, is working. As a rule, I don't usually welcome digis poking their noses into my work in the field, but it would be an honor to have you here, in the command center," Rethelt said, gesturing to the spot beside him.

Seg didn't dare look back at Ama. As eager as she was to get moving, he had only just recovered from one disaster brought on by his lack of diplomacy, he couldn't risk another by refusing the Marshal's offer,

"The honor is mine," Seg answered, and stepped closer to Rethelt. "Any difficulties?"

"None we weren't prepared for. More of those airships than we counted on, but nothing our riders can't handle. Also, they've managed to bottleneck us at zone three. The Welf are fighting fanatically, as you warned they would."

"You can shift forces around to reinforce your position there."

"I don't have much in the way of reserves to work. I hate to admit it, but we should have added more troops, as you suggested."

"Which is precisely why I contracted my own," he lied. Seg eyed the holographic map, marking the distance between his target and the Alisir temple with a glimmer of hope. "Can the raiders hold until we reach them?"

The Marshall nodded, "They're pinned down but not losing any ground. Quicker would be better, though."

Seg scooped up his helmet, "Speed is assured, Marshal."

He strode out of the field headquarters, with Ama tight at his side, and pulled his helmet back on. As he switched the comm back to Brin's channel, he turned to her, "Let's go get your father."

The sky machines of the People were nothing like the stately craft of the Shasir. Even the likeness Seg had shown her couldn't have prepared Ama for what she saw before her. Large, dark-colored, festooned with images of skulls and bones and carnage, with weapons protruding from various surfaces, this ship looked like it had crawled from a Shasir's nightmare of the Underneath. Seg guided Ama up the ramp, into the back of the craft, then shoved her into one of the seats and fastened the harness down over her before settling into his own seat.

The platoon of troops filed in after them and piled into their seats – more of Kerbin's breed, hostile and ready for action. For the first time since that night beneath Brin's cottage, she felt confident. Seg was right, with this army and this ship, they were unstoppable.

The ramp hadn't even finished closing when the vectored thrust fans kicked the craft into the air with a hard punch of acceleration. The craft flew south and made a quick strafing run over the Shasir positions before it moved on to the next objective.

What a craft! Ama's stomach dropped as it lifted off. The sharp, hard noises bothered her ears and she shook her head but the rush of flying kept her mind off them. She touched everything, the seat, the belts that held her in, the walls behind her, everything was sturdy and utilitarian. If she had a ship like this...

They banked hard and she marveled at how her body was pushed by some invisible force. It was a thrilling sensation, almost like cruising in big seas but more intense.

She looked at Seg and the soldiers in the dim orange light of the craft's belly. Their faces were set and stony, focused on the job at hand. The warriors, other than a few sideways glances, ignored her. Caj. Beneath them. Unworthy of their attention.

But you're working for me now. For me and my people. After nearly a week on her knees, the thought made her smile.

The craft nosed into a dive and Ama, forgetting her surroundings, let out a hearty "Yee-aaaa!", as she used to do when she slid her beloved *Naida* down the face of a big wave.

Seg favored her with a grin, then reached around her waist to adjust her combat utilities. "I haven't had an opportunity to teach you anything about how to use all this," he yelled into her ear over the noise of the craft, "but I don't anticipate you will need any of it. Merely a precautionary measure."

"Any luck?" Ama yelled back, her eyes directed to the comm helmet Seg wore.

He shook his head.

Suddenly the intercom chimed in, a disembodied voice reached out to them. "Craft commander to passengers. We are diverting momentarily to engage an air fleet moving south to support the Outer temple defenders. Should be quick and easy."

Seg raised a hand to his helmet, opened his mouth to speak into his comm, but the craft banked sharply. Weapons blisters opened fire. A staccato hammering from the cannons mixed with the sound of rockets igniting and the hiss of the flechette drums. Abruptly, the craft shuddered, the engine took on a strange new pitch. There was a loud bang, then another, from outside the craft.

The troops looked at each other nervously, then the lights went out inside and the craft pitched over toward the ground.

Falling. Ama knew the feeling—she had done enough high dives—but this was no plunge from the mast, and there was no water waiting to catch them.

In the dark, she groped for Seg's hand, found it and squeezed tight. She closed her eyes against the pull of the fall, the noise, the fear. The craft spun and tumbled. Someone yelled; the sound went on forever.

There was a scream of metal. And then there was nothing but blackness.

Seg worked his jaw and gasped for air. The onboard system had extinguished the fire, but it had made the air musty and sour. He fumbled around for the latch to his seat, felt it, tried to unlatch it. The impact had distorted the buckle; he groped around for his knife, pulled it free and sawed at the harness straps.

Moans and whimpers echoed in the compartment. He wasn't the only survivor. "Ama," he murmured and reached for her. She hung limply in her harness. His hands fumbled across her body and slapped at her face. "Wake up," he ordered.

She gasped and coughed her way back to consciousness. "Seg?" she called, then let out a cry of pain. "I can't move," she choked out, her voice panicked as she struggled in her seat.

"Calm down. It's just the harness." He placed a hand on her arm and she settled as he cut through the straps. When he was done, he helped her out of the seat.

The craft was tilted, she stumbled to one side. "The others...?" she struggled to regain her balance.

"I don't know." The ship's metal doors creaked as he pushed them open sideways. Sunlight flooded in and Seg steered Ama out of the wreckage. He checked her over quickly and, satisfied she was unharmed, took an amp-light from his pack and turned to go back in. "Keep watch out here, if anyone comes, call me."

He struggled back into the interior of the craft. He already knew most of the platoon was dead—nobody could have survived on the right side, where the hull was totally smashed—but he had heard a voice, moaning, and clambered through the hulk of the craft to find it.

"Help," a man said, "don't leave me."

"I'm coming," Seg shone his light in the direction of the voice. In the seat closest to the cab, he found one trooper bloodied but alive. There was nothing striking about the man's features—raiders often appeared mass produced to Seg and this one was simply a dark haired model of the square-jawed line—what was noticeable was the trooper's controlled expression and tone, despite the unnatural angle of his leg.

"Theorist," the trooper said, "what happened?"

"I don't know." He pushed his way to the cabin, "I'll be back to get you in a moment."

The pilot was dead; debris through the window had seen him off. The copilot sat stunned but alive. She looked up when Seg settled in next to her and reached for the harness.

"Kargin' junkers," she muttered and shrugged loose of the harness straps. She jerked her head toward the back, "How bad back there?"

"Three survivors, counting myself." Seg tugged at her arm to pull her off the seat, "One wounded."

She pulled her flight helmet loose and tossed it aside to reveal a tangle of unruly black hair. "How bad is the limper?"

"Broken leg."

"Fantastic. Can he walk?"

"We can splint him and help him along until we can get extracted." He gestured to the smoking instrument panels, "I gave specific orders regarding our flight path. No diversions!"

"Not my call, boss," the woman answered, with a shift of her eyes toward the dead Pilot.

"What happened?" he asked, his tone calmer.

"Debris. Those Outer airships..." she rolled her eyes, "Primitive. Structure's wood and some kind of fabric or animal hide, makes for a low d-scan profile and if we don't have clear line of sight for thermals the kargers can be right on top of us before we see 'em. This one blew up right in front of us, sucked it up straight through the inlets and the cockpit." She grabbed a survival pack, then followed Seg back into the cabin.

Outside the crashed skyship, Ama surveyed the damage. They were lucky to have survived. If they hadn't come down where they had, their descent slowed by the canopies of the old Veya trees, no one would be walking away from the wreck.

Unfortunately, the thick canopy would also make them impossible to find if Seg's people were looking for them from above.

She considered their position, where they had left from, where they were headed when they crashed, the current geography. A relatively accurate map formed in her head. It wasn't a promising map. If she was correct, they were a long way from the Secat, and deep in the heart of Welf territory.

Bad trouble.

With a keen eye and ear on the surroundings, Ama adjusted herself, pulled her hair out of her face and tugged off the heavy and uncomfortable belt load of 'stuff' Seg had strapped on her her.

After a lengthy wait, Seg emerged from the craft with two others, one of them limping. She knew from his expression that no one else was coming out. As he hopped down to the ground, he held his hand over the earpiece of his comm helmet.

"The temple blew up? Completely? Survivors?" he intoned to the microphone. "No, we're non-functional. I have three survivors here. No. Yes. Understood. Yes. Very well." Comm complete he shifted the raider's weight to the co-pilot, then gestured for Ama to follow him just out of earshot. "The Welf detonated a store of black powder under the Alisir temple, my People are trapped there."

"Your skyships?" Ama asked, already suspecting the answer.

"Are in use elsewhere and won't be diverted at this time. I won't be able to secure another gunship until the other targets have been taken and the vita has been extracted," he said, keeping his voice low.

"We can't wait here, this is Welf territory. If they find us—"

"I am aware of the danger. There is also the matter of my People to consider. The temple is our best strategy. If we can make it there and hold the ground, air support will come. Eventually. Once the gunships arrive, we'll evacuate my People and then we'll make our way to the Secat. However, we have to ensure that temple doesn't fall to the Welf before then."

Ama glanced over her shoulder, "There are only four of us and that one soldier can barely walk."

"If I can reach Brin, and if your cousin is the man I believe he is, there will be more than four of us," Seg turned himself so the others couldn't see his face. "We will finish this," he said, his expression as determined as it had been the morning he had taken over the raid planning meeting.

"I know," Ama said, steel in her gaze as it met Seg's.

Seg broke away and returned to the other survivors as he recast the frequency of his comm to Brin's channel. "Kalder. This is drexla. Answer."

There was a pause and once more Seg wondered if the comm had made it to its target or if Brin had entertained second thoughts about their deal or...

"This is Kalder...drexla. I hear you."

Seg let out a long breath at the crackling voice.

"Good. We've arrived ahead of schedule," Seg replied.

There was another pause but Seg thought he heard a laugh through the static. "Yes, brother, we figured that out from the smoke and explosions."

"We've encountered a situation. I need your support. I've got men trapped at the Alisir temple, I mean to relieve them. I need fighters, as many as you can spare and can safely travel with."

"I have only a handful. I've sent runners to gather your fifty but..." Brin's voice faded.

"I understand," Seg answered. "Extraordinary circumstances, as always. Do what you can; even a handful of men could make the difference."

"Where should we rendezvous?"

Seg consulted the holographic map of the area that he had pulled up, with the crash site and Alisir temple highlighted.

"There's a wide valley about ten kilometers south of the temple, with what appears to be a large bridge across a body of water, " Seg said.

"The Cradle Fork, yes, I know it." Brin said.

"We'll travel north-east toward the bridge and meet up there."

After Brin's confirmation, Seg disconnected, then looked at the others. "What are your names?"

"Fismar Korth, Theorist," the raider answered, with a salute.

"Shan Welkin," the woman said, "kin to the Eraranats, if it matters."

"It doesn't," Seg said. "Can you keep pace, Fismar?"

"If I have to crawl out of here I will, Theorist."

"Ama, this is your world." Seg turned to face her, "You lead. If you see anyone, you get low and signal us. We don't engage, we make our way to the Cradle Fork and link up with Brin and his men. Then we go and relieve our forces at the temple."

"What happened?" Shan asked.

"The Welf detonated a bomb under the temple. The structure is mostly shattered, and the remnants of our force are cut off and besieged. We can't pry them a warp window for twenty-six hours."

"Can they hold that long? Can we?" Fismar asked.

"They've fifty troopers and some heavy weaponry. Given a clear field of fire and some air support—" The Marshal had been uncertain as to whether the air support would be forthcoming. The precious rider that had just gone down constituted a significant portion of the raid's aerial capacity and from all accounts it seemed recovering the troops from Alisir had been assigned all but the lowest of priorities. But these troopers didn't need to know that. "Shan, can you run the sensor array?" He thrust the sensor kit into her hands.

"I guess I'll learn."

Seg unloaded his gear onto the ground. No more need for vita sensing or any other extraneous equipment. Water, a couple of ration bars, and the heavy needler he had recovered from inside the gunship would serve.

"You know how to handle that, Theorist?" Fismar asked dubiously, his eyes on the large weapon.

"I fired one in qualifications, and we'll need all the firepower we can get," Seg answered, checked the displays and dug into his memory on the operation of the weapon, as he hefted the stabilizing harness over his shoulder.

Fismar nodded and shrugged.

"We march. Ama, lead."

She set off at a fast clip with a course already in mind. The high winding buttress roots of the Veya trees would make for slow going in parts. They would have to climb over them. Alternative routes were too rocky and steep for the injured soldier. Plus, the roots would make for suitable cover if needed.

Seg's people weren't clumsy but they weren't used to negotiating the forest and Fismar was injured; Ama frequently slowed her pace so they wouldn't lose sight of her.

As they approached a clearing she heard the crackle of footsteps and waved for Seg and the soldiers to get down. When they did, she scurried up a small widgewood tree, and scouted the area. The striped back of an imheth, nosing through the brush for rodents, elicited a sigh of relief.

She gave a low whistle as she swung back down to earth and pressed forward, with a cursory glance over her shoulder to ensure the group was behind her.

At a patch of sedweed, Ama pulled out her knife and cut off four stalks. One she kept for herself, the remaining three she tossed back to the others and demonstrated to the two soldiers how to drink from them. The nectar was sweet. Good energy, especially in the heat of summer, when it was too easy to dehydrate.

Later, when they reached a small stream, she paused and waited for Seg and the soldiers. If they wanted water, this would be a good spot to stop. The limping soldier gasped for breath and was soaked in sweat. To Seg, she whispered, "Will he make it?"

Seg shrugged. "Even with the auto-med, a hike of this distance on a broken leg is nearly impossible. If he can't last until we link up with Brin, I'll leave him with his weapon. He's a raider; they know the risks when they take the work."

He crouched down to refill his canteen then fed in a cleansing tab to purify the water. He passed his canteen to Fismar and took the man's own canteen to fill.

"How far?" he asked her as he took a measured draught.

"We're over half way there, and the trail will be easier now. But more exposed, too." She turned and spoke for the benefit of the others, as she knew Seg was already familiar with some of the dangers of her world. "Keep close to the trees and try not to step on anything that looks like a pile of dirt – those are haffsa mounds. They're full of bugs that can kill you and they're really territorial."

She crouched down, scooped the water in her hands and took a long drink, then splashed some over the leather covering her dathe to help cool herself.

"Okay, let's keep moving," she leapt across the stream and waited.

Shan muttered something under her breath as they resumed.

"Problem?" Seg asked.

"Just that I'm mudslogging across a misbegotten heap of a world with a—" she made a distasteful moue, eyes toward Ama, as she hopped the stream. "Filthy water everywhere and trees and insects and poisonous dirtpiles. Other than that, I'm condition grade alpha, sir!" she snapped off a jaunty salute.

"That is good to know," Seg said. "Distract yourself by keeping an eye on the sensors so the tens of thousands of hostile Outers who would happily torture us for days on end don't find us before we find them, if you please."

Fismar slapped Shan on the shoulder as he limped past. "Welcome to the real military, skyrider."

"Karg the both of you," Shan said, as she resumed the march.

A swathe of tall grass stretched out ahead of them.

"Contact!" Shan hissed just as Ama spotted signs of movement ahead. Ama, Seg, and Fismar all went low at the same time. After a momentary gawk at the screen, Shan likewise crouched down.

"Twe—" she started to say, before Seg put up a hand and Fismar sliced a hand across his throat to indicate silence.

Twelve, she signed and pointed to indicate the direction. Seg scuttled slowly into a thicket, and Fismar followed; both readied their weapons. Shan came in with a loud rustle and Fismar leaned over and whispered to her, "If you get the Outers on us, skyrider, I'll cut your throat first."

Seg held up a fist for silence and they waited in nervous anticipation as the figures came into view.

Ama watched carefully, crouched in the grass, as the first shape moved closer. He was large, very large.

And he was no Welf.

Tensions were high, Ama stood slowly and made a low whistle, similar to a birdcall but with a pattern any Kenda would recognize.

Brin stopped and held up his hand for his men to do the same. He squinted in her direction then smiled broadly.

Ama waved at the others to come out but saw that Seg had already recognized Brin and his men and was doing just that. As she walked to meet her cousin, Ama felt her heart settle a bit. They embraced but it was not the carefree reunion of times past.

"Ama, good to see you alive," Brin said as he pulled away.

"Not as good as it is to see you, cousin," she answered. Before she could speak again, there was another set of arms wrapped around her waist.

"Tadpole!"

"Thuy?" she turned to look at her brother's face in disbelief. "What are you doing here?" she pulled him in tightly for a hug and cast a sideways glance to Brin.

"His head is as thick as yours," Brin answered. "He refused to stay with the others, as I ordered him to."

"The rest of my kin can be babysitters for women, children and old men. I don't run from a fight," Thuy answered.

"You see?" Brin rapped his knuckles against Thuy's head, "thick." He placed a hand on Ama's shoulder, "Excuse me cousin, I have a brother of my own to confer with."

Seg watched Brin break away from Ama and make his way over to where he stood. The Kenda's eyes darted to Fismar and Shan, then he offered Seg a curt, formal nod, "Eraranat." Tactful. Brin's ability to so astutely read the political climate impressed him.

"We are still a few kilometers from the rendezvous point," Seg said.

"My men move swiftly. I knew this would be your path."

Seg nodded, introduced the raiders, procured assistance for Fismar, and suggested they keep moving.

Brin moved to the head of the procession, with Seg at his side.

"It is good to see you again, brother, even under…extraordinary circumstances," Brin said, in low voice, when they were far enough from the others.

"Likewise," Seg answered.

"I have to admit I am surprised you and Ama were able to slip through the nets of the authorities."

"With your assistance," Seg acknowledged. "Neverthess, it is not a feat I would care to repeat."

"The Damiar estate at Sansin, I assume that bit of arson was your handiwork?" Brin asked, with a smile.

"Ama's actually," Seg corrected, his face stern. "In her defense, however, we had been caught in a thunderstorm and we were both quite chilled."

Brin was silent for a moment, then he broke into muted laughter. Seg lowered his eyes to the grass as his mouth twitched into a smile. The sense of familiarity he had felt in Brin's presence when they first met fell naturally into place, which surprised him.

"You and your party are lucky to be in your skins." Brin's face sobered. "Your people have stirred up the Welf something fierce. They're everywhere…and they are not pleased."

"Offending the natives is a rather large part of my job." He moved closer to Brin, "Has there been news of Ama's father?"

Brin nodded.

"Bad trouble," Seg said, in the Kenda tongue.

"Bad trouble, yes," Brin said, staring away from Seg. "The Shasir have declared Spiritual War against the Kenda. We've received word that all Kenda prisoners are to be executed beginning at high sun, tomorrow." He wiped a hand across his mouth, a thin bandage covering the stump of his missing finger. "Dagga will personally oversee Odrell's death. We've been praying to Nen for a miracle; looks like he heard us."

Seg let the superstitious reference pass, there were greater concerns. He looked over his shoulder, to where Ama walked.

"I've told the others to keep silent about the news for now, even Thuy," Brin assured him. "She doesn't need the worry and you've yet to fall short of your promises. We'll save him."

Seg nodded and looked back to Brin, "Twelve men, including yourself; what sort of weaponry did you bring?"

"All the men have sefts, a few klips, and we even rounded up some bangers. It's not much but the best we could manage in such a hurry." He frowned, "What is your thinking?"

"I'm thinking that my People's weapons were designed for simplicity and ease of use, and that a dozen more guns on the line could make all the difference," Seg said. "I'll speak with Fismar but tell me, are your men willing to follow me?"

"I have told them you are one of us – though they know not to speak of it to your people. Consider them yours. To the temple then?"

He studied Brin for a long moment. "To the temple."

As Ama and Thuy made their way up the line of Kenda, toward Brin, a familiar face surprised her. Captain Tather tipped his hat.

"Tather? So they let anyone come and fight now, do they? I had no idea my cousin was so desperate," she teased her old dock mate.

"Yes, desperate indeed if he's recruiting girls to his army."

"Oh, I owe you a half coin, by the way."

Tather cocked an eyebrow.

Ama pointed toward Seg, "You were right, the big fellow was his bodyguard."

"Thought so," he said, with a knowing nod. "I also heard your boat was burned." He pushed his chin in Seg's direction. "Anything else you'd care to share?"

She smirked at the memory of her promise to burn her boat if she fell for her Damiar passenger, then walked on. Her eyes stopped on Viren, who was busy leering at Shan.

"What are you gawking at, Outer?" Shan spat the question at him.

"My dreams made flesh," Viren answered with a flourish.

"That man is going to get himself shot again," Ama told Thuy, and shook her head as she passed by.

"She'd be worth it, though," Thuy said.

"You're in enough trouble." Ama cuffed him on the back of the head.

"Look who's talking." Thuy tugged her hair sharply.

"Ow!" she punched him in the shoulder. It felt like old times but she knew better –knowledge that pushed the smile from her lips. "Thuy, you shouldn't be here. I made Brin promise to keep you and the others safe." She lowered her head, "I've lost enough family."

"You won't lose me."

"You have no idea what you're walking into."

"And you do?" he asked.

A long stretch of silence followed.

"I'm sorry," Ama said, eyes on the ground, "about Stevan, about Fa."

"Don't be," Thuy said, the muscles of his mouth tensed. "You were right, we should have stood up to the spooks. A long time ago. We should have fought."

"Fighters don't win wars, thinkers do." Ama's tone was laced with surprise, as her eyes moved up to where Seg walked with Brin.

"Well," Thuy said and shrugged, "no matter what, after today, I'm not hiding and keeping my mouth shut anymore. Any cloud sniffers I meet will be sniffing the end of my seft."

Ama looked back to Thuy, to the faint scar across his jaw, which she had given him while they had played with their father's seft, as children. Warriors, that's what they had once pretended to be.

CHAPTER 23

With the assistance of the Kenda, the journey to the temple was made in less time than Seg expected. They were as well versed in woodcraft as the Welf, and knew the shortcuts and pathways just as competently.

The rolling hills leading up to the temple were dangerously open, with hordes of Welf scattered everywhere. Brin guided the group along a winding path that was rocky and slow going but kept them sufficiently covered.

Shrouded in dust, the sight of the Alisir temple was more of a shock than T'ueve had been. Seg could see the walls surrounding the complex were partially intact, though sections had collapsed. One of the two tall chapels that had stood at opposite corners, was gone – only a column of black smoke marked its place.

Between a cluster of rock and a pile of rubble outside the temple proper, Brin motioned to everyone to stop.

Seg surveyed the ruins of the temple. There was an unholy din arising from inside the fortress – weapons fire, explosions and piercing screams. He pulled up the holographic map once more, where the temple was still shown as intact.

He showed the map to Fismar and pointed at the blinking icon that represented their current location. The trooper nodded his understanding as Seg passed him the comm helmet to link up with the troops inside.

"Trooper Fismar Korth to defenders, have troops to assist. Southeast four-five on the temple, need cover coming in," he said into the comm.

Seg watched as Fismar listened to the response. The trooper's tenacity continued to surprise him. With the state of his leg, he had never expected, or even hoped, that the man could make the journey to the temple. Not only had he made it, he seemed as alert and ready as any of the others – a state not even heavy doses of stims could achieve. Had he not seen the very human blood leaking from Fismar's wound, he would have suspected cybernetics.

"Twelve points yeah, seventeen in all. Theorist hoping you saved him some Outers for his heavy." He chuckled, then after a moment he passed the comm helmet back to Seg, all business once more.

"Here's what we have," he drew a quick diagram in the dirt. A square, with a smaller square inside. "Our folks are pulled into a tight perimeter, back against that hill so nothing can come over and get them." He noted the protective hill with a series of hash marks. "Line's a half-crescent, set up to give themselves the best fields of fire." He drew a half circle facing toward an open area. "See how they've got a sweep on that parade ground, or whatever it is?"

"Courtyard, yes?"

"Raiders are set up to shoot anyone who comes at 'em as far out as they can before the attackers can get close and go to sticks and clubs. Problem is, the Out—Welf," he corrected, with a sudden glance to the Kenda men, "figured out not to run straight into the line of fire and changed course. There are a bunch of smashed-up buildings over to the west, where the locals can get close before the raiders can get weapons on them. That's the weak point; that's where the Welf are pushing hardest."

"If that is the case, is there a safe way for us to enter?"

"Well, there's no *safe* here, Theorist, but there's less dangerous. That courtyard is our path. Welf are west; we circle around the perimeter before we bump into them. We come across the courtyard, where our people can cover us in. We'll need to get your boys in the middle of our group so that the raiders don't gun 'em down coming in. Once we start going, we don't stop. No time to pick up anyone who goes down."

He glanced at his own leg. "Theorist, maybe I should take the heavy needler and cover you in."

"I'll carry it and cover," Seg said. "We'll make sure you get in."

With that, Seg rose and moved along the perimeter of the fight, toward the entry point. The rest fell in with him.

They pressed forward as far as they could, to wait for their moment to breach the temple.

Brin moved beside Ama. "I suppose there'll be no talking you out of following him into this mess?" he said, in the Kenda tongue, with a nod to Seg.

"Thickheaded, us Kalders," Ama said, and glanced at Thuy.

"You'll need this then," he passed her the extra seft he had strapped on his back.

"Thank you, cousin." She took the weapon and weighed it in her hand. It had been several years since Fa had first secretly taught her how to use one. An elegant weapon, the seft. Graceful and deadly.

She looked down the line of Kenda men, read their thoughts and fears, as the noise of the weapons from Seg's world tore apart the air. They couldn't know, as she did, that they stood on the precipice of a new era. An era of true freedom. Who was this stranger from another world and why should they care for his cause, they would wonder. Except Seg's cause was theirs – they were all in this together.

"My brothers," she said, then tilted her chin back, hooked the tip of the seft under her nove and sliced upward. The leather collar split in half and fell away, her dathe were exposed, for all the men to see. She clutched the piece of leather in her fist, raised it skyward, then threw it to the dirt.

"Blood for water." She raised her fist to her heart.

The men whispered among themselves, "Kiera Nen", *Nen's chosen one.*

"Blood for water," Brin repeated, raised his seft to his neck and followed Ama's example.

And so it went down the line; the words gained strength with each man. Ama pitied the Welf that stood in the way of these warriors.

Seg waited for the moment it took for Ama to finish talking. He understood the need for ceremony among some. More actually, he understood that some needed ceremony, though he didn't. There was a task to be done, a war to be fought. Who needed words?

"I bring up the rear," he said. "I'll cover. Fismar with me. Shan, you lead the way in with Ama. When you get in," he stressed the 'when', "you inform the senior commander of the situation, that these Outers are friendlies, and that we need to get them armed. If nothing else, they can provide fire suppression."

And, from the looks of it, close quarters combat support. But in all honesty, if it came to that they were all dead anyway. Firepower would win the day here.

He thought on Ama's speech for another moment. Such showmanship was not the way of the People, but then it was hardly the time to worry about unortho behaviour now. They were outnumbered and about to run headlong into what might be a death trap, some motivation would not go amiss. He turned to Shan and Fismar. "Those are our people in there, *the* People," he told them. "We don't let our own down."

Fismar looked at Seg for a long moment, nodded and, finally, seeing the seriousness of his expression, gave him a grin. Shan just nodded and muttered under her breath, before taking her place at Ama's side.

"Brin, get your people between us and Shan and Ama. Fismar, let them know we're coming."

Shan, beside Ama, did not even offer a nod of acknowledgment.

"Try and keep up," Ama told Shan. "I don't know who this senior commander is and I have no intention of being cut down by some banger-happy soldier who can't even tell the difference between a Welf and a Kenda."

"All you Outers look the same," Shan said, keeping what distance she could between them.

The entry corridor was a blasted ruin. Once, the old courtyard had been used for training Welf acolytes who would serve the Shasir in day-to-day affairs. Taken at a young age to the temple, they were raised slightly above their own kind as conduits to the 'higher powers'.

The corridor was now laden with dead bodies, many of them those same acolytes.

"If everyone's quite ready—Shan, GO!" Seg yelled.

At the word, the defending troops inside the ruins of the temple opened fire with a fresh barrage and worked studiously to keep the Welf attackers pinned down while Seg's party ran for their lives toward the defensive perimeter.

Seg paused long enough to fire up the heavy needler. A fearsome weapon, it threw concentrated spikes of explosive matter up to six hundred meters, which created large, distracting bursts of fiery death. The heavy needler was designed as much for intimidation as effectiveness, and did both quite well.

"Sector seven," Fismar directed his fire as they trotted in behind the others.

Seg pivoted and fired. Quite different using the heavy needler in real life compared to basic familiarization at the range. Quite different indeed. He saw a pack of Welf forming up to rush them from the side and stitched a burst into their midst. Screaming men streamed from the charges, bodies singed and burned.

"Go!" Fismar yelled and hobbled as fast as he could. Seg kept pace with him, profligately expending ammunition as he went.

Ama charged forward with Shan at her side, choked by smoke, the grainy air thick in her mouth. Bodies were strewn everywhere; she concentrated on looking forward and ignored the carnage. Seg had told her the invasion would be harsh; she could not have guessed how much of an understatement that was.

Explosions. Screaming. Fire. Smoke. Rubble. Bangerfire. Ama pushed everything to the back of her mind as she kept one eye on Shan and one on the path. A body sprawled in front of them suddenly came to life. The man struggled to stand upright, grabbing the heavy club at his feet as he did so. Ama passed her companion with a quick burst of speed, brought her seft upward in a smooth arc and sliced the Welf open across the torso without even slowing down.

When Shan caught up, they exchanged a quick look as they ran. *You're welcome*, Ama thought, in answer to Shan's unspoken sentiment.

Brin moved his people quickly and efficiently. Fismar provided his own fire from his huchak; electromagnetically propelled slivers tore through armor and flesh. A salvo of grenades arced in, taking out a clump on the left. One of Brin's people succumbed to a Welf throwing weapon. His comrades grabbed him in an effort to save him.

"Drop him!" Seg ordered. "He's dead." He could tell, even from his position at the rear of the line, by the way the head was tilted. Broken neck.

First kill under his command. He avenged the man's death with a steady burst into the area the projectile had come from.

"Last case!" Fismar yelled as he reloaded Seg's weapon.

Seg nodded. "We'd best move, then."

They darted through the wreckage and headed for the lines. Closer, closer. Finally, they tumbled in behind a wall of rubble the raiders were using for cover.

Shan and Ama were ahead of the rest of the group; the former gestured wildly to one of the troopers and pointed in Seg's direction.

"Theorist Eraranat?" the trooper yelled. Beneath the thick layer of dust and debris that coated every inch of her, the muted insignia that marked her as the squad commander was barely visible.

"Yes!" Seg yelled back.

"I'm the senior commander left here. Do you know if we're getting air support?" the trooper asked. Behind them, there were cries along the line. The Welf, stirred up by the latest incursion, were making another push.

"Eventually, but don't factor it into the fight yet," Seg yelled as the guns hammered again. "We'll hold with what we have. What's the situation?"

"Most of these Outers only have close quarters weapons but karg if there aren't endless numbers of the bastards. There were a few shooters in the bunch to begin with, black powder weapons…"

"Damiar," Seg interjected, speaking mostly to himself. "Welf aren't allowed to handle those weapons."

"Whatever they were, our snipers de-pop'd most of them, which disordered the rest for a short time. Too short. Now we just have to keep them from over-running us."

"Understood," Seg replied. "I've brought some fresh hands, feel free to use them where you need them."

He turned to watch as Fismar gathered Brin and his people. The wounded trooper spit out a mouthful of grey saliva, grabbed a weapon off the ground and held it out to show the Kenda.

"Alright, this is the basic K-44 gauss impeller, we call it a *'chack*. That doesn't mean anything to you. You load it like this," Fismar demonstrated. "You fire it like this." He showed them how to pull the trigger. "I'll put you with troopers. You do what you're told here and we'll get out of this alive."

When Fismar glanced back to Seg and the senior commander, Seg nodded and Fismar limped on to the dazed and bewildered troops of the People. "Look lively, you bastards! All the Outers in the Storm have come for dinner!"

Ama coughed then caught her breath as she watched the Kenda men receive instruction from Fismar – they were confused but eager. She and Shan had made it, carried out their orders; it was time to return to Seg.

As she pushed her way through the crowd, she stopped beside Thuy, who stared in awe at the weapon Fismar had given him. "It's not magic, big brother."

"Sure looks like it." Thuy turned the bulky weapon over in his hands.

Captain Tather moved past her, with his own weapon, and paused to touch his hand to his heart, then his forehead, "An honor, Kiera Nen, to die beside you."

"To *fight* beside me," Ama corrected as she returned the gesture. "And I you."

She found Seg moving rapidly along the lines of troopers and slipped quietly to his side.

Seg wasn't concerned with such trifles as proper positioning of the guns, sight lines, flanks, and other military jargon best left to the professionals. His role here, one he had adopted, was to be on the lines. He stopped to pick up some extra cartridges that were lying next to a downed trooper, then slung the needler up and moved along among the men, with Ama as his shadow.

"What's the situation?" he asked the latest bunch of troopers he met, a trio who had taken an overwatch position around the remaining shattered chapel.

"Quiet here now," the youngest answered, a boy who didn't look old enough to shave.

"You the Theorist?" a second trooper asked, a woman and likely well seasoned in battle by her demeanor. "What in the name of the Storm are you doing here?"

"My raid," Seg answered. He glanced over the edge of the rubble pile the three used for cover, "Movement."

The sniper shifted position. "Sector four, scans showing upwards of thirty. They're massing for a rush."

"Good eye, Theorist," the female trooper said. "If we've got thirty coming, that heavy needler might come in handy."

"Where do you need me?" Seg asked. The man gestured to a position a short distance away. "Come up over there, and when we give the word lay down a sustained volley on the breach south of the gate."

"Understood." Seg crouched low, darted away from the cover and into the new position. Once there he aimed the needler then glanced at Ama, who had followed on his heels, as if he had just noticed she was there.

"Watch my back, if you please," he said.

"Here they come!" came the shout. "Hold... hold... hold... HIT THEM!"

Seg watched the mass of Welf pour in through the gaps between the damaged out buildings.

This wasn't war. This was slaughter. He held down the trigger and fired a stream of needles into the mass. Men screamed and died under his guns. But if he and the others let off for a second the slaughter would invert, and the screams and cries would be theirs.

"Flankers, flankers, flankers!" a cry went up from the left. An outpost they hadn't visited yet was getting hit, up close and personal. Welf had somehow infiltrated into their midst, and troopers died noisily as the peasants swarmed them with their crude weapons. Black smoke rose from close-range weapons fire.

"Curl left and anchor, Theorist!" a trooper shouted. Seg wasn't sure what that meant precisely, but he assumed that he was now responsible for holding this section of the line. He slapped a fresh cassette into the needler and took aim.

Where are they all coming from? Ama wondered as she gripped her seft and crouched behind Seg. Every Welf in the east must have turned up for this battle. They were everywhere. She closed her eyes and hoped that Tev, the boy who had helped her, was not among them.

All she could hear was the din of weapons and the screams of the dying. And the pounding of blood in her ears.

Here and there, small groups of Welf made it through the line of fire. Not enough to do any damage but enough to create distractions.

Two were headed in her direction. Teeth bared, she ran forward over the rubble to meet them. Her seft hung in her right hand, with a deceptive casualness. The key to this weapon was to remain loose and let the blade flow.

Welf weapons were intimidating but clumsy. And heavy. As she approached the first man, Ama dropped to one knee, slid forward, then swung the seft up and across his extended thigh. When the weapon hit its apex, she reached out with the other hand, grabbed the handle, stood up, brought her right elbow back hard and drove the sharp bottom end into the Welf's gut as he dropped. She twisted the blade slightly before she dislodged it.

The second Welf was more prepared and brought his axe down in a heavy-handed swing. Ama raised the blade over her head just in time to save her skull from being split. As it was, the force of the blow knocked her backward and she scrambled to avoid the next strike that landed just wide of her leg but lost her grip on the seft as she did.

Wielding the cumbersome axe had its costs, though, and the Welf took a moment to raise the weapon and reset for another strike. In that briefest of pauses, Ama leapt to her feet and unsheathed her knife. With two bounds she reached the Welf, used the man's knee as a springboard and mounted him like a gresher. She grabbed a fistful of hair and sliced his neck open in one swift move. As the body fell, she rode it to the ground, then collected her seft and turned to make sure Seg was unharmed.

Banger fire. Something hot hit her leg. As she backed away to seek cover, she inspected the damage. A red slash about the size of her finger ran along the outside of her thigh just above her knee. She had seen enough wounds by now to know that hers was not serious.

"We've got to plug that gap!" the trooper shouted. Her arm hung limp, shattered somewhere along the way, but she held fast to her chack with the other hand. She hissed as her comrade jabbed a pneumatic injector to her neck, a shot to dull the pain.

She wasn't feeling the wound right now, if Seg was any judge of the matter, but she would soon, when the shock wore off. Seg nodded, glanced at Ama, then looked toward the shattered chapel. "If I can get to the upper level, I can sweep them."

"If you get cut off—" the younger trooper said. He didn't need to finish. The chapel had a single, narrow entry and exit. If Seg got cut off, he was dead.

"So don't let me. Come on," he ordered Ama.

He went over the top of the rubble pile and laid down a fresh un-aimed volley as he went. Welf scattered and dodged, as the surviving troops laid down fire. Seg scrambled through the debris and came around a pile to slam face-first into a large Welf. Both of them stared at each other in surprise as Seg bounced off and fell backwards. Ama rounded behind him, darted forward without hesitation, and slashed through the startled peasant. Her blade flicked back and forth as if she were dancing instead of fighting. The Welf screamed and lurched forward, blood geysered across his body. Seg hammered him in the face with the stock of the needler, to finish what Ama had started. The man went down and they hurried on into the chapel. Although clogged with chunks of fallen stone and wood, the stairway was still usable, and Seg bounded up. He sprinted to the open window and skipped around a section of shattered flooring that gaped down to a pile of bodies and rubble below.

Yes. Clear line of sight. The Welf were learning the new rules of warfare – don't bunch up under enemy guns. But this group thought they were out of the line of fire.

Seg lined up, took a deep breath and squinted as he squeezed the trigger.

From below the chapel, somewhere in the rubble of the temple, a trooper's voice called up to Seg.

"Eraranat, you can fall back now. We've got them thrown back."

How long had they been up there? Between himself and Ama they had repelled four attacks into the chapel itself – one of which had ended in a hand-to-hand fight. He was down to a dozen shots, and both he and Ama had picked up more minor nicks and injuries. He was pretty sure, from the jabbing pain, that the Welf who had come at him inside the chapel, with a mace, had broken several of his ribs. In fact, he sincerely hoped they could cover a more sedate return to the lines. Ama was limping badly, and he wasn't able to move very fast himself.

"Coming back." His voice barely rose above a whisper. Talking hurt. Breathing hurt. Moving was an agony in and of itself, a special caliber of pain. He gestured to Ama. "Let's go."

He glanced at his crono. Two hours. Two hours that had felt like an eternity. And still no word of rescue.

How much longer could they hold? Night was falling. Normally that would shift the advantage over to the People, with their advanced sensors. But against an opponent who could keep throwing endless waves of bodies?

Down to forty effectives, the squad leader had informed him over the comm. That meant forty who could pull a trigger, and half of those wounded as he and Ama were.

He hadn't thought for a second about coming here. Now he wondered if they would get out alive. He staggered down the stairway, and watched the bodies he stepped over carefully to make sure none showed any interest in coming back to life.

Bodies, that's all there was anymore, Ama mused, half dazed. The dead bodies around them and the live ones that kept attacking them. She was blood-splattered and weary.

One hand gripped her dripping red seft, the other trailed along the wall as she steadied herself. She limped her way down the chapel steps and worked to keep close to Seg. Thankfully, his injuries slowed those long legs and allowed her to stay near. This wasn't done yet and she would not leave him unprotected until it was. He was her only hope to save her father.

Some day, far in the future, she knew she would feel remorse for this battle. The Welf were not bad people by nature, they were victims of Shasir trickery, pawns of the Damiar, and now casualties of a technology they could not comprehend. Like children, they clung to the hands of their guardians with blind love and loyalty. But today was not the day for contemplative sorrow; today was about survival.

Not since the days of Theorist Lannit had Jarin seen the war room so infused with energy. Of course, the excitement generated by Lannit's multi-strike had sprung from its disastrous results – zero vita extraction and casualties in the hundreds. The enthusiastic reaction to Seg's raid, on the other hand, was of an entirely different nature. Targets had fallen easily and the boy's data was so thorough that artifacts were being extracted at an unprecedented rate.

Enthusiasm from all present, with the exception of Director Fi Costk, of course. He had maintained a respectful distance from Jarin since the launch, though even from across the room it was apparent that Segkel's unfolding success was stoking his ire.

Segkel's infiltration of the T'ueve temple had proved more fruitful than even he had predicted. Beneath the pilings of the airship docks, the troops had uncovered a trove of skulls, buried there as part of some sort of religious ceremony. The vita collected from that site alone would cover the expense of the raid.

Good thing, Jarin mused, since he noticed that Segkel's richest target, the temple at Alisir, had been lost to the Welf. Troops remained trapped inside but, now that the sources of vita were buried beneath the rubble or destroyed in the explosion, they had been all but abandoned by the House.

Vita above all. For the good of the People, they would say.

The boy had insisted on accompanying the raid, not surprising. He would have done so even if he weren't escorting Ama back to her world.

The need for control was one of his student's greatest strengths. It was also one of his greatest weaknesses.

"Where is Theorist Eraranat now?" Jarin asked the Deputy Militant and followed behind the man as he moved from the comm center to the raid schematic.

"He and two troopers have entered the Alisir Temple in zone three," the Deputy answered, then added reluctantly, "with a small group of Outers, apparently under his command."

"He went where?" Jarin asked incredulously. "No, do not answer; it was a rhetorical question. The real question is what you are doing to extract him."

"He volunteered to go in, Theorist," the Deputy said. "He could have moved north to an extraction point. He can extract with everyone else when we've finished moving the materials and caj through."

"In all likelihood, he will be dead long before then, or have you not been apprised of the situation at the temple?"

"Alisir is no longer viable for vita; we direct our forces where they can best serve the People, as per protocol."

"Theorist Eraranat is worth more than your entire force," Jarin said, his normally passive expression hardening. "You will divert whatever assets are needed to rescue him. The others too, if you so desire, but Theorist Eraranat must survive – *that* is what is best for the People, Deputy."

"You do not give orders here," the Deputy snapped. "This is my command."

"Is there a problem Deputy Militant?" Fi Costk's voice gave no hint of the poison Jarin knew filled his thoughts.

The Deputy Militant gave a brief synopsis of the situation and Fi Costk performed the role of concerned peer well enough to fool anyone but Jarin.

"Unfortunate," Fi Costk said, eyes focused on the schematic of the temple, "but I believe even Theorist Eraranat would argue the necessity of protocol in this situation. When all the vita is retrieved and all the material trans'd, by all means, send a gunship to the temple. But not one moment earlier. I have authority in this matter; Theorist Svestil is merely an observer. If he continues to disrupt the operation, have security see him out." He paused and nodded to Manatu and Gelad, who were stationed an arm's length from Jarin, "*Our* security, that is, not the Theorist's spies."

Fi Costk didn't move away and Jarin knew that the man would not allow him another second alone with the Deputy. "Authority must be respected," Jarin said, then offered a gracious bow of his head and backed away.

"He pullin' rank again?" Gelad asked, under his breath as Jarin approached.

"Thank the Storm for predictability," Jarin answered.

"Going up-chain?"

Jarin looked out across the room with a passive expression, "It is time House Master Haffset and I discussed a few matters. Alone."

As he exited the private conference room, behind Haffset's House Master, Jarin's expression was a subtle, sly smile. It had taken all of five minutes to accomplish his goal; one of the benefits of keeping one's eyes and ears open, not too mention being a scrupulous collector of data.

"What do we have in air assets?" the House Master asked the Deputy. Haffset was pale, white as death, Jarin was pleased to see. A sentiment not shared by Jarin's rival, standing next to him.

"Six gunships and four drone detachments," the Deputy answered.

"I want all the gunships."

"All, House Master?"

"All of them. Tasked to rescuing Theorist Eraranat and the balance of our forces on the ground in zone three."

Fi Costk stepped between Haffset and the Deputy Militant. "House Master, you do realize the vita—"

Haffset raised a hand to stop his speech. "I am the final authority on this raid, Director. My order will be followed without further comment or question. Understood?"

Fi Costk nodded, then shifted his eyes to Jarin. "Yes, I understand. Completely," he said. "Congratulations Theorist," he continued, "this is quite a victory for you. The CWA will be watching your protégé with great interest from now on."

Jarin had no doubts about the threats in Fi Costk's words or behind the beneficent smile. "The victory is entirely Segkel's," Jarin replied. "The first of many, I hope."

The Deputy stood stunned and speechless for a moment before he relayed the order to the comm station. The House Master looked to Jarin, who offered an approving nod before he backed away.

"He looks as if he could tear your head off with his bare hands right now," Maryel said, nodding to Fi Costk as she sidled up next to Jarin.

"Knowing Segkel, he likely believes the battle he is in at this moment is the worst he will face. I would have avoided this."

"*This*," she directed her eyes to Fi Costk, "was inevitable. What did you say to Haffset?"

"I pointed out that the Guild is well aware of the fact that his father murdered his mother in order to clear up potential succession issues and see to it that his inheritance was unimpeded, and that I hold proof of it. I told him that even if the Court of Households did not strip him of his position or dissolve the House assets, he would have a hard time carrying on with that stain on his good name," Jarin answered in a low voice, eyes forward and trained on the holographic display in the center of the room.

"Are there any secret affairs of which you do not possess knowledge, Theorist Svestil?" Maryel asked.

"I am a harmless old man," Jarin said, with a wink.

As he returned his gaze to the business of the raid, Jarin hoped he had acted in time, that Segkel could be saved — not only for his own selfish desire to see his student alive again but also for the good of the World. The raid would be a success with or without the return of its designer but Jarin knew the stakes were much greater than the outcome of one raid. The World was facing its end. Without a drastic change in policy and procedure, and a Theorist bold enough to lead the way, the Storm would swallow everyone and everything and no amount of vita or shielding would stop it. As it stood, the brash young man was the People's best, perhaps only, hope for survival.

Seg's back was against a chunk of stone that had once adorned the bell tower of the temple and now lay among the rubble. His breaths were shallow, dictated by the pain from his broken ribs. Beside him, Fismar reloaded his weapon.

"Squad Leader Coultrey's dead," Fismar said.

"Who does that leave us that's qualified to lead the troops here?" he asked.

"You, sir. And, well, me." Fismar fidgeted with the cap of his canteen.

"You can lead these men?" Seg stared at him intently. Fismar swallowed and nodded. "Then you're in command of the troops. How much longer can we hold out?"

"We could maybe throw back one more big push. Then we'll be totally dry on ammo and down to blades."

"Then we show the Welf that the People are comfortable with steel as well."

Ama scanned for her fellow Kenda, distressed to see how few remained. She stepped past Captain Tather's body, touched her hand to her heart, then her forehead, and wished him a safe journey back to Nen. As she stared down at her dead dockmate, she wondered about her father's fate.

Her people were not the only ones to have fallen at Welf hands. Seg's invasion force had dwindled as well, many of the survivors wounded, all tired.

One piece of good fortune was the sight of her brother, Thuy, still very much alive. He rested with Brin against a pile of rubble that was once a stone pillar.

Ama took a quick look around; Seg had Fismar with him and they were enjoying a momentary break from the horror. At a half jog, half limp, she hurried to Thuy and Brin and flopped down on the rubble next to them. She set her bloody seft beside her feet.

"I wish I had one of those magic talkers to call the rest of my men," Brin huffed and armed the sweat from his brow.

"No such thing as magic, cousin," she chided.

"Too bad, we could use some about now."

"We're never getting out of here," Thuy said, as he wrapped an ersatz bandage, torn from his clothing, around a jagged slash on his arm. "But it's worth it? Isn't it?" Thuy looked from Brin to Ama.

"Freedom is always worth it," Ama answered. She pulled the canteen off her waist, took a sip and passed the rest to Brin while she helped Thuy cover his wound.

"Your father would be proud of you," Brin lowered his eyes to Ama's blood and dirt-specked dathe, "Kiera Nen."

She felt a large knot in her throat and looked past Brin, to no point in particular. "I have to get back to Seg. You two stay alive."

Brin grabbed her wrist as she stood, opened his mouth to speak, then closed it and released her.

"Stay alive," she repeated and tried to smile, "we'll talk when this is done."

Thanks to the darkness, the Welf attacks had thinned and finally stopped altogether. The troops rested but none slept; Seg kept close to Fismar and Shan, the three of them silent as they waited for dawn.

Shan pulled out the sensor array and swept the area once more.

"Any sign of the Welf?" Seg asked.

She shook her head. "They're holding, for now. Think we've convinced them we're too unpleasant to deal with?"

"More likely they're unwilling to risk facing our weapons in the dark. Though they won't have that particular concern to deal with very shortly," Seg answered.

"Y'know, Shan," Fismar grunted as he shifted his body and his broken leg bumped against the rubble, "now would be a good time to find out that a former lover of yours is flying one of the gunships on this mission, and that he's been looking for a way back into your life."

Shan glanced back at him, her face lit by the faint glow of the array screen, her soft snickers breaking down into harsh laughter. Fismar grinned broadly, and even Seg allowed a smile at that one.

Fismar tore open a ration bar, leaned against the wall and chewed on the rough substance. "Guess it's okay to talk about now, since we're probably not getting out of here."

Shan rolled her eyes. "Oh Storm, not a battlefield confessional."

"Well, this one is good. And it's not that I've been staring at your ass this whole time," Fismar said.

"You haven't?" Shan manufactured a disappointed expression.

"Only when you were in front of me," Fismar admitted. "Anyway, barring certain political difficulties, I would've been in charge here, probably. I graduated from Holiseff Academy, third in my class. Had the twin pips, life was good."

"You were a Captain?"

Fismar nodded.

"And then?" Seg asked.

"And then things went sideways on the Sikkora raid. Young Master Parth, may he rot in some misbegotten Outer hell, he walked his troops into an ambush. Of course, because I was his minder, I took the blame when he came back shy most of his face and lower appendages."

"Lower appendages?" Shan asked, indicating her groin with her eyes.

"Yep," Fismar said.

"Ouch!"

"And you're only bringing this up now?" Seg asked. "Why didn't you mention your leadership qualifications when we first got here?"

"Coultrey was doing fine. Didn't need some outsider messing around in her command. Besides, I'm just a trooper like the rest of these slobs now." He waved his half eaten ration bar in the direction of the scattered survivors.

"Anything else I need to know about?" Seg asked.

"Nah, that's about it." Fismar bit off another chunk of ration bar. "Hope you've made your peace with life," he said with his mouth full.

Seg smirked, stood and walked off, shining a dull amp light to guide his path. He stepped around a large piece of rubble then turned back and shone the light on it. A chiseled face stared up at him; Seg paused for a moment to stare back. The statue of the Shasir priest that had once stood at the entrance to the interior of the temple now lay on the ground, one arm missing, one pointing off to nowhere, the lower half of the body was shattered and the many offerings that had been left at the base were now buried under piles of stone. *You never imagined this would be your fate, did you?* Seg thought as he stared at the fallen idol. Then he looked up, took in a pained breath and tasted the dust and decay in the air.

A slender silhouette walked in his direction, with a distinct limp. He knew it was Ama long before he was close enough to see her face. He also realized that, even without the limp, he would have known who it was. Everything about her body was as familiar to him now as his own – a fact that both intrigued and bothered him in some indefinable way.

"There aren't many Kenda left," she told Seg, as soon as he was close enough to hear, "but they'll fight to the end." She leaned on her seft. "As will I," she added, then once again stared off to some unknown point in the distance. "There are no skyships coming for us, are there?"

"Ama…" he reached a hand to her, then stopped and let it drop.

"At least I'm fighting now and not hiding," she said, rallying a smile. "The freedom of my people, that's worth dying for."

He grasped her shoulders, seized by sudden conviction. "We're not going to die here."

How he knew this, he couldn't say. Just a feeling that his end couldn't come in the dark at the hands of primitive Outers throwing sticks and rocks. He glanced back at the broken statue.

By the Storm, he was going to seize his own destiny. Now.

Seg stepped up to the rampart. Ama watched him as she drifted toward Shan and Fismar. Shan twisted around, to watch Seg, as well. "What the karg?"

"Gone Storm-driven," Fismar said, with a shrug. "He goes before the rest of us." He washed down the last of his ration bar with a swallow of water, then turned the canteen upside down. "At least we won't last long enough to recycle our urine. Best get your gun ready. Those Welf Outers will be coming once they hear him start in on his glorious speech."

Seg sparked a full cassette of needle rounds into the sky, where they flared and burned out dramatically.

"CHILDREN OF THE SOIL!" he bellowed. "This is the judgment of the true Lords of the Sky! The Shasir have led you false, and now the demons come to stalk you! Every soul sent against us travels with the O'scuri to the Underneath!"

He threw the needler down at his feet. "You stand against your true masters at the risk of your own souls! Where are your so-called Sky Fathers? Where are the Shasir? Their temples burn, their women lament! They are false!"

"Fis—" Shan whispered.

"Shut up, I don't want to miss him getting his head shot off," Fismar said.

Ama glanced over in Shan's direction.

"Fis, you need to look at this," Shan said.

"We have tested you in battle and found you worthy, Children of the Soil! Leave now and we will spare your shattered remnants!" Seg shouted and spread his arms wide. Welf emerged from the darkness to look up at the madman who loomed above them. Thus far none had made a move to attack. Yet.

"Alright!" Fismar shifted himself upright. "He's lured them out into the open. Best shot we're going to get to take another bunch with us." He tapped the main frequency to all the surviving troops. "Ready volley fire on my command."

"FIS!" Shan shouted. Just then, the first gunship crested the back end of the temple, running hot and silent. The searchlight stabbed out and shifted back and forth before it centered directly on Seg's back. His long shadow loomed out in front of him, stretching over the crowd like an otherworldly creature.

"BEHOLD!" Seg yelled, "The gods return!"

Fismar looked up at the gunship. "Could've done with that a couple of hours ago," he said and slumped against the wall.

Ama dropped to her knees, relieved not awed. When Seg had launched into his speech, she thought they were all dead. He couldn't have known his skyship would arrive at such a perfect juncture, could he?

Giddy from exhaustion, she laughed uncontrollably. This man, so stoic and reserved most of the time, sure had his crazy moments.

The craft lowered in a hail of noise, the engines blew a swirl of debris and dust into the air.

The Welf remained as still and silent as the rubble that lay around them. They would not fight, their eyes filling with the sight of these new gods.

"Move it! Everyone!" Fismar yelled as the first craft touched down and the large door at the stern dropped onto the rubble.

Ama clamored to her feet, then sought out Thuy and Brin. She found them wide-eyed and awestruck. "Get your men inside the craft, Brin!" she yelled as forcefully as she could. "There's nothing to fear. Go! Thuy, come with me."

Seg's people were already scrambling to the safety of the gunships, dragging the wounded along with them. Ama hobbled to the entrance with her brother, waved the rest of the Kenda along and helped them inside. Seg came in last; Ama limped up beside him, then limped back to the entrance and knocked twice on the 'hull' of the craft just before the door closed and they shot off into the sky.

"Crazy drexla," she pressed her mouth close to Seg's ear, then turned away.

"I told you, I never fail," Seg shouted, over the engine noise, curling around his aching side as he did. "We've got the gunship, now we'll go get our troops."

They were packed in tight and Seg had to make his way forward through the press of bodies to reach the pilot.

"Set down at these coordinates," Seg passed the pilot a digifilm, "I'll be disembarking there briefly with some of the others."

"You're kidding," the pilot turned his head away from the console for a brief moment to give Seg an angry stare, "this entire mission was about extracting you."

"It will be a short diversion. I've got free agency on this. I won't be going back with the invasion force just yet."

On his way back through the mess of troopers and Kenda, he stopped in front of Fismar and Shan. "I could use your services for a short while longer. I will compensate you for the trouble and," he looked to Fismar's injured leg, "your discomfort."

"Storm take me," Fismar said, "I'd come along just to see what insane stunt you pull next. Count me in."

Shan sighed, "Sure. Guess I can't let the limper get all the glory."

CHAPTER 24

T he gunships touched down on a grassy field not far from the Alisir docks. The sun, crawling back up the sky, painted the field orange, and distant columns of smoke marked the end of the Welf temple.

The doors opened and the remaining Kenda survivors limped out, except for Ama. Seg paused to speak with Brin, then pushed his way up to the cockpit.

"Right," Seg said, as he leaned on the back of the pilot's seat. "Now, we're taking on a contingent of Outers, and we're moving to a new destination. I'll get you the coordinates in a moment."

The pilot whipped his head around and flipped up his visor, "That's a negative, Theorist. I'm already facing discipline for contradicting a direct order – from the House Marshal himself. The only place I'm taking this rider is back to the main warp gate in Zone One."

Seg considered this, then jerked his head toward the lower compartment. "Then get on the other rider and return with the others." He pivoted in place, "Shan!"

"What? You can't—" before the pilot could finish, he was interrupted by Shan's arrival.

"Theorist?" Shan asked, as she picked her way over an unconscious body and up the ladder to Seg's side.

"You're flying. This fellow is leaving. Now." He directed the last word to the pilot, who remained seated. He pulled off his helmet. "Fismar! Up here!"

Fismar hobbled up the ladder. "What's going on, Theorist?"

"Two matters. One, the pilot is leaving. If he does not," Seg looked at the pilot again, "bend him. Two, you're co-piloting."

Fismar looked between the pair, then shrugged and looked at the pilot. "Bend or cut? I'm in the mood for cut."

The pilot huffed as he unlatched his harness and climbed out. "I'll be reporting this to the MRRC," he said, and bulled his way past Seg. He was barely out of the seat before Shan took his spot.

"Destination, boss?" she asked Seg, as she clipped herself in.

Seg stopped, his mouth halfway open as his eyes stared straight out of the cockpit. Then he burst into motion, patting his pockets, as he searched for the digifilm where he had stored the prison coordinates.

"Karg," he muttered, as Fismar clambered past and flopped down in the co-pilot's seat. The trooper collected a flight helmet and put it to the side, then strapped in.

"Right breast pocket," Fismar said, over his shoulder, to Seg.

Seg opened the pocket and reached inside. "Yes, how did—"

"I pay attention," Fismar said, and held out his hand. He whistled at the bloodstained film Seg passed him. "Good thing we build 'em rugged," he said as he connected the film to the onboard system. Seg leaned past him to extract the pertinent file, scrolling through the menu.

"There," he said. "You two have a right to know what's going on. We will be extracting an Outer from this prison, with the assistance of native troops who are boarding now."

Fismar pivoted in his seat. "You're beyond unortho, you're kargin' crazy," he said and gave Seg a speculative look.

"Problem?" Seg asked.

Fismar laughed. "Nah, last fight was too easy anyway. Figure now you're springing the hard one on us."

Ama whistled up to Seg, "They're here." She pointed to the back of the craft where a group of Kenda men stood outside the entry ramp, staring. Brin was at the head of the procession, Viren on one side of him, Ama's brothers, Geras and Thuy, on the other.

"I'll get the passengers secured," Seg said. He made his way back down the ladder, slowly and carefully, and limped over to Brin. They clasped hands briefly.

"We are not quite fifty yet," Brin said, "but we'll fight like a hundred."

"As I've seen," Seg replied. He nodded to Viren, then looked at Geras.

Though his dislike for Seg shone plainly on his face, like all the rest, Geras was awed by the ship in front of him. What was also obvious on his face was a lack of sleep. Not just one night but several.

"You'll take us to the Secat?" Geras asked, one hand tight around the seft at his side.

"Yes," Seg said. "Now, everyone get into seats and I'll show you how to strap in. You'll stay in the seats until we're on the ground again unless I tell you otherwise. My intent is to put us down right in the middle of the prison after softening it a bit. Once we hit ground, be ready to get out, fight, storm the facility and get our man out. Any questions?"

"Yes," Viren raised his hand, "are you going to give another speech about the gods? That last one was really...moving."

Seg turned toward Viren, anger darkening his face. He glared for a long moment, before the quizzical impishness of the other man broke his temper. He coughed out a laugh and shook his head. "We don't need the gods. We are the gods. Now sit down."

Brin stepped inside the gunship and ushered the other men in. Some, like Viren and Thuy, entered eagerly, many hung back, unsure.

"It's not magic," Ama called out to the men. At the sight of her exposed dathe, a murmur arose and the wary stragglers filed in, nodding respectively as they passed by. She worked with Seg to get the men secured in their harnesses. When she came to Geras, he grabbed her hand and squeezed. What passed between their eyes was not quite a mutual apology, but close enough.

When everyone was seated, Ama took her own seat and nodded to Seg. "Ready."

He jerked his head toward the cockpit before he climbed back up the ladder and settled into the seat behind Shan and Fismar. "Fismar, you can determine the best entry approach. I want the defenses suppressed, then put us right in the middle of the facility. These men here are infighters, let them get close enough to get a grip on the opposition."

Fismar glanced over at Shan. "You up to a shoot-pass?"

"I don't know," Shan said, "you capable of holding your own dick when you piss?" She slapped the visor down on the helmet and hit the fans, thrusting the gunship skyward.

Fismar gripped edges of his seat at the sudden acceleration. "This ain't a test flight, you know."

"Welcome to the real military, sand-stomper," Shan answered, with a grin.

Seg listened to the two bicker, over his comm, as he shifted back in his seat. He let his eyes close for just a moment, and drifted off to a loud, discordant, vibrating nap.

There were no windows in the back of the gunship, and no way for Ama to communicate with the men, which made for an uneasy ride for most of the Kenda. A few of the men threw up, most gripped their harnesses, Viren broke into peals of laughter with every turn or drop. It was with no small measure of relief that Ama greeted Shan's announcement that they were arriving at the Secat. Though she could tell, even in the dim light, none of her fellow fighters could believe the trip from Alisir to the Banks could be made so quickly.

At the sound of Shan's voice, Seg woke from his uneasy sleep.

Fismar looked out the cockpit at the approaching fortress, "Perimeter wall, four watchtowers, guard barracks at the west end, prisoner cell blocks in those two long buildings at the east end, administrative buildings scattered along the north side." He glanced over his shoulder and down to the lines of Kenda men armed only with blades, then back at Seg, and shook his head. "Don't think a speech about Outer gods is gonna do you this one, Theorist."

"You can watch my back then," Seg said.

"Everybody shut up," Shan ordered as she lined up the strafing run. "I'm taking the towers, Fis."

The trooper nodded. "You're blue on all pods, racked and ready."

She nodded, and stuck her tongue out between her lips before ramming the throttle home.

The rider accelerated roughly, the thrusters roaring as they surged toward the compound. She banked a few degrees, then squeezed the trigger. Rockets roared away from the weapon pods on the stubby wings of the rider, blazing down toward the first guard tower. Rock shattered and flew through the air in the explosion, as she soared past, juking the controls to spin the craft and kill airspeed. She switched triggers and walked a burst into the secondary guard tower, bringing it down in a hail of cannon fire. The others fell with equal ease.

"Gimme a rake on that structure at one-three-two," Fismar said, pointing at the display screen between them. "Barracks."

Shan spun the rider once more, lighting up the building. On screen, figures of men exited the building, only to flee for some kind of cover as she sprayed the building with the cannon.

"Put us in," Fismar ordered.

"Hang on," Shan said, goosing the throttles once more to drive them toward the open courtyard. The rider landed with a firm *thump* that rattled everyone. Seg was still unfastening his straps, when Fismar climbed past him. Shan banged the lever to open the loading ramp, which slammed down on the rocky soil, sunlight streaming into the darkened hold.

Ama was swept with an odd sense of foreboding as the ramp opened and clouds of dust from the exploded rubble settled around the ship. The Kenda were dazed from the frantic maneuvers and sudden landing.

She shucked off her harness and waved Brin, Viren and her bothers to where she stood. "Brin, Viren, you're in charge of the men. The guards will be confused, use that, keep them busy. Draw as many out here as you can. Thuy, Geras, take some men and search the cell block closest to us, I'll take Seg and search the other one. As soon as we get Fa, we get back on this ship and go. Spread the word."

The men gave their agreement. Ama turned to the rest of the Kenda, grabbed her seft and raised it high. "BLOOD FOR WATER!" she shouted. The battle cry jarred the men out of their stupor. They returned the yell and freed themselves from their restraints. Fismar was already at the ramp as the Kenda followed him out.

Outside, the first round of banger fire echoed. Ama stepped out into chaos. Smoke, rubble, shouts and screams; it was as if they had never left the temple. Seg was right behind her. "I need to get inside there," she pointed to one of the stone buildings surrounding them.

Seg shoved her toward cover, and crouched down as he studied the situation. Ahead, Fismar was already organizing the Kenda, barking orders and maneuvering them.

"Eraranat!" Fismar bellowed. "Get me some needles on that gatepost!"

Seg lined up and fired a salvo, two of the four arced through the window of the stone building. The weapons fire stopped as high-pitched screams erupted. He ejected the spent cassette and dug into his harness. One depleted cartridge left, with only three shots – hopefully they wouldn't even need them from this point on. Fismar darted back their way as the Kenda used the lull in fire to close with the guards. Around them, vicious close-quarter melees broke out.

Seg pointed to one of the long, low buildings on the east side of the prison grounds, to indicate their objective.

"Okay," Fismar shouted to Seg, over the din, "you and me and the girl and we'll see who we can get to follow us in."

His gaze shifted from Seg and, without a word, Fismar seized the needler that was slung around Seg's shoulder. Still attached by the strap, Seg was dragged to one side, as Fismar directed the weapon at the small airship that had appeared from nowhere but was on a path straight over the prison grounds.

"Corrus…" Ama said, eyes fixed on the approaching ship, "he was waiting for us."

As she spoke, Fismar fired the heavy needler, his shot hindered by the resistance of Seg's body. The hasty burst was mostly off-target, though one needle glanced off one of the skyship engines, which spewed silky black smoke. A bomb detached from the skyship's belly, arcing toward the ground. It went off on the other side of the rider, but the concussion found them as the rider rocked, nearly tipping on its side. The trio was blown clear away and they impacted on the ground closer to the wall.

Seg groaned and pulled himself up to his knees as the skyship circled around, trailing a plume of smoke. The needler had landed next to him and he seized it, noting the readout. Two shots. He would have to make them count. Fismar was down, maybe dead. This was his now. The skyship was slow but Shan hadn't taken to the air or fired back, which meant the explosion had damaged the gunship...or her. Either way, wounded prey, an easy target.

Needler in one hand, he lurched up the stairs to the perimeter guard wall. Ahead of him, one of the Kenda pitched a Damiar guard, screaming, from the wall, then turned and advanced down the line. Seg reached the parapet and braced himself against the wall, hefting the needler. It wasn't the lightest of weapons in regular times, and now every motion made his chest scream with agony. Two shots.

The weapon wavered in his grasp as he struggled to line up the shot; he cursed his weakness. The nose of the skyship flashed suddenly, the BOOM reached his ear a second before the wall beneath him exploded in a shower of stone. He squeezed the trigger as he fell, the ground rushing toward him.

He saw the ground coming. Briefly he felt an impact, then blackness.

Ama's ears rung painfully, sending her off balance as she tried to stand. Through the smoke, she saw Fismar's body, face down in the dirt. She looked around for Seg but he was nowhere to be found. Frantically, she stumbled to one side, hands on her ears as she tried to quell the ringing.

"Seg?" she called out, then looked up to see the skyship returning. Two sounds hammered out in quick succession – one from the skyship and one from a point behind her. Before she could turn to see the source of the second sound, there was another blast, a shout, pieces of stone wall raining down around her.

It was in this mess that she saw Seg, falling. A single needle of flame sliced through the air, narrowly missing the skyship. She limped to where he landed, as the shadow of the skyship loomed over her. The craft was trailing smoke but still functional, and it was right over the gunship.

Her eyes skipped from the approaching ship, to Seg and then to something lying very near to him. His weapon.

Clambering over a pile of rubble, she pulled the weapon from the rocks. It had to weigh at least twenty pounds and was more than half as tall as her. She had never fired a banger before but she had watched Seg do it, and had caught some of Fismar's instructions to the Kenda at the temple.

With a grimace, she lifted the strap of the harness over her shoulder, heaved up the weapon and pointed it at the skyship, her legs trembling beneath her. Her left hand groped for the switch Seg had used to make it work, then flicked it to one side. She felt a low vibration.

Finger on the trigger, she took a deep breath, aimed and squeezed.

A thin needle of flame fired from the weapon, Ama took a step back and slipped on the loose rock, dropping the weapon as she fell.

From the ground, she turned her head just in time to see the needle explode into a fireball as it connected with the front of the skyship. The craft lurched hard to one side, then spiraled down in a long, slow spin until it landed on one of the perimeter walls.

On hands and knees, she scrambled to Seg. He was on one side, half covered in gravel and rubble. His uniform was in tatters and grey dust mixed with blood, making it impossible to tell what injuries he had sustained.

"Seg, Seg, Seg," she repeated, barely able to hear her own voice above the ringing in her ears. "HELP!" she shouted into the confusion all around her. "Get up, you crazy drexla!" she shouted at Seg's unmoving body. "Get up!" she shouted again, voice ragged and hoarse.

His head lolled toward her, eyes open but vacant. Bloody froth bubbled from his lips as he wheezed for air.

Ama placed a hand on Seg's forehead. *No. I won't lose you.* She took a deep breath, stood and let loose with another yell for help.

A hand grasped her shoulder. "He's done for," the man shouted.

Ama swallowed, looked down at Seg, then to the prison that held her father. "Go back into the skyship," she ordered the Kenda beside her. "Tell the pilot we need an auto-med for the Theorist. An *auto-med*." She repeated the word slowly so the man could understand.

"Man's dead. I got battles to fight out here, spawner. You go play nurse if you want," he answered, the muscles of his face moving like taut cords, then stood as if to leave.

Ama jumped to her feet and blocked his path. "That wasn't a request," she yanked the seft from his hands, and stabbed a finger toward the gunship. "GO!"

With a dark glare, the man trotted off. Ama took one last look at Seg, afraid to admit the truth, then ran as fast as she could, on her wounded leg, to the eastmost cell block of the Secat.

The doors to the prison ward were open. In fact, there were prisoners spilling out into the courtyard. Some taking revenge on their captors, some merely walking as free men and women for the first time, faces and hands raised to the sky, tears coursing down their cheeks.

Inside, the chaos continued. Fires burned, groups of prisoners rushed guards who fought back as best they could with bangers and blades. As she dodged through the crowd, Ama scanned the faces for her father.

There was a long line of identical cells, built from stone on three sides, metal bars on the fourth. Each was dark, the only light came from lanterns along the corridor, with nothing but a covering of straw on the ground and a bucket in one corner. Room enough for a man to sleep and take a few paces, and not much more.

At one cell, she stopped at the sight of a greying head, the figure of a man hunched in the corner.

"Fa?" she grasped the bars of the open cell, but the man raised his face, eyes a dark brown instead of blue, and she resumed her search. She called out over the din, but no answers came.

It wasn't until she passed another long row of cells that she heard the sound. Faint. Not the booming voice she had grown up with, but her father's voice nonetheless.

"Ama, leave here…"

"Fa!"

A brawl between two prisoners blocked her path. "Move!" she cried, directing them with the point of the blade until they moved aside. Then the voice Ama was following went suddenly silent, which sped her legs. At a run now, she skidded around the corner, leaping over a pile of bodies as she did.

Even in rags, gaunt and dirty, she would recognize her father. As she also would forever recognize the man who held him at knife point.

"Let him go," she ordered, hand clenching her seft, stomach twisting.

Dagga took one look at Ama, then jabbed the blade into Odrell's stomach, shoved him back and let him fall to the floor.

"Came to make sure the job was done. Don't like to leave my business unfinished," he told her as he turned away from Odrell, inside the dark, stone cell.

Ama sprinted to the cell door but stopped just inside the room, one hand clinging to a metal bar. Dagga stood between her and her father, blood dripped from the tip of his blade.

"You won't get out of the Secat alive," she said, meeting his eyes.

Dagga spat at his feet, "Only rats run."

"I'm not running, Dagga," she said, and stepped further inside, seft raised.

"Good." He snapped his wrist, slinging blood from the blade across the room.

Ama reached behind her and slammed the cell door shut. Dagga was dead, no matter what happened here, he would never make it out of the prison. But she had earned the right to kill him, and she would. Or die trying.

Their bodies snaked from side to side, each waiting for the other to take the first strike.

She lunged forward, with an awkward jab. Dagga sidestepped the seft with ease and slashed his blade across Ama's forearm.

With a grunt, she backed away, dipped to one side and swung the blade in an upward arc. The handle connected with the stone wall behind her, knocking her off target. The tip caught the top of Dagga's thigh but barely scratched through his trousers.

Dagga charged and Ama scrabbled backwards as she raised the handle of the seft to protect herself. As fast as she moved, she took another slash, this time across her thigh, before she drove him back.

Behind Dagga, Odrell let out a long groan. Ama's eyes flicked to her father, curled on the stone floor, blood pooled around him, soaking into the straw. A childhood memory flashed across her eyes, the day they had learned of her mother's death, the suffering that etched itself into her father's face, as he fell to his knees. Suffering she had eased but never erased.

Ama's eyes shifted back to Dagga. She couldn't win. Dagga's skill with his blade was legendary, far beyond her own with the seft. And she was hampered by the close quarters. *He's just playing with me.*

"Come on water rat," Dagga taunted, "I got a few more Kalders to finish off today."

Fighters don't win wars, thinkers do.

Seg's voice came to her.

There are two philosophies central to our success, even against opponents of equal or greater technology. One, we know exactly what we want before we go in, and we do not deviate from the objective – with the full knowledge that some sacrifice will be required. Two—and this is established as our most effective weapon—surprise. Catch your enemy off guard, even for a second and you gain the upper hand.

Her eyes darted to her shoulder, to the wound so recently healed. Heart beating the inside of her chest, she raised her seft and, with a primal cry, tossed it through the bars of the cell door.

Dagga blinked and paused in his advance. His confusion only lasted for a moment before he sprung forward, blade arcing upward through the air.

Teeth clenched and bared, Ama lunged forward to intercept the path of Dagga's slice. She twisted her body, even as her brain screamed at her to pull away, grabbed his wrist and impaled her shoulder on the blade. The cell was already hot, from the fires burning through the building, but the sweat that poured from her body wasn't from the heat. Less than a second, that's all she had. And, in it, she forced herself back using her right hand to push Dagga away before she lifted it to the knife.

She grasped the hilt and pulled the thick blade out with a howl that echoed through every corner of the prison.

"Surprise," she muttered, and charged at him, blood cascading from her shoulder.

Dagga twisted away and dropped to one knee to reach for the backup blade in his boot. As the stolen blade sank into his throat he fell backward, his arm slashed out and cut a thin ribbon across Ama's midriff. Whatever final words he may have had for her died with the air whistling around the blade impaled in his throat, as his body thrashed and spasmed.

When she was sure Dagga was dead, Ama fell to her knees at her father's side. "Fa, I'm going to get help," she assured him, as she panted for breath, one hand clutching his tattered prison uniform. "I'm going…"

She stood, the room tilted, she raised a hand to staunch the blood from her shoulder and stumbled sideways. Dagga's knife dropped from her hand.

"Easy, little Captain," Viren's voice reached her over the creak of the cell door opening. He held out a hand to steady her, then directed her to Brin, who stood behind him. "Prow, a hand if you please?" Together the two men lifted Odrell up and carried him out of the cell.

Supported by her cousin, Ama kept as close to her father as she could, grasping his limp hand in hers as they pushed their way through the dust and smoke clogged passageways of the prison. Odrell's head lolled to one side and he whispered Ama's name.

"You'll be alright, Fa. You'll be alright..." she repeated, while tears cut muddy streams down her face.

As the group stepped outside into the light, it was immediately clear that the battle was at an end. The Kenda were finishing off the last few guards, herding the freed prisoners and collecting their wounded and dead. Ama's head turned to where she had left Seg – where he lay still, on his back, face pointed up to the sun.

Her lips trembled as she pressed them together. But as she limped closer, sitting next to Seg, she saw Fismar, the wiry man she had ordered back to the gunship, and a Kenda who looked like a child playing soldier in his father's clothes. There was an auto-med sleeve around Seg's arm and, from the gestures; she could tell the soldier was instructing the wide-eyed boy and his less awestruck companion in its use.

At that moment, Fismar raised his eyes to the approaching group and caught Ama's hopeful gaze.

"Luckiest son of the Storm I ever met." He shook his head. "He's gonna live, thanks to Tirnich and Wyan here." He nodded to the boy and older man respectively. "You don't have to stand watch, the machine, the magic's doing the work now," he explained to Tirnich, the boy. "Wyan, fix this other unit on the chop-job there, like I showed you." He jerked his head toward Odrell and passed Wyan another auto-med unit.

"What happened?" Ama asked, still clinging to her father's hand as she spoke to Fismar. "Why didn't Shan shoot back at the skyship?"

"Blind. Airship didn't register on the d-scan and the perimeter wall blocked the thermals. Took a nasty bump to the head in the first blast, knocked her out. Ended up half-choked on her harness. Good thing you sent Wyan in there or we'd be walking out of this place, which," he glanced down to his lower body, now dead weight, "some of us might have had some trouble with. Speaking of..." Fismar looked around the courtyard of the prison, then shifted around with a grunt, "we've got this, but we gotta get everyone loaded on quick, before more show up. I don't know the Theorist's plans—"

"I do," Brin said. "We return to where we came from."

"Good. Shan says, pushing it, we can get about eighty onto the rider. We lost somewhere around fifteen in the mess, so get anybody you like on there. Now."

"Of course," Brin answered. "Tirnich, give Ama a hand," he ordered the boy, then gave a set of sharp whistles to summon his men as he walked away.

Ama let the boy offer his shoulder, then squeezed her father's hand as Wyan wrapped an auto-med sleeve around his arm. "It's not magic, Fa" she said, "but it will save you." She kissed his hand and turned to see Geras and Thuy running to where she stood. Their eyes darted between their sister and their father, unsure of which was most in need of assistance.

"Help get Fa on the skyship, we have to hurry before any more Shasir show up," she said, to clear the matter.

"Where's Dagga, and Corrus?" Thuy asked, eyes burning with revenge at the sight of his wounded kin.

"Dead," Ama said, the word easing her pain for a passing second. *I hope*, she thought, as her eyes moved to the crashed skyship.

"Well, at least there's still plenty more cloud sniffers left to kill," Thuy said, wiping a smear of blood from his face with the back of his hand. "Blood for water!" he whooped, and thrust his seft in the air as he did a jumping half-turn, then jogged after the men carrying Odrell back to the gunship.

A knot formed in Ama's stomach as she watched her brother's jubilant departure. She turned her attention back to Fismar, who had summoned a group of Kenda to help carry him and Seg to the ship as well.

Fismar had been in bad shape before all this. Now she could see new wounds and his legs were both useless. Even with the auto-med, he was in better shape than any man had a right to be.

"You lot fight half-good," Fismar conceded as the men lifted him up. "Now let's get on the rider and go."

Seg groaned and rolled to his side, as the men started to lift him, his fingers questing for the auto-med cuff.

"Keep him from pulling that off!" Fismar shouted. "Damn things sting."

Limping along beside the men who carried Seg, Ama looked forward to fixing on her own auto-med. "Always have to outdo me, don't you, crazy drexla?" Ama said to Seg, then raised her head to survey the scene one last time.

Smoke billowed from every corner of the Secat. Flames licked from windows and doors. Bodies of guards, dead and wounded, littered the rubble-strewn ground – their bangers noticeably absent. The skyship hung broken on the north wall, it's guts and false majesty exposed. Men were climbing the ramp into the gunship, some in the ragged uniforms of prisoners, as Brin looked on. Those who weren't boarding the ship were filing out the gates of the prison. To freedom.

"I didn't fail, did I?" Seg whispered, startling Ama out of the observation. His eyes darted around before focusing on her.

Ama opened her mouth to reply, her voice faltered, and instead she touched her hand to her heart, then her forehead. "No, you didn't," she said, and kissed his forehead, which tasted of dust and sweat.

The inside of the gunship was packed full of bodies but they made what room they could for her and Seg. The engines came to life with a loud and satisfying roar, as the ramp closed.

"Strap in back there," Shan's voice came over the comm. "Never know what's gonna happen next on this kargin' world."

CHAPTER 25

S eg hobbled beside Brin, on an improvised crutch crafted from
a boat paddle. Grass spread out before them, ending at a large
boathouse that now functioned as an ersatz field hospital.
Beyond that, a glimmer of water was visible and the skins of Kenda
boats were silhouetted in the fading sun. The next warp window would
open in twenty minutes; Seg had used the time since their landing to
let the auto-med stabilize him, while Fismar and Shan had used the
strong backs and deft hands of the Kenda to set up the large warp gate.
The internal injuries he had sustained would need more extensive work
but Seg would be home soon enough. All of his gear and weaponry had
been removed and left on the gunship, except for the backup stunner
he wore beneath his sleeve.

"T'ueve, Alisir, Malvid, the primary temples are all down," Seg
explained to Brin. "Only Malvid remains functional as a structure,
since that was the only surrender, but you would be wise to move your
men in there, hold it, and destroy the docking pads before the Shasir
can send more skyships from their home territory."

"I have men ready to raise skins and sail north on my signal, once
your people have gone," Brin said, nodding as he walked. "We will
have four moons to establish ourselves before the ice winds arrive and
make the northern passages too dangerous for travel."

"Use them well," Seg cautioned.

"What of the military strongholds we spoke of? Ol'cania, Myan'as,
L'albor?"

"Flattened. We could ha—" Seg stopped in place, his eyes squeezed closed as he drew in a pained breath.

"You should sit," Brin said.

"No," Seg said, in a small voice. A few breaths later he resumed his walk, "No, walking, like this..." he gestured over his head with his free hand, "under an open sky, is something I may not do again for a long time."

As they approached the boathouse, Seg could make out the huddle of Ama's family. Despite the debilitating wound Odrell had suffered and his generally poor condition, they were in high spirits, the occasional peel of laughter ringing through the air. The two brothers sat on the grass, on one side of their father, who was propped up in a half-sitting position, Ama sat on the other. She held his hand and embraced him at random, but frequent, intervals. Overly emotive but Seg had to concede that it suited her.

He nodded toward Ama and her family and spoke quietly to Brin. "Her father will be fine. The wound is non-lethal. But we'll leave you an extra auto-med. When the lights turn amber, replace it with the other. It will heal the old wounds, counteract infection, and keep the new wound from festering."

"A welcome gift, thank you," Brin said, his face softening as he looked at Seg. "You're certain you won't return?"

"The laws of my People forbid it," Seg answered.

"Well," Brin tilted his head to the northeast, and watched the lines of smoke rising from the temple with a wry grin, "perhaps that is for the best, brother. There's not much left for you to burn here."

Geras had tried to get Odrell to move inside the boathouse but he would have none of it. After weeks in the Secat, he wanted to see the sky. And his children.

"Such a ship!" Odrell wheezed, his eyes directed toward the gunship. "How did you manage that, Tadpole?"

"It was a gift. From Seg. A promise, actually."

Geras made a noise in his throat at that but it was drowned by Odrell, "Well, some gratitude is in order." He coughed, "Call him over, Ama."

Ama stood and walked to where Seg and Brin stood a short distance away. "My father wants a word with you," she told Seg. Her face stern.

He hobbled toward the family, stopping before Odrell. "Yes?" he asked. "We are in a bit of a hurry to get moving here."

Odrell puffed up at the boy's rudeness, though the action elicited another cough. "Ama tells me this is all your doing." He gestured around him with a weak hand, to indicate the gunship as well as the distant smoke from the temple.

Seg turned on the crutch and surveyed the horizon as the smoke drifted into the sky and caught the wind to be carried toward the east, hazing over the setting sun. "Yes," he said with a nod, "it was."

Odrell's face creased into a smile, "Good."

Ama traded glances with Thuy, who smirked.

"Come down here so I don't have to shout, I'm half killed you know," Odrell wheezed, making a production of his frailty.

Seg hobbled closer. "Yes?" he asked, his eyes darting back toward the large automated warp gate that the Kenda were busy assembling under Shan and Fismar's guidance. First the rider would go through, then all the personnel. Very soon.

"My nephew tells me you're a Kenda now," Odrell said, his voice dropping low. "A Kenda? Nen's death!"

"Fa, language!" Ama said.

"You're no Kenda." Odrell reached his hand out, and grasped Seg's, "You're a Kalder. You're family."

Seg grasped the man's hand in turn, thoughts of leaving banished from his mind. His eyes darted in several directions as he grappled for the words, before finally choking out a simple "Thank you."

"The thanks are all mine. And you will always have a home here. Now, go on. You have important business, son. And I have stories to hear," he winked and looked to Thuy and Geras.

"I won't be back," Seg said, his voice firm as he limped away on his crutch.

Brin was standing where Seg had left him, but now a group of men, the remnants of the chosen fifty with new faces mixed among them, were gathered in front of him as he shouted out to them.

"Our brother, Segkel Eraranat, was good on his word," he began. "The Shasir are broken; this land is ours to claim. The revolution begins; our people will be free."

A cry rose up in the crowd and he waited for the men to settle again.

"Now it is up to us to keep our word. You'll not see this world again but you will serve this man under Kenda oath. Fail him and you fail me. Blood for water!"

"Blood for water!" the men called back.

"Who are they?" Seg asked of the newcomers.

Brin offered a lopsided smile, "Replacements." He rubbed his chin, "If I had more time, I'd give you better but these men were prisoners at the Secat. I've spoken with them, they know the arrangement, they've given their oath to me, and so to you. They are all fighters, from the resistance, glad to make the sacrifice."

Seg looked over them, then nodded abruptly. "Yes, I expect they are. There are a few more things we need to discuss before I leave." As he spoke, his eyes drifted back to Ama, sitting with her family – safe, happy and free.

Thuy had finally finished his retelling of the battles at the temple and the prison, and as much as Ama knew her father was delighted to be reunited with his children, the strain of his injury showed on his face. She exchanged a look with Geras, and he directed Thuy away on the pretense of moving some of the stolen bangers to a new location.

"You need to rest," Ama told her father.

"I've missed you, Tadpole." He raised a hand to her exposed dathe, "This is a sight that makes all the pain bearable. You're free. My daughter is free." She took his hand in hers and they sat silently for a moment. "You're leaving with him, aren't you?"

"I don't know," Ama said, swallowing hard.

"Yes you do."

"How can I leave you like this?" She winced as she looked at his wasted body.

"You have four brothers, three with wives that will fuss over me as if I were a child, you know that." Odrell looked to where Seg stood. "He's difficult. I can see that. But then, so are you." He smiled as best he could, then took in a deep breath. "It wasn't easy raising all you kids without a mother. Especially you. I had no idea what to teach a girl. I could have been a better father..."

"Fa—"

"But I couldn't have asked for a better daughter."

The emotions Ama had stifled flooded to the surface as she wrapped her arms around her father. "I love you, Fa. No one, on any world, could have been a better father than you."

"I love you, too, Tadpole. Now, go on," Odrell said, his eyes fluttering, "this magic is making me tired."

His eyes closed, Ama squeezed him once more and placed a kiss on his head. She walked away and found Thuy and Geras already arguing.

"Out of my way, Geras," Thuy said, as his larger brother blocked his path.

"What's going on?" Ama asked, casting an accusing eye on her oldest brother.

"Just Geras playing mother again," Thuy snapped.

"This gresher-brain thinks he's joining the fifty," Geras answered.

Ama whipped her head around, wild energy sparking into her eyes, "No! Thuy, you didn't agree to come with them, did you?"

"Of course I did, I'm not sending you off alone."

She hauled off and drove her fist into his shoulder, wincing at the pain it sent to her injury, "You idiot! NO! You're staying here."

"Ow!" Thuy staggered at the blow, more from surprise than pain. "No, I'm coming with you. You've made your decision. I've made mine. Don't tell me you're on his side?" Thuy glared at Geras.

"You're not going," Ama said. "This isn't about sides. You don't know what it's like there."

"That's what you said about the temple," Thuy countered.

"And you were lucky to walk away. You saw the dead," she reminded him.

"If it's blood you're looking for, there's enough here. We need every man who can fight," Geras added.

Thuy's eyes burned between his siblings, then settled on Ama. "You of all people should understand." He turned sharply, to join the ranks of the fifty Kenda, and was met with Viren's fist across his chin.

He dropped in a heap, out cold. Ama gasped as she watched him fall, then raised her face to Viren's.

Viren shook out his hand, "That always hurts more than I think it will." He glanced over to two nearby Kenda and pointed to Thuy, "Take him back to the boathouse and don't let him come back out here until we're gone. Tie him up if you have to."

"Thank you," Ama said.

"As I explained," Viren gave her a sly wink, "I excel at trouble. Now to speak with Brin." He tilted his head and strode away.

Ama was left alone with Geras. An awkward silence passed between them. At length, her brother spoke, "You're certain Corrus was on that skyship, at the Secat?"

"No," she confessed, "But the Shasir wouldn't send Dagga alone, without 'the hand of the gods' to keep their beloved skyship pure."

"Of course not."

They both added at once, "But make sure you find his body", "But we have to make sure he's dead". A smiled slipped between them.

"For once we agree on something," he said. "Don't worry, if Corrus survived he'll wish he hadn't."

Another stretch of silence threatened, but Geras nodded toward Seg who was deep in conversation with Brin, "Will he take care of you?"

"We'll take care of each other."

"Well then..."

"Geras," Ama raised her uninjured arm, and opened her mouth to speak, though no words came out.

"Try to stay out of trouble there, wherever *there* is," he said, and ruffled her hair, as he used to do when she was small.

"I'll try," Ama said, lowered her head and let out a low laugh.

Seg gestured toward the smoky horizon as he reached his conclusion. "Brin, believe me when I say this: I have studied the culture and history of over a hundred worlds. You think I have given you freedom. I have not. Most especially not to you. I've given you the most terrible burden a man can face – you will be their king, their ruler, whatever you choose to call yourself.

First, I would advise you to begin conjuring your own magic with the tale of the twelve Kenda that fought at the Alisir temple. 'The stand of the twelve', however you want to call it. Just remember, it doesn't matter that there were actually thirteen Kenda; the human mind responds better to even numbers. Stay with 'the dozen'. That story, properly utilized, will give you the Welf. There will be holdouts who stay with the remnants of the Shasir, but you will be able to deal with them. Take those Damiar who follow the new flow of power and use them for their wealth, resources, and connections but never trust them. Eventually, they will resume their positions under new mastery."

He paused, weighing his words before turning back to Brin.

"But to the Shasir and any Damiar who stand with them, you must show no mercy. You must exterminate those who remain and let the noncombatants flee in whatever way they may find. Send with them a message to their home territory that any who come to your land will share the same fate. They defeated you, and you waited generations for your vengeance. Do not make their mistake. You must break them and wipe them out of history so they do not fester and seethe and someday rise against you. As leader, it will be your duty to your people. You will soon learn that leadership of this type involves lying, coercion, and butchery."

His expression flattened, the evening light, now under a veil of clouds, gave his face an eerie hue. "You'll never sleep well again, Brin. I didn't give you freedom. I gave you war. What you make of it for yourself and your people will determine your fate."

Brin nodded thoughtfully, though Seg wondered how much he had taken in. He was a skilled leader but, until now, he had only led his own kind. Men who wanted him to lead them. Now he would have to rule an entire land, including his enemies.

The warp gate hummed; Fismar had hovered the rider through, now Shan was shepherding the first of Seg's new personal army to their new home. After the last one went through, the components of the gate would self-destruct, melt into useless slag and leave nothing usable behind.

Seg twisted and hobbled to face Brin again, "Blood for water, Brin of the Kenda."

"Blood for water, brother," Brin said in return.

"I can wait longer if you'd like to kiss goodbye," Viren interjected, pulled a frayed benga stick from his pocket and popped the best end into his mouth.

"You can leave now," Seg said with a wave of his free hand. "I need to speak to Ama. Alone."

"Ah yes," Viren said, "speaking of kisses. Well then, I'll just take my place in line." He turned to Brin, wrapped an arm around his shoulder and led him away, speaking in Kenda. Seg couldn't make out much but he was certain he heard the word 'woman' and caught a wolfish glance in Shan's direction.

Seg gaped at the man's back. Did he seriously believe that he would just invite himself along? He started to hobble after the insolent bastard, but was intercepted by Ama as she moved to his side.

"I've said my goodbyes," she beamed. "Except for Brin. I still have time, don't I?"

Seg stopped and sucked in a deep breath as he mustered his courage. He stared at the shifting colors of the warp gate and didn't dare to meet her eyes. "Plenty," he said, "because you're staying here."

"What?" Ama maneuvered herself so that Seg couldn't escape her gaze. "No. I'm coming with you, like we talked about. We're going to explore other worlds, we're—"

He blinked rapidly at her, his face falling. "My World will kill you, Ama. You belong here," he gestured with his free arm to the trees and water, "where the life is."

"I know where I belong." She stepped up closer to him and lowered her voice. "I thought you were dead, back there. I thought I watched you die. Why do you think I did this?" she jabbed a finger toward her bandaged shoulder, "Because I didn't care. I don't want a life without you, whatever that may mean. I belong with you."

He thought back to the words Jarin had spoken to him, and could not find fault in the old man's logic. The whispers and derision of his peers did not concern him – he had known that prejudice since he was a child. But Ama—she deserved better.

As Jarin had warned, they were caught up in the grasp of hormonal pull, and it was incumbent upon him to be the rational one. But, as he looked into her eyes, he couldn't summon the words. For the first time in his life, he found himself facing an opponent that he couldn't fairly out-argue.

"You're right," he finally conceded and lifted his hand to take hers. The look of relief on her face sent a stab of guilt through him as he triggered the stunner and dropped her to her knees. He nearly overbalanced himself as he struggled to let her down as gently as possible.

Sometimes words were not the appropriate answer.

Seg turned toward the warp gate, but his path was halted by the point of a seft pressed to his lower back. He half expected to hear Ama ordering him off her boat.

"Where do you think you're going?" Geras asked, instead, his tone menacing.

"The stunner was on the lowest setting; she'll be awake shortly, with no damage," Seg said, freezing in place. He was in no shape for combat, but he would take a swing with the crutch if it came to it. "Take her home. She'll find someone else and be better for it. As you wanted."

"What I wanted," Geras said, standing taller, "was for my sister to be happy. Unfortunately, she's happy with you. So, you'll take her with you."

"Your entire clan is insane," Seg grumbled. "If I turn, will you not kill me?" Without waiting for the answer, he shifted himself around to face Geras. "Whatever feelings Ama has developed for me will fade."

Geras smirked, "You have a lot to learn about my sister. The first boy who ever tried to kiss her walked away with a black eye. She's been chasing away men ever since. Her family and her boat, that's all she ever cared about—until you."

"Listen, I would rather," Seg started to say, before his voice faltered. "She should..." He shook his head again. "She—"

He looked down at Ama, who was slowly waking from the stun.

"It will be difficult to explain what just happened," he said at last, his voice a strange blend of hope and sadness.

"My sister seems to do well with *difficult*," Geras said, with a deliberate eye on Seg.

"What...where..." Ama shook her head, then rose to her feet uncertainly. She looked from Geras to Seg, then down at the seft. "I missed something."

"We were resolving a few matters," Seg said. He reached out to Geras, who hesitated a moment before clasping his hand. "Blood for water, Geras Kalder."

"Blood for water, Segkel Eraranat," Geras replied.

Seg nodded toward the gate, where the last of the Kenda were filing through. "Go on, Ama. I'll be right behind you."

Most of the men were through, Ama hurried to the gate, which glowed even more brilliantly now against the darkened sky.

Brin was waiting on one side of the metal arch. "So, the wild, vagabond captain still roams."

"To seas undreamed of," Ama replied, before they embraced. "You'll be a good leader, cousin," she said, when she pulled away.

"Seg is right. It is a burden," he sighed. "This world will miss you, Tadpole. As will I."

Ama bit her lip and turned her head in the direction of the warp gate. A light, summer rain began to fall. Water from the sky, would she ever know that again?

"Go to him," Brin said, his voice low.

And so, she did.

The last of the men were through. Seg held out his hand to Ama, to guide her through the warp gate again. There was no need for the gesture, she had been through before. This time there would be no rough decontamination. She actually stepped ahead of him. Nevertheless, he did not let go of her.

His men would be waiting on the other side. Not caj. He had taken them in voluntary service. More like mercenaries. Whatever the men were, he now had a body of warriors to work with to achieve his goals. To change his World.

Ama stepped through the gate, with one final look over her shoulder. He stepped in behind her, taking one last breath of the moist, salty air as he did.

His first raid. It had worked. Not in all particulars, but that was only to be expected. Planning was one thing; life was another.

Life was a bloody business.

ABOUT THE AUTHORS

Kristene Perron is a former professional stunt performer for film and television (as Kristene Kenward) and a self-described 'fishing goddess'. Pathologically nomadic, she has lived in Japan, Costa Rica, the Cook Islands and a very tiny key in the Bahamas, just to name a few. Her stories have appeared in *Canadian Storyteller Magazine, The Barbaric Yawp, Hemispheres Magazine, and Denizens of the Dark*, among others. In 2010 she won the Surrey International Writers' Conference Storyteller Award.

She currently resides in Nelson, BC, Canada but her suitcase is always packed.

A career nomad, **Josh Simpson** has driven trucks through the lower forty-eight states, treated and disposed of hazardous waste, mixed mud as a stonemasonry laborer, failed abysmally in marketing, gotten on people's nerves as a safety man, and presently gets on their nerves even more using nerve release techniques in musculo-skeletal pain relief.

He lives amidst the scrub and mesquite of West Texas, cohabiting with the requisite writer's minimum of two cats. Warpworld is his first published novel.

H ere is an excerpt from **Wasteland Renegades**, the second book in the **Warpworld** series from authors Kristene Perron and Joshua Simpson.

Turn the page and follow Ama, Seg and the Kenda through the warp, to a world fighting for survival from the Storm – a world where orthodoxy rules, change comes at the highest cost, and an unforgiving wasteland holds the only hope of freedom…

Available spring 2013

WARPWORLD: WASTELAND RENEGADES
Warpworld II

The World
Year 863 of the Well

G rand Marshall Devian Bendure held her helmet by its strap, dangling from her hand, as she surveyed the remnants of her forces. Etiphar's Expeditionary Corps had barely managed to extract the Family Household, and at the cost of three quarters of their troops and riders. She had nearly two hundred troops left, not counting hastily impressed House employees who were little better than fodder for the guns.

Legions. House Etiphar had once been able to call upon entire legions of troops. Their own forces were among the largest of the House armies and, with their financial resources, they could quickly augment themselves with a vast armada of independent raider charters. On a war footing, House Etiphar's devoted troops and resources would have allowed them to face any potential opponent on the World.

But not the *entire* World.

Now, a rocky outcropping offered the survivors of House Etiphar temporary shelter from their enemies. The wastelands of the World, however, were not a place of safety. The threat of the Storm was minor—their riders were well equipped with Storm cells—it was the land and its inhabitants that gave even the most battle-hardened raider good reason to keep a wary eye on the land, the sky and even the rock. Everything that lived outside the protection of the shielded cities

471

had evolved to survive in an environment of scarce resources and the scourge of the Storm. *Hostile* was barely sufficient as a description for the wastelands.

Danger above, below, and on all sides.

The rider engines growled in low idle. Even now the remaining forces of House Etiphar had to be ready to evacuate, yet again, if their enemies located them before they were ready to make their final move. Technicians labored to repair damaged equipment. Troops checked their weapons, redistributed their ammunition.

House Master Urvish Etiphar, the only Person of authority above her, touched the Grand Marshall's shoulder lightly. "Will this work?"

She looked at him, mouth open for a moment as she processed the question. "Yes. Yes it will. Julewa Keep can be fortified. We carried away enough anti-rider weaponry to prevent our enemies from attacking directly. We can hold Julewa until the end of time, House Master."

Their *enemies*, Devian mused, now consisted of nearly the whole of the World's population.

"Thank you, Devian. I knew I could count on my people. What about the ones living in the Keep?"

Devian shook her head. "Escaped caj and bandits. Julewa's been abandoned for over two hundred years. Rocks and spit."

"Carry on then," he ordered, with a wave of his hand, and returned to his family.

Devian pulled the helmet back onto her head, bucking the strap into place as she turned away to hide her revulsion. It was the House Master's damned fault they were in this place. Urvis Etiphar knew he could trust his people, but the People knew they couldn't trust Urvis Etiphar.

Now every raider unit on the World wanted Etiphar blood.

She reached a hand to her helmet to activate the comm but hesitated. She knew what was waiting, the cacophony across the comm channels as the remnants of her troops prepared for the assault. The final charge of House Etiphar, most likely, and this one had to succeed. She flipped the small switch and was bombarded with voices.

The World
Year 976 of the Well

Voices. Ama stepped into the warp gate, the temporary passageway between worlds, and was swarmed by voices. Her second crossing to Seg's world and, just as before, she felt as if she was being pulled, stretched in all directions, her insides twisted, her ears assaulted by voices, distant and desperate. Only, this time, the voices were getting close, scratching past whatever defenses her mind used to keep them out. Not thousands, either, but millions. All telling their stories and Ama hearing every one at once.

Below the noise, she sensed, was peace. She longed to dive down there, to escape the din. But there was something else, something lurking just below that layer of peace. Something monstrous, hungry, ready to devour her.

I'm trapped, Ama thought, a knot of panic forming in her stomach.

The pulling and stretching threatened to tear her skin open. If only she could move – forward to Seg's world, or back to her own, it didn't matter which. She strained against the force holding her but her body didn't budge even a hair's width. How long had she been here? Hours? Days?

Then, like a cork freed from a bottle, she burst out through the gate and fell, gasping, to her knees. Her left hand found the floor—smooth, metallic—and sent a stab of pain up into her shoulder. She would have collapsed if it weren't for her right hand. She looked up to see it still clasped in Seg's. His eyes, that silvery brown colour that reminded her of the winter coat of a volp, were fixed on her with a mixture of concern and puzzlement.

"How long were we in there?" she panted.

Seg's eyes narrowed slightly. "A second or two." He studied her for a moment. "Ama? Is something wrong?"

She caught her breath then glanced around.

"I'm fine," she answered. Not wholly a lie, now that she was free of that Nen-cursed warp.

Ama pushed up from the floor. She could see they were in a decontamination chamber, though this one was big enough to accomodate the metal skyship that had attacked the Secat and carried eighty men to freedom. Shan Welkin, the woman who had piloted the skyship, was making a slow survey of the craft, inspecting for damage.

But Ama was not interested in Shan. She swung her head to the left, where fifty men, all Kenda like her, took in this new world. Some huddled together, others raised their sefts—long staffs topped with curved blades—ready for a fight. Their voices echoed in the chamber as they muttered among themselves.

She picked out Viren Hult and, unsurprisingly, he looked merely amused by the scene. Unlike her, he seemed *very* interested in Shan, as he slapped his friend Prow on the back and pointed toward the skyship.

Young Tirnich, who had helped Seg and the raider Fismar at the Secat, wandered through the crowd in a daze. His eyes and mouth were agape at the sights around him. But where Tirnich's expression was one of boyish wonder, the majority of the men looked on with obvious suspicion and fear.

"It's a trick!" one of the men shouted in the Kenda tongue. "Brin spoke nothing of this!"

The outburst rallied some of the others who protested, raised fists, banged their sefts against the floor.

Out of the corner of her eye, Ama saw a crowd of men and women in white suits that covered every inch of their body—the decontamination crew, medicals, guards—waiting against the wall opposite the men. One of the white-suits raised a weapon and stepped forward.

"I gave you orders!" Seg shouted, teeth clenched at the pain of the effort.

The white-suit hesitated, then stepped back.

Ama walked as quickly as she could, limping slightly, to the crowd of Kenda. "Honor your oaths to Brin! My cousin did not deceive you," she said, in the secret language of her people.

Ama's reminder calmed the men somewhat, though uncertainty remained firmly on their faces. One of the youngest, a boy who couldn't have been more than fifteen or sixteen, could not move his wide eyes from the waiting decon crew. Ama felt a swell of pity. Seg had brought these men here as part of some plan to change his world and she knew he would protect them, but to his eyes there was nothing to fear in this room.

As Seg arrived at her side, she whispered and pointed to the white-suits, "The first time I came to your world, I thought they were demons. It was terrifying."

He nodded. and turned to face the Kenda, then indicated the chamber with his hand. "This is a room for cleansing, to ensure we do not bring sickness from your world to ours and to shield you from any potential poisons." He gestured to the white-suits, "Those are men and women. They wear special protective clothing, that is all."

At Seg's explanation, men lowered their sefts. Hostility was replaced by a natural wariness, and they began to look less like a pack of cornered animals. In contrast, the white-suits, held in place by Seg's orders, muttered more loudly and looked through their visors at Seg, with growing unease and contempt.

"Get to the part about the women and the drink!" Viren shouted to Seg. The chamber echoed with Kenda laughter.

Seg scowled but did not respond. Ama stifled a smile. Coming from any other man, Seg might have laughed as well, but Viren had gotten under his skin from their first meeting.

Ama regarded the Kenda more closely, now that the alarm had diminished. They were not precisely the band of warriors Seg or Brin had hoped for.

There was a small contingent who had fought at the Alisir temple and, later, helped storm the Secat. These men sported bandaged limbs, their clothes were torn and bloodied, and dark circles ringed sleepless eyes. Yet, no matter how fatigued and wounded, a good meal, a visit from a healer and a full night's sleep would soon set these men right.

However, a larger number would need more time and care to heal. These were former prisoners of the Secat, who had only been freed from a life of horror and neglect that very morning. Their dull grey prison uniforms hung loose on their frames, giving them the appearance of children playing dress-up, but their hollow eyes and sunken cheeks made it clear that once those same uniforms must have fit well, even snugly. They scratched at parasites, crawling in their hair and on their skin. Fresh wounds and old scars stood out, silent testament to the treatment the prisoners had received at the hands of their Damiar guards.

Scattered among the fifty were a few who were not yet bearded and still others with a noticeable portion of white or grey in their chin whiskers. Too young and too old.

A 'Westie crew', Ama's father would have called these Kenda. Boat captains in the Western Islands of her world were known for hiring bedraggled and sea-worn crewmen, all in the name of saving a coin or two.

"We've arrived," Seg stated, when the men had quieted again. "As I have explained, these processors must cleanse you before we move you into your new home. That will require—" he paused for the slightest moment, "removing your clothes."

As Seg spoke, the auto-med hooked to his arm chimed, a small pulsing tone that rang out in the silent room. The men muttered again at this bit of 'magic'. With a look to the sleeve, Seg waved a dismissive hand. "It's nothing, pay it no mind."

As if answering him, the sleeve chimed again, a sequenced, continuous beeping. An orange alert flashed on its screen, in time with the beeps.

He was overdoing it. His body needed more medical attention than the auto-med could provide.

With a look of disgust, he tapped his fingers on the sleeve. Red, blue, then amber lights flashed in protest as the machine keened at him, before the screen finally went dark.

Ama frowned but he deliberately avoided her gaze.

"You will unclothe and let these people cleanse you," Seg continued. He paused, looked to the white-suits then back to the Kenda. Ama could see he was drawing on some memory.

"No hurt white clothes people," he said to the men, in his broken Kenda.

"Unless I authorize it," he added, in the common tongue.

He looked from man to man, let them feel the weight of the moment. "White clothes people hurt Kenda," he pointed at the group, "yes, hurt back."

The white-suits looked to each other as Seg spoke a language their chatterers had not been programmed to translate.

"Ama is in charge of you for now, until I return. She speaks with my voice. Understood?" Seg asked the men, in the common tongue once more.

Under normal circumstances, the Kenda would never agree to a woman as their leader, even for a short while. But what resentment existed was quickly dispelled as men pointed to her newly revealed *dathe* – the slits of skin on her neck that marked her as unique among her kind. *Kiera Nen*, they murmured and nodded, some with obvious reverence.

"White clothes people say question," Seg went on, in Kenda, his voice strained, "you answer no." He shook his head to demonstrate. "Say you: 'Talk Ama'."

Ama understood this to mean she would be the lone voice here. The men were not to answer any questions Seg's people might ask them. *Clever man.*

The white-suits looked disdainfully on the *unortho* spectacle: a Theorist of the Guild speaking the strange, lilting language of barbarous Outers. They murmured among themselves, their thoughts clear in any tongue.

"When you are done here, you will be taken to your new home in a…in a type of cartul called a 'mass-trans'. The driver will not speak to you and there are no windows to see outside. This is for your safety." He paused, struggled for breath. "I will come for you." That was all he could muster.

He's lucky to be alive, never mind making speeches. At the thought, Ama's shoulder throbbed where she had taken Dagga's blade. She adjusted the auto-med that circled her arm, pulsing medicine and speeding healing. A chastising beep warned her not to fuss with it further.

"Crazy drexla," she whispered to Seg as he turned. She offered her good arm, but he waved it off as he limped toward two white-suits – medicals who waited with a slim table on wheels, braced with shiny metal. A stretcher, Ama guessed. As with everything on Seg's world, it resembled no stretcher she had ever seen.

"I didn't have it so easy the first time I came through," she said, glancing back to the Kenda.

"You weren't armed," Seg wheezed, and she knew he was making a joke despite the deep folds of his brow and the sweat that rose on his skin.

Perhaps it was the drugs washing through Seg's system or perhaps he had ceased to care what his people thought, but he grasped Ama's hand even as the medicals urged him to lay down on the stretcher. "Watch over them," he forced the words out now; his forehead was shiny with perspiration, his face a deathly white.

One of the medicals stepped forward. Behind his mask, his eyebrow arched as he regarded Ama, "Theorist, I have to insist—"

"You'll have to stay with them until…" Seg grit his teeth, winced, took a breath.

"Until you know we're safe. I know, I understand," Ama finished and raised a finger to her lips to silence him, for all the good it would do. "Enough. You need to go now."

"I will c—" his hand went suddenly limp in hers.

She gasped and reached a panicked hand toward him. Just then the second medical pulled a silver, tube-shaped instrument away from the back of Seg's neck and nodded to his partner as he caught his patient mid-slump. Whatever the instrument was, the medical had used it to knock Seg out. Tricky, but Ama was glad. Seg would have gone on making speeches and directing everyone present until he collapsed.

The medicals maneuvered him up onto the stretcher. She leaned in to place a kiss on his burning forehead but they yanked the stretcher, and Seg, out of her reach.

Only their eyes were visible behind the masks, but there was no mistaking the looks of disgust as they hauled Seg away from the filthy Outer.

So, Seg had made arrangements for her and the men. To keep them safe. After all, she and her fellow Kenda were considered *caj*, slaves in the eyes of his people. *Unprocessed* and *unregistered* slaves. And even if she didn't fully grasp the meaning of those two words, she knew that Seg had made a powerful enemy in CWA Director Fi Costk. That man would hurt the young Theorist any way he could. If he could take Ama away, or any of Seg's new Westie crew, he would do it.

Ama shook her head to clear the thoughts.

Seg made you a promise; he keeps his promises.

There were more important things to deal with now. Including the fight threatening to break out between the Kenda and the white-suits.

Jarin Svestil, Senior Theorist of the Cultural Theorist's Guild, Selectee of Education and Council member, rubbed his eyes and stifled a yawn. His fellow Theorist, and clandestine companion, Maryel Aimaz, stood beside him where he sat.

"Despite your stance on the use of chemical enhancements, if you insist on forgoing sleep any longer I highly recommend you consider a dose of stimulants," Maryel said, with a note of impatience.

He didn't have to look up at her to know she was frowning, or that her eyes were as fixed on the monitor in front of them as his own were.

"Nothing a cup of greshk cannot remedy," Jarin answered, lifting a steaming cup to his lips.

He had chosen to view the intrans of his former student, Theorist Segkel Eraranat, from the privacy of his office – one of the few places he knew he would not be observed, where he could speak freely.

On the screen, a rowdy group of Outers clustered together in the decon chamber. He glanced up at Maryel and offered her a wry smile.

"I don't know why you're smiling. Everyone with any bit of influence in the World is likely monitoring this feed right now. Your prized pupil is showing yet again that he is the very definition of unortho," she said, her voice sour and clipped. "The CWA will make use of this."

The smile faded as he nodded in assent to her words. Maryel was not only a Senior Theorist and member of the council that led the Guild, she was also one of the Lead Questioners in post-raid analysis. Normally, for completed raids, the Question was little more than a formality, a superficial study of the successful areas of the raid and how the process could be improved.

As with all things Segkel, however, nothing about his Question would be normal.

Unortho was a word Jarin had known well would haunt Segkel's career. Nevertheless, he had cultivated that very trait in the boy because the survival of the People and the World would require new, unorthodox ideas and methods.

"The vis feed is being trapped," Jarin assured his companion. "As best we can, we will contain this. At present, Segkel's image can survive a certain amount of unortho."

"At present, yes, but we both know the CWA thinks in the long term. They will use moments such as these to chip away at his image." She gestured to the screen and pursed her lips.

Jarin sighed, all traces of good humor evaporating. "He has complicated matters, agreed. But I knew, we all knew, allowing him the freedom to act on his instincts and intelligence would complicate everything. Genius burns like fire, Maryel."

"You could have chosen a less alarming metaphor." She crossed her arms and let out a sharp gust of air through her nose.

He shook his head as he turned back to the screen. "It would serve us to remain alarmed, I believe. In the interest of staying ahead of these matters.."

"Fifty Outers. Fifty! With weapons, no less. And an order specifying they not be processed, grafted, or even registered. Forgive my language, but what in the name of the Storm is Eraranat thinking?"

Revolution. Jarin pushed the word to the far corners of his mind. No, not Segkel. Even the headstrong protégé had his limits. For all his unorthodoxy, Segkel was a true Citizen of the World.

"I believe we will have answers soon enough," Jarin said.

"Indeed," Maryel agreed, lifted a digifilm from the desk and crossed to her seat to make notes. "Theorist Eraranat may dazzle the primitives with his speeches but they won't get him far in the Question."

Jarin watched Maryel for a moment, out of the corner of his eye, then returned his full attention to the monitor once more.

He leaned forward and squinted. Amadahy. The girl was unmistakable, even if her gills weren't visible on the screen. By the automed sleeve on her arm, the state of her attire, and the tangle of her long, blonde hair, it was obvious she had taken part in the battle at the temple. Segkel, battle-worn himself, held her hand and they spoke conspiratorially. As young lovers often do. Jarin's mouth turned down at the sight and he felt a surge of anger. *Segkel, I warned you not to bring her back.*

This would not end well.

"Hold."

Ama stopped at the sound, turned to find the source, and was shocked to see raider Fismar Korth heading toward her. *Rolling* toward her, that was, in a chair with large wheels on each side.

"Why are you still here?" she asked, shaking her head. "What—" she gawked at the chair, mouth hanging open, unable to finish her question.

Fismar had taken a beating in the various battles on her world. When she had last seen him, less than an hour ago, he had been unable to move from the waist down.

"Medicals will get their claws in me soon enough," Fismar said, in a tone that suggested he considered treating his multiple injuries nothing more than annoying interruption. "Had worse, anyway. I want to watch these boys a moment."

The 'boys' were a group of about ten Kenda, most from the ex-prisoner contingent, who had their sefts raised and pointed at the decon crew.

"Fools," Ama sighed. "Seg told them to unclothe and let the workers clean them. I have to stop th—"

"*Hold*, I said." Fismar clamped his hand around her wrist. His other hand held the wheel of his chair to prevent it from rolling forward.

"Seg put me in charge until he returns," Ama protested, tugging against his grip.

"Wait and watch." Fismar held firm. "You're dealing with troops. Or what're going to be troops, unless I miss my guess. Your Theorist is a weird one, unortho as the Storm, but he's got a plan here."

"I don't think his plan is to start a war in this room."

The Kenda shouted and rattled their sefts. The decon crew took nervous steps backwards, as white-suited security personnel, scattered through the decon chamber, stepped forward.

Just as Ama was about to launch another protest, Fismar pointed to a solitary Kenda, pushing his way through the scrum with a purpose. "Him," Fismar said, and released her wrist.

The man had dark hair, almost black, which made Ama suspect there must be some Welf or Damiar blood in his line. The hair was pulled back in a ponytail, the style of those who spent their days in the wind and spray. A cargo hauler perhaps? He wasn't as brawny as some but carried himself as if he were twice his size. His eyes were two dark, unmovable stones.

As the crowd parted for this man, Ama felt a twinge of recognition. He wasn't from the temple or the Secat, he didn't wear a prisoner's uniform, he wasn't one of Brin's workers (that she knew of), but he looked familiar nonetheless.

"What about him?" Ama asked Fismar, conscious that she had lowered her voice and that, somewhere inside, she was answering her own question.

The dark haired man grabbed one of the shouters by the collar, a newly freed prisoner from the Secat, catching his hand before his seft could curve back toward him.

"The man explained his purpose, brother," the dark haired man said. "Let these people do their work."

The ex-prisoner with the blade turned to voice his objection but something in the dark haired man's face made him silent.

"They want to take our sefts! They defile the names of our ancestors!" another ex-prisoner shouted.

"I wouldn't mind doing some defiling of my own," Viren said, with a lecherous glance toward Shan, who was still at the skyship.

"Our sefts are sacred!" the man continued to protest.

This outburst was met with a snorting laugh. Viren Hult stepped forward, chortling and clearly enjoying the spectacle, "You didn't even have that seft until this morning, old timer. Hardly long enough to make anything sacred."

"Show respect," the black haired man tightened his grip on the first ex-prisoner's collar to prevent him from lunging forward, then turned his stony glare on Viren. "This man suffered in the Secat for the freedom of his brothers, while you played cards and whored your way through T'ueve."

He widened his focus and spoke to all the Kenda, his tone low but commanding. "We are not animals! We gave our oath and our honor to this man, Segkel Eraranat. And, through him, to Brin Kalder. We are Kenda and we are on a far shore where our names and the names of our ancestors are meaningless." He let go of the ex-prisoner. Then his mouth twisted into a savage grin, as he glanced down between his legs and winked, "Let's show them what the true weapons of men look like."

Ama shook her head as the men laughed and hooted.

Viren turned to the man beside him, "Prow, I do believe that... *pirate*...tried to insult me."

"Wouldn't be the first," Prow said, stroking his ample chin.

"You wound me," Viren pressed his hand to his heart, then turned his attention back to the black haired man. He fixed the man with an overly large smile and held out his own seft for the white-suits to take away for cleaning. "Not animals, no. Civilized, we are," he said, when the weapon was removed from his hands. "From the mouth of Cerd Jind himself, Nen take me."

"Jind," Ama whispered.

"That mean something?" Fismar asked.

There was a low murmur among the Kenda. Some of the men raised their index fingers and touched their left eye. A few stepped away from the black haired man.

"Cerd Jind was a criminal on our world."

"And...?" Fismar shrugged, "Seems you like you have a few of those in this bunch."

"This is different," Ama said.

"Look lively, deckies!" Viren called out, as he unlaced his trousers, "Let's see who's carrying the biggest weapon!"

Without another word, Cerd Jind, the black haired man, picked up his seft and handed it to the decon crew, then pulled off his shirt. The scars and lean muscles could have belonged to any of the Kenda; the tattoo was a different story.

Spread across Jind's back were swirls of black ink. Though highly stylized, any Kenda would have recognized the symbol as a drexla – the lethal, poisonous predator that hunted in the Big Water. Ama's calf bore two scars left by drexlas; not many could say they had escaped such an encounter, twice. But the ink was more than a symbol of a water creature, it was the mark worn by those Kenda who betrayed their own and ran with the pirates of the Rift Tribu.

Why would Brin trust a man like Cerd Jind? A man who had murdered and stolen from his own kind.

"Well, no bloodshed. That's a first from this crowd, I'll wager," Ama said, forcing lightness into her tone. She turned her eyes from the Kenda men as they shed their clothes, just in time to mark Shan's approach.

"Did I miss the animal show?" Shan asked, as she stepped up beside Fismar's chair. She spoke only to Fismar and was careful to keep her distance from the 'Outer'.

"Think you would've learned something by now, skyrider," Fismar said as he engaged the wheels on the chair. "Fighters are fighters, wherever they come from. These boys ain't troops, but they *are* fighters."

"Yeah, yeah, kargin' Outers all look the same to me," Shan said, scratching at the unruly mop of black hair that jutted out from her head in every direction.

Fismar waved the medicals over at last.

"Enjoy med-leave, sand slogger," Shan called to him.

"Stop by the RQ and we'll drown the dead," Fismar answered, with a look back over his shoulder.

"Long as you're paying," Shan said.

He gave Shan a wink, then shifted his eyes to the Kenda and gave them one last thoughtful look.

Shan unzipped her flight suit, sighed and muttered, "Kargin' decon."

Ama looked left and right. The white-suits were already at work, hosing and spraying and brushing.

"Shan…" Ama began, shifting her weight from side to side.

"Are you still here?" Shan spat. "Go get scrubbed with the other caj. Go on." She made a shooing motion with her hand.

Ama backed up a few steps, turned her head toward the mass of naked men, then turned back to Shan. "I'm not caj and I don't wan—"

"Listen up," Shan's eyes burned, the upper half of her flight suit hung around her waist, "because the next time you talk to me, or even look at me, like you're a Person, I'm gonna put you on the ground. I've played nice because you belong to the Theorist but the raid's over. Get it?" She scowled as she eyed Ama from toe to head, then her eyes cooled faintly. "Besides, you ain't got any equipment those worms over there haven't seen before. Well, except for the—" she gestured to the dathe on Ama's neck. "Quicker you get it done the quic—"

"Less talking, more unveiling!" Viren shouted. He stood about fifteen feet away, fully undressed, hands on his hips. Some of the Kenda laughed, some turned away, some turned to watch, more than a few exchanged whistles.

Shan's eyes fired up again but, Ama noticed, the pilot's cheeks flushed pink.

"Shut your kargin' hole, Outer!" Shan shouted, then turned to Ama. "That one has a big mouth."

Ama considered a reply but Viren beat her to it.

"Goddess of the Sky! I beg your forgiveness." Viren spread his arms wide, "Come let me shower you with repentance!"

"That's it," Shan growled under her breath.

She stomped away. Ama thought she might leave the decon chamber but Shan stopped at a rack and pulled a large chack off a shelf. As she marched toward Viren, all the other Kenda, and a few of the white-suits, backed away. Viren's smile never faltered, even when Shan jammed the muzzle of the gun into his naked chest.

"One more word, Outer," Shan said, firing each word at him as if it were its own weapon. "One more and I fill you full of spines."

Viren offered Shan the kind of look a boy might give the Lesson House instructor after being caught truant. The moment her shoulders relaxed, his eyes roamed to her chest, which was only covered by a thin undershirt, then caught her gaze again and directed it downward, between his legs.

"You filthy—"

"Return to the decon area!"

The booming command, from one of the white-suits, halted Shan's outburst.

"You're kargin' lucky," she said, as Viren strolled back to the rest of the men. He was quickly led away by the white-suits and Shan tossed the chack onto the shelf under security's watchful eyes.

As she walked to the far end of the chamber, her eyes flicked to Ama just once. And though she still wore a look of disgust, Ama thought she saw embarrassment in that derision, too.

Alone now, Ama swallowed down her discomfort and started the long process of removing her clothes. Her injuries made the task almost impossible; her left arm hung useless thanks to the knife wound Dagga had inflicted.

Frustrated, she lowered herself down on the cold metal ground and struggled to unlace her boots. "I forgot how much I hate this place," she muttered to herself.

"Kiera Nen?"

Her head jerked upward at the name. Two merry eyes shone down on her. *Kiera Nen*, prophesied savior of the Kenda. Some of the men had taken to addressing her that way since she had revealed her dathe. Ama had borne it at the temple, when their lives were at stake, but the thought of carrying on with the name was too close to Shasir trickery for her liking. She had fought with her Kenda brothers to rid their world of false gods and prophets; she had no intention of becoming one herself.

"Ama. Just call me Ama."

"Tirnich Kundara," the boy said, "I was at the Secat."

"You helped with Seg's auto-med."

"Is that what it's called?" he asked, gesturing to the unit on Ama's arm. Tirnich was down to his waterwear but if he was embarrassed it didn't show. "Thought you could use some help, too."

His look was so earnest and innocent; Ama found herself agreeing without hesitation.

"Brin didn't want me to come here. He said I was too young," Tirnich chattered as he helped unlace Ama's boots. "Then everything happened at the temple and such, and I guess he saw I could fight, so he let me join. It's pretty exciting. I bet I'll have some stories for stories for for Pica, that's my baby sister, if we ever get to go back home. Do you think we will?"

No, Ama thought. *This is home now.*

"Maybe someday," she answered.

"I hope so. I bet we do. Not that it really matters, though I'd like to see Pica again."

Ama smiled. However naïve Tirnich was, his optimism and joy was like wind filling the skins of her boat.

Efectuary Jul Akbas clicked her fingernails on the smooth surface of her desk. The desk was void of all objects, as she ensured it was every evening before she returned to her residence in the CWA city of Orhalze. *Clear desk, clear mind*, she always reminded her staff. Lazy and careless, that is how she thought of most of her underlings. People in general, for that matter. How some made it up the ranks with their deplorable work ethic and sloppy personal habits was both a mystery and a source of annoyance to Efectuary Akbas.

The man on the monitor before her was a prime example. *Theorist Eraranat.* As the name entered her mind she felt the muscles of her face constrict and twitch.

Eraranat had dismissed her, not once but twice. He had made a fool of her in front of her peers. This boy, this smug, sloppy boy, had dared to set himself above an Efectuary of the Central Well Authority? And, in the process, this arrogant young Theorist had undone the years of effort it had taken to win a place among Director Fi Costk's inner circle. Thanks to him, she had been reassigned to a position of little importance and even less chance of promotion. Eraranat would learn that the woman he had trifled with knew and lived the Fourth Virtue of a Citizen: Supremacy.

The intrans vis feed from the Eraranat 001 Raid came through on her monitor in jerky, staccato chunks. There was no audio. She suspected Eraranat's mentor's hand in the poor quality of the feed. Nevertheless, she watched, closely.

She watched the gunship come through the gate. Eraranat had commissioned his own rider but this was not it. Noteworthy.

She watched the wounded raider and the rider pilot pass through, capturing a still frame of each in order to research them later.

She watched a stream of Outers armed with prim weapons pass through the gate. Unrestrained.

She watched Eraranat lead a female Outer through the gate. One of his two trophy caj. He had taken the Outer back to her world and then returned with her. Why?

Tomorrow, she would dissect the feed. Tonight, she wanted raw impressions. A method that had proved effective in her years of surveillance.

Eraranat stands in front of the Outers. Then he limps to the medicals. (Injured. How?) The medicals load him onto the stretcher. Then the...

Wait.

She halted her nail tapping and pressed a button to reverse the feed at half speed. The figures moved backwards, almost comically.

She stabbed a button to freeze the feed, then another to play it again, still at half speed.

The trophy caj walks at Eraranat's side. Their lips move to indicate they are speaking. The Theorist stops, turns slightly, and takes her hand.

He takes her hand.

Akbas stopped the feed. As impossible as it was to believe, she could not deny what was in front of her. The gesture was not one of master to slave, or owner to property. Affection, this was what Efectuary Akbas saw.

"Degenerate," she said aloud, with an urge to spit. Though she would never.

The act was disgusting. It was also, she mused with a thin, hard smile, damning. She trailed her fingernail over the onscreen body of the Outer in a distinct 'X'.

And, again, something made her pause.

She captured a still of the moment, used her finger onscreen to center the image on the Outer, then magnified it. As the face of Eraranat's caj expanded, the image quality lessened. Even so, through the fuzzy details, there was something too familiar about the features. Aside from the digifilm of data she had collected on Eraranat, Akbas knew she had seen this face before.

From her desk drawer, Akbas withdrew the Eraranat data film, slid it into the base of the monitor and tapped the screen to split it in half. On one side, the grainy face of the caj remained; on the other, data and images of the Theorist scrolled by.

Akbas's eyes zipped left to right, left to right, absorbing, comparing. *Where, where, where?*

There was a vis still of Eraranat in Haffset's raid planning chamber. Her teeth ground as it appeared and, perhaps to remind herself of the importance of this work she now did, she froze the image.

All the players in the room were known to her. She had memorized names, faces, titles, and any other information she considered pertinent. Theorist Jarin Svestil sat at the outer ring, though she had never allowed herself to imagine his influence was limited to that realm. His 'aide' Gelad sat on his right. Was anyone fool enough to believe the former raider was merely an aide? At Gelad's knee, was his caj, the one she had questioned him about. In the seat next to Gelad—

No. Wait.

She centered the image on Gelad's caj and expanded it until the face filled its half of the screen. On the left half of the screen, Eraranat's caj. On the right, Gelad's. And while Gelad's caj wore a thick collar, had a face covered in intricate black designs, hair twisted and hidden in coils of red fabric, the features were unmistakable. These two images were of the same Outer.

And now she had her answer to the question that had kept her awake too many hours since that day: How had Eraranat retrieved the raid planning data?

Every muscle tensed, not just those in her face. How had this detail eluded her? They had used the caj. Somehow, they had used Eraranat's caj to smuggle out the data.

"Storm-rotting bastard!" she shouted, smacking both palms against the desk hard enough to sting. Her hands rolled up into fists as she fought the urge to rip the monitor from the desk.

Instead, she pressed a button and Eraranat's face filled the screen. Palms flat on the desk, she leaned forward until she was almost nose to nose with him. "I see you now." Her eyes narrowed, "I see right through you."

74127818R00275

Made in the USA
Columbia, SC
26 July 2017